THE SILENCE

THE
SILENCE

Alison Bruce

Constable & Robinson Ltd
55–56 Russell Square
London WC1B 4HP
www.constablerobinson.com

First published in the UK by Constable,
an imprint of Constable & Robinson, 2012

Published in this paperback edition by C&R Crime, 2013

A copy of the British Library Cataloguing in Publication
Data is available from the British Library

ISBN 978-1-47210-194-5 (paperback)
ISBN: 978-1-84901-786-2 (ebook)

Typeset by TW Typesetting, Plymouth, Devon

Printed and bound in the UK

1 3 5 7 9 10 8 6 4 2

Iakona,
Ko aloha makamae e ipo,
Aloha no au ia 'oe,
Alekona x

PROLOGUE

July 2007

Saturday, 14 July 2007 started hot, and stayed hot. For the six plain-clothed officers waiting out of sight behind an empty house in Histon Road, Cambridge, there was no choice but to attempt to ignore the dual discomfort of sweat-damp clothes and the stench of unemptied food bins.

DC Michael Kincaide was less than impressed, and only his boss's conviction that this operation would lead to the arrest of Roy Kelvin had persuaded him that it would all be worth it.

Apart from DI Marks, Kincaide was the most experienced officer on the current team and, even after a wait of almost two hours, he was determined to lead the others in a quick and decisive arrest as soon as the moment presented itself.

After two hours and five minutes, Kincaide's radio came to life.

Ten turns through the network of streets to the other side of Madingley Road, a man called Ratty was sitting on the grit-strewn tarmac that ran between two long rows of facing lock-up garages. He had his back to a low, partially collapsed wall, and the only things in front of him of any interest were a half-drunk can of Strongbow and an open tin of tobacco. Ratty was muttering disjointed words which sounded like the mumblings of a hopeless alcoholic. The words emerged all mashed by a mouth that had lost too many teeth and too many nerve-endings. The one person who never seemed to find it difficult to understand Ratty, without reading his lips, was crouching on the other side of the wall.

'What can you see?' Goodhew whispered.

'I'll cough – all right?'

'You cough all the time.'

'All right, I'll stand up, and then you'll see my hand on the top of the wall.'

'Don't draw any attention to yourself.'

Ratty swore twice, and the next few words were totally unintelligible, then: 'I told you before, I never get involved.'

'And *I* told *you*, you didn't have to stay. You showed me which lock-up, and that was enough.'

A few seconds later, Ratty erupted in a volley of coughs, and beyond him Goodhew heard the unmistakable squeal of an up-and-over garage door.

So much for subtle signals.

Goodhew scrambled over the wall and ran towards the Lexus, parked facing forwards inside the fourth lock-up to the left. He stopped about six feet in front of the car and held out his warrant card.

'Police! You are under arrest!' Goodhew shouted.

In response came the sound of the engine gunning. He repeated his instruction just as the driver slammed his foot full on the accelerator and released the clutch.

Goodhew didn't have time to jump out of the way. But then he didn't need to. Only the driver's side of the car moved because Goodhew had already clamped the other back wheel, and the full power of the XE20's three-litre engine propelled it into the passenger-side wall of the garage.

The driver killed the engine and burst out of the car, but he was coughing too hard to run and Goodhew brought him down and cuffed him within a couple of yards of the front bumper.

Goodhew had no idea what the damage to the car might be but, judging by the amount of tyre smoke in the air, he suspected he could add four bald tyres to the aggravated burglary charge. He'd left his mobile for Ratty in case there was a problem, but Ratty was already gone and Goodhew's phone lay unattended on top of the wall.

He rang DI Marks.

Marks answered, saying, 'It's your day off.'

'Sorry, just how it worked out, sir. Didn't have time to call it in.'

Marks didn't acknowledge the excuse and then, in the background, Goodhew could hear him speaking to Kincaide on the radio. Marks was instructing him to bring his team over to join Goodhew.

Then Marks was back. 'Kincaide's not happy, but I'm sure you'll have worked that out. Stay there till Kincaide relieves you, then go home. And report to me in the morning.' On reflection Marks didn't sound too happy either but, by morning, Goodhew suspected that his boss would be more pleased to have Roy Kelvin off the streets than displeased about having one extra officer turning up uninvited.

Once relieved, Goodhew walked homewards, stopping at University Grocers in Magdalene Street for a can of Coke and a copy of the *Cambridge News*. Roy Kelvin's arrest would provide tomorrow's headline, but for today he was happy to just sit in the sun on Parker's Piece and catch up on any other local news.

As Goodhew sat reading on Parker's Piece, the same hot sun was scorching the wide tarmac that ran along Carlton Way. Like much of Cambridge, the street was totally flat. Regularly spaced trees had been planted when the houses were built half a century ago, but they had still not grown sufficiently to provide any decent shade. True, there was shade in the bus stop, but its metal roof and frame caused the air to be intensely hot, and even the broken windows refused to let a draught through.

Joey McCarthy knew these things; in fact, he reckoned he still knew everything there was to know about hot summers on the Arbury estate, though it was a long time since he'd lived here. A long time, too, since his natural aptitude for anything connected with a computer had first opened the door to the possibility of a proper 'career'.

Not that he'd wanted one, but it had taken only a few short contract assignments to show him how easily the application of skills he cultivated on his home PC, combined with tidy dress and the kind of bullshit he usually reserved for visits to his grandmother, could be converted into actual currency.

Real cash.

So he'd peeled away all the unwanted layers of his former life. He'd thrown away the idea that if you didn't want the cheap replica you had to nick the real one. And if you couldn't nick it, you couldn't have it.

He had broken off contact with most of his former friends, kept contact with his own family to a minimum. They didn't seem surprised by his lack of interest in them, but their expectations of anything in life had never been that high.

Joey had rented a large apartment halfway between the Cineworld Multiplex and the train station. It came with private parking, and shortly afterwards he had filled that space with a black Audi. It was two years old but top of the range.

Of all the layers he'd stripped away, one he had never quite managed to dispense with was Arbury itself – the Carlton Arms in particular.

The best pint is always the one in your first local, or so the landlord said.

But Joey knew, and admitted only to himself, that his real reason for going back there was to measure the ever-widening gulf between his success in life and the mediocre existence that he'd nearly been condemned to. He loved the way the regulars pretended not to notice his car as it swung into the car park. He accepted each nod of greeting as he strode into the bar, knowing that, behind their brief smiles, they felt the same sort of envy that he'd grown up feeling every day of his teenage years. He guessed that they looked at him with contempt. He knew exactly why, knew what it felt like to be on their side of the fence and felt proud that he'd left them behind.

* * *

Joey left two hours later, by which time the only remaining punters were male, and too absorbed in some European football game to pay any attention to his leaving.

'Cheers, mate,' he threw over his shoulder, in the direction of the landlord. If he got a reply, he didn't hear it.

He'd parked halfway across the car park, under the branches of a cherry tree where he hoped the car would catch plenty of shade but not too much birdshit. Joey pulled his keys from his pocket and aimed them towards his Audi, pressing the remote.

Nothing happened, so he guessed he was still too far away.

As usual, he cast his gaze a little further, just to see whether there was any sign of anybody casting an admiring glance in the direction of his vehicle. A woman, eyes down and ear bonded to her mobile, turned in from the main road and went inside the pub, still talking.

The car was about fifteen yards away when he tried again, but still no response. He pressed the button a couple more times, then studied the key, half wondering whether the battery was going flat. When he looked up again, a familiar figure stood in his path.

Despite the fact that this was their first contact in . . . he really didn't know how long, Joey found his lips curling into the same sneer that their encounters had always prompted. 'What d'*you* want?'

'Are you interested in politics?'

'Politics? What the—?'

'I'm not. Except for that moment when it suddenly gets interesting, like when one of them gets caught out – you know, put on the spot in front of a reporter. I always want them to get caught lying, but I stop listening and instead, watch their faces. And that's how I judge them. And that's why I came to see you.'

'About what?' Joey couldn't imagine why he now felt threatened, but he instinctively planted his feet squarely, shoulders-width apart, and felt himself puff out his chest and bulk up his shoulders. 'Seriously, when have I ever had anything to say to *you*?'

'I meant it literally. It's just to see you, to look at you. Do you really think I'd want some meaningless dialogue either? I only came to watch your face.'

Joey scowled. 'Just piss off.' He stepped to one side, wanting to get into his car and go.

'I know *everything*.'

The last thing Joey expected was any physical intervention. He knew he was the stronger of the two, and he doubted the owner of such precise hands would have the guts to lay a single finger on Joey's sleeve, yet those three words halted him with the same force as a punch to the guts.

He turned slowly, trying to maintain his mask. 'You don't know anything about me, so what are you getting at?' He was sure that his face remained expressionless, but knew his eyes were darting about uncontrollably.

For several seconds neither of them spoke, or moved, until finally, Joey stepped back, a small rebalancing of his weight, nothing more. 'You mean back then, don't you?'

'What else would I mean? We've barely seen each other since, have we?'

'It was just an accident.'

'Just an accident? And what would you say to me if I said I knew it wasn't? I'm standing here in front of you, and I'm telling you I *know* what happened – every detail. Now you are the politician, the one with the chance to tell the truth. And I am the audience, the one who is watching your face to see if you lie.'

Joey thought he had an aptitude for reading people, especially when, like now, he considered them a soft touch. It was always easy to spot when childlike fear had been visible too long into adolescence, and had then been picked upon by the stronger ones in the pack. But a single look told Joey that the eyes that returned his stare were dilated with something far more potent than fear, or even anger.

Resolve.

Then Joey half smiled: did the kid really think they were about to square up for a fight? 'Stop wasting my time.'

No reply.

'It's madness.' Joey tapped his temple a couple of times. 'You were never going to let it drop, were you?' He pushed past and, this time when he jabbed at his remote control, the central locking responded with a muted beep.

'It's a nice car.' A pause. 'I mean, I don't really like it – too pretentious. You'd only drive a car like that to a pub like this if you were trying to make a statement, one that you couldn't manage by turning up on foot.'

Despite knowing he ought to go, Joey turned his back on the car. 'And your point?'

'Brand new, top-of-the-range Audi which only unlocks at the fourth bloody attempt? I don't think so.'

Joey was caught between the urge to step forward, and further into the confrontation, and an unfamiliar but stronger urge to get into his car and drive away. So instead he didn't move.

'So I'm thinking there's nothing wrong with the technology, which means there has to be something wrong with your aim, perhaps, and your level of soberness without doubt. So what's the truth I see? You're not somebody who has learned a sense of responsibility, or really suffered, or knows any compassion.'

Joey scowled. He realized that this was the moment to speak, but there was nothing he could say that would ever be genuinely heartfelt or truthful. So he stayed silent. And unmoving. And, in his remaining seconds, he was aware that his quick wits and speed had deserted him when he needed them both most.

He became a spectator as, with no sign of a stumbling childhood or awkward adolescence, his assailant moved closer.

The reversal of the roles was absolute, and Joey finally understood the power that a bully wielded from the point of view of the stunned prey.

This was action without hesitation. No self-conscious wavering, just a single fluid movement from pocket to hand to neck. A 6-inch thin shaft of flathead screwdriver, rubberized handle. No slip or resistance, through skin, into artery.

Joey's eyes were wide, his mouth wide, his blood pumping. It splattered across his driver's side window, and he reached towards it, his fingers sliding through slippery wetness as he sank to the ground and died.

ONE

Libby wrote: *Hi, Zoe, thanks for the friend request. How are you? I heard you died.*

'Doing well for a dead person. LOL.'

There was a gap of a few minutes before Libby replied. *Sorry, that was bad taste.*

Then there was a gap of a few minutes more.

'I heard about your sister,' Zoe wrote. 'You know she was in my year at school?'

Of course. Your profile picture comes from your class photo. I think you're standing just behind Rosie. She's got a funny look on her face, told me once how you pulled her hair just as the flash went off.

'Yeah, I was in the back row and we were all standing on gym benches. The kids in her row were messing around, trying to get us to fall off. Mrs Hurley saw me wobble and yelled at me. I tugged Rosie's hair to get my own back. I reckon that was Year Seven or Eight. I don't remember seeing Rosie much after that.'

Libby had hesitated over the keyboard. She didn't want this to become nothing more than awkward and pointless chit-chat. She had an opportunity here and, although she guessed it was going to be difficult to get things started, she knew that she needed to do it.

I have a proposition . . . a favour, I suppose. You see, I don't have anyone to talk to. Rosie's death left a hole, but there's more and, if I'm honest, I'm struggling a bit. I've tried writing it down, but it just doesn't work. I get so far, then I'm stuck. So I wondered if I could message you?

'Do you think that would work?'

I don't know, but I'd like to try. I thought you might ask me some questions, prompt me to look at things differently. Or maybe I just need to let things out, I'm not sure. The point is, I need to talk.

Those first messages took up little space on her computer screen, yet Libby felt as though getting even that far had taken up the equivalent effort of a 2,000-word essay. She had worked hard to balance her words, to load them equally between truthfulness and understatement. *I need to talk* had been a tough admission, as it stank of being unable to cope. The last thing she had wanted, through all of this, had been to load anyone else with any part of this burden. But she now accepted that it was the only way to move forward. She thought of Nathan and wished she could speak to him – or her parents even, but they were almost as inaccessible as her brother.

And what about Matt?

No, when she looked at him she recognized what other people saw when they looked at her. It was a hollowness that scared her.

She read Zoe's 'Okay' and nodded to herself. This was something she had to do.

I'm not sure where to start, she told Zoe.

'Begin with Rosie.'

Libby took a deep breath. *Rosie, Rosie.*

Rosie was in your year, Nathan was one year below, and then there was me, two years below him. I'm 18 now, just to save you working it out, and I'm at sixth form college. The course is a bunch of 'A' levels and the college propectus calls them a 'Foundation in Accountancy'. I'd always wanted to work with small children, but I assumed I'd just leave school and get a job in an office or something.

Instead I chose this course. I gave them all the spiel but, in truth, the only reason I'm doing it is because they were the same 'A' levels that Rosie took. She was going to get a degree. She wanted to be a primary school teacher one day, and I bet she would have managed it.

I'm explaining it this way because it shows what Rosie and I were like; how we were similar but different. On a parallel track except I was always a little bit behind, and a little bit in her shadow.

'But she was three years older?'

Yes, and I'm almost the same age now, but I still haven't caught up with her in so many ways. And you're misunderstanding me if you think I feel that's a bad thing. I was happy in her shadow: it was always a safe and comfortable place to be.

For my entire childhood I could look up and see Rosie and Nathan. Rosie teased Nathan, and Nathan teased me; that was our pecking order. And if Nathan ever upset me, Rosie stepped in, or the other way round.

I can't remember one single time when I didn't have one or other of them to look after me.

Anyhow, now I feel like I need to follow in her footsteps, at least for a little while. I'm not ready to let go of her yet, so I sit in the same lectures and try my hardest to get grades as good as hers. That's what got me through school. It's like she's been there before me and I can feel her looking over my shoulder. She says 'Go on, Bibs, you can do it.' No one calls me Bibs any more, and I wouldn't want them to.

Then after a gap of almost twenty minutes, Libby added, *Can I message you tomorrow?*

'Of course.'

TWO

What do you know about Rosie's death?
'Just bits and pieces – you know how fragments of information fly about.'
Can I tell you?
'Only if you want to.'

The short version is that she went to the cinema and never came back. The short version is important to remember, because to me that's how it happened. I was in my bedroom – my hair was three or four inches longer then, and I was straightening it. Rosie heard me swearing, came into the room and finished the section that I couldn't reach properly.

I told her she looked nice, but I was too wrapped up in my own night out to pay her much attention; later that night, Mum and Dad asked me what she'd been wearing and I just couldn't remember. I knew that, when she put the hair straighteners on my dressing-table, I noticed that she'd had her nails repainted a slightly metallic shade of purple.

And that's really all I could remember. I can't remember which cinema, which film or if she said who she was going with. I can't remember a single word she said, just the touch of her fingers as she separated the strands of my hair, and the colour of her nails as she finished.

I tell myself that I can't remember all those things because I never knew them, that she'd never shared the details with me. I don't believe though that she would have ever gone to watch a film on her own. And I find it equally hard to believe that I wouldn't have said, 'Who are you going with?'

I went to the beauty salon a couple of weeks later and bought a bottle of that same nail polish. I've still got it in my drawer.

I returned home just before 1 a.m. I came back in a taxi and, as it pulled up, I noticed the lights on in our front room, with the curtains open. I could make out Mum and Dad standing apart from one another. It was only a brief glimpse but I felt uneasy and hurried inside.

Nathan was there too. You can see our kitchen as soon as you walk through the front door and he was standing by the kettle, pouring boiling water into three mugs.

'What's happened?' I mouthed at him.

'They tried to ring you because they can't get hold of Rosie. But your phone was off.'

In that case, I reasoned, they wouldn't get hold of me either, would they? Why were they so worried about her when they weren't worried about me?

I can't really remember how I felt at that moment. I think I wondered why there was this amount of fuss. Or maybe I realized something was up. Mum's always been a bit paranoid, and Rosie had only passed her driving test a few months before.

Dad called through from the front room and asked me what Rosie had said to me about her plans for the evening. Mum snapped at him, told him to get to the point. He snapped back.

Then he turned to me and started, 'It's probably nothing, but . . .'

Even now those words always fill me with dread.

Rosie had told Mum that she'd be back by eleven. No biggie on its own, but Nathan had been playing an away match for the Carlton Arms pool team, and she'd promised him a lift home. Her phone kept going straight to voicemail, so he waited for her till 11.30, then rang our parents as he walked home.

Like I said, it never took much to make Mum start worrying, and this was plenty. Nathan said she'd made Dad phone the police at half-past midnight. I suppose there wasn't much the police could say at that point, except to let us know that they'd had no incidents involving anyone called Rose, Rosie or Rosalyn, or with the surname Brett.

Straight after I got home, Mum told him to call the police again. He was kept on hold for a while, and said they were being very polite and understanding, but I could tell that they'd left him with the feeling that he was totally overreacting.

I don't know if you remember much about my dad, but he's a stubborn bloke, and when he makes his mind up about something, it's really hard to get him to shift. 'That's enough now,' he decided, and demanded that we all go and get some sleep.

So of course Mum started to argue with him, and he refused to budge. I looked at Nathan, and he just raised his eyebrows. It wasn't like we hadn't seen it all countless times before.

We left them there to wrangle, although I don't remember hearing another sound from them.

I lay down on my bed fully dressed, and let the rest of the house think I'd gone to sleep. I heard Nathan's door close, and imagined him in the next room, doing exactly the same. I don't think I slept at all. Maybe it wasn't like that, but that's how I remember it.

If I did stay awake, it wasn't because I was scared for Rosie. I didn't believe for one second that I'd never see her again. It was more that I kind of felt out of kilter.

Funny phrase that: out of kilter. I don't even know what a kilter is. And that's the point. I knew something was up, but I didn't have enough experience to guess . . .

Libby's intended words had trailed off to nothing. The minutes ticked by as she tried to finish the paragraph, but didn't think she could. For a moment she was tempted to delete the whole page, but that would amount to avoiding talking about Rosie. She could promise herself to type it again, but she knew that it wouldn't happen.

She pressed 'send'.

Zoe's reply was typically short: 'Can you tell me what happened?'

Libby gave a little smile. In Zoe's photo she had cropped dark hair and the type of face that looked serious even in the middle of a grin. Zoe didn't need her messages surrounded by frilly words. This was exactly the reason she had picked Zoe to talk to; with her it was okay to be blunt, which in turn took away the excuse to give up. Libby typed quickly.

They found Rosie's car first, parked up on a bridge crossing the A14. Her body was about half a mile away down on the carriageway. She'd been run over. More than that, actually, but I think, to explain it all . . . I just can't do that right now.

Can I just say 'multiple injuries' and tell you the rest some other time? The press referred to it as suicide.

The police were more cautious and listed other factors: bad weather, poor visibility, heavy traffic and so on. The A14 is notorious for its high accident rate. They never found out what had really happened. At least that's what they told us, but I have a feeling that they did know. They just couldn't prove it, and in the end, the verdict was left open.

I couldn't grasp it at first. It didn't seem possible. Even at Rosie's funeral it didn't seem real, then finally, when I understood that she really was dead, the questions started to form in my head. Little things at first. *Had she ever made it to the cinema? Which film had she seen? Who had she gone with?*

I asked myself: *what was it that had prompted her to drive out anywhere near the A14?*

I also wondered how long it'd taken for her to die. I didn't go to the inquest, Mum and Dad were there, but I could hardly ask them. It's questions like that which make me worry that I have become overly morbid.

My list of questions grows, and I can't stop it. And when I don't have proper explanations, I start to invent the answers. It's a bad habit and I feel like my life is only half lit now, and instead of

14

looking to the light, I'm turning towards the darkest corners. I've got it into my head that there is some evil lurking just out of sight. And I'm straining to see it.

You see, I thought things couldn't get worse, and that losing Rosie was enough.

In fact, it was enough. But what has happened since is too much.

THREE

Charlotte Stone knew the history of the Regal Cinema. She knew that it had opened in 1937 and managed to survive for sixty years, through the Second World War, a name change, and even a fire in the mid-1980s. Competition from new movie houses had come and gone, with their rise, demise and conversion into bingo halls. In the end it was the opening of the multiplex in the Grafton Complex that led it to closing its doors in 1997. However, the Regal was a survivor, and re-emerged two years later with its lower floors turned into the Regal pub, and the upper floors converted into the three-screen Arts Picture House.

Charlotte Stone loved the old building's interior – the curved staircases and the grand Art Deco light-fittings – but most of all she loved it because it was situated slap bang in the middle of St Andrews Street, not too far from her bakery counter job at the town centre branch of Sainsbury's, but also near the shops she liked to browse, the busiest bars and her favourite pizzeria.

She and Holly left the auditorium and returned to the bar for a post-movie drink, picking a small table halfway along the lounge, with a black-and-white poster of Vivien Leigh looking down on them. Vivien's eyes were dark and clear, defined by perfectly separated long lashes. Charlotte looked at her friend and, despite the subdued lighting, she could clearly see dark smudges round her eyes.

'Forgot your waterproof mascara?' she asked.

'It's a good film.'

'*The Notebook*'s a classic, made even better because we're here, right?'

'Okay, okay, I can see that watching it here has more atmosphere than seeing it on DVD. But I'd still have cried at home. I like films wherever I watch them – even on a plane I still enjoy them.' Holly smiled. 'I already know what you're going to say next.'

'What?'

'What your dad always says.' Holly slouched back in her chair, with her arms lying along the armrests and her fists planted squarely one on each side, '"It's like drinking a good beer from a plastic cup".'

Charlotte giggled at the accuracy of the vocal impression.

As Holly's mobile started to vibrate, she picked up her shoulder bag and reached for her phone. She glanced at the caller display. 'Your brother.'

Charlotte stopped mid-laugh, and quickly reached forward to take the phone. 'Matt? What's wrong?'

Matt's voice sounded tight. 'I couldn't get hold of you. Where have you been?'

'The Picture House with Holly. I turned my phone off.'

'You could have left it on silent, then you'd have noticed that I'd rung. You know how I start to think . . . Anyway, Holly didn't turn hers off.'

Charlotte bit her lip and silently counted to three, hoping to calm him. 'I expect she forgot,' she said quietly. 'We can't answer phone calls in the cinema, Matt. Or text, either,' she added, pre-empting his next reproach. 'Have you been drinking?'

'No.'

'What, then?'

'You think I can't feel anything unless I've got some alcohol in me?'

'That's not what I said.'

'You just more or less said it: if I'm upset, it means I must be drunk. No, I'm sober – which usually means I will do anything

17

possible not to think about it, but it's always there. How couldn't it be? It takes alcohol to numb it just a little bit, and why is it so terrible if sometimes that's what I need so that I can start to understand things.'

'Matt, please . . .'

He was audibly crying now. 'That's all I want to do, just to understand a little bit, so I can move on. How am I supposed to study or plan things for the future, when there's nothing there.'

'Matt, listen to me—'

'Why? Why, Charlie? You don't know any more than me. There's nothing you can tell me, or promise me that means . . .' Her brother's voice disintegrated into sobs, then silence as he disconnected the call.

Charlotte dropped Holly's phone on to the table. 'I need to go.'

She threw on her jacket and snatched up her bag, glancing just once in Holly's direction. She saw her friend's disappointed but accepting expression, and then left without another word.

Charlotte ran down the stairs and out on to the wet pavement. She'd done this before, too many times to count now, but perversely such a response felt increasingly urgent. She didn't buy her father's *Cry wolf* theory. Did that mean that, one day, there could come a point when she was the only one still listening to her brother?

She switched her mobile phone on even as she ran, then stuffed it straight back in her pocket. By the time it was ready to use, she'd be almost there.

She turned right down Emmanuel Street, raced through the bus station – and on to the open green space of Christ's Pieces. At the far end lay some tennis courts surrounded by a high mesh fence.

Despite the coolness of the evening, she knew that's where she'd find her brother.

He was crouching on his heels, holding on to the fence for balance. His head was bowed, and he was silent. She was aware that she'd seen her little brother almost every day since his arrival in the world a month after her own fourth birthday. She knew him better than anyone. Certainly better than their parents did, and maybe better than his best friend Nathan ever had.

He already knew she was there, but he didn't look up.

She ran to the fence and kicked at it, about a foot above the ground. 'Bastard.' She kicked the fence again, causing a ripple that rattled loudly behind him. 'Why don't you ever think about how *I'm* feeling?'

Matt mumbled something but still didn't look up.

'Every time you do this, it scares me. Matt – listen to me. You need to get some help – more than just me, as I'm not an expert. There'll be a student welfare officer or someone, a proper counsellor . . .'

He lifted his head. 'Like I said, *you* understand. What's the point of me speaking to some complete stranger? They can have all the qualifications, but they never met Mum, they never met Nathan.'

She shook her head. 'You're not listening to me, Matt. I *do* understand, I understand so well that, when you phone me and you sound distressed, I get scared. *Really* scared. And when you phone and can't get hold of me, you get scared too. We are both the same, but we're getting out of control. We have to find a way to help each other, not make things worse.'

'I don't know where to begin. Do you?'

'No, but we need to start to get over it.'

'Like Dad, you mean?' She heard the tightness in his voice.

Charlotte's anger had been subsiding, but she couldn't help reacting, and her temper surged again.

'Because he enjoys a drink with a friend, or a night out, you think he's happy?'

'Happier than when she was alive.' Matt scrambled to his feet, reaching into his pocket and pulling out a badly folded bundle of A4 printouts. 'We need somewhere with more light.'

He led them down the narrow alleyway between the Champion of the Thames pub and kebab shop, and stopped in front of the glowing kebab-shop window. He opened out the sheets of paper and thrust them towards her.

Stress and cancer link confirmed by scientists.

She only had to look at this first heading to know that every page would offer evidence of the same theory. 'You have to stop this, Matt. It's no one's fault she died. You can't blame Dad.'

'He gave her a hard time.'

'No – you just thought he did.'

'How many times did you come home from school to see she'd been crying? Or looking sick with worry? There's nothing else that could make her that unhappy – only Dad. And if it wasn't him, why didn't he fix it?'

Charlotte opened her mouth to argue but Matt got in first, grabbing back the sheets of paper and waving them in her face.

'I've bookmarked loads of it. It's all over the Internet, and it wouldn't be if it wasn't true, would it?'

'The Internet's full of crap.'

'When it suits you, it is. I've seen your search history, Charlie, and you're just like me except you want to find the answer somewhere else.'

Charlotte turned and looked up the street in the direction of the house Matt shared with the other students. His gaze followed hers.

Suddenly Charlotte had had enough. Now she just wanted him to go home.

No, that wasn't true. What she actually wanted was for him to *come* home, to make peace with their dad and stop asking her questions that she couldn't answer, or couldn't face asking herself. She turned back to him, but he continued to look away.

'Why don't you fix it, Matt? Come home, and talk to Dad. He'd answer your questions. I know he would.'

Matt shook his head then started to walk away. Charlotte followed.

It was only a few yards, but in that time Matt remained silent. Charlotte guessed he was angry with her, thinking she'd pushed it too far this time. But when he stopped just outside his front-room window and turned towards her, she realized that he had started to cry.

She grabbed hold of him and held him tight. Through his tears he sobbed the truth, and told her his biggest fear.

FOUR

Libby looked out from the window of her first-floor bedroom in the student house. She was the youngest of the seven housemates and the only one still studying for A levels. They were a mix of first-year students attending Anglia Ruskin University, second-year students at Cambridge University and one post-grad American. Her name was Shanie and somehow she managed to be the least worldly-wise of them all.

Libby and Matt had been involved in choosing the house. A quirk of the fact that it was their two fathers who had control of the purse strings and had been anxious to find accommodation that they all agreed upon. It hadn't mattered to her that Long Road sixth form college was a mile and half across town. By the time she had convinced her dad that this house would be just a few short steps home from almost every night out, he'd dropped his objections to her daily bike ride to and from classes.

Libby preferred this side of the city. Her window faced in the approximate direction of her childhood home in Avbury. She couldn't see it and it certainly wasn't where she wanted to live right now but that didn't mean she wasn't glad to know it was there. The foot of her bed abutted the windowsill, and she lay across it, with her face close to the glass.

She was a fraction over five foot three in height so found lying across the bed as comfortable as lying on it lengthways. She was propped up on her elbows, with her fair hair scooped away from her face.

The others were downstairs playing poker and she'd declined the game, saying she had an assignment to finish. It was actually true, but there was nothing like some pressing coursework to give her the urge to check her emails. Normally this would result in a couple of hours lost while bouncing between her inbox, eBay and Facebook, but after the first email her thoughts drifted to Matt.

They were close, and usually he talked to her, but not tonight.

Something was bothering him – but that was a stupid thing to think, for when was it *not* bothering him? Tonight though, bad thoughts had drawn him in and she saw the pain written on his face. He'd gone to the fridge, raiding Oslo's shelf for a can of lager, then, after a couple of swigs, had tipped it into the sink in disgust. He'd opened and shut everyone else's food cupboards, finally settling for a bottle of vodka belonging to one of the girls.

He then knocked back about four shots in the quickest time possible.

Libby had watched him from the doorway. She assumed he knew she was standing there but, as he turned to leave the kitchen, he seemed surprised when he realized he'd been observed. Still he said nothing, brushing past her and hurrying along the hallway, slamming the front door as he went out.

She waited a few minutes, then she sent him a text. He didn't reply, so she decided to leave him alone, for the time being at least.

After answering one email, she went to the window and checked in both directions, then returned to her PC and sent the next email. As the evening wore on, the gaps between each email expanded as she spent longer by the window. It was over two hours since he'd left when she relented and sent him a second text message. She placed the mobile on the narrow windowsill and watched out of the sash window as she waited for a reply.

There was plenty of banter coming from downstairs, and she wondered who was winning. She usually made it to the last three players and it sounded close to that point now. Shanie kept on top of the dealing, reminding everyone which player was the big blind, the small blind, and telling the dealer to 'burn a card' several times during every hand. Shanie was still in then, since she usually disappeared to her room once her chips were gone. Libby could hear Jamie-Lee's perpetually loud voice, too, and decided she too was still in play. Then there was Oslo – she couldn't actually hear him, but he rarely missed the final hand.

Most weeks it took them at least a couple of hours to get to that point. She picked up her phone to check the time: just after 11 p.m. Where was Matt?

Half an hour later she spotted him, walking back, from the opposite direction of town, followed by his sister Charlotte. He stopped outside the front of the house to talk to her.

Libby moved away from the glass, but lying lower on the bed and watching over the lip of the windowsill.

The two weren't saying much. Libby could see he was upset, but that might be a good thing. Everyone said crying helped. Some said it to her in a tone that implied they were giving good advice. Others said it in voices tinged with suspicion; they'd noticed that she seemed as though she hadn't shed a tear. And they were right – she hadn't, but that didn't mean it wasn't right for Matt to cry.

She pressed her right index finger on to the glass, touching the spot beyond which he stood. Anything that helped him hurt less was fine by her.

Her finger was only there for a moment before she withdrew it. She rolled on to her back and stared at the ceiling instead.

At seventeen years, eleven months and four days old, she knew she had plenty to learn. But the advantage of growing up in a home with two older siblings was learning even as they learned. She'd seen first-hand why some good ideas were doomed to fail, and why some successes only came after making mistakes.

She had also learned that there were always options, even if none was desirable. And there were always answers, too. Answers and options vying for importance. She had learned so much from Rosie and Nathan, so losing them was like having every page of her

23

memory scattered to the wind. Each family milestone now meant nothing, the petty rivalries no longer existed, and the two people who had taught her the most had left her alone to teach herself.

Libby was dreading her birthday for, in just a month, it would be followed by the day when she had lived longer than her oldest sibling, and the path from then on out would truly be untrodden.

Answers and options. Her future was full of them.

Once she had the answers, then maybe there would come a time when she felt the need to cry. But right now she couldn't, and wouldn't. She had her reasons, and no plans to share them.

FIVE

Matt opened the front door quietly, his first thought being to avoid the others and slip off to his room. But, as usual, he found himself drawn towards the buzz in the kitchen. Seven of them shared the house and all but Libby had been playing poker around the table.

'All right?' He nodded towards them.

Meg and Phil were out of chips and responded immediately, but Shanie and Oslo were too engrossed to even look up. The fifth, Jamie-Lee, gave a thumbs-up. 'I'm in the last three,' she pointed to a dwindling pile of chips, 'but only just.'

'Cool.'

The house was old, and he guessed it'd been extended several times over the years. This extended room was a knock-through between one of the original reception rooms and a later addition of a kitchen.

Matt forced himself to drink a pint of water. It tasted foul but, after the amount of alcohol he'd drunk, it was either that or vomiting later. Knowing his luck, he'd have to put up with both.

He moved back to the dining area end before somebody got the bright idea of using him as a waiter.

He eyed his housemates and realized that the scene reminded him of the poker-playing dogs in the famous paintings by Cassius Coolidge. He had never noticed that before. Maybe alcohol was enhancing his artistic eye. The walls had that same shade of pub red as in *A Bold Bluff*, and the ceiling light which hung over the table looked like a little green Chinese coolie hat. They even had full-height bookshelves stacked with titles that everybody needed but nobody seemed to read.

Meg had to be the rough collie: similar hairdo for one thing, bright and sharp featured too. It suited Phil to be the bulldog, small, solid and stubborn looking, whereas Oslo bore more resemblance to a Labrador/Alsatian cross than he did to a St Bernard or Great Dane.

Matt smiled to himself as he realized his analogy was running out of steam, for even in his head he wouldn't dare compare either Shanie or Jamie-Lee to one of the bigger dog breeds. But the image was there now, so, for the sake of diplomacy, he substituted breeds, making Jamie-Lee a lively and affectionate red setter and Shanie a keen-to-be-loved retriever.

'Hey, Matt, what are you thinking?' Jamie asked.

'Nothing, why?'

'You've got a stupid look on your face, like you're mentally undressing us or something.'

'What, all of us?' Phil piped up. 'At the same time? Sicko.'

Then Meg intervened, 'Leave him alone. He's drunk.'

Jamie lifted what was left of his large glass of cider. 'So what. We've all had a few, haven't we?'

'Difference is, he looks like he's been bawling his eyes out.'

Jamie stiffened. 'You are so crass sometimes, Meg.'

Meg shrugged. 'What are we supposed to do, sit here pretending we haven't noticed? Matt looks like shit and who hadn't spotted it? Hands up.' She looked around the room before concluding, 'It was hard to miss.'

'Meg. Hush up, now,' Shanie hissed. Her American accent contrasted sharply with the other voices and she seemed embarrassed, even though she didn't need to be.

Meg remained defiant. 'Didn't put your hand up though, did you?'

'No, I sure didn't.' Shanie's voice quivered, clearly reluctant to get involved.

'No, I sure didn't.' Meg attempted to mimic her, but her accent came out closer to Tennessee than Indiana.

Meg continued to bait Shanie until part of Matt felt he should intervene – but he didn't. It might have been the comments about himself that initially provoked this spat, but he guessed that these two would have kicked off at some point in the evening anyway. They usually did.

Meg was a waiflike bottle-blonde who wore skinny black jeans and check shirts, baseball boots and black nail varnish. She drank beer from the bottle and cited Tank Girl. Nothing prompted her to speak up like a moment calling for subtlety.

By contrast, everything about Shanie, from the tone of her voice to the curve of her bust, was gently rounded and natural. Her world view was well intentioned and serious.

The two girls were so incompatible it was almost a joke putting them under the same roof.

Matt could see that Shanie had now had enough of Meg as, with barely a change of tone she interrupted the other girl, 'You want my opinion? You are a complete bitch. Ugly all the way through.'

'So I'm just being direct, and now I'm a bitch?' Meg grinned nastily then turned to Matt. 'I think she fancies you.'

Shanie stared down at her playing cards as Oslo and Jamie made a show of restarting the game. It seemed as though everyone was waiting for her to take her turn, and Matt watched her struggle with her feelings.

After a long minute, Shanie dropped the cards and rushed out of the room.

Matt drew a heavy breath, but didn't follow.

No one did.

SIX

I'm sorry I left it for a couple of days, but I needed a breather after my last message. But talking to you is doing me good, Zoe.

'I think you should carry on then. Tell me what happened after Rosie died.'

OK then, but I'll need to explain my whole family, not just Rosie.

We lived in the same house, down that funny cul-de-sac where the road bulges into a circle at the end so that cars can swing round. We call it Banjo Street, which is what my dad christened it when he was a kid. I doubt much has changed since you lived on the estate; apart from some replacement double glazing and newer cars, I think it looks pretty much the same.

My dad grew up in this house, moved my mum in, married her, then stayed put until my grandparents went into a residential home. My mum and dad have been together since they were teenagers. They're not very adventurous, but no one else around here is.

I used to be really proud of them, feeling sure that they were really solid because, however many times they fought, they never talked about splitting up. But when you're a kid you don't see much of other people's lives. Well, I didn't, and I thought that everybody else's parents were pretty much the same, and the ones that got divorced must have hated each other even more than mine did.

Maybe they didn't hate each other back then; it could have just been years of frustration and disappointment that turned into mutual distaste. Hating each other started with Rosie's death.

And if part of their logic for staying together is that they are doing it for their children, then the spiteful streak in my personality says they're now almost off the hook.

Two down, one to go.

Shit, where did that come from?

I'm sorry, sorry, sorry.

The inquest, investigation and funeral planning seemed to drag on for weeks, and through all that time my parents mastered a fake civility towards each other. They hugged, cried together and talked for long periods in hushed tones. It was unnatural for us, like living with two strangers. And obviously it couldn't last.

Nathan's best mate was Matt. Our family has always known theirs, so they went through school together. I started following them around and they didn't tell me to clear off, so I suppose they felt sorry for me. Matt's mum had died of cancer a few months earlier, and the three of us would always hang out together.

It was funny but we didn't ever talk much.

Usually we would distract ourselves with the Internet, or a DVD or some unstimulating computer game that would allow us to communicate via top scores and new challenges. We couldn't do that on the morning of the funeral, of course.

Nathan and I sat with our parents all through the service. We are not a churchgoing family though, and the interior of the Good Shepherd Church would have looked unfamiliar if this hadn't been my second funeral there in just a few months.

Last time, Matt had sat at the front.

The church was built at the same time as the rest of the estate. It seemed as though the architect's remit had been to design it as if a good proportion of those hundreds of new households would be attending there every week. The result was something that resembled the plainest of chapels accidentally built entirely to the wrong scale. I imagine that most weeks the vicar preached to a congregation that consisted of just half a dozen parishioners, each one politely occupying their own pew.

But today the church was full. I turned and scanned the congregation, and spotted Matt sitting very solemn and upright on a pew near the back. In the rows between, I saw plenty of faces I barely recognized. There's nothing like a combination of youth and tragedy to fill a church, I guess. Matt saw me and gave a little nod of acknowledgement. He'd warned me that it was too soon for Rosie's loss to sink in, and as I looked at him, I could see that losing his mum had left him looking more battered than anyone else present.

This was the first time I had lost anyone close to me, I wasn't sure how I was feeling and, until I worked it out, my instinct was to keep it private. I kept my head bowed for most of the service, and made it through to the end without crying. Maybe Nathan had the same idea, as he gripped my hand hard, but I never heard him sobbing.

It was just a very small group of family and close friends that came back to the house with us. They were Mum and Dad's close friends, as neither Rosie's nor mine were invited. Matt and his sister Charlotte were brought along by their dad, then there were the grandparents, the wedding-invite list of aunts and uncles, and a few other old schoolmates of my dad's that I suspected he'd barely seen since he married Mum.

I think Charlotte felt awkward, because she disappeared into the kitchen and made tea and coffee with Aunt Jess. Nathan went out for a cigarette. He found a can of lager and stood on the patio, can in one hand, packet of fags in the other.

Matt and I sat side by side on the settee, each holding a mug of coffee and pretending to be adults, while the adults stood in groups making small talk. I found myself staring at the back of someone's dark grey suit. There was a grease mark on one elbow, and I must have been staring at it for a while.

I was suddenly aware that Matt had spoken after he nudged me. 'Well?'

I shrugged.

'Do you want me to hang around?'

I shrugged again, and he took that as a yes.

I realized then that the room had almost emptied and it wasn't long before he was the only visitor left. He'd spent so much time in our house by then that my parents no longer noticed him. They had certainly given up tempering their behaviour when he was around, and the mood there changed within seconds of my father shutting the door behind the last guest.

There was a smash from the kitchen and, before either of us could get up, my dad shot across the front room just fast enough to witness the destruction of a second item from their only smart tea set.

'How could you stand there talking to your old school buddies as if nothing has happened? Did they even know Rosie? Most of them had never even seen her since she was a little kid. And what about me? Out here trying to make polite conversation with their fucking wives, when all I want to say is, "You have no fucking idea how I'm feeling." If they did, they'd have had the fucking decency to stay away, instead of standing here in my fucking kitchen . . .'

'Fucking kitchen' was accompanied by another smash.

'Making fucking small talk . . .'

Another smash.

'And leaving me to wash their fucking tea cups.'

Dad made it across the kitchen before anything else was broken. That was the point where he might have been able to dissipate her temper with a show of compassion or understanding, or even a bit of both. But that had never been his way.

'Why is it all about you, Vicky? I had them here because I want support but, no, all you can do is twist it round so I've done something wrong. Just look at yourself.'

'So it's my fault? I wasn't the one forever pushing Rosie to do better.'

'No, you were the one holding her back. I wanted her to get a good job, to get out—'

'You pressured her!'

'Encouraged.'

31

I looked at Matt, screwing up my nose, knowing we were probably still at the prettier end of the fight.

He smiled in a way that said he felt sorry for me. 'We could get out of the house now?' he suggested.

'We should stay for Nathan.'

'A DVD, then?'

I nodded, but neither of us made a move for another ten minutes or so. I closed my eyes and listened to my parents, as they became increasingly vindictive. Then, when he couldn't stand hearing any more, Matt dragged me to my feet. 'You choose the film. I'll get Nath.'

As it turned out, he didn't need to. I hadn't even reached the top of the stairs when I heard the back door burst open, then slam shut again, and Nathan's voice cut right through the house.

'You're never going to stop, are you? We've spent our whole lives listening to your screaming matches. And when you weren't fighting, we were all holding our breath waiting for the next round. When I was little, Rosie would hear me crying. She was probably only seven or eight years old and trying to look after me.'

I heard someone moving round the kitchen. I imagined Mum and Dad repositioning themselves, trying to change their body language from confrontational to parental. I knew it was a bit late for that and, with barely a pause, Nathan continued, 'Always so wrapped up in yourselves. That's all you've ever been, and now you're wondering what happened to Rosie – whether she killed herself and how each of you can blame the other.'

'Nathan!' That was Mum, echoed, a moment later, with less surprise, by my dad.

And Nathan shouted right back: 'You're surprised? Surprised I've finally spoken out? Or what?'

Nobody spoke, then I heard Nathan heading towards me. I stepped to one side as he barged past me on the stairs. He grabbed his jacket and pushed past me on his way back down, too.

There have been times since then when I imagined that he'd later wished he'd touched my arm, or given me some other sign of solidarity, but he didn't. And I know it would be wrong to paint it into the picture.

He left the house and, although there were other times after that when we talked, I can't remember them as clearly. The day of Rosie's funeral became the last vivid memory I have of Nathan.

SEVEN

Dear Zoe,

This weekend has been strange. *I've* been strange.

I like having people around me. They don't tend to die when they're right in front of you, for one thing. There I go again: dark humour.

I like having people around me for comfort, and even the ones I don't like much distract me from the thoughts that stalk me when I'm by myself. But this weekend I chose to be alone, and that in itself was strange.

It started on Friday with the good intention of shutting myself in my room and working on my assignment, but ended with me splitting my time between messaging you and watching the real world out of my window. I spied on Matt and his sister Charlotte from the end of my bed and then, after he'd gone indoors, I still lay there just listening to my housemates squabbling downstairs and watching the trickle of people who find a reason to potter through King Street late on a Friday night.

I heard him come up the stairs, so I crept across the room and quietly locked my door, then sneaked back over to my bed and pretended to be asleep when he knocked. I actually lay with my head on my pillow and my eyes shut, as though that made it more believable for him, and I smiled to myself when I realized how farcical it was.

When I woke up on Saturday morning, it was barely six o'clock as I slipped downstairs and raided the fridge for yoghurt and orange juice. By the time I took my plate back upstairs, it was also loaded with toast and Marmite, two chocolate muffins and an apple.

I've been on detox days where you have nothing but fresh water for twenty-four hours. I don't know if it does much but, by the end of it, I have noticed a certain feeling of being refreshed. I made it to the kitchen and back without seeing another soul, and when I shut my bedroom door behind me again I had the idea that it might be nice to just stay in there, completely undisturbed, for the rest of the day. A kind of 'people detox'.

Of course, it was nothing against Matt or anyone else in the house, and just to be sure that he didn't worry about me, like I would worry about him if the tables were turned, I sent him a text which read *Gone shopping in London, text me if you need me xxx*

Just to make sure he knew, I sent it to Jamie and Shanie as well. Between the three of them, he'd get the message. He hates shopping, and I've made the forty-five-minute trip on the train enough times for him to think I wasn't acting out of character. He did text me back twice, but once I was confident that his alarm bells were genuinely disabled, I settled down with a book, a blanket and my food stash, and had the whole day to myself.

Believing that no one realized I was at home left my conscience clear of the urge to be sociable, or domesticated, when I actually felt like neither. For the first time I noticed how the house had its own sounds and rhythm. Even when everyone had gone out, I could still hear the gentle creaking of the nearest tree in the garden, the breeze in the chimneys and the sighing of doors and sash windows.

In the quietest part of the afternoon I heard footsteps on the stairs, wary and hesitant. They stopped on the landing outside my door, then crept up to the next landing and paused there, too. I moved closer to my bedroom door, standing with my ear close to the jamb. I heard a key turn in a lock upstairs where Phil and Oslo have their bedrooms.

It hadn't sounded like either of them. Phil usually trudged while, as often as not, Oslo's steps were short and hurried. For that reason,

I carried on listening. I heard the first door shut and relock – then, to my surprise, I heard the second door being opened, too. I looked up at the ceiling, towards the point over my head where I guessed the person now stood. After a minute he or she moved further into the room, and after another minute back towards the door.

I heard the door being re-locked, then the footsteps coming towards me as they returned down the stairs.

Sometimes the obvious only becomes obvious to me, as it unfolds. This was one of those moments.

My face was still an inch from the doorjamb as the footsteps stopped outside my own room. I saw the magnolia paint smear on my round Bakelite handle wiggle by a quarter of an inch in each direction as the door was tried. Then I heard a key slide into the other side of the lock.

I drew a sharp breath, but apart from that I didn't move. I looked longingly at the bolt, but I knew it was noisy. Stupidly, and illogically, I was still pretending to be out.

The key rattled in the lock, then I heard some jangling, as if there was a whole bunch of them. They tried again – maybe with a different key, I don't know. But I suddenly realized their problem was my key, which thankfully still sat in my side of the lock.

After a minute, the footsteps moved on. I heard them enter and leave Jamie's room, Matt's and then Meg's. I exhaled slowly, wondering why I hadn't just shouted 'Bugger off, this is my room!'

Shanie's room's on the ground floor and I heard them disappear down there, in and out of her room too. I slowly slid my squealing bolt safely home then, and for the next few minutes I listened for the front door and watched the street outside, but never saw anyone leave.

Finally I decided that I was alone in the house again so I relaxed and had another hour of peace before gradually everyone returned. Of course, I can't tell anyone, even Matt, what happened without confessing that I never went out at all. I'll pretend I've read a warning for all students to lock their rooms. I don't know any more than that, anyway. And I'm not ready to give up spending time on my own, now I've found that I'm such good company!

EIGHT

Dear Zoe,

Does it matter that I don't talk to you about Rosie and Nathan? I hope it doesn't because I have other things filling my head now, things that I need pushed to one side before I can concentrate on the events that have already taken place.

No one has seen Shanie since poker on Friday. I wasn't in the room so I only know what happened second-hand, but it sounds as though a bit of banter exploded and Shanie stormed out. Meg was pleased to see the back of her, but when Shanie didn't come back for a second night I'm sure that even bitchy little Meg felt a pang of conscience. Let's face it, Shanie is thousands of miles from home, so unless she's found a friend we've never heard of, it's a choice between coming home to us or . . .

Well, I don't know what I'd do.

I don't think she's the type to randomly pick up a guy just for convenience, and she said the guys on her course were 'all zit-ridden geeks'. It didn't seem to occur to her that she herself is about as geeky as a girl could get, cute though in a kind of my-dad's-a-history-professor type way. I don't think she'll be with a bloke for anything less than being hit by a bolt of true love, and if she really had found 'the one' she would have stopped sulking about Meg and told us not to worry.

Actually, I wasn't worrying, not until today. She never turned up at college, according to Jamie, and Shanie always looks down on our frequent truancies. She thinks we're showing disrespect to the opportunity for education. I can hear the twang of her accent as I type these words. I've explained that they factor in 10 per cent pissed days and 10 per cent just-can't-be-arsed days as part of the curriculum. Lighten up! We've all told her that one way or another but she won't budge. She's evangelical about it, so when Jamie texted me to say she didn't know where Shanie was and had found out that she hadn't shown up at class today, I did feel the first twinge of something uneasy.

I phoned Jamie and tried to get her to come back here, so we could talk about it, but she was adamant that something bad has happened.

'I need to go to the police.'

The first time she said it, it shocked me. I never again want to see a policeman standing on our doorstep. As she spoke the words, my stomach lurched just like it does on a fairground ride. As if I was being thrown back in my seat and then propelled forward into some unseen drop.

'I need to go to the police.'

She said it again. Obviously I had not reacted the first time. So I muttered, 'No, it'll be fine.'

Then she rattled off all the reasons why it wouldn't be fine – why Shanie's disappearance could not be anything but serious. Her final words were, 'I am going to the police,' and by then I couldn't think of anything to say.

She's there now, and I am here holding my breath, and wondering how far Matt and I are about to plummet.

NINE

PC Sue Gully didn't smoke. She had tried it a couple of times but it felt unnatural, like she was playing at being someone else. She'd been about sixteen at the time and it had never appealed to her since, though once in a while she found herself slightly envious of the smokers' routine. It looked like a good excuse for a ten-minute break, some fresh air and a chat with a clique of mates who shared the same habit.

She returned now to Parkside Station after having spent the first six hours of her shift waiting to give evidence in a shoplifting case, only to have the case adjourned when the defendant claimed she was pregnant and about to faint.

Caitlin Finch had also been pregnant and about to faint ten months ago when she'd been cautioned for a breach of the peace, eight months ago when she'd received a second caution, and five months ago when charged with stealing six litres of vodka from the local off-licence. Stuffing those inside her coat had been the nearest Caitlin had ever been to displaying a pregnancy bump.

Sitting through the farce of Caitlin's melodramatics, and the court's politically correct show of taking her seriously, had made Gully want to spit. She considered standing up and making an honest comment about the stupidity of the situation, but it seemed to her that a sudden outburst of the truth would have been considered a bigger no-no than the entire pile of Caitlin's lies.

Gully's first thought now was to attempt to salvage a few hours of valuable work and to cram as much into them as possible, but on her way back into the building she had passed the usual clutch of regular smokers and realized that, had she been one of them, the first thing she would now be doing was lighting up, and then expelling some of her frustration along with the cigarette smoke.

She couldn't imagine getting away with just wandering around outside for ten minutes here and there; she'd look like a skiver and, more to the point, would feel like one too. She didn't have anything against smokers, not really, but at that precise moment it seemed as though the bad habits were the ones most likely to get rewarded.

She was clutching a two-inch-thick folder containing paperwork regarding Caitlin Finch, and the first thing she did was to return it to her desk, slotting it back in its own section of the deep drawer containing a zigzag of suspension files. She gave the front of the drawer a hard push and it slammed home with a satisfying snap. But that did nothing to dissipate her deep-seated frustration.

'Good day then?'

The voice belonged to DC Kincaide. She turned to find him standing in the doorway, with a fairly convincing look of concern slapped on his face. Perhaps this was one of those rare moments when he was genuinely interested.

Unlikely.

She continued to scowl. 'Crap, actually.' She avoided any further eye-contact and squeezed past him into corridor.

'I've got time for a coffee?'

She pretended she hadn't heard and just kept walking, hoping to make it out of earshot before he offered the almost inevitable jibe about women and their PMT. She might have felt compelled to retaliate. Gully decided she needed a cigarette, even if it was just a metaphorical one.

Outside was overcast and cold, but the air felt clearer for it. She stood by herself and leaned against the brickwork, a few feet away from the wall-mounted ashtray. There she let herself seethe for as long as it would have taken to smoke two Rothmans King Size.

Frustration ruled her some days; she didn't know how to tread the fine line that ran between saying too little and too much, and sometimes found herself embarrassed by her own abruptness. When she remembered, she stayed quiet until she had thought her words through, but there were always people, like Kincaide, who made her feel pressured into saying the wrong thing.

Like the court officials too. From the moment today when the delays started, she'd had that same anxiety; if she'd attempted to make a case for proceeding, she was nervous of it exploding into a full-scale rant about Caitlin Finch being a liar and wasting everyone's valuable time. So instead she had spent most of those six hours stewing.

She shot a dirty look at the ashtray, and the slot underneath it where genuine smokers posted their half-extinguished dog-ends. So much for a cigarette break: perhaps it was the lack of nicotine, but it really hadn't done very much for her at all. She turned towards the rear entrance and spotted Gary Goodhew entering the car park from the footpath on Warkworth Terrace.

'You look happy,' he said. In essence it was the same comment as Kincaide's, but Gully knew that this time it would have no side to it.

'Wasted a whole day in court. That Finch girl had everyone running after her.'

'Come on, Sue, that's exactly what you were expecting.'

'No, I said I wasn't looking forward to going to court, and you said, "What's the worst that can happen?" I wasn't *willing* it. I was so wound up that I came out here.'

'The virtual cigarette break?'

Gully must have looked bemused, so he carried on without waiting for her to answer.

'Don't we all do it at some time or another? You know, taking ages to get coffee, or a lost twenty minutes in the records archive or standing out here trying to imagine a bad day disappearing up in smoke. There's a bench just across the road from the station, on Parker's Piece, and I used to sit there regularly, until Marks moved his office and gave me a rocket for looking like I wasn't busy.'

'I suppose you told him you were out there thinking?'

'Absolutely.'

'And he bought that?'

'Not for a second. And I promise you, you don't want one of his lectures on the shortage of police resources and the impact caused by wasted man-hours.'

'But Caitlin Finch wasted more of them.'

'You know my grandmother?' It was a rhetorical question. 'Well,' he continued, 'she's a big fan of all that karmic balance stuff. She would argue that Caitlin Finch is wasting everyone's time because she is wasting her own, and that your wasted day will be rebalanced by something worthwhile.'

'And you buy into all of that?'

'I can't decide. Logically no, but I don't feel comfortable totally dismissing the concept either.' Goodhew smiled, while simultaneously managing to look serious. 'Especially when it provides such a useful tool for avoiding the virtual fag break.'

Gully nodded. 'Yes, it would be justice if Caitlin Finch really did get pregnant one day and suffer the worst case of morning sickness on record.' They walked through to the downstairs lobby together, and then Gully headed for the stairs, pleased to note that Goodhew was following the same route. 'I get so wound up sometimes,' she confessed. 'I've worked so hard making sure that I've been thorough with every item of paperwork, but I can't stop feeling that it will all go wrong at the last minute. What if I've missed something?'

Goodhew halted in his tracks, waiting until she stopped too. 'Did you stub out your imaginary cigarette? And did you do anything with the imaginary butt?'

Gully shrugged, then admitted, 'I imagined putting it in the bin. Is that what you mean?'

'Exactly. So you do have an eye for detail, you finish the job, you're thorough . . .'

'That's bollocks.'

'. . . and slightly unhinged. Would you feel better if I go through the stuff with you and prepare you for any questions you might get asked?'

Gully wondered whether saying, 'Yes,' would be like asking for help. She hated the idea because, whatever needed doing, she wanted to be the one to work it out. She didn't even like reading an instruction manual, which was about the most anonymous help she could possibly receive. Even so she heard herself ask, 'When?'

'Now? There's an hour till the end of our shift, and I can work on a bit longer if that suits you.'

She knew the offer arose out of Goodhew's diligence rather than any sudden desire to spend his off-duty time in her company, but still Gully felt the familiar warmth of her cheeks suddenly reddening. Luckily that happened frequently enough to go unnoticed.

Once back at her desk, she retrieved Caitlin Finch's file and placed the contents in a stack between them. Goodhew read through the papers, occasionally stopping to ask her questions.

By the time he reached the last page Gully was close to believing that she would be able to deliver a statement and be comfortable with any cross-questioning that followed. 'Thanks, Gary, I really appreciate it.'

Perhaps she should buy him a drink just to say thanks properly, but she hesitated. She didn't want him to read anything into it, but then again, she wouldn't read anything into it if a male friend made the same offer to her. Unless she suspected that he really liked her. *Damn, damn, damn*, why did she always make things more complicated than they needed to be? *Do you fancy a drink?* No, she needed to steer away from the word 'fancy' and probably also the expression 'quick one'. She decided that *Have you got time for a half?* probably indicated the right ratio of colleague/friend and was about to try it out loud when the phone began to ring.

It was Sergeant Norris, on the front desk. 'Who's up there at the moment?'

'Just me and Goodhew.'

'You'll do, Sue. Pop down, if you don't mind. There's a Jamie-Lee Wallace here, concerned about a missing housemate.'

'I'll be right there.' She put down the phone.

'Okay?'

'Yes. Someone's lost his lodger – probably run off with the rent money.'

Goodhew re-stacked her papers, then pushed his chair back from the desk. Gully quickly left the room before she could start debating with herself whether to wait for him to walk with her down the stairs.

All the way to reception her thoughts stayed on Goodhew. It was a crush undoubtedly, one that had hung on for too long now, and had more to do with her lack of boyfriend than the reawakening of teenage hormones which managed to hit almost every time they were alone together. And the main result was that she felt very angry with herself.

Gully banged at the reception door with the heel of her hand. It swung open in a wide arc that gave her a full view of the waiting area, and simultaneously reminded her of the dangers of making assumptions; Jamie-Lee Wallace was no irate male landlord on the hunt for a missing tenant, but a young woman aged about twenty, whose long dark hair was tied up in a neat braid. She wore jeans and a burgundy hoodie, and although her clothes looked newly laundered there was still something unkempt about her appearance.

The girl stood uneasily in the waiting area, surrounded by empty seats, and as soon as she spotted Gully she hurried towards her. 'Thank you for seeing me.' She spoke calmly and clearly, her voice at odds with her worried expression.

Plenty of people remained restrained in the face of fear or pain, and Gully fully expected her next words to begin: *It's probably nothing but . . .*

She was wrong.

Jamie-Lee grabbed her hand like she was about to shake it, but instead held on to it, as if she was determined to keep Gully close. 'One of the girls in our house-share is called Shanie. I think she might be dead.'

TEN

Sergeant Norris had initially used the word 'missing' and, between Gully leaving her desk and arriving at reception, it seemed that Jamie-Lee Wallace had upgraded the girl's status to 'dead'.

'Missing or dead?' Gully asked sharply. 'Which is it?'

'Missing. She's missing – but I'm scared she's dead.'

Gully guided Wallace into an interview room and directed her towards the nearest chair.

Jamie-Lee began to speak before either of them was seated. 'I live in a house in King Street, where I'm a student and so are the others. There are seven of us in the house; six of us moved in together at the start of October, and Shanie arrived at the start of this term—'

'Hold on.' Gully dumped her notebook on the table, sat on the chair beside it and didn't speak again until she had her pen poised ready to write. 'I need to start with some basic details.'

Jamie-Lee nodded.

'Your full name?'

'Mine?' The girl looked surprised for a moment. 'Jamie Leonora Wallace.'

'Date of birth?'

'First of November, 1992.'

It was Gully's turn to look surprised, for up to that moment she had assumed Jamie-Lee was closer to her own age, and a half-decade adjustment suddenly made a big difference to the way she viewed this young woman. True, there was nothing overly mature in her features; the maturity was all in her manner. When Gully spoke again, she let her voice soften a little. 'And your friend Shanie's full name?'

'Shanie Faulkner – that's all I know. I guess it's short for something.'

'What's her date of birth?'

'I don't know that either. But she's twenty-two, and her birthday fell just before Christmas.'

'Do you have a home address for her?'

Jamie-Lee shook her head. 'She's from Merrillville, Indiana. Due to go back there next month, I think. Look, you can check all of this with her college, can't you?'

'Tell me when you last saw her.'

'I already told you, on Friday night, the sixteenth – about midnight, I think. We were in the kitchen playing poker and she got annoyed . . . nothing really, just bickering, but she stormed out of the house. None of the others have seen her since.'

'The other people in your house-share, you mean?' Gully wrote the word 'occupants' on a new line and double-underlined it. 'Aside from you and Miss Faulkner, who else is currently living at that address?'

'Meg DeLacy, Marcus Phillips, Libby Brett, Matt Stone . . . and Oslo. He's Norwegian, his first name's Gunvald. I think his second name's spelt G-J-E-R-T-S-E-N because I've seen that on his post, but he's happy with "Oslo".'

'And all these people were present when she left?'

'Yes, except Libby. She was upstairs, but everyone else was together in the house.'

'Did Shanie give you any indication of her plans for the weekend?'

'No, I doubt she really had any. She has a degree in software design, graduated last year but she's continuing to study. She's still attending her old university in the States, but she was given the chance to come here for thirteen weeks, and wanted to make the most of the opportunity. Shanie doesn't go out much – in fact, she seems to have made a point of avoiding anything in the way of a social life. I like her but she's a bit of a boff. I reckon she doesn't really know how to just let her hair down and have a laugh, so I don't think it would have happened accidentally either.'

'No boyfriend, then?'

Jamie-Lee snorted, '"Proud to be a virgin", apparently.'

'Apparently? You don't think she was, then?'

'Sorry, that was my personal comment on that philosophy. The rest of us don't walk round wearing T-shirts that say either *Glad I lost it* or *Ashamed to be a slapper*. She wouldn't have morphed into some kind of reckless party person overnight. She likes rules and structure and nothing much that's frivolous.'

'I see,' Gully said slowly. 'So if there had been a sudden change of plan . . .'

Jamie-Lee nodded vigorously. 'Yes, she would have told us, and definitely contacted her course tutors, since it would need to be something pretty catastrophic for her to miss any of her classes.'

'Catastrophic?'

'*Dead* was an exaggeration, I know, but it would still have to be something serious. I mean, something out of her control, which is preventing her from getting in touch with us.'

Gully kept the rest of her questions brief. Jamie-Lee Wallace didn't strike her as someone who was readily prone to panic; instead she came across as pragmatic, the kind who provided an ear for other people's problems. From Gully's experience, people like that only sought help when they genuinely felt there was trouble.

'What happens now?' Jamie asked.

'I'll go back to the house with you, find out whether any of the other housemates can provide any more information.'

'They can't.'

'I still need to ask, and I'll need access to her room. Who has a key?'

'The landlord, I suppose.'

'No one else?'

'I don't know – maybe Rob. He's Matt's dad, and he sorted out

47

the lease, so he has all the details.' Jamie suddenly looked defeated. 'I should know these things myself, as I'm the one who always organizes any repairs. But I just ask Rob, as I don't even know the landlord's name.'

It took less than five minute to drive from the police station to King Street. The road was narrow, lined with townhouses that had been restored or replaced over the past few hundred years. There was only one gap available between the parked cars, so Gully pulled up to the kerb and glanced back at Jamie-Lee, who sat directly behind the front passenger seat.

'Okay?' she asked.

Jamie-Lee nodded. Then silently they moved towards number 42A.

It was a pretty but tired-looking cottage with dust-covered rendered walls and windows that looked slightly out of alignment. The front door opened and a figure appeared in the doorway, glancing in their direction then withdrawing quickly. Gully had just enough time to catch sight of a dark jumper and a mop of sandy hair over untamed sideburns. 'Who was that?'

'Oslo. He's gathering everyone together in the main room.'

The hallway was decorated with palm-leaf embossed paper that had been painted over in a shade of dark mulberry. No lights were on, but the furthest door on the left-hand side of the short corridor was ajar and a shaft of bright daylight shone through it. Gully could hear the low murmur of voices and followed Jamie towards them.

As she entered the room, the tiled floor gave way to thin carpet and the walls turned an even gaudier shade of raspberry. She couldn't escape the thought that the choice of décor had resulted from shopping in the bargain bin. All six of the students now faced her, three male and three female, and, at first glance it was hard to imagine a more mismatched bunch.

Gully introduced herself, then chose a chair on the longer side of the kitchen table, before inviting the others to sit. Instead of just picking any available seat and sitting down, the housemates manoeuvred their chairs until they all faced her directly as a group.

Gully had managed to lodge their first names into her brain, as well as jotting them down in her notebook. She'd even written them on the page in the order that corresponded with where they were now sitting. Meg was sharp featured, with her hair dyed a completely uniform shade of corn-blond. She sat on the far right next to Phil, who already displayed the spreading physique of a middle-aged man, and a receding hairline to go with it. Meg tilted her head closer to his and whispered something, the whole time keeping her black-lined eyes fixed on Gully and, as she spoke, his gaze followed suit.

Jamie and Libby occupied the middle two seats with Matt and Oslo further along. Libby was small framed and small featured, with fair bobbed hair which stopped just below her jawline. Matt was solid and broad shouldered like a rugby player, but Oslo was of average height, though looking taller due to his gangly frame.

Gully studied their impenetrable expressions, and guessed this seating arrangement was nothing more sinister than leftover childhood habits, but they still looked remarkably like a judging panel.

'Firstly, we must track down the landlord, but it would save time if any of you had a key to Shanie's room.'

No one spoke, but all glanced at one another and shook their heads. On asking them a couple more questions, she soon realized that they either didn't like talking to her, or, alternatively, had a collective knowledge of zero. *They're just a bunch of teenagers*, she reminded herself. Just the same as the drunken ones she could face any evening or weekend: some meek and some confrontational, but often vulnerable or emotional. Teenagers who were rarely experienced enough to recognize the growing unease that broke out at the start of an investigation. Gully could feel it now; something felt awry.

'Look, I may need to speak to you all individually, but right now it is important that we locate Shanie Faulkner quickly. As soon as

49

we establish that she is safe and well, I won't need to take up any more of your time. But until then . . .'

Gully paused, irritated by the sight of Meg smirking at her as she whispered something to Phil again. It was clear to her that Meg thought that a policewoman only a few years older than herself deserved absolutely none of her time. Whether it was ageism, sexism or simply a dislike of the police was irrelevant.

'Megan? Do *you* know where Shanie is?' Gully's voice was sharp and the other five turned towards Meg.

'No, of course I don't.'

'Do you reckon she's safe?'

Meg shrugged. 'I don't know, do I?'

'And you don't care either, do you?'

Gully had intended only to prod Meg into paying closer attention, but hadn't actually expected to see the expression of earnest indignation that now painted the girl's features more boldly than her overdone eye make-up ever could.

'That's not true,' she protested.

Now it was Phil's turn to smirk. He muttered, 'Right.'

Focusing her attention on Meg, Gully continued, knowing she now had the others' full attention. 'I already have her mobile number, and details of the course she is studying. What I need from all of you now is everything else: names of her friends, her favourite hangouts – anything that could help us find her more quickly.'

No one rushed to answer, but the flicker of something reached her. It reminded her of looking into a river and only spotting a shoal of fish when one turns against the direction of the rest. Then they all turn instantly, and there's no way to tell which one was the first. These people either *knew* nothing or had made up their minds to *say* nothing. All but one of them. There had been a ripple of movement, but at the time her attention had been fully on Meg, and she only knew that it had come from someone sitting to Meg's right. Anyone but Meg, in fact.

Gully fell silent, holding their stares. It took just seconds for Libby then to speak. The words came suddenly and simultaneously as her body language transformed her from a meek figure slouching low in her chair to a neat and precise young woman, sitting very upright.

'Someone does have a key,' she said firmly, delivered as a plain fact with no room for doubt in her voice.

'How do you know?'

'I told everyone I was going out one day, but I was here all the time and I heard someone entering Shanie's room.'

'When was this?'

'Saturday, during the day. It could have been Shanie but, no, I don't think so. It sounded to me like a man, but I don't know why. Whoever it was went into all the rooms.'

There was a stir of disquiet amongst the others.

'Into our bedrooms?' Meg asked.

Libby nodded.

'Why didn't you tell us?' a male voice muttered. Gully wasn't sure which of them had said it; Phil and Oslo both glared at Libby, and Matt looked unhappy.

Libby ignored them all, then her expression changed. 'There was something today, too,' she said slowly. 'I walked into town earlier, and when I came back I thought the house was empty. But then, as I started to unlock the front door, I heard a strange clatter. I called out but there was no one. I didn't relate it to Saturday, I just thought it was one of those odd things that happen.'

She finished the sentence as if she hadn't planned to say anything further, but almost immediately continued. 'I'd bought some milk,' her tone had changed and she sounded puzzled now, incredulous even, 'and when I took it through to the kitchen, I noticed something else.'

She hesitated, her lips pursed as though they had no intention of letting her speak. Colour drained from her face, then almost as quickly, it rushed back. Gully got up and moved towards her: this wasn't someone pausing for effect, trying to relish a self-important moment. Libby looked away, focusing now on a far corner of the cheap carpet, as if suddenly unable to meet anyone's gaze.

'I thought it was in the fridge but I couldn't work out where it was.'

Gully lowered herself on to one knee and spoke quietly, just to Libby. 'Where *what* was?'

'I couldn't find it.'

Gully tilted her head, trying to coax Libby into looking at her. 'Libby, what couldn't you find?'

'In the end I opened the window, and then forgot all about it. There was a smell . . .' Libby turned her head slowly, her limpid blue eyes seeming to beg for this moment to end. 'I just assumed something in the fridge had turned bad; there's always something past its sell-by date in there.' She drew a couple of quick breaths and hurried to get out the rest before the words jammed in her throat. 'I smelled it as I came through the front door. It was faint, disgusting, but it went once I got a breeze circulating. That's why I didn't think . . .'

'Think what?'

'That it was in the hall not the kitchen.'

'And can you describe this smell?'

Libby's nostrils flared slightly as though a fresh wave of the stench was hitting her. She closed her eyes, as her fingers dug into the fabric of her skirt. 'Rotting meat.'

ELEVEN

Hi, Zoe

I need to explain how weird it was.

I hadn't planned to say anything. One minute I was sitting there, sandwiched between the others. Inconspicuous, I thought. PC Gully hardly seemed to notice me, because several times her eyes skimmed over me like I was just the comma separating the other members of the group.

Jamie, Oslo, Matt on one side.

Meg, Phil on the other.

Her gaze barely touched me until I spoke. I had no plans to say anything. In fact, I doubted there was much point in me being there at all. All I intended to do was stay in my room, available if I was needed but separate enough to protect myself.

I should have learned by now that refusing to accept that something's happening doesn't actually make it go away. My dad has always said how the piper needs to be paid. That's crap. What has our family ever done that requires so much reparation? But I agree with him enough to know that staying in my room would have been just a temporary fix; because I could have avoided facing the police now only to be forced into a one-to-one meeting later.

That was why I joined them, sat in the middle and kept quiet, because I really did have nothing to add. Or so I thought. Until I heard them talking about the key to Shanie's room, and everyone agreeing that no one had one. Keeping quiet would have been like telling myself I'd just imagined it. That goes against the grain for me.

I'm studying accountancy, so maybe that's why I have to keep my own ledger balanced. I like the idea of details being correct, with meticulous accuracy, checking and cross-checking. I'm careful but not a perfectionist, nor do I have any intention of becoming one, but consciously letting something drop is very different from missing it entirely, and I wasn't about to collude with whoever I'd heard rattling my bedroom door by pretending I could ignore it.

That's how I'm summing it up now, but at the time it was an instinctual response. 'Someone has a key,' I'd blurted out. Everyone stared at me, and then I had to explain that I'd never been to London. My description of crowded trains, tube-train delays, congested shops and everything, right down to the non-existent Danish pastry in Starbucks, had all been a total lie. It had made sense at the time but I couldn't explain my logic in the face of so many suspicious stares.

I'd hurt Matt.

He tried not to show it but his expression showed it enough for Jamie to comment on it, and briefly everyone's attention switched towards him. I scratched around for the right thing to say, but empty space filled the gap where I usually kept my ability to think straight.

Then I remembered this morning: the noise of something falling over. Silence as I stood in the hallway. And then that faint but terrible smell. I pressed my hand over my nose and mouth, then gingerly moved it away by an inch or so, and sniffed again.

Something gone off in the fridge maybe? Or a dead mouse rotting under the floorboards?

I checked the fridge. Nothing.

I never mentioned the mouse idea to PC Gully. For, if it had been a decaying animal, surely the smell wouldn't have faded away like that?

Even now that thought keeps doing circuits around my brain.

I had walked back to the spot where I'd first smelled it.

I still could, but it was noticeably fainter. I opened the window and forgot about it until the moment when I needed to distract attention from Matt, then it snapped back into my head.

It felt a convenient diversion, and I couldn't shake the sensation that the others thought I was making it up. PC Gully didn't though, and her manner changed abruptly.

She phoned into the police station, conversing in terse bursts amid the returning bursts of dialogue and crackle that came from the other end.

She then asked Jamie to make drinks, and told everyone but me to stay where they were. I was allowed as far as the doorway of the main room, just to point a few feet down the hall and confirm to her which room was Shanie's.

'Why's her bedroom on the ground floor?' Gully queried.

Halfway between the front door and the lounge and kitchen; it would have been the room I think one of the boys would have taken if they'd had the choice. 'It was supposed to be a study room, but when Shanie arrived it was the only place to put her.'

'Okay.' I couldn't tell if PC Gully was listening; she moved close to the door without actually touching it.

'You think Jamie's right to be worried, don't you?' I asked.

'Shanie's behaviour does seem out of character, so I think Jamie was right to call us.'

A stock answer, no doubt.

I wonder if police cadets are handed a book of useful phrases: cleverly worded sentences that manage to prepare people for the worst without extinguishing all hope.

We remain positive . . .

Concerned for her safety . . .

Our investigation is ongoing . . .

I don't hold that against PC Gully; it's her job, after all. How was she to know that she was talking to a seventeen year old who had already heard the top hundred phrases from that same bloody book.

'You don't believe she's in there, do you?' I asked.

'I will need to see inside her room,' she replied, as if that were enough of an answer to shut me up.

I persisted: 'I don't see how it would be possible.'

'I'm sure we'll be able to locate the other holder of the key shortly.'

'No, I meant how could she be in there?'

Her cheeks reddened but, apart from that, any other sign of warmth disappeared and her face became expressionless. 'Please rejoin your friends.'

Someone rapped hard on the front door just then and Gully waved me back towards the main room as she turned to answer it. I didn't budge; in fact, I had no plans to move and realized I was gripping the doorframe so hard that my fingers ached.

She put her eye to the spyhole, then pulled away in an instant, reaching for the catch. I was only seeing the back of her head, but I could tell she was both surprised and relieved.

However, by the time they were face to face, she just sounded irritated. 'Why are you here?'

He spoke quietly but I was close enough to hear his reply. 'I was talking with Norris when you called in.' The man who had entered the house looked about Gully's age, a little older maybe. Short hair, cleanshaven, casual clothes. Reminded me of a medical student or a bartender. Okay, that's a bit diverse; the point is, he didn't remind me of a policeman or any kind of detective. He neither shook my hand nor told me I should do anything that might include releasing my hold on the doorframe. He introduced himself as DC Gary Goodhew, then turned back to Gully.

'That wasn't an answer,' she insisted.

'You requested assistance with the lock?' he replied.

'Yes, but I didn't expect you.' She released a ponderous sigh. 'Whatever . . . let's get on with it. What do you know so far?'

'Shanie Faulkner's gone missing and the quicker we get access to her room the better.'

'But we can't just force the door without damaging the lock. And if you break in through the window you'll add glass, external debris

56

and God knows what to the scene. We can't risk disrupting forensics.'

He glanced back at me and I retreated into the doorway by a few inches but I could still hear them whispering.

'Sue, stop stating the bloody obvious and just slow down. Look, this lock is really old – and it wasn't designed for a bank vault.' A pause, then, 'Do you know what this thing is?'

'No.'

'Watch.' He must have meant 'watch' as in observe, not as in Rolex, because a moment later I heard a metal-on-metal shuffling followed by the unmistakable sound of the lock bolt sliding aside.

I glanced behind me into the main room and found that everyone else seemed to be staring over at me. I must have looked like someone who'd been posted there as a makeshift door guard.

'What's going on?' Jamie mouthed.

I shrugged and Phil looked like he was about to stand up. I shook my head quickly and raised my finger in the 'wait' gesture.

'Who came to the door?' Oslo asked before I'd had a chance to turn away.

'Another policeman.'

Then Meg: 'What's he doing now?'

Something told me that it would be unwise to make any comment that might bring them all spilling out into the hallway.

'Hang on,' I whispered.

As I stepped out from the lounge doorway, everything hit me at once: Shanie's open door, the artificial light from Goodhew's phone, bouncing off the bedroom walls, the way Gully moved towards me – and the smell.

Most of all, the smell.

Gully grabbed me and turned me round in a single manoeuvre. She was only an inch taller than me but I felt weightless, as though she'd lifted me right off the floor and just handed me over to Jamie.

Jamie dragged me to a chair in the kitchen area. 'Sit down.'

I knew her routine by now. I'd be given tea and wisdom. I'd be asked if I was feeling okay, and treated as if I'd suddenly developed a disorder making me liable to sudden disintegration.

I just did as I was told, while all around me hell was unleashed. Jamie was trying hard not to cry, while Oslo started talking about natural processes and how long she'd obviously been dead already. Phil remained silent; so did Matt. And Meg sobbed loudly, as if she really had been Shanie's bestest bezzie, or however she might have described it.

The police presence swelled like increments in the Fibonacci series. First Gully, then Goodhew, then two more uniforms . . . and a few minutes after that, another three, including the boss. He was older than the rest, thin in a steel-rod kind of way. He introduced himself as Detective Inspector Marks, and I got the impression that he thought that would put me at ease, but by then, I was unable to know how I felt.

After that there were others, too, but all we were thinking about by then was how soon we could get on with whatever was going to come next.

PC Gully stayed in the room with us, fielding questions. 'We will need a statement from each of you,' she repeated.

'Separately or together?' Meg asked.

'Separately.'

'Can I have someone with me, though?'

'Yes, but as I just explained, it can't be Phil.'

'So we're suspects, then?'

'Significant witnesses.'

'No, we're suspects. If you thought we were innocent, you wouldn't now be trying to stop us talking to each other, would you?'

'We need to have statements that are made independently.'

'So Phil speaks to you first, then sits in along with me and he doesn't speak at all, what's wrong with that?'

'We may need to revisit the various statements.'

'So now we can't talk to each other at all?' Meg's mood was fast escalating towards a full-blown screaming match, but the only thing missing was an adversary. Gully remained resolutely patient, and none of us tried asking Meg to calm down; because we knew better. Without warning, Meg changed tack. 'So how did she do it?'

'Meg, I'm sure you realize why I can't comment on—'

'Was she hanging, or what?'

'Meg, please lower your voice.'

'Has she been dead since Friday?'

One look at Gully's face would have told Meg that she stood no chance of an answer, so she turned to me. I was still sitting on the same chair, but with my knees raised to my chest and my arms clutched round them.

'Libby, what did you see?' Meg shouted suddenly.

I pressed my forehead flat against my knees and stared at the fabric encasing my thighs. I pictured a mouse, and I pretended that it had been the cause of it all. A dead grey mouse, with its form and features fading. A mouse left with more dignity than that glimpse of Shanie I had caught reflected in her bedroom mirror.

TWELVE

Both Matt and Libby were picked up from Parkside by Matt's sister Charlotte, and the contact address now given for both also belonged to Charlotte. Brimley Close was a cul-de-sac of post-war semi-detached homes, once carbon copy three-bedroom, two-reception houses, but now embellished with a variety of extensions and improvements. Number 14 looked tidy but tired, maintained but not polished; everything about it said 'domestic' and Goodhew wasn't surprised to learn that it was the house inhabited by the Stone family throughout Matt and Charlotte's childhood.

Charlotte was about five foot four; she was dressed in battered jeans and a pink scoop-necked top. Her hair was light brown and blessed with exactly the kind of curls that straight-haired people spent a fortune trying to replicate, and which she had probably spent hours trying to tame.

She shook his hand, then led him along the short hallway and into the lounge. The room was dominated by an oversized flat-screen television and a chunky three-piece suite. The TV was new enough for the instruction manual to still be in use, as it lay on top of several issues of the free weekly paper and a pile of letters resting on their empty envelopes. By comparison, the sofa and armchairs seemed twenty years out of date. They had been uniformly upholstered in a leaf-patterned chenille, using a colour palette that might have been entitled *shades of goat and cow*. When

Goodhew first sat down, and each time he moved, a fresh plume of dust took to the air.

'Are your parents home?'

'There's only Dad now. He's at work.'

'And where is that?'

'He works for a landscape gardener, so they'll be employed somewhere local. I'd rather wait until he gets home.'

'No one's told him yet?'

'No, not yet,' Charlotte replied. 'I wanted to get Matt and Libby settled in first.'

'Libby's staying here?'

Charlotte jerked her head in the direction of the front window and the cul-de-sac beyond. 'Libby's parents live at number 57, but she doesn't want to go home.'

Her eyes flickered as she seemed to read his expression – accurately as it turned out. 'Matt and Libby aren't in a relationship, if that's what you're thinking. They have separate issues to deal with, and both decided they'd take the opportunity to try living away from home.'

'What kind of issues?'

'Personal. Ask them if you like, but I just didn't want you misconstruing anything from the outset.'

It was then that Goodhew decided that he would speak to Libby first.

THIRTEEN

Libby Brett reminded Goodhew of one of the characters in the game *Who Is It?*, with features that were neat and symmetrical. Her hair was cut into a jaw-length bob.

Does your character have blue eyes?

Yes.

Fair hair?

Yes.

Dangly earrings?

Yes.

Then it must be Libby!

Her full name was Elizabeth Dinah Brett and she'd be eighteen on her next birthday, though she could have passed for about fourteen if she'd wanted to. The earrings were little silver flowers, and were the only frivolous things about her appearance. She wore a blue cotton shirt that made her look as though she'd just removed her school tie.

The note about her said she was studying accountancy 'A' level along with English, business studies and critical thinking. Her expression gave away very little so perhaps that was one of the entry requirements for identifying the future tax advisors amongst them.

'She killed herself, didn't she?' Libby said.

'It's too early to say.'

She gave a little snort, half disgust, half disrespect. 'I thought you'd have made up your mind by now.'

'No, it's the pathologist who—'

'Not *you* the individual, I mean *you* the police.'

'What makes you think we decide on the outcome before we have the facts?'

Her expression closed a little more. 'I never said that.'

He changed direction. 'Do you think Shanie was depressed? Had something upset her?'

'If I had to guess, I'd say that Shanie spent her whole school life as the nerdy kid in class. Probably wishing she got looks instead of brains.'

Goodhew realized then that he had only seen one low-res photo of Shanie and apart from that, only had the time spent with the body to go on. As far as attractiveness went, neither had given him much of a clue.

'A kid like that often ends up feeling embarrassed about their academic ability – like a tall person who stoops over time. And that's why I don't think she did it.'

'Did what?'

Libby's eyebrows gave a little twitch, a hint that she thought he was missing the obvious. 'That's why,' she explained patiently, 'I don't think she killed herself.'

Goodhew ran back over her previous sentences. He'd obviously missed the point somewhere. 'You'll have to explain.'

'Okay.' Libby didn't actually seem at all put out by his slowness to grasp her theory. 'If you've spent your whole childhood feeling like a misfit, don't you, kind of, get used to that being the norm?'

Goodhew shrugged. 'I'm not sure about that.'

'If you woke up one day and suddenly everyone treated you like a different person to the one you'd been all your life, that would seem odd, wouldn't it?'

'Of course.'

'Shanie was used to being the geeky, studious one. She wouldn't have been surprised that we found her a pain in the backside at times, but we also made the effort to include her, and at the same time she is here doing a course that recognizes her ability. So this was probably the best time she'd ever had as a student. Now do you understand?'

Goodhew nodded, but he didn't agree. If only the steps to suicide were so clearly signposted before the event. In his experience the trigger usually came from problems that weren't so obvious to everyone else.

'And how was your relationship with her?'

Libby bit her top lip while she considered the question. 'The first couple of days she was here I couldn't stand being in the same room. She asked daft questions about everything, from posting a letter to catching a bus. D'you know how some people get you helping them with simple things and before you know it you're indispensible? My instincts told me not to let her latch on. Maybe I was wrong, but she didn't seem quite on the same planet as the rest of us. She always dressed like a "before" on a makeover show, her hair needed trimming and she didn't bother with make-up when it would have done her a favour.' Libby threw up her hands. 'I'm being honest and I sound like a bitch. But it didn't take me long to realize that she didn't pay attention to those things like other people, because they weren't important to her. Whenever she stopped hiding behind her high IQ she could be pretty sweet.'

'You liked her then?'

'She grew on me enough that I would have felt something when she left. Left properly, I mean.'

Goodhew dropped that line of thought abruptly. Instead, he looked down at his notepad until he was certain that the silence between them was beginning to seem uncomfortably long. Then with equal abruptness, he asked his next question. 'How would you describe yourself?'

'Pardon?'

'Sum yourself up in two or three words.'

She looked confused.

'For example, would you describe yourself as honest?'

'I think so.'

'Tell me about your trip to London.'

She shook her head. 'This is crap.'

She was right, but Goodhew's aim was to give things a little shake just to see what, if anything, fell out. Hard facts and straight answers were just a bonus. 'So you were in your room all the time, but you pretended to be out?'

'That's right. I didn't want to be disturbed.'

'Fair enough, but lying about a visit to London seems extreme.'

'So is calling it "lying".' She looked as though she felt suspicious of him.

Goodhew changed tack. 'Is there a reason you and Matt have chosen to study in Cambridge? Most people don't decide to stay in their home city, do they?'

She shrugged. 'Some do, I suppose. Maybe I didn't want to move away.'

'But neither of you wanted to live at home either.'

She drew a new breath as if she was about to say something, but no words followed. 'I decided I was old enough to move out,' she muttered finally.

'And that's financially possible?'

'Yes.' She wasn't about to volunteer anything further.

'How do you afford it, Libby?'

She hesitated. 'Matt's dad and my dad rented this house. With what the others pay, it's almost covered. My mum and dad help out. Matt's dad chips in a bit more so sometimes Matt pays for things.'

'And your relationship with Matt?'

'Relationship? What is this, some kind of personal vetting? There is no "relationship".'

'So Matt was a stranger to you when you moved into the house on King Street?'

She smiled at the surface of the desk, before looking back at Goodhew. 'Sorry, I misunderstood.'

'That's okay.' The sudden softening of her demeanour was interesting.

'I've known Matt for years. We lived down the road from each other when we were kids. We're good mates. *Best* mates.'

Goodhew stifled the urge to point out that Matt had been such a good mate that he'd been sent texts claiming she was seventy miles away in London. 'It says here that you are studying accountancy?'

'Yes, that's right.'

'You're seventeen. Not a degree then?'

'No, A-levels. They call it a foundation in accountancy but I know someone who took the course and it's just a good combination of A levels.'

'And then what?'

'English? Social Science?' She hesitated. 'I realize I have a way to go before I qualify, but every step counts.'

'You must be the youngest at the house.'

'Yes, but you know that already, I'm sure.'

If he'd been shown a photo of Libby and asked to guess her personality based on looks alone, he would have gone for timid. But if she had insecurities she hid them well. She seemed quietly self-assured; completely unflustered by this interview.

'So tell me how you found yourself involved in a house-share with a group of degree students.'

'Through Matt. He knew I was looking for somewhere.'

'But you're local – wouldn't it have been cheaper and easier to live at home?'

Libby shrugged. 'Does it matter?'

Goodhew shrugged too. 'It's just background detail, part of putting together a bigger picture and making sure everything fits.'

'My A-level choices have nothing to do with Shanie, or what happened to her.'

'I would be surprised if they did, but understanding the people she lived with will help us understand her life from her perspective.'

'And why she killed herself?'

'At this stage—'

She gave a short, dismissive snort. 'I know – "ongoing enquiries", "too soon to comment", et cetera, et cetera.'

'Can you think of anything you noticed that might indicate Shanie was depressed or upset?'

'Some people don't need a reason.' Everything about her had stiffened suddenly, therefore Goodhew knew that he had touched a nerve.

'Most do,' he replied softly.

'According to what source? Some police training guide?' Her expression darkened further but her voice remained quiet. 'Don't you think it would be kinder to accept that suicide can happen for no good reason? Why should we be made to feel the guilt of wondering why Shanie killed herself and be left wondering whether there was anything we could have done to prevent it?'

'No one is trying to put the blame on you – any of you.'

'No. If she killed herself because something about living with us made her so fucking unhappy, then we wouldn't be normal if we didn't feel responsible. I'm sorry she's dead, but if she did kill herself, I hope she did it for no reason whatsoever. I hope it turns out to be a purely selfish and illogical act that no one could have predicted or prevented. None of us deserve to be the victims of this.'

When she had finished speaking, she drew her hands together, covering her stomach. As she did so, her expression returned to its earlier guarded state. He guessed that she had probably opened up more than she had intended, and consequently, would be better prepared next time, and less likely to do so again.

FOURTEEN

Matt Stone was a couple of inches taller than Goodhew. His frame was broad but he still managed to be lean in a way that indicated that his metabolism burned calories quicker than he was able to consume them. His eyes had a natural droop at the outer corners, and Goodhew could see that even when Matt was happy, he would retain a rather soulful look.

'Is Libby okay?' were Matt's first words.

Goodhew replied with a brief nod. 'How long have you two been friends?'

'We grew up on the street.' His voice sounded unnaturally taut, and he stopped after the first sentence to cough, as if making a deliberate effort to slow the question which followed. 'What did Libby say?' His shoulders were tightly hunched and he rocked ever so slightly as he spoke.

If Matt could have managed any kind of cheerful smile, he would have had the kind of face that could have landed him a job as a kids' TV presenter, and he would probably be blessed with boyish good looks into his thirties, if stress didn't finish them off prematurely.

Goodhew didn't answer immediately. It was an odd question.

The sitting room was completely square apart from the chimney breast which protruded by eighteen inches from the same wall that housed the door. The TV stood right in front of the fireplace, but the top of the mantelpiece was still visible and on it three framed photographs were displayed. There was an old school photograph each of Matt and his sister Charlotte, and in between stood a group picture of them with two adults who looked like their parents. It had been taken in a studio and was intended to be an informal shot of them sitting together on the floor. Matt's dad looked uncomfortable, as though he'd registered the obvious farce of two adults and two uncooperative teenagers pretending that sitting in a tangled heap was an everyday event. While the others all gazed directly at the lens, he sat to one side and had been captured in the act of being absent.

Finally Goodhew replied, 'Was there something you were expecting her to say? Is there something in particular that she should have told me?'

Matt shook his head.

'You travelled back with her from the student house,' Goodhew said. 'Didn't you ask?'

'She didn't speak much. No, actually she spoke but it was just chatter. She doesn't like silences when she's feeling stressed.'

'But she spent Saturday quietly enough.'

It was hardly noticeable, but for a second Matt's face clouded. He shrugged. 'It was an odd thing for her to do. I would have left her alone if she'd said. I mean, it's not as if we hang out together every second of every day. I didn't think it was like her to lie.'

'Maybe she hasn't been caught out before.'

'No . . .' Words began to form on his lips, but he wiped them away with the back of his hand. 'No,' he repeated more firmly. 'She doesn't play games. Not with me.'

Tension had returned to his voice. The first time Goodhew had heard it, he attributed it to distress over Shanie and concern for Libby. But Goodhew now recognized it as rising panic. Matt's distress hung around him as if it had been his companion for far longer than the brief period that had elapsed since the discovery of Shanie's body.

'I wanted to know whether she said anything about *me*?' Matt demanded.

'Such as?'

'I thought she might say that I had expected something like this. And I thought, if she said that, then you'd be looking at me like I had forced the pills down Shanie's throat.'

'What pills?'

'I don't know.' Matt's voice became quieter. 'She'd do it like that if she had killed herself. She wouldn't cut her wrists or hang herself, she wouldn't have gone for the messy, chaotic "out". She was talking recently about some actress who had killed herself with booze and pills.'

'She discussed suicide?'

'No, I think the topic was weird death stories, and Shanie mentioned this actress who thought she'd be found glamorously draped across the bed, but instead of that she vomited on the way to the bathroom, skidded in it and died after cracking her head on the toilet. Too much alcohol made Shanie vomit. So she wouldn't have gone for that, but pills on their own? Maybe.'

'You do believe she might have taken her own life, then?'

Matt tilted his head to one side and surveyed Goodhew for a moment. 'I'd never have predicted it, but now it's happened, it doesn't seem so mad. In some ways she wasn't very worldly – always reminded me of a schoolkid even though she was older than me. Isn't that the type who think they're somehow going to be in on their own wake, their own book of condolence, and stuff like that?'

Goodhew felt sceptical and Matt spotted it. 'I'm not kidding. Some teenagers don't have enough grasp on what permanent means; they don't see suicide is forever.'

'Seriously?'

'Absolutely.'

'But *you* do?'

Matt nodded.

'And you were expecting "something like this"?'

'I had a feeling . . . I'd had it for weeks, I couldn't get it out of my mind. Almost willed it to happen – not to Shanie, though. There was tension . . .'

Goodhew looked up sharply, 'In the house?'

'No, I just felt it all around me but I don't know why.' Matt hung his head and stared at the carpet through the narrow gap between his knees. 'It was probably all in my mind,' he conceded. 'I don't remember very much of last Friday. I'd drunk way too much but was actually sobering up when I came home. Meg and Shanie were laying into each other, but Meg's always confrontational. She likes to say things to get a reaction, and Shanie hadn't learned to ignore her. Meg would be fine if she didn't think she was a total princess.'

'So they didn't socialize with each other outside the house?'

'None of us did much. Meg liked vodka shots, Shanie drank pints. Meg liked nightclubs, Shanie would go to a pub to read.' It seemed to be Matt's final word on Shanie and Meg's incompatibility.

'Which pubs?'

Matt shrugged. 'Definitely up our road. We made a joke one night about entering a team in the next pub crawl.'

'The King Street Run?'

'Even Meg said she'd be up for that.' He gave a very small smile, but it was enough to transform his face for a moment. It vanished as quickly as it arrived, and for the rest of the interview Matt kept his elbows planted on his knees and his gaze fixed on the top of the coffee table between them.

He used a lot of words to say very little; sometimes he struggled to find the right ones, picking his way through the minutiae of life in the student house, anxious not to misrepresent any of his housemates through a careless comment. Right now he was searching for a tactful way to ensure that his description of Meg's casual sexual relationship with Phil didn't sound like he was judging or insulting her.

In the middle of a suspicious death investigation, did Matt really think that non-violent consensual sex would raise any eyebrows? Goodhew's gaze drifted back to the three photos over the fireplace. His hour spent with Matt had coloured them differently.

Meanwhile Matt's search for the right words had petered into silence.

Goodhew took the chance to fill the gap. 'When did your mum die, Matt?'

'Four years ago in May.'

'What happened?'

'Cancer. It was advanced already when it was diagnosed. She seemed to vanish right in front of us.'

'And you miss her?'

'Shit.' Matt slapped his palms on to his knees, then slumped back in the chair. 'She was my mum – of course I miss her. She was too young, and I was too young, but d'you know what I'd say to her if she walked through that door now?'

'No.'

'I'd tell her she picked a fucking stupid time to go. I'd tell her how it had opened the way for shit to flood over me from every side.' With a single move, Matt was on his feet, poking an accusatory finger at Goodhew through the silence that suddenly filled the room.

'Please sit back down, Matt.'

'Always on your terms? I don't think so.'

'Matt.' Goodhew's voice hardly rose above a whisper. 'Sit.' And, in contradiction to his determination not to, Matt did exactly what he was told. 'You're in a pretty volatile condition, Matt, so I'd prefer to have someone else in the room with you.'

'I'm fine.' Even Matt didn't sound convinced.

'What about your dad?'

'He's out at work.'

'Gardening, Charlotte told me. I could find him.'

'Gardening?' Matt snorted. 'He's far more likely to be at the Carlton Arms. Drinking pints with his mates is his answer to everything, apparently. I don't want him here.'

'Okay,' Goodhew said slowly. 'Charlotte, then?' She had brought her brother and Libby home, but Goodhew still wasn't sure how well this suggestion would be met. She hadn't offered to sit in at the start of the interview.

'She's with Libby. Can you talk to Charlotte, then to me? I don't want Libby left alone, right now.'

'What about *her* parents?'

'They're the last people she needs. Ask Charlotte why – she won't get wound up like me.' Matt crossed to open the sitting-room door, but stopped just short and turned back to Goodhew. 'I'm sorry I get like that. I can't help it. Have you ever had to keep reminding yourself how you ought to behave?'

'How you should be reacting?'

'Yes, yes. I know that Shanie's death should be traumatic, but I've ended up in this bubble where nothing quite gets through to me. Then, once in a while, something small makes me react. It's like all my emotions blow up over the wrong things, and I'm not in control any more.'

FIFTEEN

When Charlotte returned to the room, Goodhew realized that she shared the same naturally cheerful features as her brother; she didn't exactly exude joy but she certainly seemed less burdened than Matt. Whenever she smiled, it reached right up to her eyes, making them curve into warm crescents.

'I'm glad you wanted to speak to me. I was actually hoping I could have a few minutes of your time.'

'Your brother asked me to speak to you, actually.'

'Okay.' She paused to think for a moment. 'Okay,' she repeated, sounding as if she'd made a decision. 'I didn't really know Shanie. I've met her a couple of times, but nothing more than a "Hi", and I'm not going to even begin to consider whether or not she was hated, depressed or irresponsible.'

'But you're concerned about Matt?'

'And Libby too. Matt will only be okay if Libby is, and vice versa.'

Goodhew guessed his expression alone made it obvious that she needed to offer him a better explanation.

She glanced towards the window at the other end of the sitting room. 'I'd like to show you something.'

He knew how Marks would feel about him taking off at a tangent and, by Charlotte's own admission, she wasn't likely to be pointing out anything remotely linked to Shanie's death. He therefore should have said, 'No.'

'Fine,' he replied.

She led him down the back garden and then through the gate opening on to an alleyway that ran behind the houses.

'We've known Libby's family most of our lives. I went to school with her sister, Matt with her brother, and Libby was always the little kid who tagged along after us wherever she could.'

'Matt told me to ask you about his outbursts.'

Charlotte stopped, her length of curly hair taking a second longer to fall still. Only then did she reply. 'Detective, I'm not giving you our family history just for the fun of it. I'm explaining why Matt is in such a mess, and when I get to the end I'm going to ask for your opinion.' She leaned back against the wooden fence. 'Do you know how our mum died?'

Goodhew nodded. 'Cancer. About four years ago?'

'I think Mum must have known she was ill for a while; she became remote and stressed. She and Dad argued quite a bit and he couldn't seem to lift her out of it. When we were finally told she was ill, I think she knew it was terminal. But Matt just didn't accept that she wouldn't recover. She was in a hospice at the very end, but he carried on like nothing major was happening until the last twenty-four hours. Then, right at the end, he grabbed me . . .' Charlotte clutched at the sleeve of her jersey near the top of her left arm. 'For the first time he sounded distraught.' She turned away from Goodhew and continued along the footpath. 'He said, "She's not going to make it, is she, Char?"' She shook her head. 'Said it like he'd only just realized, and despite me and Mum and Dad trying to get him used to the idea, he really only believed it at that moment. It feels as though that was the start of Matt's problems.'

'Losing a parent at that young age is going to be tough.'

She screwed up her nose. 'Mr Cliché.'

'Hmm, sorry.'

'And I suppose time heals everything?'

'I really wasn't being dismissive.'

'Fair enough.' Charlotte had a ring on the third finger of her right hand. She rubbed it with the tip of her thumb. It looked like an engagement ring and he wondered whether it had belonged to her mother. 'Matt became increasingly withdrawn and moody,' she continued. 'Now *I'm* reaching for the clichés. I had some bereavement counselling, but he wasn't interested. I read up on grief, and it seemed to me he was going through the classic stages. I thought we'd just have to wait it out and then I'd get the old Matt back.' She grinned suddenly, instantly becoming vibrant again. 'He's always been so funny – annoying in this charming way, if you know what I mean.' The smile vanished as quickly as it had arrived. 'Nathan and Libby also had problems at home, and we knew Nathan was finding it particularly hard, but no one thought . . .' Again her voice trailed away.

They'd only walked about one hundred yards before she stopped again. She pointed at the fence immediately to the right of the path. He noticed she didn't actually look at it though. 'What can you see in that garden?' she asked.

Goodhew was tall enough to be able to peer over the fence without any difficulty. The house itself had originally been identical to Charlotte's family home, but its post-war elevations had been rendered and painted cream, and the windows and doors looked as though they'd been replaced about ten years ago. At some point since then, the owner had given up; the grass was knee-high, outstripped by sturdy thistles and flat-leafed nettles. Tentacles of dark green ivy had curled across a weathered pile of unlaid decking and woven their way up around the legs of a rusting barbecue which looked close to disintegration. Curtains covered the two upstairs windows; maybe they had been drawn earlier to block out the afternoon sun, but Goodhew doubted it. The fabric was either faded or behind glass clouded by the heavy patina of neglect.

'Abandonment,' he answered finally.

'That's where Libby's parents live. If you look at the back garden, you can see what her home life is like.'

Around the edges of the long grass it was still possible to see the curve of old flowerbeds and the crumbling remains of a broken stone planter. 'If it wasn't always like that, what went wrong?'

'Libby and Nathan's sister Rosie died within months of us losing Mum. Then Nathan killed himself.'

The final four words came so abruptly that Goodhew took a second or two to fully grasp them. 'When?'

'Three years ago. At the time it felt as though it would destroy Matt, and maybe it would have done, if he and Libby hadn't had each other.'

'And that's why they look out for each other then?'

'They think they do, but how can they when they're both so vulnerable?' She bit her bottom lip as she reflected for a second. 'They *talk*,' she added, as if those two words explained everything.

'That's not a good thing then?'

'They fuel the wrong ideas.' Charlotte pointed in the general direction of Libby's parents' house. 'I hate them. They were always spiteful, selfish people, but Rosie, Nathan and Libby were decent kids. Now Libby is the only one left, and she can't stand living in that house with its locked bedrooms and her parents drinking and fighting every day.'

As they began to walk back towards Charlotte's home, Goodhew decided to nudge her back on topic. 'You were saying they get the wrong ideas – but about what exactly?'

'Matt refuses to believe that Nathan committed suicide. I asked the police to double-check, but even that wasn't enough to convince him. Sometimes I think I'm getting through, then Matt starts off again. He keeps going over it and over it. Meanwhile, Libby keeps asking him why it happened, saying there has to be a reason.'

'Trying to rationalize is part of dealing with trauma.'

'Now they think everything, starting with Mum's cancer, is all part of the same chain of events. I've tried listening, agreeing, arguing . . . everything. Matthew and Libby moved into that student house as a compromise. My dad and Libby's parents both agreed because it would give Matt and Libby some independence but without too much risk. Or so they thought.'

'And Shanie Faulkner's death changes all that.'

'Totally.'

'We'll be allowing everyone back into the student house shortly. Will they want to return?'

'Libby will. She can't go back home. And Matt will go where Libby goes.'

'But they're not *seeing* each other?'

'No, and Matt had no involvement with Shanie either, but he'll still take her death very badly. He couldn't live with himself if anything happened to Libby.' They were almost back at Charlotte's garden gate when she stopped and turned to face Goodhew. 'And having watched my mother die, I would never use that expression lightly.'

'What happened to the brother, Nathan?'

'An overdose. Took about four packs of paracetamol and washed them down with a huge amount of spirits. They found him on the road to Oakington, and . . . What's the matter?'

'Nothing,' Goodhew lied.

His memory was good, he knew it was and he trusted it. He had never considered himself prone to blotting out any of the memories he found hardest to face, but here was the proof.

Rosie plus Brett plus Nathan had not connected for him, but suddenly the name 'Oakington' welded them together into a single event.

'Why did he go to Oakington?' he asked. Then he listened carefully as she told him her version of the story that he already knew.

SIXTEEN

Goodhew considered pulling out Rosie's file and making himself reread all the notes on her death. And forcing himself to look at the photos too.

He knew it would mean steering clear of anyone else involved in Shanie's case, or he would run the risk of trying to explain to Marks why he was wasting time on an old case so totally unconnected with their current enquiry.

Worse still, he didn't know the reason himself.

Instead, he phoned his friend Bryn O'Brien and arranged to meet him at D'Arry's in King Street at eight.

Bryn had arrived at twenty past, and downed his first bottle of Peroni before managing anything more than an initial greeting.

Goodhew had picked a table near the window, but Bryn spent most of that first bottle of beer studying the restaurant interior. The food was broadly European, the stone floors reminded Goodhew of the Med, while the low ceilings and the lighting glowing from wrought-iron candelabras said Bavaria, or maybe Prague. The whole building had burned out a few years before, but it had been rebuilt, giving it the air of somewhere that had evolved over many decades.

Eventually Bryn nodded slowly. 'I like it in here.' He continued to gaze down the length of the room, adding, 'Great legs on that waitress.' Then finally, he turned to Goodhew. 'It's no coincidence that we are here and you've been working on a dead body fifty yards up the road, is it?'

'Perhaps I just like it here.'

'Have you noticed how some waitresses move quickly, with lots of little steps, but they're facially serene, like energetic geishas?'

'And I suppose you've always had a thing for energetic geishas?'

'Do you really want to know, or instead do you want to tell me what's bugging you?'

There had been a time when Goodhew had kept everything to himself. Occasionally he would open up to his grandmother, but beyond those times everything stayed firmly private. He had moved on from there, made slow but deliberate progress to make his life less isolated. There were now times when he confided in Gully, and others when he discussed things with Bryn but, as he tried to choose his opening line, he became aware that this wouldn't be one of them. Right now he wished he'd stayed at home, door locked and with nothing but his jukebox for company.

The main course arrived and Goodhew saw that Bryn had ordered a rare steak that was already seeping pink into the surrounding gravy. Bryn peered at Goodhew's plate with an equally critical eye. 'Is that some kind of veggie meal?'

'Goats' cheese flan.'

Bryn frowned. 'Now we look like we are on a date.' He pressed the flat of his knife against the meat until the blood oozed. 'I'm the bloke, by the way.'

Goodhew replied, at least he assumed he did, but later he realized that he had stopped talking somewhere along the way – some time after Bryn had put pressure on that sirloin and the deep red had seeped further into the gravy.

There had been only two times in his life that Goodhew had seen a dead body and recoiled. He hated succumbing to that reaction, and on both occasions had felt a deep disgust at himself. A corpse deserves respect: that had been one of his grandfather's serious and abiding messages. A body is no longer good or evil; it has ceased to be anything but an embodiment of the human form, and the way it is treated reflects on the living.

It deserves dignity.

Goodhew heard those words before he'd ever faced a corpse and they'd stayed with him like his ingrained knowledge of multiplication tables or the alphabet.

Whenever he was confronted by a body, he made sure he paused long enough to acknowledge the person lost, and silently offer his respects. He knew it probably didn't stand up to careful analysis, but that was what he did. Sometimes to recoil was natural, but he also found it unforgivable.

Francisco Silva had regularly driven his lorry from Holland to Peterborough and back again. He knew how a delay in ferry sailings would affect his driving time and equally how any delay on the notoriously congested A14 might impact on his journey from Felixstowe. He timed the UK-bound trip so that whenever he was approaching Cambridge and the North he had made up just enough time in his tight schedule to be able to afford to sit for an hour in the backlog of any accident without his stress levels accelerating beyond comfortable.

Whenever he had to wait any longer, the story changed. He began to fidget, listening to the traffic reports, frustrated that they couldn't give any more accurate update than, 'There's an accident resulting in an eighteen-mile tailback.' In a situation like that, he would eventually climb from his vehicle and ask other drivers what they knew.

Invariably, when they finally moved again and eventually trickled past the accident scene, the visible remnants would be little more than broken glass and crumpled bonnets. For an actual fatality, the road would close completely, and the six lanes of traffic would be left to pick their way through the string of thirty-mile-an-hour villages that littered the route.

Francisco was not an habitually impatient man, yet he did not understand the necessity of closing the road for so long. And what he didn't understand, he did not sympathize with.

On 21 October 2008, the trip had worked out much the same as on so many previous occasions. The roads were busy, but the traffic flowed freely, and Francisco's lorry tucked into the slipstream of an artic belonging to a removal firm; the phone number on the back said it was based in York. It was driven precisely on the speed limit, so he'd have been perfectly happy to sit behind it until the Peterborough turn-off.

The two vehicles ate through the miles that way, passing Ipswich, Bury St Edmunds and Newmarket, through the rush hour and into the dusk. As the A14 passed Cambridge and veered north, the traffic still flowed. Francisco tapped a cigarette from his pack and opened the window in readiness.

Until that moment, the names Oakington and Dry Drayton had been irrelevant to him, just anonymous titles appearing on a couple of signboards. They were so insignificant compared to Peterborough and Amsterdam, or the other major points along the way.

Less significant still than São Miguel do Rio Torto in Portugal, where he'd been born and hoped to spend his retirement.

There was rain in the air, so he set his wipers to sweep the windscreen intermittently; they made the return journey about once every minute. Visibility was good.

Suddenly the trailer in front of him shuddered, and Francisco just had time to tighten his grip on the steering wheel and extend his brake foot before he saw the stricken trailer start to slew. Something tumbled from its darkened roof into the glare of his own headlights. It was there for a split second before it fell in front of him.

Not something . . . Someone.

A moment of colour. Clean clothes. Fresh blood. He slammed on the brakes, rigid and frozen as his lorry continued to travel, sliding towards the back of the trailer in front, parallel for a moment then closing fast as the lorry travelling behind cannoned into his rear.

Francisco's cab crumpled, folding around him, the windows exploding in all directions, the seat and steering wheel inexplicably moving together, pinning him in between. Then the lorry was on its side, damp tarmac grating his door and sending sparks through the driver's missing window.

A short time later, through his dimming consciousness, Francisco picked out the blue lights, all the emergency services, but most of all a young policeman who called to him through the little tunnel that had once been the nearside window.

'The fire brigade will free you as soon as possible. Can you hear me?'

Francisco nodded. 'I need to get out now.' It hurt him even to speak. 'Where am I?' he asked.

'Just outside Cambridge.'

'I think my legs are trapped.'

'Your lorry has been involved in a collision with two others. We'll get you all out as soon as possible.'

'And the girl?'

The young policeman's gaze darted warily around the remains of the cab. 'In here?'

'It's why we crashed.' Francisco intended to say more, but his voice was overtaken by a groan accompanying a spasm of pain. 'Under,' he gasped. He barely recognized his own voice. 'Under,' he repeated.

The policeman's hand gripped his own and the remnants of his last cigarette flaked from his fingers.

'Where is this?' Francisco mumbled.

'Cambridge,' the policeman repeated.

'No,' he grunted again, louder this time. But somehow he sensed his voice had weakened. 'Where exactly?'

'Near Oakington.'

'Oakington and Dry Drayton,' he whispered, remembering the signboard. Suddenly those names were as relevant as São Miguel do Rio Torto.

Finally he understood all the other delays, the chaos – the havoc he'd always been so impatient to see scooped off the road with undue haste.

He gripped the policeman's hand more tightly. 'She's underneath,' were his final words.

SEVENTEEN

The three lorries had come to rest in a skewed zigzag. The first one hung over the central reservation, its trailer section sliced open by the second lorry. All the efforts involved in a carefully packed house-move were spilled across the outside lane. The top of a coffee table lay flat on the road. Goodhew saw no sign of its legs.

Headlights from the emergency vehicles had been hastily replaced by floodlights, and Goodhew wriggled back out of the crushed cab into their full glare. A paramedic walked towards him.

'He just died,' Goodhew informed her.

'And are you okay?'

Goodhew followed the woman's gaze, and saw that his clothes were now heavily stained. 'It's the driver's blood. He was trying to tell me that he'd hit a woman. Said she was underneath.'

The bright pools of artificial light were compact and distinct, fading into complete darkness within inches of their perimeter. The paramedic stared at the black gap between two sets of wheels and where one side of the felled lorry lay almost flat on the ground. 'Call me if you find anything,' she muttered, then walked away without looking Goodhew in the eye.

The third lorry had jack-knifed and come to rest with its cab relatively undamaged. It was the rear half that had taken the brunt of the impact, decelerating from fifty-five to zero within yards as it tore into the undercarriage of the lorry in its path. The result was a narrowing 'V', an acute angle of scrap metal and 36-inch-high tyres.

The whole crash scene seemed overrun with emergency crews cutting, tending and directing, but no one seemed to notice Goodhew. He hesitated, he knew he should tell someone what he was considering, but if they delayed him it might be too late. He wanted to believe that, by some fluke, someone could still be alive under there.

Although the trailer lay on its side, it was no longer entirely rigid, and the impact had buckled it just enough to allow Goodhew a crawlspace. He lay flat on his stomach and, with his mobile phone in his hand, extended his arm in amidst the wreckage and took a photo. The flash lit the space for a moment, then he quickly withdrew his arm. The timer revolved for a few seconds and then the photo appeared. The light had reflected off the wet tarmac, blanching the image, but Goodhew saw what he'd been looking for. It was a smudge of orange, out of focus but clearly fabric.

He folded his hand around his phone and dropped back on to his stomach, then he slid further under the toppled vehicle. The gap was tight, narrowing further in. Every few inches he had to stop and check his route, using the meagre light from the phone's screen to see for the next couple of feet. As he moved forward, he had to keep his head low, his cheek only an inch from the greasy tarmac.

He made it another yard forward before realizing that the gap between the wreckage and the ground was starting to reduce. It was also becoming more difficult to tilt his face up in order to see where he was heading. If he went much further, it might be impossible to back out again, then he himself would need to be rescued. But equally he felt he'd already come too far to turn back. He took several new pictures with his phone and finally managed to take one that gave him the answer. The orange fabric was clearer now, and he could distinguish part of an arm and her fingers. They were dirty and bloodstained, but still intact.

He held the phone a little further from his face, squinting as he

85

tried to identify anything that might confirm a definite sign of life. Or death.

At that moment Marks's number flashed up on screen, and Goodhew realized his own odds were not so great.

'Where are you?' Marks barked. 'I'm at the scene now.'

'I'm under the lorry, sir.'

'You need to get out right now.'

'There's someone under here.'

'Goodhew!'

'I'm nearly there.'

'It isn't safe, there are procedures that must be followed. And you're not going to find anyone alive under this mess.'

Silence.

Then the beam of a flashlight swung under the lorry, and hit Goodhew full in the face. 'Get out now, Gary.'

'I can't.'

'It's not a request. Out. *Now*.'

'I'm sorry, I can't move backwards,' he lied.

'Bollocks. I know the position of the lorry, Gary, and it gets narrower as you move forwards.'

'It's harder to back up.' Goodhew drew a deep breath. 'Shine the torch on her, please, sir.'

'I can't bloody well see her.'

'Stick your arm in further and I'll direct you.'

'I can't see anything if I do that.'

'It doesn't matter – I can. Okay, okay, round to your left . . . Stop! Now, slowly, left again. Stop.'

By craning his neck, Goodhew could see the furthest point of torchlight, a narrow beam that clipped the edge of a metal strut, before landing to give him a partial view of a woman's face. He could see her cheek and ear, her jawbone and neck. 'I can reach her,' he called out.

They were still on the phone and, though just yards apart, Marks might as well have been a mile away.

'That lorry's not stable, I want you out of there.'

'I don't think I can. Look, if I'm with her, they'll only need to work on one spot and, if she's not dead, I might be able to help.'

Marks didn't actually say it, but Goodhew could imagine his boss's exasperated response: *Don't be stupid, of course she's dead.*

It took Goodhew almost twenty minutes to reach her, pressing himself ever flatter to the ground as he wriggled forward.

He had spoken to her several times during the last ten minutes, but there was no response. Finally he got close enough to touch her. She was over to his right as he lay on his stomach, his face level with the back of her head.

'Can you hear me?' he whispered.

He slid his hand over and around her cheek, to feel for any hint of breath. He cupped his palm close to her nose and mouth. But there was something getting in the way. He felt around more urgently, then realized that whatever it was led to her mouth. It went directly inside. He didn't want to move her, but she needed to breathe, no matter what other injuries she'd sustained. He lifted his own head as far as possible, and turned hers towards him.

And despite the bad light, he saw the thing forcing its way through her open mouth. Not going in but coming out – *what the* . . .

And that was when he recoiled, pressing his face to the tarmac and struggling to breathe. He wanted to fight his way out from under that lorry, just to escape it. But that was impossible: he was just too exhausted and too tightly wedged in to go anywhere.

His mobile rang again, and he answered. He could hear himself carefully explaining the situation to Marks, his voice on some kind of autopilot and doing a poor impression of calmness.

It took another two hours for the wrecked lorries to be lifted. Goodhew didn't think he'd moved in all that time; even when he'd spoken to Marks, his face had stayed put, his eyes fixed on the road surface. It seemed like the only thing he was able to trust right then.

He told himself to look at her again, to try to understand what he thought he'd seen and silently offer her body the *respect* it deserved. Instead, he didn't lift his head again until he felt a hand tugging at his shoulder, and heard the firm voice of the paramedic he'd spoken to earlier.

'Gary.' Her voice was insistent, as if it wasn't the first time she'd spoken his name. 'Come on. That's right.' She spoke as though he was being coaxed from a ledge. She helped him to stand.

He did exactly what he was told, but beyond that struggled to gather his thoughts. It was as if some part of his brain had switched off and would take several attempts to reboot.

He muttered something.

'You weren't under a bed.' She laughed – a false noise that didn't suit her. 'That's your shock talking.'

She had one hand on his elbow and the other pressing into the small of his back, manoeuvring him towards a waiting ambulance. By the time his head began to clear, he was sitting inside the vehicle with a thermal blanket draped around his shoulders. Marks was there too, with an expression of angry relief written on his face.

'Strickland's examined the body, taking her back for autopsy . . .'

Goodhew wasn't really listening. 'Did you see her?'

'Strickland told me. He's insisting on having a word with you. Ah, here he comes.'

Goodhew nodded. As far as he knew, Strickland was the most humourless and pedantic man on the planet, but he was also a very thorough police surgeon who would never waste any of his time just to hand-hold a junior officer.

Strickland was to the point. 'DI Marks thought it important that you had some kind of understanding of the condition of the body. One of the injuries sustained by the young lady was a huge crushing force sustained to the abdomen. Certainly, I would say, enough to cause death – although it is possible that she had already been fatally injured at that point. Needless to say . . .'

Gary hung his head and stared into his filthy hands.

'. . . it was likely to be the result of the wheels rolling over her, and simple physics tells us what that kind of enormous pressure will exert on soft tissue. Her diaphragm would have ruptured and her oesophagus would have compressed a little, but intestines are extremely plastic. The first time you witness intestines expelled through the mouth, well, it's certainly weird but with the forces involved, not as improbable as it would seem.'

Goodhew had his hand raised, willing Strickland to stop. He'd understood as soon as Strickland had mentioned *simple physics*. It was Strickland's favourite phrase when he wanted to demonstrate the frailty of the human body.

But Strickland had continued with his explanation, while Goodhew pumped hand-sanitizer on to his palms, and tried to expunge the feeling of raw intestines against his skin.

Three years on and it was a memory he had never chosen to revisit, until forced on him now by the realization that he had ended up face to face with Rosie Brett's little sister and the remains of the family home. Until then the memory had been lodged in the part of his brain called forget-it-ever-happened.

Goodhew's dinner was virtually untouched, but Bryn was gone and in his place sat Gully.

'I've only been here a couple of minutes,' she began. 'Bryn rang me because he was worried.'

'Really?'

'I don't know why you're surprised. You didn't even see him leave or me arrive. He made a good call. He said you'd become totally vacant, like you weren't here at all.'

'No, I was just thinking.'

'Bollocks, it was more than that. I just saw it, remember? Most of us don't go that far away, even when we're on annual leave.'

Goodhew managed to smile. Gully was a good antidote to self-pity.

He went over to the bar and returned with a pint of lager and a large glass of Bacardi and lemonade. 'Cheers,' he said. He leaned forward, lowering his voice. 'Libby Brett's brother and sister both killed themselves.'

'Yes, I know. I found that out this afternoon when I went to visit her course tutor. I thought he might be in a good position to arrange some extra support.'

'There's a big heart under that uniform, after all.'

'Yeah, right. I was actually thinking more about our workload. Less witness trauma probably equals a clearer statement, which probably equals less paperwork.'

'That big heart?'

'Yes, I know, it's made of granite.'

The waitress approached their table holding a dessert bowl, napkin and spoon. 'Hot chocolate orange pudding?'

Goodhew pointed to Gully's side of the table. 'It's a treat for your soft side.'

She took a mouthful, then paused before the second. 'I'm concerned for Libby because she's been through so much, but I wouldn't joke if I really thought she was a risk.'

'See, you're as soft as they come.'

'Piss off, Gary. If this wasn't Jaffa Cake heaven, I'd walk out now. Just go back to thinking. I'm not interrupting this just to talk to you.'

EIGHTEEN

I'll tell you one thing, Zoe. I never expected all of this when I started emailing you.

We've been allowed back into the house.

I wasn't expecting that. I thought it would remain sealed, with tape across the doors and the PC on guard at the front step, at least until the end of the investigation.

So much for TV and my imagination, I guess.

And at college I seem to have gained this weird kind of notoriety. The favourite question seems to be whether I find it creepy going back to a house where someone killed themselves.

And, no, I don't.

Each time I reply as if that's the first time it's been brought to my attention, I never go on to say that being back here is a comfort. It is, especially here in my room with all my own things.

Matt didn't want to come back, but I think he did it for me. He's been in my room a bit more than usual, talking about Shanie mostly. We both worry in case she was alive for a while, and trying to get our attention, but we're also determined not to dwell on that until we're told more. DC Goodhew had a quiet word and reassured me, saying that it looked like she'd been dead for most of that weekend.

He talked to Charlotte, and I know she would have told him all about Rosie and Nathan. They went for a walk somewhere, and he was white faced by the time they returned. He looked at me as though he felt sorry for me.

Thanks, Charlotte.

No, that's not fair. I'm genuinely pleased that she told him, and thankful for everything Charlotte has done to try to convince people that Rosie and Nathan would never have killed themselves. I'm just angry that, in the end, she seemed to reach the conclusion that they did. And now she wishes Matt would accept it, too.

And Matt does waver about it sometimes.

'If they didn't kill themselves, Libby, what are you saying?' That's been a question that he's asked with increasing frequency.

The word 'murder' sounds so extreme that I hesitated before using it. Could that really have happened? I sat on the fence a bit with my reply: 'Someone made it happen,' I said.

'Someone made them kill themselves?'

I'd only made it sound even more unlikely.

'No, someone killed them,' I said quietly. It sounded as improbable as a fairy sneaking into your room at night and taking teeth from under your pillow, leaving money behind. Was I just a kid wanting to believe the fanciful over reality?

'Who?' Matt asked.

'I don't know,' I answered miserably. I could feel that I would regret it if I lost my nerve. 'They were murdered.' I voiced the thought, and realized it didn't sound ridiculous at all. 'They were murdered and I don't know why, or who would have done it.' My strength of conviction alone has been enough to keep Matt on side.

But, for all Charlotte's doubts, she is determined to find something that might give me conclusive proof. She understands that it's the only way I will let it drop and, more importantly from her point of view, my own peace of mind will give Matt the answer he needs so that he can begin to get on with his life.

Charlotte is strong and single-minded, and 'conclusive proof' is all I want, too. But I reckon it will give a different answer to the one she expects.

She believes DC Goodhew can help, but wouldn't say any more

than that. I can guess what she's thinking. I hope she genuinely likes him, as I don't want to see her make the same mistake twice.

As far as this house goes, I feel like I'm on suicide watch. Jamie scares me, she's taken it so badly. Of all the people here, I do wonder why she returned. She averts her head from Shanie's door whenever she walks down the hall and lowers her voice if she needs to say Shanie's name. I can hear her crying in her room, and listening to an endless stream of angsty music. If I hear her listening to Coldplay, I'm calling an ambulance.

The others aren't so bad and, yes, they all came back. Oslo's gone on one of his sick photography expeditions. I would have thought he might have given that a rest in the circumstances. Funny, really – when the police let us back in, he was crapping himself in case either of his precious goldfish had died.

Meg and Phil are together even more than usual. I don't understand their relationship. They have this way of acting around each other that makes me feel they're part of their own private club. I can be in a room with them, and then leave with a feeling that I'm the subject of a private joke between them.

I thought that sounded paranoid until Jamie said she felt like that too.

I don't think I like either of them very much, but I can't shake the feeling that I'd like them to like me. It's a shame I'm not studying psychology: none of this is on the accountancy syllabus!

Hang on, now their two-person club is not sounding quite so happy. Shit. I'm not staying here to listen to this. Why don't they remember that Phil's room is straight above mine? Perhaps no one realizes how much I can hear in this house.

Or maybe we can all hear the same, but I'm the only one who's actually paying attention.

NINETEEN

Phil's room was small with just a narrow strip of carpet on either side of the double bed. At its foot was a slightly larger area of carpet where a chest of drawers stood with its back to the wall. In the narrow space left between that and the bed, Meg and Phil were standing almost toe-to-toe.

She was shocked at the fury she felt towards him. 'I told you to leave her alone.'

'It's none of your business,' he snorted.

'I had to find somewhere else to sleep, while the police were going through our house.'

'For fuck's sake, that's not my fault.'

'Nothing's your fault in your eyes. Has it occurred to you that you hurt her? That this whole mess might be your fault?' She knew she was goading him now, but she didn't care.

But he came straight back at her. 'Just as likely *you* pushed her to it.'

'Fuck you, Phil.' Meg wanted to leave, but she wanted an explanation even more. 'I did nothing to her that she didn't do to me.'

'Meg, you picked her up on everything, every chance you had. If you couldn't bitch at her, you blanked her or sidelined her.'

'At least I didn't screw her.'

'Since when do you care?'

'She wasn't even pretty.' Meg's mouth pulled itself downwards. 'There was something about her that made me cringe. I'd just look at her and want to vomit.'

'That's pathetic.'

'Why? She made no effort with her looks, her hair was a mess, she dressed like a slob . . .'

'Meg. Just give it a rest.'

'No. You can screw who you like, Phil, but I don't have to like them too. And you didn't have to do it here. In this house. In that bed.' Meg's voice began to waver. She didn't want to cry, she just wanted him to know how angry she was.

Phil's expression suddenly shut down. 'So what about you and Matt?' He sounded calm at first, but then began his vent in earnest. '*That* was in this house. On your bed, and loud enough for people to hear in the centre of Cambridge. Did I have a problem with it? No.'

'I was drunk.'

'Not as drunk as he was, I'd bet. He spent the first two weeks here looking totally ashamed.'

'Thanks, Phil.'

'Okay, okay, I'm sorry. Meg?' He reached out to touch her but she pulled away. 'It was the heat of the moment, all right? I didn't mean it.'

'Worried that you said too much? You're quite happy to sleep with me when it suits you, so I'm sure you don't find it *that* unpleasant.' She was pleased to see how uncomfortable he looked, and rewarded him by glaring more fiercely. She didn't want to give in to him and she hated the suspicion that she probably would. 'The police will find out she wasn't a virgin.'

His eyes hardened again. 'And what – arrest me? I don't think so.'

Meg had hoped he would deny it, though she couldn't explain why. Couldn't even begin to form another coherent thought. She backed towards the door. 'I hate you, Phil.' And, as she said it, a lump formed in her throat.

His response was a sharp laugh. 'So much for friends with benefits,' he shouted after her, and clicked his door shut in her wake.

* * *

Jamie-Lee kept crying; the tears came and went in unpredictable waves. Earlier she'd walked along Sussex Street and ordered a jacket potato at Tatties. She'd then taken a seat near the window and idly watched customers drift in and out of the music shop opposite. With a clear view of the sales counter, she soon realized that guitar picks seemed to be their biggest seller.

Guitar picks and sheet music; half the sales were one or the other and she occupied herself for a while trying to predict who amongst the customers would buy which item.

It was an innocuous way to spend half an hour. And it was that very thought that set the tears rolling again. Who was she to while away careless minutes after what had happened?

She had thought she cared about the other housemates, but did she?

Did she really, when one had taken to her room and died while she herself had been too wrapped up in guitar picks or sheet music or whatever that particular hour's diversion had been.

She turned away from the window, only to catch the eye of the couple sitting at the next table. She bowed her head and sobbed quietly into a serviette, until one of the waitresses leaned across and asked, rather redundantly, whether she was all right.

Her response was to push back her chair and dash for home.

She opened the front door just as Libby was hurrying out. The younger girl looked at her with almost equal despair, then, instead of leaving, Libby grabbed Jamie and the two of them clung together.

Finally Libby spoke. 'I thought I was okay. But I'm not.'

'I know,' Jamie murmured. 'It hurts so much.'

TWENTY

Goodhew's Bel-Ami jukebox was set to random play, but so far he had barely noticed any of the 45s that had clicked and whirred their way on to the turntable. The room was dark and, behind him, his window looked out on Parker's Piece and across to the police station.

The verdict on Rosie Brett's death had been left open since there hadn't been any conclusive evidence that she'd planned to kill herself by jumping from the nearby bridge into oncoming traffic. But Goodhew read 'open verdict' as 'Well, she might have done' – and he didn't see how any family could ever step out of the shadow of uncertainty hanging over those words.

Goodhew had given evidence at the inquest, and he could remember her parents; they had sat side by side, but were conspicuously separate in their posture and reactions. Her mother kept wanting Rosie's dad to say more, while he just wanted it all to be over. She looked like someone trying too hard, but behind his smart suit was a man who seemed to have given up on trying at all. Even then, Goodhew had begun to wonder whether Rosie's home life had been miserable. And now he knew.

The single changed again and this time he listened to the jukebox's mechanical routine and waited to hear the next track.

Nathan Brett stole his concentration first. Pulling Nathan's file should have been the first thing he'd done after he came back from talking to Charlotte.

Goodhew turned towards the window, and Parkside Station. He didn't want to distract attention from Shanie's case, but felt compelled to find out more about Nathan. Apart from the lobby area, the station looked quiet. It usually was at this time of night, when most of the officers on duty were either out of the building somewhere, or running back and forth dealing with the latest drama to fall through the front door.

Goodhew unhooked a pair of binoculars from behind the open curtains and trained them on the foyer. There were five people presently there, four looking patient and one pacing; he guessed everyone had their hands full. He scanned the rest of the building and the only person he spotted was DI Marks, standing alone at his office window. He held a mug in his right hand, and his left was buried deep in his overcoat pocket.

It was a minor point, but why had he stopped for coffee after putting on his coat? And if he had only just arrived, why had he been motivated to turn up in the middle of the night?

Goodhew grabbed his own jacket and headed for the door. He paused only to switch off the jukebox, halting The Ventures' 'Perfidia' mid-flow.

He crossed Parker's Piece playing out the final bars of guitar in his head and wondering at the lengths he would go to for the sake of curiosity.

Goodhew reached his boss's office door and found Marks standing in exactly the same spot.

The man spoke without turning. 'I saw you walking over, you know.'

'I fancied a cuppa and not much beats our drinks machine. Can I get you a refill?'

'Sit down, Gary.'

Goodhew pulled a chair towards the window and sat with his arm resting along the sill.

Marks gave him a sideways glance. 'You belong on the far side of the desk, Goodhew.'

'Would you like me to move?'

'No.' He paused. 'Yes, actually. I have a report on Shanie Faulkner. I'd like you to take a look, as you're here.'

They settled into their usual positions on opposite sides of the table, and Marks turned his PC screen in Gary's direction. 'I have the video footage of the autopsy.'

Goodhew merely nodded. 'Oh good,' didn't seem like quite the right response.

Marks slid Shanie's file in front of him. It was already thick, considering the case was only five days old.

'I just have the preliminaries.'

'I know,' Goodhew replied, then added, 'you just said so.'

Marks gave him a sharp look, so Goodhew reached for the photos taken at the scene. He studied them closely and found everything as he remembered it. Shanie lying on her side, dressed in jeans and a T-shirt. The T-shirt had ridden up to expose her bloated midriff, as though the swelling of her body had lifted it to one side.

It was the clothes he was studying now, rather than the body. Her sweatshirt had the various Cambridge college crests displayed in rows across the chest; otherwise it was a bold purple and looked new. Her jeans were either well-worn favourites or bought to deliberately look that way.

Goodhew held his hand a couple of inches away from the photo and, by blocking his view of Shanie's face, it was possible to picture those clothes in a different situation.

'Did she smoke?' he asked.

'Not cigarettes. Some marijuana use.'

She had very few personal items in her room, and only enough clothes to fill a medium suitcase, some toiletries and her MacBook.

'No books?'

'About two hundred on the Mac, but that's being analysed separately. The rest of the inventory is listed there.'

Goodhew pulled it out of the pile of documents and set it to one side, cross-checking against it from time to time, as he looked through the rest of the photographs taken in Shanie's room. The inventory was thorough, and listed everything down to an empty cheese and onion crisp packet and a bus ticket to Madingley, both found in the waste-paper basket, as well as the Boathouse Bitter beer mat used to protect the desktop from a succession of damp-bottomed coffee cups.

Finally he moved on to the autopsy notes. Initially he scanned the report: she'd been drinking and her blood-alcohol would have been a little over twice the drink-drive limit, at the time of her death. She'd taken sleeping tablets too, and an empty Zimovane blister pack had been found on the floor beside the bed, most of the contents having made their way to her stomach.

Goodhew's attention strayed briefly from the page to Marks, and back again. He had a feeling that Marks's thoughts were largely elsewhere at the moment.

Goodhew reread the report more slowly the second time, then when he finished he saw that he had his boss's full attention. 'I'm not sure what I was looking for,' he began.

'That's fine. Just tell me what you did see. Just brainstorm it.'

'There's a note somewhere, right?'

Marks nodded and wiggled his mouse until the screen woke up. 'I have a PDF of the screenshot.' He double-clicked a couple of times, and a snapshot of the Facebook profile page popped up. He pointed to the screen. 'At 11.52 she changed her status to: *don't make friends with the hot girl. She's still a b**ch.* Then, at 1.26 a.m. she changes it to: *Cambridge is just like Merrillville. Neither likes a misfit.*

'Then she sent a single message to her mother, Sarah Faulkner.' Marks double-clicked again and another PDF popped up. 'Read it for yourself.'

Goodhew leaned closer, even though the sparse words were easy to pick out from across the desk.

Dear Mom,

I've been so unhappy, and all I think about is how very much you want me to succeed. I could have phoned you, I guess, but how about all the times I was miserable at highschool and you didn't notice?

You will be okay, Mom. I can see your face now, and I know how you keep going, no matter what. I love you, but I've had enough of being ugly and clever and pretty and stupid all at once.

'There's a lot of anger there,' Marks observed. 'And the suicide note on the social networking site is pretty common for kids of that age. But . . .' His voice trailed away.

'But?'

'I think the coroner will go with suicide.'

'But you're not happy with that?'

'I don't know.' Marks strummed his fingers on the desktop. 'I just don't feel totally convinced.'

It was unusual for Marks to raise concerns in such an open way. It made Goodhew wonder whether Marks was questioning the findings or actually questioning his own judgement. Goodhew couldn't think of a way to broach the question without sounding like a psychotherapist or a junior officer radically overstepping the mark.

Marks continued to frown. 'Give me your thoughts on Shanie Faulkner,' he said.

Goodhew turned the first photo towards his boss. 'Shanie was socializing with her housemates and yet this is what she was wearing. Her personal belongings are virtually devoid of beauty or styling products. She owned two pairs of shoes – trainers and walking boots. No dresses at all, one blouse and everything else was either jeans, T-shirts or sweatshirts. It is fair to say that Shanie did not put fashion or personal grooming far up her priority list. But the sweatshirt worn in this photo looks brand new, that colour is unusual, and I'm guessing it's more than just a bargain picked up from the market. She didn't buy this because any old shirt would do; it looks like she specifically bought a Cambridge University shirt because she was enjoying her experience here. Or maybe it was a gift. Either way, she chose to wear it and, if she really had developed a strong dislike for Cambridge, it seemed to me that it happened after she got dressed that day, or at least it hadn't been bothering her much, earlier.'

'What else?'

'Why didn't her mother respond to her Facebook message?'

'Both her parents are currently en route from Chicago, and they land at Heathrow at 6 a.m. We can get their statements first-hand then.'

Goodhew flicked through to the end of the post-mortem report: *cardiac arrest due to respiratory arrest due to Zimovane and alcohol poisoning.* 'That seems quite straightforward.'

'They're running further toxicology tests too.'

'Then that's all we can do at the moment, isn't it?'

Marks remained unconvinced.

In the entire time Goodhew had known DI Marks, his boss had proved decisive and matter-of-fact at the most emotionally testing moments. When he appeared distracted, it was only while following a case-related train of thought. If he was ever uncertain, he hid it well. And when he asked advice, it was to gain expertise or an alternative viewpoint, never because he was asking someone else to take the lead.

Obviously that wasn't what he was asking of Goodhew now, but somehow it still felt that way.

'You've seemed very preoccupied recently, sir.' Goodhew spoke the words carefully, bracing himself for the knock-back he had no doubt his superior would swiftly deliver.

Instead, Marks simply looked curious. 'Have I, Gary?'

'I assumed you were worried about something.'

Marks's eyes narrowed. 'Something about this case?'

'No.' Goodhew hadn't yet been able to put his finger on what it might be, but it suddenly struck him. 'Something parallel but not part of the case; something that is making you think this is suicide, but stopping you from following that line wholeheartedly.'

'I think you enjoy too much off-duty snooping, Gary.' Suddenly there was only coldness in Marks's voice and no hint of the unspoken encouragement that Goodhew often felt his boss placed carefully between the lines.

Goodhew remembered Marks's daughter – how old was she now? Sixteen? Seventeen?

'Is it Emily, sir?'

'Not even close.' One corner of Marks's mouth twitched with a smile. 'Just come back to me with the full low-down on that sweatshirt.'

Goodhew knew the truth about the devil being in the detail, but he somehow doubted that Satan had done much lurking in a Cambridge University sweatshirt, which was precisely why a town-centre outfitters wasn't going to be his first stop the next day. Probably not the second stop either.

TWENTY-ONE

Don't most people reach a point when, however briefly, they wonder if they still want to live? Knowing they can choose can be the only thing that pulls them back from the precipice. It's that affirmation of the control they still have over their own destiny that makes them decide to push the idea away.

Word for word, that was pretty much the opening paragraph that had appeared in the student newspaper last January. It was upbeat and empowering – and full of patronizing shit.

It encouraged the use of helplines and support groups, and explained how restricting the sale of paracetamol to smaller packs had reduced the incidence of 'unplanned suicides'.

If it's intentional, it's planned – right?

The article was shit.

Shit, shit, shit.

Meant for all those who wanted to find reasons not to, the ones who vented their anguish through repeated drafts of an apologetic explanatory note, only to find they'd then got enough out of their system to chuck the letter in the bin. They'd probably rewrite it during the next drunken binge, over and over, until they'd done the dance between advice and suicide note enough times to leave that phase behind and go on to live average, untroubled adult lives.

It was all shit.

Who stops to debate, once you *know* what you are doing next?

Not me.

TWENTY-TWO

For several years, Goodhew's favourite spot at Parkside had been an unused desk at a second-floor window. It was in a recess which once housed one of IT's hub cabinets, a fridge-freezer-sized unit full of cables and flashing lights. The gap alongside it had been too big to leave empty but too small to be considered useful; the desk that had been slotted in there was due for disposal, but both the view and privacy had been great, at least until the advancement of technology dispensed with the cabinet and the vacant area had come to the attention of Sergeant Sheen.

Goodhew headed there next. Sheen had added two new shelves to the rear wall, filling them with a series of bulky lever-arch files. Sheen had one folder open on his lap, and glanced up and back to the papers without comment.

'Come to see your old hideout?' he murmured.

'Hmm, I like what you've done with the place.'

Goodhew left it at that, and waited for Sheen to finish whatever he was reading. The vital point when dealing with Sheen, Goodhew knew, was acknowledging Sheen-speed.

The man was just a few years short of retirement and he'd undoubtedly spent his whole adult life working slowly and thoroughly. It was a habit ingrained in him as much as his Fen accent and stubborn expression.

Sheen was a hoarder of information; he held on to everything, from rumours and anecdotes to hard statistics. He'd been dragged reluctantly into the computer age, but had almost instantly become an Internet junkie. Of course, that didn't mean he'd ever ditch the paper copies of all his notes. Digitizing information was one thing, but being able to spread pages on a desk and have different layers of Biro and creasing triggered his brain in a way no PC monitor ever would. Additionally, Goodhew knew that there were some pieces of local information that were retained in Sheen's memory alone.

Finally Sheen removed his reading glasses, pushed back his chair and addressed Goodhew. 'How are you going to challenge my poor old brain this time?'

'With a long shot. There's a family in Brimley Close, three kids, but the eldest died three and a half years ago, open verdict but suspected suicide, then—'

Sheen interrupted. 'Family name?'

'Brett.'

Sheen nodded slowly. 'Rosie and Nathan. I remember.' He turned towards his new shelving and selected the third file from the right-hand end. 'This is what my red book has become.'

Sheen had outgrown his red book at least a decade earlier, but at Parkside Station 'Sheen's Red Book' was practically a brand name. He dumped the file on the desk, and flipped open the front cover. 'Rosie and Nathan,' he repeated. 'You know I followed that at the time. Not Rosie's death so much – she was the first.' Sheen paused, studying Goodhew for several seconds before he spoke again. 'It was you that went under that lorry, wasn't it?'

'Yes.'

'Then you must remember Nathan?'

'No.'

'Really?' Sheen didn't look convinced. 'I think of you as one of the people to ask about old cases – your brain files data just like mine does.' He held up a photocopy of a newspaper article. 'Don't this ring a bell?' The headline read *Second Tragedy for Suicide Family*. 'Not very compassionate, is it?'

Goodhew frowned as he read it. The page was dated 6 December 2008, but was as unfamiliar to him as tomorrow's news:

106

A teenager found dead beside the A14 has been named as 18-year-old Nathan Brett. Tests have shown that his death was the result of a drink and drugs overdose. His family were too upset to comment, but police have confirmed that his death is being treated as suicide.

It is the second tragedy for the family whose eldest daughter Rosie, 18, also died after falling from a bridge further along the same stretch of road.

Friends say that Nathan had become very depressed after his sister's death. Police are not seeking anyone else in relation to the incident, but would like to hear from any witnesses who may have seen the teenager in the hours immediately before his death.

'No one contacted us,' Sheen added, as if he'd been reading at exactly the same pace as Goodhew.

'I really don't remember it.'

'And why the current interest?'

'The younger sister, Libby, is one of the flatmates sharing the house where Shanie Faulkner died. I'm just getting background so that I'll be careful when I speak to her.'

'You're snooping, then. I'm not your DI, so you don't have to be coy with me, you know.'

Goodhew flicked the page. 'Is there any reason why you remember them so well?'

Sheen slipped his glasses back on and switched his attention to another press clipping in his folder. There was a photo this time: Rosie and Nathan both grinning at the camera like they were pretending to hate loving each other – or maybe the other way round. Whichever, Goodhew remembered similar moments with his own sister. It was a pose that shouted 'siblings' even more than their physical similarities, which seemed to stop at their shared features of straight noses and matching cowlicks at the left-hand side of their fringes.

Rosie's expression had the kind of openness that said 'volunteer worker' or maybe 'student representative'. Positive. Enthusiastic. Pleasant to meet.

Except in the crawlspace under a motorway pile-up.

She smiled broadly at the camera. Goodhew thrust the picture back at Sheen, who propped it against his telephone. 'I've been here my whole career and I s'pose, now and again, I start to think about the kind of cases I've never come across, like a firearms rampage. Obviously I hope it never occurs here, but the fact of the matter is that it will happen again somewhere, one day. So whenever I hear a case like that in the news, I wonder whether it will be us next.'

'You must be a riot at office parties.'

'You poke fun, but we all have morbid thoughts, don't we?'

'Guess so.'

'Bet you wouldn't share yours, Gary, and I bet they're darker than mine.' He didn't wait for a reply. 'Bridgend, remember that?'

'A spate of teenage suicides, right?'

'Yup – don't ask me what makes 'em do it. I steer clear of all that psycho-whatever-it-is but I heard they often stick to the same method and so, when I saw that Nathan was found on the same stretch of road, I had the feeling he'd been heading for that bridge where his sister jumped. A bit too much Dutch courage though, and he doesn't make it further than the grass verge.'

'Two cases isn't enough for a cluster.'

'Cluster, eh? So you *do* know a bit. Nope, two ain't a cluster. There were twenty-four in two years in Bridgend, but they couldn't have had a third one until they'd had the second, now could they?'

Sheen's logic was, as ever, a little on the straightforward side, but no less effective.

'You're not trying to link this new one, are you?' Sheen asked him. 'That's quite a lot of time between deaths, you know. And a different method.'

'Alcohol again.'

'The rest of it though? Seems very different to me.'

Goodhew was still holding the notes on Rosie and Nathan as he stood up, but he knew better than to ask to borrow them. 'Any chance you could keep these handy?'

'They are not leaving this area though.'

'I know, I know.'

'And I'd think very carefully about linking your new suicide to these ones.'

'It might not be a suicide.'

Sheen brushed the remark to one side. 'If you link them together, the press will jump on it, and the last thing you want is other kids joining in. And you don't want to be pissing your boss off at the moment, either.'

'I think he expects it.'

'Seriously, Gary, steer clear. You never know what stress is rumbling around at the top.'

TWENTY-THREE

The weather settled down to being warm and still. It was most likely a one-day wonder, and so Goodhew arranged to meet his grandmother for coffee at one of the outside tables at Don Pasquale's on Market Hill.

He arrived first and had already been served with drinks and a selection of pastries by the time he saw her approaching from Rose Crescent. A man was running behind her, carrying a parcel. It was flat and square, and wrapped in brown paper. He called out and she turned to face him, halting him in his tracks. He seemed apologetic as he handed her the item. The man looked to be in his forties but, even from this distance, Goodhew could see there was a slight flirtatiousness in his manner.

And, as ever, he knew his grandmother would be warm but uninterested in equal parts. She accepted the package, no doubt declining his offer to carry it for her, and continued towards Goodhew.

His grandmother was quick witted, worldly wise, and could still turn on 'glamorous' better than many woman half her age. She exuded the kind of sensuality that still garnered frequent double-takes from men and women alike. She'd met Goodhew's grandfather when she'd been in her early twenties, and Goodhew really knew little more than that, but could imagine his grandad must have pulled off something pretty darn sensational to have grabbed her attention.

Maybe a bank job.

That was a bad joke, even to himself. His grandfather had left him a large inheritance and, although he'd been assured by his grandmother that he didn't need to worry about its origins, he doubted he'd feel comfortable until he knew for sure where it had come from.

He'd delved back as far as 1972, and now knew that the family wealth was older still. Bank robberies he'd neither looked into, nor ruled out. And anyway, he was pretty sure that his grandmother hadn't married a man just for his money. Or vice versa, come to that.

He'd given up asking and, while she wasn't to be drawn on that particular subject, she was willing to discuss any other that Goodhew chose.

She kissed him on the cheek, then took the chair opposite him, leaving the package on the one in between.

'Guess what it is,' she said.

'Okay,' he said slowly. 'If you'd been in the gallery up there and purchased something today, I don't think the guy would have needed to run up the street after you. You're never that absent-minded, so I think he saw you walking past and ran after you with a purchase that you'd been waiting for and was ready to collect.'

'Which could have been something I bought there,' she pointed out.

'Unlikely.' He shook his head. 'You would have picked it up when you bought it, and you wouldn't buy a painting without seeing it in the flesh. Unless of course they were framing it, too.'

'Fair enough,' she conceded.

He snapped his fingers. 'I think,' Goodhew added quickly, 'it's a black-and-white print of some local scene that you've taken in for framing.'

'Because . . . ?'

'It's the same size as the photograph of Skaters' Meadow hanging above the desk in your apartment, and there's enough space beside it for another one. In which case you'd probably pick something

111

similar – the same photographer even, local guy . . .' For a moment the name escaped him. 'Sean Crawford,' he added finally. 'How did I do?'

His grandmother shrugged. 'Three out of ten for deduction, nine out of ten for insider knowledge. I refuse to be impressed. Now what insider knowledge are you hoping to get from me today, Gary?'

'How good's my memory?'

'Well, dates and numbers, it's pretty close to photographic. Names and faces?' She thought for a moment before answering. 'Trickier to say but above average, I'm sure.'

'And events? Would you be surprised if I told you I'd attended a road accident but didn't even recognize the victim's name when I heard it mentioned a few days ago?'

'Depends when the accident occurred.'

'That's not the point.' They were seated just a few feet from customers occupying the next table, so he leaned forward and whispered, 'I lay next to the body for hours. I wrote reports about it. I was a witness at the inquest.'

His grandmother smiled sadly. 'Rosie Brett?'

'*You* remember.'

'You know how the brain filters out whatever it can't deal with.'

Trusting his own judgement had become a cornerstone in Goodhew's life, and he based his decisions on it. So how would that work if he couldn't trust his own mind?

His grandmother put her coffee cup back on its saucer, then turned it so that it was completely square, with the handle pointing off towards home.

'Sometimes,' she continued, 'I think it's better that way. I like to tackle one obstacle at a time, and if that's the only way my subconscious lets me deal with problems, I wouldn't complain. Don't lose track of the job at hand, Gary. Is Shanie Faulkner considered a suicide or not?'

That made Goodhew sit up. 'You know which case I'm working on, then?'

'I do like to keep abreast of the latest. So tell me.'

'There's no way of being sure what happened yet. On one hand, it's hard to see a pattern of depression, or anything immediately stressful in her current situation but, you know what, it's amazing how comparatively minor dramas escalate for teenagers.'

'Well spoken, old man.' A tiny smile touched his grandmother's lips. 'My sister killed herself.'

'Did she? When?'

'She was twenty.'

Bits of family knowledge were scattered throughout Goodhew's memory. Maybe he had no worries about mental recall, after all, because on cue they tumbled from each recess and converged like iron filings heading towards a magnet.

An old black-and-white photo, two teenagers sitting on either side of the wheel of a continental kit fitted to an American convertible. His mate Bryn O'Brien would identify the vehicle instantly, probably with stats on engine size and a few appropriate anecdotes. As far as Goodhew could remember, it was sporty-with-chrome rather than huge-with-fins.

It was obvious that one of the two girls had been his grandmother, but less clear which one. They'd both been wearing Capri pants and thin angora sweaters. Their poses were wannabe Diana Dors, or maybe Lana Turner.

He'd once asked his grandmother about the photo, but she had smiled in the same way then as today and tucked the picture forever out of sight.

He reckoned that had been about ten years ago.

His paternal family tree stopped at his grandparents. He knew nothing about their childhoods, upbringing or schooling.

But now he remembered a battered copy of *To Kill a Mockingbird*, the words *Happy Birthday, Scout. Love, Mayella* written on the title page.

And a plastic sailboat brooch amongst the real jewellery. And the uncharacteristic tears she'd shed at his sister Debbie's twenty-first birthday photo.

Iron filings. Scattered and insignificant by themselves.

'What was her name?' he now asked.

She gave her head a tiny shake. 'Her reasons made sense, but they weren't good enough. It was nothing that wasn't fixable, but it was too much for her at that moment.'

'What did she do?'

Again no direct reply. 'I tried to find a reason to believe she hadn't done it, any excuse. But it wasn't an accident. It wasn't murder. And it wasn't a cry for help that had gone wrong. Sometimes the answer we want is the one we can't have, and it took me a long time to accept that.' She touched his hand. 'Who she was and what she did won't ever answer your questions about Shanie. Suicide doesn't have to make sense to anyone except the person who commits it. I spent a long time wondering whether, on a different day, she might have chosen another option, but eventually I realized I had to let it go.'

'How many years did it take for you to see it like that?' A rhetorical question for both of them. 'There's nothing to point to murder, at the moment.'

'But?'

Yes, there had been a definite *but* in his voice. 'Something obvious, I think. Something that flashed into my head and back out again too quickly to pin down. It's there like a half-remembered line of lyrics.'

'Too few words to Google?'

'Something like that.'

'I hate it when that happens. I usually play something else, then my memory comes up with the goods as soon as I'm not consciously trying to think of the answer.'

Simple logic, simple philosophy. Goodhew spent the next ten minutes watching the nearby market: people, hundreds of them, crossing and recrossing the square, shopping, lunching, visiting. All of them driven by each one's individual purpose. Time lapse would turn them into blurs, streaks of movement, patterns of activity in and out among the classic façades of the evolving city.

That was him and his grandmother too.

He pushed events along, while she respected that sometimes they only happen when the time is right. She stood still long enough to observe.

He saw again the student house in freeze-frame. The dust hung in the air, undisturbed. The fridge door stood wide open, revealing half-used cans, fresh yoghurt and out-of-date tomatoes.

Uneaten tuna dried on to a bowl.

Cold coffee in a mug in the sink.

Unwashed tea-towels on the windowsill.

Goodhew's gaze swung round slowly. A pot plant. Takeaway cartons festering on the table. A fat fly licking its feet, a thousand inverted Goodhews being transmitted via its red apposition eyes. All this he let his imagination paint until its focus finally returned to his grandmother.

'The smell of the body came and went, apparently.'

She shrugged.

The door fitted tightly. Someone went into her room at will. They had a key. Knew she was dead long before we were called.

Goodhew said a quick goodbye to his grandmother and left Don Pasquale's, breaking into a run as he headed for Parkside Station. And all the way, he cursed himself for taking so long to notice something so very obvious.

TWENTY-FOUR

In the milliseconds before Tony Brett's fist connected with his wife's jaw, he felt a familiar rush of emotion: the pumping pressure over-bubbling when it could no longer be contained. Even if that meant violence. Blood. Destruction of someone he now hated.

This wasn't the first time either. He'd lost count of the times he'd hit her, and also the ways she'd damaged him. That wasn't an excuse, but it was a fact. The damage she'd done and the damage he'd done to himself ran neck and neck.

Neither did he need analysis to educate him about triggers or warning signs or counting backwards from ten, or any other fucking precaution he was supposed to learn in order to resist beating the crap out of her once every few months.

He had a choice: fix the problem at its root, or not fix it at all.

He couldn't now go back two and a half decades, and finally oblige his dad who had hoped that Tony would buck the family trend of no qualifications and manual jobs. *Grab the chance of university, son. Make me proud.*

But Tony hadn't wanted to make anyone proud. He wanted to hang out with the older boys, bunk off school, drink cheap lager and loiter with intent. He could see them all now, feeling arrogant at the time but probably looking pathetic.

Scratch 'probably'.

Undoubtedly.

He'd been making a point back then, asserting his independence, showing his dad that he would be doing things on his own terms. His dad acknowledged no respect for any of Tony's so-called independence, and what should have been a two-week rebellion stretched into two terms. Enough to screw A-levels, never mind university.

Tony blamed his dad. Blamed Joey and Len for encouraging him to skip school, and Ross for joining him.

The front two knuckles were purpling already, and Vicky's top lip had split. He blamed her too. Once she'd been pretty, in a brittle way. Sharp, demanding and cocky. She should have been the final push of the rebellion, the girlfriend he would love to shag, then love to hate when it turned sour.

Instead she got pregnant. He knew he'd got her pregnant, and he knew how he had a pattern of laying blame and never taking responsibility. He hadn't really had to marry her. Or father two more children, or stick it out when their relationship turned 90 per cent sour, and 10 per cent spite.

But the children had changed it all. It turned out that he never found the determination to do anything unique in life, outside raising them. They were his salvation, the meaning and direction and future all rolled into one.

'I said, "No wonder they killed themselves",' she shouted.

He thought: 90 per cent sour, and 10 per cent spite? He needed to revise those figures; there wasn't even that much love between them now.

'Two down, one to go, Tony.'

Even now she could still shock him.

'I never pushed them into it.' He was shouting, but could hear his throat gagging with emotion.

He punched her again, catching her full in the nose. He wanted to hit her hard enough so that she understood his pain. He couldn't go back and fix everything that had brought them to this point. He now accepted that he couldn't fix it at all.

He hated her. God, how he hated her. He wanted to blame her

for every second of the hell they were in, but he wasn't that stupid. Whatever had driven two of their three children to suicide lay at his door, too. And that was another reason he continued raining blows down on her. For his own sanity, he wanted to destroy them both.

Vicky didn't seem to care. Just like his dad, she refused to acknowledge his pain, glaring in defiance and spitting hate back at him, through the blood and the bruising.

The thought that he might kill her flashed into his head.

I don't care.

What about Libby?

Libby. Their last child.

He crumbled then, dropping backwards into the nearest chair. Sobbing till he couldn't catch his breath.

Vicky stayed in the same room. She sat on the floor with her back against the opposite wall, her bloody face pressed into her blouse. She cried, but quietly, and neither of them spoke. They were like that for several minutes, then there came a loud knock at the door, the squeak of the letter box, and a clear voice: 'Mr and Mrs Brett, this is the police. Open the door.'

Goodhew was already most of the way to Brimley Close when he heard the report of a domestic disturbance. He responded instantly, and pulled up outside the Bretts' house in under three minutes. By then it was silent, but that was no surprise; most domestic assaults are over quickly, although a few seconds of being punched can feel like an eternity, and it had undoubtedly gone on far, far longer than that.

A Mrs Harper had called it in after several minutes of standing close to their party wall and weighing up whether it was 'just one of the usual verbal spats'.

She met Goodhew at the kerb. 'Will you be all right by yourself?'

He doubted she'd be able to provide much in the way of physical back-up and reassured her that he'd be fine.

'They're wicked to each other,' she added as he opened the gate and stepped up to their front door.

'Coming.' Tony Brett answered his knock. He looked spent and, as soon as Goodhew entered the sitting room and saw Vicky Brett, he could probably guess the point of impact of most of the blows Mrs Harper had overheard.

Maybe it was the resignation on both their faces – Tony Brett's weariness, Vicky Brett's lack of outrage – but the scene made Goodhew feel despair above any other emotion. Was this so typical of their daily lives that it no longer caused more than the smallest ripple? He sighed, and made Brett bring him clean towels and a bag of frozen peas. He wrapped the peas in the towel and kept them against Mrs Brett's face while they waited for an ambulance. He read Brett his rights, too, arresting him for assault and cuffing him.

And throughout, neither raised an eyebrow.

Shock maybe. Maybe not.

'I was already on my way here to ask you a little more about Libby – for one, why she's returned to student accommodation rather than home. But I'm guessing this is a big part of the reason?'

'It's not going to help, is it?' Tony Brett conceded.

'I'd say that's a slight understatement,' Goodhew replied.

Mrs Brett still said nothing. Even in her swollen and bloody state she seemed like the kind of person who would want to 'keep up appearances'. That kind of attitude was so common, but so frustrating, and any minute now she'd probably suggest that no charges be pressed against her husband.

'I am one of the detectives investigating the death of Libby's housemate, Shanie Faulkner. Do either of you know whether Miss Faulkner had any connection with your two elder children?'

They both shook their heads. Until that moment, Goodhew hadn't been able to recognize either of them from Rosie's inquest. Since then they had aged, shrunk and morphed, until barely resembling their former selves. The head-shakes were the same though – vacant, as though the question wasn't really intended for them.

'I spoke to the rental agency, and it appears you and Rob Stone are the official tenants of that house.'

Tony Brett nodded. 'They know we've leased it for use as student accommodation. Rob and I sorted it out between us.' As if discussing property and money felt safer, his tone had begun to settle by the end of the first sentence. 'Matt and Libby wanted to study elsewhere – outside out of Cambridge, I mean – but I was worried about Libby leaving home so soon.'

Mrs Brett cut in with, '*We*, Tony, *we*,' and he corrected himself.

'Tell me about that house, and how did Shanie come to move in?'

'Rob was happy to pay more of the rent. His wife died last year, and there was life insurance. He's blowing the lot now. He is really screwed up.'

Mrs Brett's snort of cold laughter was delivered with perfect timing.

'Yeah, Vicky,' he snapped back, 'we're all screwed up. I'm not so thick that I don't get the irony.'

'At least he doesn't punch the fuck out of his missus.'

'Bit fucking difficult when she's dead.'

'Enough!' Goodhew said.

But it took more than either the assault or the frozen peas to silence Mrs Brett. 'You liked Mandy a bit too fucking much. Bastard.'

Tony Brett turned his face towards the furthest corner of the ceiling, then with forced calm he dragged his attention back to Goodhew. 'I knew Mandy from school, and we became friends again through our children. That's all. She was a lovely person and I doubt Rob will get over losing her, this side of liver disease. So both families have suffered loss. Including our children. And if Matt and Libby are helping each other through it, that's fine by me. I can see that they aren't about to start healing while they're living at home.'

Goodhew heard Mrs Brett draw breath, but thankfully she managed to keep silent this time.

Tony Brett continued, methodically describing the advertising for, and selecting of, new housemates. 'Only Shanie was different, she was just in the house on a short-term basis. I don't know how it came about. Rob said it was arranged as a favour for an old friend.

I didn't ask any more. I didn't see how another girl in the house would have any impact on Libby. I certainly didn't feel I needed to meet her first, like I did with the lads.'

Goodhew could hear the sirens now and knew he didn't have many more minutes alone with the Bretts. 'Have you heard from Libby today?'

She shook her head. He nodded. 'Text this morning.'

'And when did *this* particular fight begin?'

His turn to give a hollow laugh. 'About twenty years ago.'

Vicky Brett moved the bag of peas away from her face but her voice remained muffled. 'I accused Tony of pushing them to it.'

'Rosie and Nathan? Is that what you think?'

'No.' She pressed the towel back to her face for a couple of seconds, catching a bubble of blood from her left nostril just as it popped and dripped on to her upper lip. 'I don't think anything any more, I just lash out.'

The ambulance arrived with a patrol car following so close to its back bumper that it looked like it was being towed. Goodhew knew PC Gardiner's driving when he saw it. What he didn't need right now was assistance from a graduate of the DC Kincaide school of policing. PC Gardiner habitually drove in two modes, *go* and *stop*, and switched from the first to the second within a couple of feet. Goodhew brightened when he saw PC Yeates in the passenger seat.

'A domestic turned nasty,' Goodhew told him.

'Those two are known for it.' Yeates shrugged. 'I'll take it from here.'

'Thanks. Can you update DI Marks after Brett has been processed?'

Yeates seemed a little sceptical about that part of the request, but Goodhew had every intention of speaking to Rob Stone before his boss gave him a reason why he couldn't.

'And if you want Rob Stone, you'll need to get down the Carlton Arms,' Yeates added. 'Third barstool on the left.'

The paramedics moved Vicky Brett into the ambulance almost at once, as keen to get her away from her husband for her mental health as for her physical well-being, Goodhew guessed. He also

121

guessed that whatever was occurring between Mrs Brett and her husband was a small dark window showing just a glimpse of the actual picture.

Goodhew was about to drive away, when PC Gardiner tapped on his window.

'Paramedic says the wife doesn't want to press charges.'

'And did you tell her how it doesn't work like that any more?'

PC Gardiner shook his head. 'Sorry, I wasn't sure about that.'

The kid looked about nineteen, and nowhere near cocky enough to be Kincaide's understudy.

'It's okay. Just go back and let Mrs Brett know that it's no longer her decision. We'll be sending a female officer to interview her as soon as she's been checked over. Her injuries will serve as the evidence.'

When he'd been a kid, Goodhew had imagined that adulthood was something that occurred overnight, sometime around the age of eighteen, like walking through a door from childhood and being given an invisible certificate that confirmed you now held all the skills necessary for the remainder of your days. He'd been at primary school when he'd begun to suspect that was a fallacy, and any last doubts had been erased just before his twelfth birthday when his grandfather's death had first introduced him to the adult realities of funerals and divorce and loss.

Was it any wonder that some kids didn't make it through that door, that some family transition screwed them up beyond their ability to cope? Had Shanie, Nathan and Rosie all drifted into the uncharted waters of adulthood and then found it impossible to swim back out?

He'd jumped to his conclusions about PC Gardiner based on two or three instances of watching his less than admirable driving skills. He didn't like to admit to himself that he'd been too quick to judge when what PC Gardiner really needed was the kind of support and guidance he seemed to be now receiving from PC Yeates.

One thing Goodhew knew for sure: he felt bloody old and burdened today. Twenty-seven? He felt more like fifty.

TWENTY-FIVE

The Carlton Arms was the kind of pub that Goodhew usually liked to visit, professionally at least. The place was essentially honest, a kind of public house equivalent of does-what-it-says-on-the-tin. The signboard outside advertised darts, pool table, live screen sport and home-cooked food.

The punters would be mostly locals, and predominantly regulars. Any trouble was likely to be a long-brewing feud more than a random scrap. In all of that there was a rough and ready dependability with which Goodhew felt at ease. And that, in essence, was the main reason that he entered the pub without giving any thought to his own safety.

There was a pool match underway. About a dozen men – no women – were clustered around the pool table. A handful of more serious drinkers sat at the bar. The third barstool on the left was actually occupied by the only woman in the place.

Goodhew spoke to her first. 'I'm looking for Rob Stone.'

'Police?'

'Yes. I was told I might find him here.'

'Having a smoke.' She nodded towards the sign marked *Gents*. 'Back door's that way.'

She turned round to her pint before he had even had a chance to say thanks.

The smoking ban had encouraged drinkers into the beer garden more than the landscaping, parasols and summer barbecues had ever done. However, apart from two guys standing in the doorway while holding their cigarettes outside it, there was just a lone figure out there tonight.

Rob Stone. Aged forty-nine.

There was a smouldering cigarette in his ashtray and a half-drunk pint in front of him. He stared into it as though he expected a genie to appear and grant him his deepest wish.

Or maybe he had already drunk enough to be able to see the genie and that was the problem. Goodhew took the seat facing him and waited for Rob Stone to look across. The patio lights were bright enough to see Stone clearly and, if the picture was adjusted to eliminate beer poundage, smoker's wrinkles and a defeated body posture, it was obvious that he had been a strikingly handsome man in his day.

Stone glared. 'Why are you squinting at me like that?'

Goodhew introduced himself.

Stone was unimpressed. 'Worked out you were one of them.'

'Why?' Goodhew hated the idea that he could be identified as a detective so quickly. For one thing, it reduced the whole point of being plain-clothes.

'Unless you're a talent scout from the visiting pool team, who else would come in here to see me?'

Fair point.

There were many types of drunks, a full spectrum from volatile bingers to the prematurely aged who came complete with alcohol-induced senility. Stone's expression seemed to suggest he used beer like a reverse telescope: it kept everything distant and slightly out of focus. Self-preservation maybe.

'What d'you want, then?' he asked.

Goodhew explained his connection to the Shanie Faulkner case. 'You jointly rented that house in King Street.'

'My son lives there. He's studying.'

'I know. So how did Shanie Faulkner come to move in?'

Stone blanked the question. 'Do you know why Matt's studying?'

Goodhew shook his head.

'If he went and got himself a job, he'd have to pay me to live at home, or else move out and cost me nothing. Instead of that I'm paying because he is studying. He thinks he's punishing me.' Stone pulled a face that, partly at least, included a wry smile. 'He thinks he hates me.'

Stone's voice had a woolly edge to it, but the sentences themselves seemed coherent. A reverse telescope didn't make things invisible though.

Goodhew wanted to show interest without pushing, so he just echoed the statement back. 'Matt hates you?'

'His mother was ill with cancer, and he thinks I killed her.'

'How?'

'Well, he knows it was cancer that actually got her, but thinks it was my fault she contracted it. I made her unhappy, and it was that stress that caused it. Or so he's decided.'

'Is that possible?'

'Medically? Yeah. Apparently there are websites and discussion forums that say so, therefore it must be true.' Stone hadn't touched his beer since Goodhew joined him; now he made up for it by gulping down the rest of the pint. 'God bless the Internet, I say.' He finished the cigarette next, with several equally intense puffs. 'I'm getting another pint.'

Goodhew followed him into the bar. Stone was talking now and it didn't seem to bother him that everyone from the landlord to the opposing pool team would hear all about his family crisis.

'We can go somewhere private,' Goodhew offered.

'God, no. Matt's temper's no secret in here, is it, Trev?'

The landlord shook his head obligingly as he filled a pint glass with Old Speckled Hen. Goodhew caved in and ordered lemonade. With ice.

'When you talk about your wife being unhappy, do you mean your marriage was unhappy?' Goodhew kept his voice low, uncomfortable at the idea of asking questions in a public bar. He needn't have bothered.

'Me and Mandy?' Stone laughed, and it sounded genuine until the last moment when it took on a hollow edge.

He crossed his fingers and held them close to Goodhew's face. 'This was me and Mandy; the best woman in the world and she picked *me*. D'you know what gets me – wanna know?'

Goodhew nodded.

'There have been times when I've felt like I'm the cat with the cream, the one who'd got his life sorted. I've even given mates advice, feeling I'd done something that set me apart – as if a happy marriage and great kids were mine because I'd somehow earned them.' Again the hollow laugh. 'But life's like a bloody credit card: if you have all the good stuff up front, it feels to me that the repayments are loaded with one hell of a lot of interest.'

'So she wasn't unhappy.'

'Mandy was naturally cheerful – one of those warm people that gets huge pleasure out of small things, know what I mean? Charlotte and Matt used to be that way too. And we said we told each other everything, but I know there was one thing she held back.'

'What was it?'

Stone narrowed his eyes, as if weighing up how much of an idiot Goodhew really was. 'If she'd told me she wouldn't have been holding it back, would she?'

'I thought someone else might have known.'

'No. This was something private. A preoccupation that ate away at her sometimes. She'd get this look. I asked her plenty of times over the years but she always said, "I'm fine, don't worry." Just once I pushed it and she said that if she ever admitted to having a secret, she wouldn't then be able to keep it from me. "So, Rob," she said, "The only thing that matters is you and me are okay. And we are." That was the end of it. The subject was completely closed.'

'There's a big difference from your wife seeming worried or withdrawn, to your son's idea that you made her unhappy, isn't there?' Goodhew mused.

'All I can think is that Mandy had lost her mum and aunt to breast cancer, and I wonder whether she feared it. She said not,' he shrugged, 'but I don't know now. Point is, there was a lengthy period between her first visit to the doctor and her second or third hospital visit. We didn't open up to the kids during that time. We decided to wait till we could give them something definite. Can you imagine the tension in the house for all those weeks? Unbearable. We bickered in front of the kids. Then, when they were out, we'd talk about our fears. Apart from that, I don't understand any reason Matt would have for thinking I made her unhappy.'

Stone swilled the last couple of inches of beer around in the bottom of his glass. 'If that's all you want me for, I'll get off home now.'

'I was asking about Shanie Faulkner remember?' Goodhew prompted.

'Shanie's like the others, there to share the costs and helping Matt and Libby put a couple of miles between them and home.' He drifted off subject immediately. 'It's bollocks.'

Stone finally drained the glass then thrust it towards the landlord. 'Matt's grieving. I don't know how a teenager starts to get their head round it. I'm his dad and I don't know where to start. Stupidly big hole Mandy left behind, you know what I mean?'

Everybody's grief was different, but Goodhew looked at Stone and was pretty sure *he* did know.

'And if Matt's way is to lash out, who am I to tell him he's doing it wrong? Better than this, eh?' He pointed at his empty pint. 'I know Mandy and Sarah messaged each other right up till the end, so when she phoned me, I really wanted to help.'

'You've lost me. Who's Sarah?'

'Shanie's mum. Dead Shanie from America.'

'So Shanie came to stay because your wife and her mum were friends?'

'BBFs or BFFs or whatever it is.' Again, the laugh.

'A favour to your wife?' Goodhew said it almost to himself, trying to pin down the uneasy feeling lurking in the shadows of his mind; as if someone with the whole picture was watching him struggle to make something up from just the first few fragments.

Stone leaned towards him, close enough that his heavy features filled Goodhew's entire field of vision. 'Sarah will be like me now. You don't just lose the one you love. Friends care, but they don't know what to say and it comes out stilted. Or else they don't say anything at all.' He continued his list of those he'd lost, along with his wife, including Matt, but not Charlotte. As hard as Goodhew tried to keep up with the list of colleagues, old schoolfriends and assorted relatives, his thoughts kept drifting back to Mandy, and the preoccupation she'd never shared with her husband. Perhaps it involved him. Maybe she'd discovered something about him that she wasn't supposed to know. Or maybe it was the other way around, and she'd been afraid of telling him something about herself. He wondered whether she would have confided in Sarah about this.

Goodhew turned to leave, then hesitated. Shanie was dead and the only reason she'd been in that house at all was because of Mandy. Who was also dead. And however Shanie had died, there had to be a reason.

He would later struggle to remember much more about his visit to the Carlton Arms. He had asked Stone more questions; he must have done because Goodhew could remember himself sitting on one of the bar stools. And later watching Stone leave.

Then he had left too. But somewhere between the front entrance and his car, he heard a heavy crack. A splitting sound. The gravel rose to meet him.

He blacked out before he hit the ground.

The next thing he saw were several men, and behind them the approaching flash of a blue light blinking in the darkness.

He heard a woman's voice. 'Gary, can you hear me? Gary? The ambulance is here.'

TWENTY-SIX

Regaining consciousness in hospital usually meant that the first thing visible was the ceiling. Recessed lighting, tiles embossed with a little squiggly pattern, and a powder-coated curtain track. Maybe there was a patient's suggestion box where he could ask them to add a sign up there that said *Welcome to Addenbrookes.*

He blinked slowly . . . and when he opened his eyes again he realized that the sun streaming through the blinds had moved on by an hour or two.

'Keep them open this time, Gary.'

He twisted his head to the left and found his grandmother sitting on one of the visitors' chairs holding an open copy of *Maxim.*

'Am I concussed or are you really reading that?'

'Both. How are you feeling?'

'Coming round slowly.' He pulled himself into a sitting position, moving very slowly, waiting for something to hurt. Nothing actually did for the first few seconds, then a dull thudding kicked in just above his right ear. He reached to touch it.

'Stitches.' She put the magazine on to his lap. 'Interesting article on Scarlett Johansson.'

'Did you buy this for me or yourself?'

'Neither. Bryn dropped it by.'

'He's been in?'

'Yup, and Gully too. Even Kincaide.'

'Why Kincaide? Did he think I wasn't going to pull through?'

'Very funny. Came for a statement. Fat chance. And Bryn said you had another visitor here when he arrived. A young woman with, and I quote, "a dazzling smile and rampant curls".'

'Charlotte?' That made sense, it was her voice he'd heard in the car park.

'Bryn seemed to like her.'

'But he would.'

'Exactly.'

His conversation with Rob Stone remained hazy, but as his head began to clear he thought about Mandy and Sarah. Sarah Faulkner's flight was about to land.

'What time is it?' He asked the question out loud even though there was a clock clearly visible in the corridor. It was a white analogue, and though it told him it was seven it didn't seem as though either the morning or evening option could be correct.

'Quarter to seven,' she confirmed.

'Evening?'

'Yep, you were out for about twenty hours. Not bad for an insomniac.'

'I need to get back to Parkside.'

Maybe it's just that a parent and grandparent have different attitudes, or maybe that was just his own grandmother, but he didn't either expect or receive the stay-in-bed-and-rest dialogue. Instead, 'I'll call a taxi,' was all she said.

And in less than ten minutes they were heading towards the city centre.

'And Marks sent you a text.'

Goodhew checked his phone. *Don't go feral. I want to speak to you as soon as you are fit to be discharged.*

He guessed his grandmother had already read it. 'Did the doctor say I was fit to be discharged?'

'I didn't hear him say so.'

'Me neither.'

'Problem is, Gary, I texted him back and told him you were leaving in any case. He'll be waiting in the incident room.'

'Thanks.' Gary pulled up the Internet on his phone, and used the last few minutes of the journey to search online images.

TWENTY-SEVEN

The display of photographs connected to Shanie's death had grown since Goodhew last looked.

Marks sat with his back to the door, simultaneously facing the photographs and Goodhew's reflection in the window beyond. He swivelled his chair around slowly. 'So what happened to you last night?'

'Obviously someone hit me, but beyond that, I don't have a clue.'

'What did the doctor say? Or did you leave the hospital before you found out?' Marks glared.

Goodhew realized that his previous tone had sounded a few shades too indifferent. 'I started looking into the background of one of the other students, and I let myself get distracted.'

'Remind me what you were supposed to be doing?'

'Tracking down Shanie Faulkner's sweatshirt.'

'And?'

'I believe it came from Giles and Co. on Trinity Street. That design is one of their own and it appears that they are the only place to stock it. They sell them online too. I'll go in and try to work out who bought it, and when. It will have to be tomorrow now though.'

'Hallelujah, Goodhew remembers an instruction.'

'Sir?'

'Theoretically you could have still been in a very serious condition today. You were bleeding heavily when you were found. A few hours like that and I would have been down by one whole time equivalent.'

'It's so comforting to be thought of as a manpower statistic.'

'It comforts me if you've finally recognized that it is exactly what you are. The young woman who found you?'

'Charlotte Stone.'

'Why was she there?'

'I don't know. I'd been speaking to her father there, so maybe she turned up to find him?'

'No matter, Kincaide's going over to take her statement later. You'll also need to make one.'

A little more of the conversation with Rob Stone was coming back to Goodhew now. 'Did Shanie's parents arrive?'

He nodded. 'They came into the station first thing. Shanie was their only child.' Marks picked up a folder, tipped out some loose pages, tapped them into a neat pile, then placed them back inside, before closing the flap. Again he was distracted and again Goodhew's thoughts were drawn to Emily Marks, his only child.

Goodhew nudged him. 'Were they aware of Shanie displaying any suicidal tendencies in the past?'

'No, not at all. But her mother . . .' Marks sighed. 'She's one of those women who kept questioning why Shanie had done it to *her personally*.'

'And the suicide note leans that way.'

'That's true.' Marks's voice tailed away. 'She didn't come across as a tremendously maternal woman, left me with the feeling that it could have been difficult for Shanie to confide in her if she was having problems.'

'But she *was* upset?'

'Yes, absolutely. No suggestion of anything less than heartfelt grief. Have I ever told you about Emily's cat?'

This abrupt change of subject threw Goodhew for a moment, but it didn't really matter; Marks often asked a question without expecting a reply.

'He'd originally been a stray and one night he decided to curl up under the warm bonnet of a parked car shortly before the car's

133

owner drove to work. The lady pulled over when she heard unidentified bumping and squealing, and rushed the injured animal into the nearest vet's. It lost a leg and most of its right ear. It was malnourished, flea ridden and worm infested – and do you know what they wanted to call it?' He paused, but only for effect. 'Lucky. Personally I could think of far more appropriate names. My wife suggested Mangle ... The point is, Gary, I could call you Lucky after last night. Lucky your injuries weren't worse. Lucky you didn't bleed to death, and so on.'

Goodhew knew where this was going and nodded slowly. 'But you can think of far more appropriate names?'

'You leave here on a hunt for the stockists of a purple sweatshirt displaying crests of the various Cambridge colleges, and somehow that turns into one arrest and one hospitalization at the first address you decided to visit, and your own hospitalization at the second. Officially I abhor the way you behave, but I enjoy seeing what gets flushed out in the process.' Before he could say anything else, his mobile rang. It vibrated on the desk, and wriggled an inch or so before Marks snatched it up.

'Yes?' Marks stared at the desk-top for several seconds, then at Goodhew. 'The same house?' he asked the caller.

Goodhew strained to hear, but Marks turned away and stood with his attention now fixed on the street below. For several minutes the stillness of the room was punctuated only by monosyllabic questions.

'We're coming,' he said finally and snapped the phone shut.

Goodhew knew instantly that Marks had reverted to his usual official persona. 'Another death,' his boss revealed.

'Who?'

Marks shook his head. 'In the car.' Goodhew found himself following him down the corridor, proceeding at slightly less than a jogging pace.

'Phone Gully and pass the sweatshirt thing on to her. How are you feeling?'

'Fine.'

'Right, you're coming with me. Don't screw up – or bleed in my car.'

134

TWENTY-EIGHT

So one of them was dead.

Goodhew waited until they were in the car park before he considered repeating his question. On the way down the stairs he'd gone through the list of occupants.

Which one?

Trying to guess felt like a macabre game, like a game of dead pool where he was the only player. A niggle of superstition warned him against it: would the wrong choice be like willing something fatal on that person? He decided it wasn't a game he wanted to play but, even so, two names had risen to the front of his mind by the time he and Marks had reached the car.

Libby and Meg.

He told himself he'd just picked the two most fragile-looking housemates. He knew nothing of Meg's background, but in the last forty-eight hours had become over-familiar with Libby's.

'Who died?' he finally asked again.

'Meg DeLacy.'

'How?'

Marks pulled out of the car park and executed the two left turns that took him on to East Road before he replied. 'From the little I know, it sounds as though there are similarities to the Shanie Faulkner case. She'd been quiet and some of the others became

135

worried so they broke in and found her lying on her bed. They called an ambulance immediately, but she was pronounced dead at the scene. That's it, so far.'

TWENTY-NINE

Her dad was out but Charlotte Stone still answered the knock at the front door without stopping to consider who might be there. She felt her welcoming expression close down and shrink away when she saw DC Kincaide.

He spoke first. 'DI Marks sent me to take a statement.'

'Great.' She was no expert at fake smiles but aimed for something sour and sarcastic and was fairly confident that she pulled it off.

'You alone?'

'Unfortunately.' She stepped back, pushing the door further open with her shoulder, and left him to close it behind him.

She led Kincaide into the kitchen, preferring the formality of straight-backed chairs and a table between them. She directed him to the nearest chair, then bought herself a few minutes' breathing space by making instant coffee. She didn't look at him again until she passed him his coffee.

'So why you?'

'Luck of the draw.' He shrugged. 'So what happened at the Carlton Arms?'

She settled in the seat opposite him, relieved that Kincaide's focus seemed to be purely professional. 'I went to look for my dad, but instead I found your mate in a puddle of blood.'

'Colleague,' he corrected sharply.

'So he's the one you don't like?' She knew that the last thing she should be doing was referring, however obliquely, to her past conversations with Kincaide.

He acknowledged nothing further. 'Let's get this over with, right?'

'Absolutely.' She meant it, as she said it, but there was an added tension in Kincaide's voice now, and she found it irresistible not to poke at it. 'So what's wrong with Goodhew, then?'

Kincaide pretended to ignore the question, so she asked it a second time. He worked his tongue around his top teeth, as though the answer was wedged between his right premolars. Finally he replied, 'Your dad is a regular at the Carlton, right?'

'You know that already.'

'So why did you go down there?'

She glared, remembering all too clearly just how much she disliked Michael Kincaide. He had bitterness buried deeply inside him, but he was capable of hiding it well. 'I worry when he stays out too late. I wanted to be certain that nothing had happened to him.'

'So you weren't being controlling?'

'No, I don't think so – but then I would say that, wouldn't I? Why don't you ask my dad whether he thinks his daughter's a manipulative bitch.'

'I didn't say that.'

'You didn't say that *today*.'

'For fuck's sake, Charlotte, I just want to know why you were in the car park. I need to find out what happened to DC Goodhew and whether you witnessed anything, however small or insignificant.'

'Now I know why they sent you. "Let Kincaide go, he's the expert on small and insignificant".'

'You used me.'

Charlotte was on her feet so abruptly that the table trembled and coffee slopped from the mugs. 'Get out.'

'Sit down. *Now*.'

'*You* manipulated *me*. You never had any intention of helping us. You abused your position.'

Charlotte saw his expression change instantly. Gone was the hurt vanity, the dented ego that showed itself in his macho posturing.

She'd cut deeper this time. Those last four words had done it: he'd taken them as a personal threat.

A single swift move of his hand and she found herself thrown back into the chair. It rocked back on two legs and for a moment she was sure she was about to go sprawling across the floor. She grabbed at the edge of the table and managed to keep herself upright.

Kincaide remained on his feet, with his right fist close to her head, until she had made it clear she had no plans to get up again.

They stared at each other uneasily.

'Do you think that's acceptable?' Her tone was quiet, cowed even, but she refused to let the moment pass without saying something. Kincaide didn't react at first, then he dropped back into the chair opposite, and briefly hung his head.

'I've never done that before,' he said.

'Well, the trick will be to avoid doing it again, won't it?'

'I'm sorry.'

She hesitated, keen not to reignite anything, but at the same time determined that she wouldn't be left fuming at what she had not had the guts to say. 'You just came very close to crossing a line. You need to make sure you don't kid yourself that the line's moved a bit, next time you get near it.'

'Meaning what?'

'You're not stupid. Work it out.' A short silence followed. What mattered most now was the assault on DC Goodhew. 'I didn't see anything,' she continued. 'I thought at first that the car park was empty, so I walked towards the main entrance. Then I don't really know whether I spotted something out of the corner of my eye, or maybe heard something, but I glanced round and saw an arm. And when I moved a little closer, I recognized him. I ran to the pub door, shouted for help. Then went back to him.'

'And you called an ambulance?'

'From my mobile, yes. And I assume they called the police or ambulance from inside the Carlton.'

'We have the time of your call. How soon after discovering Goodhew would you say you made it?'

139

'Straightaway. Two minutes at the absolute most.'

'And you'd say the car park was empty for approximately how long before you found DC Goodhew?'

'Another minute or so as I crossed the road. Tops.'

'And where did you find your father eventually?'

'Back here. When I got home, he was asleep on the settee.'

'Not worried about *you*, then?'

Charlotte stiffened. 'You weren't ever really prepared to help me, were you?'

'I did exactly what you asked me to do, and there was nothing to tell you. But instead of accepting that, you just kept pushing.'

'No, you strung me along. How many times did you tell me you were waiting for a chance to look at this, that or the other document? The coroner's report first. Then results from Forensics, yet another witness interview ... You dragged it out for weeks, Michael.'

'You heard only what you wanted to hear. I told you right from the start I couldn't find anything. How could I, when there was nothing *to* find. Why is that so hard for you to live with? They're not even your own family.'

'Matt is my brother.'

'Yeah, Charlotte, you've made my ears bleed over that one already.'

'Well, you lied to me about plenty of things, but until tonight I still felt you had a common thread of decency.' This time when Charlotte stood up she was determined that their conversation really was over. 'There's so much less to you than meets the eye, Michael.'

She pulled open the kitchen door, then realized that they weren't alone in the house after all. Matt and Libby stood side by side in the hall.

Matt peered beyond Charlotte, into the kitchen, then back at her in disbelief. 'What the hell did you do, Char?'

But, behind him, she was certain that she saw Libby give her a small but definite nod.

THIRTY

Dear Zoe,
I know I do all the talking, but it helps me, it really does.

Sometimes Charlotte seems in denial. Sometimes I truly did believe that she thought Rosie and Nathan had killed themselves. The problem with all of this is wondering if I would believe the full truth if I came across it. In my mind it's a conspiracy, like Marilyn and Kennedy and Presley all rolled into one.

I take people's words at face value, the first time I hear them, then repeat them to myself and find another stance and, finally, they are turned over so many times that I eventually discard them as nothing more than static in the bigger picture.

Tonight I saw that Charlotte and I really are on the same side. She probably doesn't favour one truth over another the way I do, but the fact is there is only one truth and she knows we haven't had it all revealed yet.

I didn't hear everything that went on between her and the policeman, but I was there for longer than she realized.

And I'm not going to make any moral comments. As far as I'm concerned, if she slept with him it shows her determination. And I think he's not the kind to go out of his way without getting something out of it for himself, but I know Matt will dwell on it even if I don't.

Matt dwells on everything.

Should I tell him that I know he slept with Meg? And why should it bother me? Because, if I'm honest, it does – but then the other part of me wonders why it doesn't bother me more.

Maybe I don't have feelings for him, or maybe I'm no longer capable of having a normal range of feelings for anyone, or anything. Is it possible that emotional reserves are like eggs? It's one of those mind-blowing facts that I was born with all the eggs I'll ever produce already inside my body. What if all the feelings I'm capable of having were there from birth, too, and I don't have any left for the rest of my life because they were all used up on my family.

My family?

My dad put my mum in hospital today. That was supposed to be the first thing I should write; instead, it's lower on the list than my fertility.

Joke.

Actually, I don't know what to think. It's not the first time he's hit her, but this time he was arrested and charged. I'm relieved, I suppose. I don't want Mum hurt. Neither do I want them to split up. Sometimes I wish someone would thump *me* – it might be a relief to hurt for some other reason, and at least with a *physical* injury I could watch myself heal.

Well, that's kind of a joke, too. Not a very good one, I suppose, but like the rest it has a sliver of truth in it.

Matt was coming with me to the hospital tonight to visit her. I wanted to visit my dad in custody, too, but I don't know whether I'm allowed to yet. Matt didn't want to visit my dad, not even to keep me company, not even as far as the door. He's more black-and-white than me; he won't make it up with his own dad so I guess he'll hate mine forever too.

Anyhow, it seems like the visit to the hospital is out of the question now. Matt and Charlotte are having some kind of heart-to-heart and that detective is still attempting to pin down her statement on the injured officer. He was attacked not long after arresting my dad; if my dad had any friends left I think that one of them might have done it out of warped loyalty.

142

Funny thing is though, one of Dad's only mates was attacked at pretty much the same spot. I hadn't thought of that until this very second. Mind you, he wasn't a close mate, because the really close ones gave up after the second funeral.

Oh fuck. I hate my life.

Sometimes I really wish for something significant to happen, but it would take something pretty huge to pierce this constant numbness. Yet I have days when I think that I want it to happen, no matter how bad it is. Anything to move me somewhere else.

Then I remind myself that this isn't numbness. It's an overload of self-preservation and I really *don't* want something bad to happen, even when I think I do. I just thought it, but I didn't mean it. Sorry.

THIRTY-ONE

Marks felt there was little doubt that Meg DeLacy had committed suicide and, up to a point, Goodhew couldn't help but agree. It definitely looked that way.

Megan lay mostly on the bed, one arm dangling over one side, and a foot protruding from the other. She'd managed a partial suicide note. It began as a status update on her Facebook profile: *hey guys, I no wot u all think but I neva meant 2 upset Shanie. Soz babes.*

It carried on with notes scribbled on a sheet of paper next to her keyboard. *Shanie was a bitch but she didn't know better and I didn't want her dead. Neither did Phil.* Then, *It was no biggie, would have been forgotten if she hadn't died,* and *I wasn't being a bitch but now she's dead I look like such a cow. How do I come back from that?*

There were empty drugs packets on the bed, the computer desk, and also one on the floor. Some were painkillers, but most were sleeping tablets, and two drinks bottles kept each other company in the waste-paper basket. One had contained Sambuca and the other a cheap brand of vodka.

Half a bottle of Southern Comfort lay on its side next to the bed and some had leaked on to the carpet.

Marks shook his head. 'I'm not surprised she didn't get to finish that bottle if she really had gone through the rest.'

Meg was sprawled on her back, her face tilted to one side, with a trail of vomit around her mouth and nose. It was still wet where it had pooled in the soft well of the suprasternal notch.

'First thought?' Marks asked.

'Squalid . . . and depressing.' Goodhew studied the room for a few seconds longer, noting the dirty laundry in the corner, the unopened packet of digestive biscuits on top of the portable TV, the red marks scribbled on the calendar.

They looked like assignment-due dates, extensions and final, final deadlines. 'Based on first appearances, it seems genuine,' he remarked finally.

'Emily tells me that some kids at her school talk about suicide as if it's a cool thing to do. She says they don't really get it, because they think that they're going to witness the aftermath, watch their friends crying for them, and so on. It's so wasteful. They just don't seem to grasp the permanence of it.'

'Really?' It wasn't the first time that Goodhew had heard this theory, but he still found it too unlikely to fully accept. Without a shadow of doubt he himself had understood the frailty of death from the age of eleven when his grandfather had suddenly died. Un-learning a lesson like that seemed impossible.

'We've already had contact with the family, and they acknowledged that she had intermittent emotional problems throughout her adolescence.'

'If that's the case, I'm sure that, between her former teachers and her GP, there'll be reports to corroborate it.'

'Subject to forensics and toxicology, I am satisfied. That goes for Shanie Faulkner, too.'

Goodhew nodded but he was far less convinced.

Marks picked up on his scepticism. 'We've had confirmation from her doctor that Shanie not only sought advice about feeling unable to cope with the pressure of her studies but had also raised concerns about her making a trip to the UK by herself. Her doctor is willing to make a statement to that effect.'

Goodhew nodded again and continued to agree with Marks until slipping from the room looked like a viable possibility.

Once again, the house was quiet, but this time the retreating students had left more than shocked silence in their wake. There was fear here now.

There were people he knew, his grandmother one of them, who liked the idea that buildings retained memories, that an imprint of events could be left within the fabric of the walls.

He didn't buy it. The whole concept belonged with the kind of new-age philosophies that he would believe as soon as he had proof. And not before.

Despite that, there was definitely more than just dust hanging in the air.

He already knew which room belonged to which student, but if he hadn't, it would have been as easy to deduce as each of them having a photograph pinned on a tag and hanging from a hook on the centre of their door.

The girls' rooms were particularly easy. Jamie-Lee's erupted with energetic colours and quirky kitsch. Libby seemed determined to colour or disturb her environment as little as possible. Her room was neat, and everything from her clothes through to her notebooks and toiletries could have been picked for their low-key and almost inconsequential appearance.

No doubt too many assumptions based on a few incomplete facts had to be a bad thing, but on the other hand, who in the house but horticulture student Matt would have owned a bookshelf with titles ranging from *Science and the Garden* to *A Handbook for Horticultural Students*? The books were well used, the corners battered and the edges of the pages grubby as if they'd been hauled from classroom to allotment, and back.

By the same token, a single glance at Phil's bookshelf said 'science' in a way that Jamie-Lee's selection of gossip mags and chick lit never had. Phil's personal flavour seemed to be physics. Goodhew selected a couple of volumes at random, both of them creaking open as if it were the first time. He slid them back into place.

Goodhew sat on one corner at the end of Phil's bed. He wouldn't have much time before Marks called him away. He needed to find something – anything – that might explain why Shanie's door had been repeatedly opened during the hours after her death. With each room he entered he was moving further from Shanie's room and still had no idea what he might be hoping to spot. He scanned Phil's room carefully and, as with the other bedrooms, his gaze stopped at the laptop. Turning on a suspect computer was a whole other ballgame. As soon as it booted up, evidence was lost: with every file accessed, more details still would vanish, and details of any remaining information would be wide open then to accusations of tampering.

Still, it was tempting.

'Gary, what exactly are you doing?'

He hurried through the doorway before calling down to his boss from the head of the stairs, 'I'm just checking through the building, making sure nothing looks out of place.'

'How much longer?'

'I'm coming now.' As Goodhew said it, he crossed the small square landing to the final door. He turned the handle, but of all the rooms in the house this was the only one currently locked.

'Just the open rooms, Gary,' Marks shouted up. 'Off-limits if they're locked right now, you know that.'

Goodhew sighed. Sometimes Marks could tune into his thoughts with uncanny accuracy. It took him about twenty seconds longer than the end of Marks's latest instruction before the lock mechanism surrendered to his trusty skeleton key.

'Gary?'

'Yes, sir, I heard you.'

He pushed at Oslo's door with the tips of his fingers. The window was small and square and covered by a pair of heavy brown curtains. There was a beige stripe running down the centre of each of them, and it was through this that the daylight glowed. At first Goodhew stayed very still and after a few seconds tuned into a soft humming just to his right. On the opposite wall, a large frame hung over the bed, the aluminium-coloured sides clear enough against the

147

dark wall; picking out the subject of the photo it contained took a little longer. It looked like some kind of animal, maybe a dog.

Goodhew reached one gloved hand towards the light switch and turned the dimmer gradually until the picture took shape. One second later, he had racked it up to full power.

The photo-frame extended to approximately the width of the bed and was about two feet high. It consisted of five large photos, each very similar to the last. The subject was clear now: it was a fox. A dead fox. In the first image it lay with its body parallel to the gutter and its head resting on the kerbside. The camera seemed to have focused on a small patch of fur right between the eyes which still stared out dully.

Between photos two and five, those eyes had dulled further, shrinking away and disappearing into little black pits.

By the third photo it was obvious that the fox's body had been disturbed; its head and brush had barely moved, but everything in between looked close to disintegration. The final shot kept the same angle on its face, but there was little else left besides crushed fragments of pelt.

Goodhew had taken several steps towards the photographs before he looked around the room and found himself staring at two similar shots, both 10×8s. One showed a dead badger being picked over by crows; the other a trail of feathers leading to the headless corpse of a pigeon.

The humming he had first noticed came from the pump inside a fish tank standing near the foot of Oslo's bed. The entire tank was about eighteen inches long but Oslo had managed to deck it out in a style best described as 'Halloween meets Vegas'. A layer of black marble stones carpeted the tank's floor, with a wavy pattern of gold pebbles running like a footpath from end to end. Thanks to a tasteful selection of ornaments, the lucky fish were able to swim from golden Sphinx to crystal Eiffel Tower via a sunken pirate ship and a shrunken head. The head itself housed the pump, and every couple of seconds its mouth opened and closed, emitting a lively string of bubbles between its missing teeth.

Two mismatched goldfish stared out at him, probably wishing for the more dignified surroundings of the hook-a-duck stand at the fair.

In fairness to Oslo, the room was the most dust-free part of the entire house, and the fishes' view of the outside world looked mark-and fingerprint-free. A small triangle of shiny paper jutted out from under one corner. It was its skewed position in relation to the tank that first caught his eye, but it was the familiar shade of blue that made him take a second look.

Boathouse Blue.

He remembered it from the catalogue of Heritage paint colours that he'd worked through while deciding on colours for his hallway and stairs. But more importantly he remembered it from just a few minutes earlier in Libby's room.

He changed to latex gloves, and although they were thin, it still took him two or three attempts to grip the protruding corner and ease the photograph out.

And there it was, the inside of Libby's bedroom. One of her books on accountancy lay open and facedown on the bed. Two pieces of paper had been balled and thrown in the direction of the waste-paper basket. The bin itself contained another textbook and more rejected work. He saw the little things, a half-drunk mug of coffee which had been stirred by a broken pencil. A small calculator, the kind banks give away, submerged in a glass of water. And the drawer was left open just enough to reveal a stash of Red Bull, chocolate and Pro Plus.

Goodhew understood.

He flicked the photo on to the palm of his other hand while he considered the implications, his gaze focused further afield than any point in the room until he was done. Then, with a start, he moved towards the bedroom door. 'Sir!' he shouted downstairs. 'I think you need to see this right away.'

THIRTY-TWO

Gunvald Gjertsen, aka Oslo, had his arms folded across his chest and his body stretched out in the chair so that only his shoulders and the top of his thighs seemed to be making contact with it. No doubt a body-language expert would have a term for it, but Goodhew couldn't imagine there would be anything more appropriate than 'the uncooperative plank position'. Oslo was trying hard to pull off a facial expression that smothered the interview with a blanket answer of '*Whatever*', but Marks and Goodhew had been with him for over an hour now and it was about time Gjertsen began to waver.

Goodhew simply started the round of questions all over again. 'Tell me about the photos.'

'I did that already.'

'You didn't tell me everything.'

'They're private. You broke into my bedroom. You shouldn't have done that.'

'There's no point trying to play that card. The photo was in your room and I had every right to check the house.'

'My room was locked and I rent it as my private area. Just because you have a right to be in the house, doesn't mean you have the right to enter a room that is mine and mine alone.' He swung his glare over to Marks. 'I'm right, aren't I?'

Marks had deliberately stayed in the back seat on this one,

slipping out of the room a couple of times to make phone calls then quietly returning without interrupting Goodhew. 'If Goodhew forced entry, or if the court were to decide that he should've waited for a search warrant, then any evidence he found in your room could be considered inadmissible. DC Goodhew is quite aware of this rule and, as I gave him specific instructions not to enter a room that was locked, I am confident that proper procedures would have been followed.' Marks's attention snapped on to Goodhew. 'Detective?'

Goodhew concentrated his eye-contact on Gjertsen. 'I walked straight into your room without any impediment. It seems to me that you're more concerned with your reputation than with the fate of your housemates.'

'You broke in.'

'That's enough.' Goodhew had planned to demonstrate endless patience with Gjertsen – to plug away with facts and logical questions until Gjertsen accepted that telling the truth was the most pragmatic thing to go. Goodhew had now gone off the idea. 'You're hung up on the thought of your photographs appearing as a headline-grabbing piece of evidence, and I can't work out whether you're excited that it would give you some kind of phony kudos as a photographer, or that you're scared that your disgusting behaviour will be laid out in front of everyone you know.'

Gjertsen's expression said it all.

'Right,' Goodhew continued. 'So you won't be pleased if I ask your family, friends, course tutor and classmates whether they were aware of your habit of sneaking into other people's bedrooms and arranging their personal items?'

'I never damaged anything.' The first admission so far.

'Can't you see how intrusive it is?'

'*I* didn't break in.'

'No, you had a key.'

'I didn't.'

Goodhew paused to regroup. 'Why do you like to photograph roadkill?'

'Don't know.'

'That's not true. You're sufficiently proud of those pictures that you frame them and display them on your wall. You're not keeping them secret – in fact, you have a Flickr account. They are on public display so it makes sense that you've thought through your arguments.'

'I didn't kill the animals, you know.'

'Look, I'm not judging – I just want answers. We all have more things to do than sit here for the next forty-six and a half hours while we go backwards and forwards over the same questions.'

Gjertsen's gaze wandered towards the high, frosted window.

Goodhew clapped his hands together. 'Oslo, this isn't about you. It's about Shanie and Meg. They're dead and you are implicated.'

'I don't know anything.'

'Stop telling us what you don't know, or what you didn't do. You have a passion for photography. Good for you. At some point you decided that it was interesting, exciting, artistic or whatever to find dead animals in the street and photograph them. You also fed your voyeuristic streak by breaking into private rooms and photographing people's personal possessions.'

'I didn't break in.'

'You broke in. I'm using *your* words. You thought I had unlocked the door and you accused me of breaking in. I *know* you have a key. We have a witness who can testify that you have a key.'

Goodhew kept talking but he knew that Gjertsen had stopped listening at that point. The man's eyes were flickering like crazy, probably rewinding his denials and trying to find a way to respin them without losing all his dignity. Still Goodhew kept talking, chipping away at him with a stream of incessant questions, hoping to interfere so much with Gjertsen's thoughts that he just gave in.

It took about ninety seconds before Oslo raised his hands in defeat. 'This is a freaking nightmare. Okay, I've screwed up. I just want to sort it out now.'

'In your own words then?'

Oslo nodded. He shuffled his bum back in the seat until he sat fully upright then cleared his throat as if he'd suddenly become the keynote speaker. 'Everybody needs a niche – well, everybody in the arts at least. I want to be a photojournalist, that's the plan anyway. But first I need to get a portfolio and I was looking for something different, subjects that were a little controversial. I tried a few things. I thought I was doing okay with urban decay but, when I started to look at other examples, I realized that my photos were like a cliché of a cliché.'

'So you hit on the idea of roadkill?'

Oslo's eyes lit up, and sudden his natural enthusiasm was enough to knock some of the pompous artiness from his voice. 'You saw my fish? Torlyn's the big one and Holstein's the small one. He's actually Holstein the third. When the first Holstein died, I realized I didn't have a photo of him so, when I bought Holstein the second I made sure I took plenty of them together.'

'Holstein one and two?'

'No, Torlyn and Holstein. Then Holstein the second died. Don't know why, as I actually care for them really well.'

'Go on.'

'Straight away he looked different. Obviously dead, but as if something else had vanished; as if his personality had left him. And, before you comment, I do realize that fish don't have one, not exactly. So I photographed him. Then again a few hours later. It was fascinating.'

'The start of your niche then?'

'Did you see the other Flickr roadkill photographers? They find a body and photograph it once. Very often it's about the contrast between the dead animal and the landscape: they depict the hostility of life in the wild or maybe the vulnerability of animal against machine. I haven't come across a single photographer who does what I do. I go back, day after day, and capture the journey the animal's body makes after death. You saw the fox on the wall, right?'

Goodhew nodded.

'I chose those photos from about a hundred that I took. I kept going back until it was impossible to tell which smears and fragments originally belonged to the fox. It's like watching an animal become invisible as it merges back into the rest of the world.' Oslo looked at Goodhew expectantly.

Goodhew raised his eyebrows slightly and did his best to nod with an expression of encouragement. He guessed Oslo wasn't used to being overwhelmed by excited photography fans; the nod was more than enough to keep Oslo talking.

'But it's no good having only one talent; photojournalism is about capturing the news – that means people, situations, anything really. So I knew I had to get better at the human angle. Poignant shots, shots that told a story . . .'

'Staged photos that invented a story?'

'Whatever. If I'd photographed Libby's room as it is, then what? It would've been dull, so instead I'm showing the real person – outwardly in control, but underneath she's a conflicted and tortured soul.'

'Right.' Goodhew got it; photojournalism with most emphasis on the *photo* and little on the *journalism*. 'And you were slipping in and out of everyone's rooms?'

Oslo nodded.

'Where d'you get the key?'

'There used to be a bunch hanging in the kitchen. I was one of the first to move in, so I had them copied.'

'I'll need to take them. Who has that original bunch?'

'One of the dads, Libby's maybe, but more likely Matt's dad Rob. He's fixed more things round here than Tony has, but at the end of the day that's who we rent from, so they should know who's got the keys.'

'How long have you been sneaking in and out of the other rooms?'

'Can I just say I really object to you calling it sneaking – it makes it sound creepy. I totally think they would have been fine about it if they had understood the integrity of my photographs.'

Goodhew had been aware of a short mantra repeating in his head, telling him to listen, learn and understand. The last statement had overfilled each of the three quotas. 'Actually, I really, really object to you using the word "integrity". You are one stop short of claiming to be misunderstood and a victim of circumstance, and if I hear either of those phrases coming out of your mouth, I will do my best to work out exactly how many offences you can be charged with.'

Oslo briefly looked indignant but swiftly replaced it with a sullen, 'Fine.'

'So cut the pompous, self-serving crap.'

'I said fine.'

'How long have you been doing this?'

'Since I moved in – whenever everyone else had gone out.'

'And what about Shanie?'

'The same thing. She arrived from the States, crashed out for a few hours then went out. Everyone else was out so I just added her room on to my round.'

Round? Goodhew only just managed to keep quiet.

'I remember that one, because it was a good shot. I called it *American Traveller.*'

'Good title.'

Oslo nodded in agreement and already the enthusiasm had slipped back into his tone. Goodhew sensed the moment was now a good one. 'When did you find her body?'

'Whose body?'

'Saturday? Sunday maybe?'

Oslo's nodding had been replaced by a headshake that was as quick and rhythmic as if he was following world-class table tennis.

'And before you say anything, let me explain. You told me about the photographs, admitted that you have access to every room in the house and that you have been in those rooms trying to build up a portfolio of photographs. If you really want to get this sorted out, answer the question now. Otherwise, I have more than enough to arrange for a search warrant and I will confiscate all your equipment.'

'Saturday. I found her Saturday morning, but I swear she was

155

dead by then. I didn't plan to mislead anyone, but I thought I'd be under suspicion. The person who finds the body always is, aren't they? And I started panicking because I thought of all of those cases where people have been wrongly arrested. I knew that no one would believe me if I said I was just taking photographs.'

'Even though you'd be able to show them the rest of your *work*?'

'Like I said, I panicked.'

'I don't believe you. That excuse is straight out of the kind of dodgy newspaper that will probably employ you at some point. Yes, you were scared to be caught out but I think you instantly saw an opportunity . . .'

Oslo's face began to pale.

Goodhew continued. 'Lucky you, because what you now faced was the perfect combination of both photography subjects: all the reasons you photograph roadkill, beautifully incorporating the human angle. I doubt you even let yourself consider the importance of giving Shanie's family the chance to say a decent goodbye to her.'

'It wouldn't have made any difference. She was dead.' There was no conviction in Oslo's voice now, but not enough shame either.

'I bet there's a huge difference between the Shanie Faulkner in your first photo and the state of her body in the last one.'

'You know what? I'll show you my photos with my blessing. You'll get them anyway. Yeah, I know I should have reported Shanie's death, but those photographs are unique. Controversial yes, but cutting-edge too and—'

'Shut up.' Goodhew spoke slowly and clearly, adopting a tone that sounded overly formal, but it was as much about controlling his own anger as silencing Oslo. 'Mr Gjertsen, I appreciate your offer of full cooperation, since your statement will form an important part of the evidence into the enquiry surrounding the death of Shanie Faulkner. It will also be used to assess whether or not you can be charged with obstruction.'

Oslo looked shocked.

Goodhew didn't react. 'We will conduct a search of your room at 42A King Street, Cambridge, for the purposes of obtaining the photographs you have offered to hand over. But I also warn you that our search will extend to the recovery and confiscation of any photographs and digital images that are being held on your behalf.'

It was enough. Oslo had already worked out that it was better to hand over every copy of the photos he had taken inside the King Street house in return for keeping his collection of roadkill shots.

Goodhew hoped Oslo would be charged with at least something, anything to subdue that arrogance. He reminded himself that everyone had redeeming features, but he still couldn't convince himself that Oslo possessed any trait more charming than a slightly creepy affection for Torlyn and Holstein III.

THIRTY-THREE

Marks had gathered together the key members of the investigation team in the incident room. Amongst them were DCs Kincaide, Young, Charles, Clark and Goodhew himself, and PCs Sue Gully and Kelly Wilkes.

Sometimes when Marks gave a briefing he used the full array of flipchart, wipe-board, notes and photographs. Today he was taking a more minimalist approach and although he held a clutch of A4 sheets in his hand, they remained folded in half, as though he had no intention or need to refer to them. Goodhew thought he knew what the announcement would be.

'As of this morning, the deaths of Shanie Faulkner and Meg DeLacy have officially become suicide investigations. Toxicology results confirm that Shanie Faulkner died from heart failure directly attributed to an overdose. Initial tests on Meg DeLacy indicate a very similar scenario, and her medical history supports the likelihood that she took her own life.'

So that's it, then? Goodhew wondered.

No one else in the room looked surprised. In fact, the typical reaction was: *Box Ticked, Case Closed, Move On.*

Kincaide spoke next. 'I took the statement from that Charlotte Stone girl, who claims she doesn't know anything about the genius who cracked Goodhew on the head.' He paused to allow the quip a moment to settle in. DC Clark obliged with a short snort of a laugh.

'And, as there is no reason at all to connect the incident with the other deaths, the assault on Goodhew will form a separate investigation which has yet to be assigned. I want to point out that I have nothing else to tie down on the Faulkner case and, therefore, I am immediately available to work on another case.'

Usually this kind of manipulation fell on deaf ears with DI Marks, but today was clearly different. 'That's fine.'

Kincaide hesitated. 'It was just a suggestion, sir. I don't actually mind continuing.'

'You *do* mind. You're just not sure whether you want it now I've agreed so easily.' That amused Clark too.

Marks wasn't about to dwell on any of it. 'Clearly with our caseload I intend to move all but a handful of you on to other investigations. Despite all the coaching and attempts to change attitudes, some of you are woefully lacking in enough tact to be trusted with families of suicide victims. Yes, Kincaide and Clark, you hear your names. At the other end of the scale we have DC Goodhew who secretly wants to adopt every bereaved family he encounters. Gully?'

She reddened instantly. 'Sir?'

'You're staying on it, also Charles and Young. The rest of you . . . Goodhew, what now?'

'I can't remember what happened just before I was attacked, but I know I was talking to Rob Stone and planning to take a formal statement from him, so I thought it might be a good idea if I still did that.'

'You're not about to add "for closure" I hope?'

'No. I thought that when the conversation started to cover similar ground it might help me to recollect something about the minutes before I was knocked out. Equally, it might remind Rob Stone of something.'

'He's a piss-head,' Kincaide muttered. 'He won't remember anything.'

Goodhew didn't argue, instead waited for Marks to speak, and was grateful when, 'Okay, that's fair enough,' came back as the

159

boss's less than enthusiastic response. Marks hesitated, then added, 'Nail that today then – you're rostered off tomorrow. When you get back on Wednesday, I'll have something entirely different for you.'

The meeting broke up a few minutes later, and Goodhew caught up with PC Gully in the corridor.

'What's got into Marks?' she whispered.

'Why ask me?'

'You always know more than I do.'

'Not this time.' He tried to catch her eye but she kept walking without looking once in his direction. 'I'm surprised *you* picked up on it.'

'You think I suffer from perception myopia or something?'

'No. You've worked with him less than I have, that's all,' Goodhew said.

'If I'd only worked with him twice, I'd have spotted the difference. He's . . . I don't know.'

'At the end of his tether? Irritable?'

'No. It's like whatever's bugging him is to the exclusion of everything else. Could be anything. Maybe it's a family matter,' Gully said.

'That was my first thought, but I've changed my mind.'

'Why?'

Goodhew shrugged. 'Perception incompetence, I expect.'

Finally Gully stopped and turned to face him. 'Actually, I was being serious.'

'Okay – well, so was I. Marks has occasionally mentioned his family without a trace of anxiety. It's at work that he doesn't seem himself. That's all.'

'Isn't it more interesting if it's work related?'

'How?'

'You might think it's morally unacceptable to snoop into his private life, but anything connected with Parkside's fair game. Right?'

'No.'

'Bollocks. Just share the gossip with me and I'll keep you up to date on the King Street deaths.'

'Are you trying to blackmail me?'

'I prefer "bribe", Gary.'

'That's devious but doomed. I'm not even going to try to work out what's bothering Marks. I'd prefer to be tied up with you on the King Street case.'

'Of course you would.' Gully blushed. It was an odd habit, and so frequent that he rarely noticed it now. Other people still commented, but this time the rush of pink to her skin was intense and unmissable. She turned her head away to face down the corridor, and said something he didn't catch, then turned back to him. 'Besides, there isn't a case any longer, Gary. It's closed, remember?'

THIRTY-FOUR

Rob Stone bent over the flowerbeds, but instead of digging the trowel into the ground he pressed its tip into the fold of tree roots protruding from the soil. He leaned his weight on it so that he could balance on the balls of his feet and watch his boss through the gaps in the hebe.

Colin had been cornered by the manager. For all the gardening contracts Colin held, Rob reckoned 80 per cent of the care homes were run by overweight, dictatorial females, and this one was no exception. They always wanted to find reasons for discontentment; even a perfectly planted flowerbed would warrant nothing more than a grudging, 'Very nice,' followed by, 'I think they should all be planted that way.' Dissatisfaction was usually demonstrated by the delivery of a stern set of I-know-best instructions while a job well done was rewarded with a sour smile, and yet more instructions, and higher odds of failure the next time.

Phyllis Koza didn't just fit the mould, she *was* the mould. One of the residents had told him her surname meant goat. Rather than using her first name he always referred to her as Mrs Koza after that. He gained quiet amusement from the mean-spirited connotations of her name.

It was petty but he had felt the glare of her distaste from the very first introduction, as though she'd already made up her mind that he just didn't deserve the chance to return to work.

He'd wondered whether Colin had told her about his drinking and she was actually one of those women who considered alcohol the devil itself, and condemned anyone who drank even a little, never mind a man who regularly drank too hard. Whatever deficiency she'd seen in him, she'd obviously spotted it from the first, so he understood Colin's suggestion that he should concentrate on the flowerbeds furthest away from the main building.

Colin had no problem with women like her. He'd listen politely to their instructions, and his knowledge of design and species seemed to win them over every time. Maybe genuinely knowledge-able gardeners were just hard to find, and if that was true Rob was glad that Matt had decided to study horticulture.

As she spoke to Colin now, she kept casting sharp glances in Rob's direction. None of her words reached him, however, so in the end he turned back to the weeding and waited for Colin to fill him in.

Colin strode towards him, unhurried, but Rob could see the tension in his friend's expression. 'I don't understand you, Rob.'

Rob shrugged. 'What have I done now?'

Colin was careful not to raise his voice above a whisper. 'Rob, you can't just go around with that aggressive attitude, slamming things down and swearing under your breath. We're working on the gardens of an *old people's home*. This is supposed to be the space where they can sit outside and relax. This space is supposed to be peaceful and therapeutic.'

'Sorry,' Rob muttered.

But Colin wasn't finished. 'Instead of associating their time out here with something positive, they're witnessing the fallout from your personal life.'

Okay then, a simple sorry wasn't going to be enough. There were very few things about Colin that ever grated on Rob, but sometimes he wished the other man could relax his personal code of conduct, even if only by a little. 'So I'm just releasing pent-up anger on the flowerbeds and that's getting on your tits? So what? Perhaps it does me good to take it out on the weeding.'

'The customer isn't paying for you to indulge in your therapy.'

'Oh, I see. You're sympathetic only when it suits you. When you want to give me a shoulder to cry on, you're there, but when it interferes with your business, that's different.'

'Don't be ridiculous. You are here working for me because I have given you an opportunity to get back on your feet.' Colin was still whispering, but it had become more intense. 'If you're going to insist on throwing your chances away, you're not throwing my business away with it. I'm not going to go down the drain just because I've stuck my neck out and tried to help you.'

'Well, I never asked you to.'

'Oh, for fuck's sake. No, you never asked me to. How long have we been friends? You were there for me when I needed support, and I haven't forgotten that.'

'Debt repaid. Good for you.' Rob heard himself talking and knew it sounded like he was doing his best to set fire to bridges he never intended to burn. Momentarily he wondered whether it was his habit to test everyone and everything he knew to absolute destruction.

Colin's tone remained calm, though Rob knew he was angry. 'I didn't know I'd ever get the chance to repay your friendship, but I'm glad I have, and I'm actually not going to just abandon you. But, and it is a big but, I have spent my entire working life building this business and you need to respect that. You are either polite to our customers or do what we agreed and work down the other end of the garden.'

Colin's code of conduct. Colin had decided that Rob should stay away from the customers. Decision made. Set in stone. As far as Colin was concerned, Rob was in the wrong.

'I've told you before, there's loads to do. Just stay where people won't bother you and where you won't bother them.'

'Right, so I'm not fit to be in front—'

'We've had this conversation, Rob. You've turned up at work drunk – fine, but it means you can't drive the van, you can't drive the mower, you can't do half the things I would like you to do, right? But I know you have a drink problem . . .'

'Well, thank you. Why not announce it to the world.'

'Oh, for God's sake, everybody knows you have a problem. There's not one person here who hasn't seen you down by the river finishing off a four-pack at lunchtime, or sitting on the pub bench and getting back for work an hour late.' Colin took a step back. Literally. And when he spoke again, his voice was quieter but no less forceful.

'I also know that you've always worked hard, you *are* a hard worker, you are a decent person – so that's why you're still with me. That way, you have the time to sort things out. And the opportunity.'

Rob knew the spiel but was still festering about being sent to the end of the garden like some misbehaving infant-school child.

Colin then scowled. 'Fuck it, Rob, am I just wasting my breath?'

'Probably. Probably totally wasting your time.' He paired the words with a lopsided and sarcastic smile since, after all, he *was* being made to feel like the naughty kid in class.

'Rob, you are doing my fucking head in. All I am asking is that you show enough respect so that I don't lose work. I don't care if employing you doesn't help me turn a profit but I do care if you push me under. How can I make it clearer?'

Rob's expression didn't change. He knew the next words before Colin even opened his mouth.

'What do I have, Rob, tell me? What, apart from this business? Exactly nothing. You have your kids, and they need you. I want us both to come out the other end of this and find some way to make some sense of our lives. I don't want to be standing there drunk like you in five years, because you've lost your kids and I've lost my business.'

'Fuck off. I'm not going to lose my kids.'

'They lost their mother, and now they're being forced to watch their father disintegrate. Don't you think they need you to get it together, right now?'

Rob shook his head, but not because he disagreed. *Getting his life together?* He'd thought through it plenty of times, started and

165

restarted mental lists of the things he needed to do to avoid wrecking his health, risking Matt and Charlotte's future, facing financial ruin. Just thinking about them exhausted him; he never once managed to complete the list even though he knew every item on it was an imperative. Even regular housework and shopping for food had become mountains that were too steep to even contemplate. Each time he saw Charlotte packing away shopping or folding laundry he felt the gap between them was stretching to an impossible divide.

Admitting that his mental strength had deserted him amounted to saying, *I can't look after you, Charlotte. You need to care for me now.*

Rob shook his head, because these days it only contained words like *can't*, *sorry* and *impossible*.

Colin stared at him, waiting for what? An apology? An admission of failure?

'Rob, just take ten minutes. Walk along by the river, just calm down, then come back and we'll sort it out.' Colin wanted to help but Rob was beyond asking for any more sympathy.

'Don't worry, I'm going. It's obvious you don't want me round here contaminating your customer's garden.'

He was outwardly belligerent but Rob felt something new cutting through. It was an emptiness that he hadn't felt since the first weeks after Mandy's death.

Colin kept talking. 'I'm just asking you to take ten minutes away. Fifteen, twenty – whatever, just come back and respect what I'm trying to do here. Respect my customers and my business, and respect yourself, Rob; respect yourself enough to give your kids their dad back.'

An emptiness descended that felt like it would swallow him. He heard himself shout. He didn't know what he said, just wanting to hear his voice above the desire to fall to the ground and just stop. If this was what hitting rock bottom meant, maybe he should welcome it. Maybe though, this was just the start of the final collapse.

Colin kept talking. 'Rob, look, I don't want to be here making a scene. I have not turned Matt against you. I haven't turned anybody against you. I haven't turned Charlotte against you, but eventually she's going to turn, mate, because they need you and you're not there for them.'

'Oh, same old record . . . same old, old, old, old record. You know what? I'm out of here.' Rob heard the shake in his voice. 'I am *out of here*. You know, maybe if everybody didn't treat me like this kind of wreck, I'd show them how I could get back on my feet without Charlotte running around after me and without you giving me some hand-out of a job that I'm supposed to be eternally grateful for, and then blame me when things go sour with your business. I'm not your scapegoat and I don't need minding by my own child, so yeah . . .'

Suddenly he ran out of things to say. The words were still racing round his head but too churned over to come out of his mouth in any coherent way.

He threw down the trowel. It landed point first in the soil. Somehow that wasn't aggressive enough so he kicked it and it flicked through the air, hitting a stone bird-table. The corner splintered off with a sharp crack. He threw down his gloves too and turned his back on Colin.

Rob headed down the slope towards the bottom of the garden, where he could scramble over the low fence and head for the river. He even resented the idea that the river had been Colin's suggestion. He stalked towards the towpath, finally understanding that this pain had a long time to run.

THIRTY-FIVE

It took Goodhew over an hour to track down Rob Stone and his boss, Colin Wren, to the grounds of Ferry House in Water Street, Chesterton. Even when he saw the van complete with business name parked outside, he still wasn't convinced he would finally catch up with Rob Stone. Maybe it was the last memory of this drunk and isolated man that left him wondering whether he would really find him capable of working in harmony with anyone else.

He was directed around the back of the building where the long and narrowing gardens sloped down towards the river and a view of the tow path on the other side. He could see a man working alone but it wasn't Rob. He approached and saw that the gardener was taller and slimmer than Stone but of a very similar age. Goodhew thought Rob looked old for his years, but this man also had the look of someone to whom time hadn't been kind. With Rob it was the alcohol: the blotchy complexion and unhealthy eyes that saw him slipping prematurely from middle age. With Colin it was due to a life in the outdoors, where the skin hardened into an expression that shouted of physical fatigue.

He looked up as Goodhew came close by, but only straightened when he realized that the approaching footsteps belonged to someone looking specifically for him. Colin didn't speak, just nodded.

Goodhew introduced himself and Colin nodded again but this time in understanding rather than greeting.

'Are you the officer that was attacked at the Carlton pub?'

'You heard about it?'

'Rob told me – he was worried that it would be pinned on him. He can have a temper when he's been drinking, but he just gets mouthy, and by the time he's wound himself up enough to have a pop at anyone, he can barely coordinate his breathing, never mind his fists.' He fell silent for a moment then added, 'Rob's not here.'

'I thought he was meant to be working with you today?'

'Well, he is . . . *was*. I sent him off on a break, so he should be back shortly. But that was an hour ago, maybe more.'

'So he's at lunch then, early lunch?'

'No.' Colin rubbed his forehead just above one eyebrow. 'Rob's struggling at the moment. I told him he should get some space – you know, straighten his head out, I suppose.'

'He's struggling how? I'm sorry, I don't understand. Is he drinking at work or . . . depressed? Restless, aggressive – what?'

Colin hesitated for a second as though trying to make a decision. Sometimes when they did that, people were running through all the tactful ways to answer, the ways to avoid that can of worms that so often lurked behind a simple answer to a simple question. And quite often, like now, Goodhew would see them give up, deciding that the tactful answer would be too complicated, would lead to something even more complicated later on; they were usually right and Colin Wren was no exception.

After this hesitation, Colin relaxed and just told it how it was.

'Rob lost his previous job. He had time off when his wife Mandy was ill, then more when she died. He started drinking heavily then. I think losing Mandy was too much. It wasn't just the drink, he wasn't reliable any more – he couldn't concentrate. He was a welder at the time and, let's face it, it's a job where you've got to concentrate. He was working at a garage and the jobs were getting behind. He told me he reached a point when he was relieved when they let him go.'

'So he was confiding in you through all of his.'

'I've known him since school. He's always been a hard worker, a

169

good employee too, as far as I know. He never worked for me before but I think he's been one of those straight-up guys who just turn up and do a good job. But now he felt he'd gone too far the wrong way to pull himself up. He had to start somewhere else and so he left I suppose under a cloud. He then tried several contract jobs but he couldn't hold them down, and I was watching him fall to bits.'

'Is that when you employed him?'

Colin nodded. 'They always say that two years is the big turning-point. When you're grieving the first year, it's the loss, and the second year it's the anniversary of that loss. After that, things get better so I figured I'd stick with him through that. I have contracts, care homes like this, the grounds of buildings; places that require a mix of skill and hard labour. Rob seemed perfect – he doesn't have to go face to face with people. I thought he'd have space to think and still be working. It all made sense to me.'

'But something went wrong?'

'Look, I'm not admitting defeat at this point, but it's a struggle, and several of the care homes have asked me politely about him; they're not tremendously happy with him being in contact with some of their residents. He's not dangerous, but sometimes he's aggressive in a verbal way. He wouldn't hurt anyone, but he has a slightly confrontational way about him, and he's turned up several times after lunch when he's obviously had a few too many to drink or even first thing in the morning.' Colin stared at the ground for a moment then back up at Goodhew. He looked apologetic. 'That type of thing will end up damaging my reputation.'

'Is that what happened today?'

'It's what happens too frequently, if I'm honest. If a job goes well, it goes well. If I have a problem it's always about Rob, and that chip on his shoulder is growing so huge he can't pull himself out from under it. It's in my interest too that he just keeps his head down and steers away from the customers, but today . . .' Colin shrugged. 'At first he seemed fine, but soon he was muttering to himself. I couldn't even work out the words, but he was internally sorting things out and swearing under his breath. He was working on a flowerbed that was a bit closer to the house, up at that end by the patio. He was filling it with bedding plants – it's the job of the day. All Rob had to do was move some tools from the van, collect the plants from the greenhouse, take them down to the flowerbed and plant them up. Little things kept going wrong, which turned into a vicious cycle. He's flustered so he's clumsy. He's clumsy so he swears. He swears in a way that sounds aggressive, and he's heard by a couple of residents who complain to the manager.'

Colin made a ta-da gesture with his hands, but didn't actually say it.

'This is a really good nursing home and they keep their grounds maintained for the residents all year round. Even in the winter we still have a few things to do here. The greenhouses here have been restored. My point is that this isn't any old contract – I need to keep them happy.

'The manager doesn't want somebody wandering around in the grounds and using bad language, even if it's only to himself. From Rob's point of view, he probably wasn't even aware that he was doing it, but that's no excuse. He knew I was annoyed. By the time she spoke to me, he'd cleared off further from the house and was keeping his head down.'

'So you argued?'

'I was just trying to make him see that it wasn't a way he should behave. I'm not stupid – I know that when he's angry, it's about what's going on in his head, not about the garden and the residents and all of that. I therefore suggested he took time out and went down by the river – have a walk, clear his head, all of that.'

'And he's still down there?'

'Well, he hasn't been back. You could go down there and look, I suppose. You might want to check out the pubs, the tow-path.'

'Are you planning to let him go?'

Colin rubbed the bridge of his nose with the back of his wrist. If he'd been trying to push away the fatigue, he failed. 'I can't keep on like this. I want to find some way round it. I can't lose my customers. But I can't lose my mate either.'

THIRTY-SIX

The nearest two pubs were the Green Dragon and the Pike and Eel. Goodhew checked there first but neither of them had seen Rob Stone. So much for the obvious assumptions. Goodhew walked along the tow path for about twenty minutes, away from the city. And walking at pretty much the same pace that the river flowed.

Goodhew turned round when he was almost opposite the Plough in Fen Ditton. He decided that it was unlikely Stone had walked this far, or if he had, had kept on walking. He was about halfway back when he spotted the figure in the distance sitting in the grass of the river bank.

Goodhew squinted. He saw no sign of fishing rods, or bait boxes. He walked a little further and when the man came into focus he was able to pick out the shape of Rob Stone's features. Although facing the river, Stone seemed to be staring across it at Stourbridge Common. He didn't look round as Goodhew approached.

'They once used to hold the biggest fair in Europe there, did you know that?' Stone didn't wait for an answer. 'Used to be a couple of days and then it grew until it lasted almost a month. It was famous – they probably couldn't imagine it no longer existing.' He tilted his head in Goodhew's direction, not quite looking him in the eye, but almost. 'What is the point of anything, if nothing lasts forever? Whatever you build crumbles. Whatever you don't build doesn't matter.'

'Mr Stone.'

'Yeah, yeah, I know. Pointless drunken ramblings.'

There were three empty cans lying next to Stone's feet. The fourth of the pack was in his hand. He'd arranged the empty ones so they were side by side with the labels positioned at precisely the same angle.

Goodhew guessed this must mean that Rob had been there for more than a few minutes and if that was the case, he must have sat down pretty much as soon as Goodhew had passed the first time.

'I walked this way a few minutes ago.'

'Yeah, I saw you. I wasn't in the mood.'

'But you are now?'

'Yeah. No, I can't be bothered to get up. I can't be bothered to.' Stone pushed down the corners of his mouth. 'I just can't be bothered.'

'D'you remember when I came to speak to you at the Carlton Arms? I went outside and shortly afterwards I was attacked.'

'Yeah, I heard.'

'Well, two things. Firstly, I don't remember our conversation before, not clearly, though I know we were talking about Shanie. Secondly, I know you've also said you don't remember seeing anything, so I just wanted to check.'

'Check, as in catch me out? Or check to see if some memory emerged through my drunkenness? No, when I said I don't remember, I don't remember – and if I said I saw nothing, I saw nothing.'

'Okay, fair enough.' Goodhew sat down beside Stone and joined him in looking out at the river. 'But I might remember something if we go back over the last conversation about Shanie.'

'Ha, do you think I remember any more than you do? I remember us talking about Shanie but nothing else.'

'I will need to take a formal statement about how Shanie came to be in the house. But could you at least think about whether anyone saw you leave the Carlton?'

'I don't know.'

'Look, try to remember. There were people inside. There was some pool match on and the woman at the bar . . .'

'No, I don't remember. Ask them.'

'Okay, how did you get back home?'

'I walked – it's not far.'

'No, but your daughter Charlotte came looking for you. She must know the quickest way from the pub to your house as well, but you didn't cross paths?'

Stone smiled; it was accompanied by a short snort of amusement. 'Well, that's simple, because Charlotte would go the lit way, while I go up the back alley. She's sensible, I'm the stupid fucker that comes home with dogshit on my shoes and a head that's banging so much I don't know if I've been clouted or not. Great.'

'Well no, it's not really, is it? At the moment all I have to corroborate your statement is Charlotte's statement saying where you were. That's not much help.'

'I didn't hit you over the head, you know.' Rob tried draining the final can even though he'd made a show of draining it just a few moments before. He held it in his hand, crushed the middle of it then folded in the ends and finally concertinaed it so it made a disk about an inch thick. Then he did the same with each of the other three cans, and stood up.

'I bet you think I'm messing my life up. I am, I know I am – however, I haven't turned Matt against me.' Stone spoke slowly at first, as though the thoughts were only revealing themselves to him a moment before he spoke them. 'Matt is me, Matt is who I was before he was born. He's got the same anger that was already in me before all of this happened. I don't have some big chip on my shoulder because I've lost Mandy. I've always found life a mental struggle. Charlotte, she's different, she is like her mum. She wants to care and nurture and show everybody that there is something better in the world. And I make that worse.' Stone's words emerged uneven, spilling from him in irregular volleys, but the sentences themselves were becoming surprisingly coherent. 'I lean on her good nature and let her take care of me in the way I don't take care of

175

myself, and all the while I'm thinking, my god, she deserves so much better. She does, you know. She deserves so many things I can't give her and so does Matt.

'Now I'm talking, so that means I'm just a burbling drunk shooting my mouth off. Isn't that the way we are? Passive aggressive? I'm either offending people or talking garbage and offending them with that. Don't worry about a lift either. Colin will take me or I'll walk. Either way I could do a lot worse.'

'We're not finished yet, Mr Stone,' Goodhew told him. 'Shanie Faulkner, remember?'

'What about your own injury?'

'I'm not really interested in that right now.'

Again the snort of laughter. 'Well, you're a fucking arsehole then, aren't you? You're judging it on how badly you were hurt and how quickly you recovered. Maybe if you'd turned your head a little, or landed badly, or if my Charlotte hadn't found you, you could be dead or in a right fucking state. Whatever the outcome: same man, same attack.'

'I wasn't dismissing it, but my focus is Shanie.'

'And the other girl, Meg?'

'Of course.'

'No, no it's not. I see something in your expression. What's with you? Both cases should be treated the same, but they're not.'

Goodhew shook his head.

'Liar,' Stone said. Then: 'Charlotte and Matt think like you.'

'Think what?'

'That Shanie wasn't the type. Never was.'

'There isn't a type.'

'And who taught you that? It's bollocks. This fucking life crushes me but I'm not the type. If I was, I would have done it. And you? Are you the type?'

Goodhew didn't answer.

'No, I didn't think so. You never met Shanie but you don't buy the idea that she killed herself: it's bugging you. You don't think it was an accident either. You really think someone killed her?'

'Why would they?'

'I'm not the fucking detective here, I'm the fucking alcoholic, remember?' Stone's uneven speech had gone: both his thoughts and words had suddenly sharpened. 'But even a fucking alcoholic can work out when his own kids are in the shit. I think the least you can do is hear their concerns.'

'Fair enough.'

'And don't throw "fair enough" at me and think that's the end of it.' And before Goodhew could respond, Stone demanded, 'Did you have Lego when you were a kid?'

'Yes, I did.'

'I had a whole box of it. I had names for the different pieces, like "eighters" and "flat fours". I even didn't need to check if I had a "see-through twelve-er", I just knew. Didn't matter how many times I tipped it out or churned it over, I knew what was there.'

Goodhew nodded; he knew too.

'That's Charlotte and Matt, and everything connected with these deaths. They've stored every thought, question and discussion. Without examining the whole box of Lego, how do you know what you can build from it?'

THIRTY-SEVEN

When Goodhew woke the next morning, he knew it was early. The room was too grey for 5 a.m. but the traffic was too quiet for six. He lay on his back, staring straight up at the indistinct shape of his ceiling lampshade, aware of the things he hadn't done. He hadn't taken Rob Stone's statement – nor spoken to Matt and Charlotte, as he'd eventually promised.

Instincts. He'd made a promise to himself to listen to them, and right now that was vital. He needed to clear his thoughts, not muddy them further, and to achieve that he needed time on his own.

He made himself some coffee and sat on the floor with his back against the battered leather settee. His jukebox played quietly, its valves humming almost as loudly as Goodhew's brain. He cupped the mug in both hands and it was almost cold by the time he started to drink.

As far as he could remember, he'd been about twelve when his interest in understanding people and fascination with crime had crystallized into the desire to become a detective. The job was always full of surprises.

But Lego? He hadn't seen that one coming. Nor Rob Stone's sudden and eloquent outpouring. Bryn would undoubtedly come up with some convoluted analogy between alcohol and the fuel supply in a carburettor: too little and it spluttered and didn't respond, too much and it flooded and wouldn't work at all. Something like that anyway.

For a few minutes he allowed himself to wonder at Bryn's apparently simple take on life, and the depths of thought that Bryn's views sometimes revealed. Then, once in a while, he'd make a throwaway remark that was equally illuminating. *A dazzling smile and rampant curls.* The words flashed back into Goodhew's consciousness and in his mind's eye, the image he held of Charlotte took on a new clarity. Suddenly every feature, from the curve of her cheek and brightness in her eyes, through to the sound of her voice as she'd tried to revive him, felt as though they'd communicated far more than he'd first realized.

This was no good. He tried to ignore any further random thoughts of Charlotte but, despite his best efforts, she refused to entirely leave his mind.

Damn Bryn.

Goodhew made a mental note to give his friend a call then pushed himself back to considering the Lego he himself had owned as a child. He'd kept his in a dark blue translucent plastic tub that had started life in the 1960s as either a futuristic umbrella stand or a groovy kitchen bin. It had been relegated to toy storage and could hold so much Lego that Goodhew had never managed to fill it up past the halfway mark.

Rob Stone was right; he too had known exactly which pieces he possessed, but he also knew that the only efficient way to put them together was to tip them into a heap in the middle of the floor.

Goodhew asked himself about his current options. One was to accept that both Shanie and Meg had committed suicide. Marks was the boss and had years more experience. Goodhew trusted him. The first option, then, was to trust Marks's judgement and let it go. But that didn't sit right: the picture was hanging together, but he was sure that whatever was holding it in place wasn't enough to withstand too much shaking.

Linked suicides, or murder?

The whole problem, with both the case and the Lego analogy, was a lack of all the necessary pieces.

And, put like that, it was suddenly simple.

THIRTY-EIGHT

Police stations of any size were never deserted. Maybe the front desk would be briefly unattended or the corridors silent at various times, but there would always be someone somewhere in the building. Goodhew moved quickly and with purpose. He reached Sheen's desk without crossing paths with anyone.

At first glance, Sheen's method of information-gathering seemed erratic and incomprehensible, but Goodhew had seen enough of the multi-coloured arrow-happy diagrams to know that nothing would appear on a page without having a connection – no matter however disparate the information appeared. Sometimes just following the arrows led to the answer; other times it only helped when Sheen provided the translation.

Goodhew turned on Sheen's computer and searched for any details Sheen had logged that cross-referenced with suspected teen suicides, Brimley Close or the Carlton Arms. Then he took down one box-file at a time and began rifling through the physical files. Each time he found a page of interest he slid it out carefully, photographed it with his phone then slipped it back in exactly the same place.

He needed to be both accurate and fast, but each time he checked the clock the hands had jumped forward another handful of minutes. The building would be filling from seven, and absolutely anyone who knew Sheen would smell a rat if someone other than Sheen was seen anywhere near his files.

The absolute deadline would be the arrival of Sheen himself at 7.30.

Twice he heard sounds in the corridor and ducked under Sheen's desk. No one appeared; thankfully, Sheen had been moved to pretty much the most secluded spot in the station.

Goodhew replaced the last file, switched off the PC and made it into the corridor just as the big hand jerked its way on to 7.25. He checked through the banisters on the second-floor landing: Sheen was crossing the first-floor landing and heading up, so Goodhew hurried to the other end of the second floor and left by the public entrance.

The Kite is an area of Cambridge named for its shape, and Goodhew cut through the back streets from Parkside Station at the Kite's southern tip to Maids Causeway on the northern edge.

Many of the large houses were still family homes, or had been split into flats but were residential nonetheless. Braeside sat between two of these houses, and from the outside appeared to be the home of a slightly poorer – or possibly more eccentric – relation. In fact, the building was home to several health-related resources, including a chiropractor and more recently an osteopath. Goodhew was looking for Elizabeth Martin, the psychotherapist whose treatment room was situated on the first floor. He looked up at the half-lowered bamboo blind with the half-closed curtain behind; no visible lights, no sign of movement.

He'd come on the off-chance, planning to leave a note if Miss Martin wasn't available. He had a pen but was rummaging through his pockets for any piece of paper more substantial than a grocery receipt, when he became aware of someone close behind him.

'The curious detective,' she said.

And he looked round to see Elizabeth Martin herself eyeing him. She was a woman in her mid-fifties, with grey-flecked blond hair and a passion for knitwear. Skirt, top, scarf; all knitted. Even her boots had a roll-over top that looked knitted too.

Beach holidays must be tricky.

'Curious? As in nosy?' he enquired.

'And slightly odd.' Unless he was imagining it, there was mild humour in her tone.

'Thanks.'

She pulled a bunch of keys from her bag and used the largest to open the front door. A second, newer one, opened a door beyond, which led to stairs and the floor above. 'I have an hour before my first client – will that be long enough?'

'I should explain why I'm here.'

'Bit difficult if you don't. Go up then, explain while I make coffee.'

'I don't need one, thanks.'

She followed him up the stairs. 'To which you hope I'll say I won't bother either, so you get the most out of your hour – but if I don't start with a coffee you won't get anything from me at all. D'you want one now?'

He decided he did, and in less than five minutes they were seated in her consulting room. It was like he imagined a session might be, with herself in the more upright chair with the wooden arms and high back, while he sat in a lower softer chair, upholstered in a soft green velvet and positioned within easy reach of a large box of tissues.

He had already explained the bare bones of his enquiry while the kettle boiled and now she sat with her pen poised over her notebook as if he was about to give the answers to her rather than the other way around. Maybe she needed to hold the pen and pad in order to think. 'Epidemics of suicide?' she murmured. 'You could just read a book, you know.'

'I've read some – heard comments. I'd just like it first-hand.'

'Fair enough. So you have four deaths that are possible suicides. They weren't part of the same group of friends, but each person knew at least one of the others?'

'Correct.'

'And you just want general background?'

'Yes, please. Without knowing specifics, the kind of questions you'd want to ask and the kind of background information that you would take into consideration.'

'Okay, I understand. Have you heard of the term "suicide cluster"?'

'It was mentioned at the station.'

'Well, when I use the word "cluster" I'm talking about both suicides and attempts that are linked in some way. So, for instance, maybe there is a group of suicides at one college or in a particular community.'

'Geographically linked.'

'Possibly. They might also be grouped by time, as in impact suicides where an event such as the death of a celebrity or the collapse of a bank seems to provide the stimulus.'

'So by place or event?'

'Yes. It's usually referred to as a link by time or space – space meaning place.'

'There's another term I've seen mentioned: *contagion*.'

Miss Martin nodded. 'When talking about suicides, the words "contagion" and "cluster" both relate to a situation of multiple suicides, but are actually quite different. The cluster is the way the group is related, while contagion is a theory about cause. As the name implies, it's the idea that a suicide has been triggered in response to an earlier suicide.'

'It's catching, you mean?'

'In essence, yes. But I must stress that it's a complicated subject, and as far as I'm concerned, the contagion idea is unproven. There are key groups that tend to be more vulnerable: students and psychiatric patients, for example. But these people may naturally gravitate towards grouping with similarly minded individuals, and my personal view is that it is the propensity for depression amongst those connected to the first victim that puts them at risk. In the sense that the initial suicide acts as a catalyst, that could be argued as being contagion – but any notion that a person who has never before suffered from depression or suicidal tendencies would be suddenly overtaken by a desire to kill themselves is nonsense.'

Elizabeth Martin offered to talk Goodhew through some published papers on the subject. He declined. He was just about keeping up with her, but had the feeling he ought to find a few medical students to hang out with before he tried keeping pace with a fully fledged consultant again in the near future.

'This case I'm dealing with . . .'

'The one in the papers?'

He nodded. He hadn't seen any news for several days but knew Shanie's death had been referred to on the billboards. Unless he had a specific reason to check a media report on an active case, he kept well away from the press. It was hard enough to keep his thinking straight without tripping up on other people's supposition.

'And there were two cases before, and one since?'

'Potentially, yes. There's a gap of over two years between number two and number three, though.'

'But numbers three and four are just days apart?'

'Correct.'

'Unless number three was particularly close to either of the first two and had, for example, been finding it difficult to cope since their deaths, I'd feel sceptical about considering that they might be linked. Incidentally, I saw no mention of related suicides in the paper.'

'I don't believe they've made a connection yet.'

'Better if it stays that way. Once the media starts with the dramatic headlines, these things take on an identity of their own. Boredom, lack of belonging and impulsivity can make people do things they won't then live to regret . . . But, more crucially for your case, I think you should consider Shanie Faulkner as an unconnected case.'

'Okay.'

'With number four, you need to consider whether the third death alone provided sufficient stimulus to link them.'

'Possibly two pairs of suicides, then?'

Elizabeth Martin nodded, but had suddenly become distracted. She rose from her chair and crossed to a small oak writing desk next to the door. With a tug the front opened to reveal four bundles of newspapers, each held together with a thick elastic band. 'I like to keep the previous four weeks; it's surprising how much local news

185

is discussed during sessions. Here we are.' She pulled the band from one bundle and flattened the copies out on the writing surface. She had her back to him so that the pages were partly obscured by her body.

As he hadn't been invited to join her, Goodhew stayed where he was.

'Do you always separate work from work like this?' she asked him casually.

He wished he had joined her then, as he would have liked to witness her expression as she spoke. 'Like what?'

She poised, with a page half turned. 'Take tasks away from the job then come back with them later.'

Even though she wasn't looking at him, Goodhew shrugged, then replied, 'Sometimes.'

'Don't you think I recognize avoidance when I hear it?'

'Sorry?'

'You, question after question, but still avoiding giving me a straight answer. Obviously you've heard of a square peg in a round hole? Well, you're potentially a peg of many shapes; you may still develop in many different ways. Interesting to see, when so many dies are already cast.'

Goodhew fidgeted. Might have even reddened slightly. Certainly didn't know how to reply. 'The suicides—'

She waved him quiet, then turned to face him. She held one particular copy of the *Cambridge News* in her hand, but her attention was directed fully towards Goodhew. 'Have you considered some counselling yourself?'

'For what?'

He imagined her emitting a tut.

'For the things you find difficult.'

He shook his head. 'I hadn't expected a sales pitch.' And he knew he would feel disappointed if that was where this was heading.

'So cynical. Seems to me you're split between wanting to fit in and feeling drawn to challenging the status quo. Am I right?'

He heard himself sigh.

'Why *did* you join the police force?' She waited for a few seconds more, then slapped one hand with the now folded paper held in the other. 'Shanie Faulkner, your number three?'

'Yes.'

'I take it the evidence is pointing at an overdose, accidental or otherwise? I'm not scared to voice my opinion, Detective, as I am not a consultant on this case, nor do I have any more background than the press report and the information you have given me. I am actually a scientist and as such would far rather work with facts than supposition. *However* . . .' She emphasized the word, then paused for full effect. 'The post-graduate course on which she was enrolled suggests she was an extremely bright student, and that attending this course was a real feather in her cap. Medical history?'

'A vague reference to depression, nothing detailed as yet.'

'Okay, that would be a key consideration. Without that, though . . .' She paused. 'I'd be doubtful, unless you found she'd suffered some kind of major trauma, physical or emotional. Without that, I would take plenty of convincing.'

Goodhew saw her glance at her watch. He checked his own and found he had used up all but ten minutes of his hour with her. He gathered his thoughts, but she stopped him before he had a chance to ask the next question.

She smiled. 'You know, there are actually only fifty minutes in a therapist's hour, so I'm throwing you out now.'

He stood to leave and reached out to shake her hand. 'Thank you, I really appreciate your time.'

'You will consider what I said though, won't you?'

'Don't worry, I'll be thorough.'

'Not her situation, Gary. I mean yours.'

THIRTY-NINE

Goodhew was the first to arrive at the public park in Arbury Road. It included a small slide, one swing and plenty of wood shavings, all enclosed behind smart red-painted railings. Seemed to him that rather too much had been expended on health and safety and not enough on the items that would actually encourage kids to play.

It was a warm morning but the place was empty. Being a lone male hanging around a children's play area made him feel a little conspicuous. It took him several minutes of switching his attention between watching passing traffic and checking his mobile before he spotted a second, larger playground beyond some trees.

He headed over and immediately saw that Libby and Matt were there already.

This area was better equipped, and even had a few children playing on the climbing equipment. A blue steel beam ran horizontally about six inches off the ground, topped with Frisbee-sized stepping stones. Matt and Libby each sat on one of them, facing one another with their knees almost touching.

They stood up as soon as they saw him, and moved over to the nearest bench. Goodhew followed them, sitting at one end while Libby sat in the middle.

He explained that the deaths of both Shanie and Meg were being passed to the coroner with police evidence supporting a suicide verdict. Neither of them said much, so he couldn't work out whether they'd heard this already or didn't expect anything else. Libby eventually spoke first. 'We're not going back to the house. I'm back at home with my mum, Matt's staying at home too. Jamie's gone back to Devon. She's abandoned her course.'

'Oslo and Phil?'

Matt shrugged. 'We don't want to see them again.' He frowned suddenly and glanced at Libby. 'I don't, anyhow.'

Libby picked up on the thought. 'I love Jamie, but I don't see how we'll ever keep in touch, because I think the shadow hanging over us will always be too big. It's just one more thing that can't be fixed.'

They were all silent for a moment or two. Goodhew wondered if Matt was, like himself, silently agreeing but not knowing the best way to put it.

'As for Oslo and Phil, I don't think I care one way or another,' she confirmed. 'I didn't really know either of them. They hung out together a bit but maybe only because they were living in the same house. Phil and Meg were the close ones.' Libby shot a glance at Matt but immediately turned her attention back to Goodhew. 'I know Phil slept with Shanie.'

'Where did you hear that?'

'From the stallion's very own mouth.' She studied Goodhew's reaction closely for a moment. 'I thought you detective people were unshockable.'

'I am surprised, that's all. And he told you this?'

Libby managed a wry smile. 'I overheard him and Meg fighting. They were loud – and pretty frank.'

'When was this?'

Libby began to speak, but Matt cut in quicker. 'In case you need to know, Meg and I had sex during the first week of college.' He started the sentence speaking to Goodhew, but by the end of it he was facing Libby. 'I'm sorry, I should've said.'

'Why?'

'I felt guilty not telling you.'

'*She* didn't have any qualms telling Phil about it.'

'Well, I just thought . . .' Matt's voice drifted into silence. Eventually, both he and Libby turned their focus back on Goodhew.

It seemed like they either wanted him to change the subject, or clear off.

He copied down Jamie-Lee's mum's home number from Libby's mobile phone, then started walking back towards Arbury Road.

'Wait!'

Goodhew turned. Matt hung back, but Libby was running towards him. 'I forgot to say, Shanie was going to meet someone. I think it was the same week she died, but I don't remember which day. She came back home from the pub, complaining she'd wasted her money buying a drink for someone who didn't show.'

'Who?'

'I asked her, but she just shook her head and said it was no biggie.'

'Male or female?'

'A man . . . no, I'm not sure. I don't know whether she actually said *he* or whether I just assumed it was a man.'

'D'you know which pub?'

'Something close by, I think. She said she'd waited half an hour, and I remember thinking she was exaggerating because she hadn't even been out of the house much longer than that.' Libby didn't move and Goodhew waited for her to add something else. In the end she said, 'That's all I know. I'm sorry . . .' The inflection on the final word made it sound as if it wasn't at the end of the sentence.

'There's something else?'

A quick nod. 'My sister . . .' she swallowed. 'I was too young to go to her inquest.'

He wasn't prepared to guess what she wanted to say, or ask, so he just waited. By the time she found the right words, she was close to tears.

'I heard you tried to save her,' she managed finally.

'But I couldn't . . .'

'I understand . . .' The words caught in her throat and she fought against them until she was able to speak again. 'I understand it was instant.' She steadied her breath before speaking again. 'There was no chance you could – but you stayed with her. I had terrible dreams afterwards.' She squeezed her eyes shut, heavy tears dropping on to her cheeks. 'But however bad I dreamed it was, there was always someone trying to reach her. When you did that for her, it turned out you did it for me too. I just wanted to thank you now.'

Goodhew reached his car and left it parked while he phoned Jamie-Lee Wallace. Their conversation was brief, punctuated by awkward silences at the other end. Goodhew could tell from her tone that she really wanted to help. He could also tell that, every time she couldn't answer a question, she felt as though she was letting him down.

Jamie seemed to have some insight regarding each of the housemates; her observations of their personalities tied in with his own.

'Do you think Shanie could have been more deeply involved with any of the other housemates?' he asked.

'I'm not actually bi-sexual, but there are moments when I feel a little *ambivalent*.'

'Ambivalent about men, or curious about women?'

'Good question, Detective. Let's just say I can look at a woman and appreciate in her what I would appreciate if I were a lesbian. Makes me think men have it lucky. But the fact that the idea of sex with another woman doesn't arouse me is probably what's going to keep me heterosexual.' A pause. 'Are you still there? Does that make sense?'

'Er, yes.'

'Shanie *didn't* appreciate the female form. I think she found the whole thing of being human a bit odd.'

'Really?'

'You know, like some nerdy people can't get their heads round the function of a pet?'

'Go on.'

'I think Shanie liked interaction, but didn't quite get it either. All I'm saying is, I'm one hundred per cent sure she wasn't into girls.

191

And I reckon she hadn't got further than a little dabbling with the boys.'

Goodhew pulled up outside Rob Stone's house, but Charlotte wasn't home. He tried her mobile, leaving a message for her to call him.

He'd just left the car back at Parkside when she replied. He let it ring three times before he picked up, wondering whether her actual voice would banish the thoughts of her that had drifted in and out of his mind for most of the day.

'Hi, this is Charlotte. Stone.' She added her last name when he didn't immediately reply. He imagined she was smiling.

'When can you talk?' he asked.

'Right now, if you like.' Wherever she was standing sounded empty. 'I can come to the station.'

'Where are you?'

'Clearing out the King Street house.'

'Really? Then I think I'll come to you.'

The house had been rented by Rob Stone and Tony Brett solely for the use of their children; someone had to sort it out now that it wasn't needed. He didn't know why he felt surprised that the task had fallen to Charlotte; there didn't seem to be anyone else.

It was a short walk up to Christ's Pieces where the footpath across the public gardens took him directly on to King Street.

He could spot the house as soon as he turned in to the street. A row of dustbin sacks and cardboard boxes were lined up against the front wall. The door opened before he had a chance to knock, to reveal Charlotte clutching another black sack in each rubber-gloved hand. She had pulled her curly hair into a loose pony-tail, and wore jeans, work boots and the tattiest looking T-shirt he could remember seeing since his grandmother had dragged him along to a student fashion show.

She dumped the bags alongside the others, before speaking. 'Go in, but it's a real mess.'

He went through to the kitchen. 'What's happening with the house?'

192

'Going back to the agents. It has to be in the same condition as when we took it on. They'll clean it for about three hundred quid but I said "no way".'

He'd seen worse but it was a long way short of being clean. 'Can I give you a hand?'

'Why?'

He didn't stop to consider what Bryn might advise him to reply. Goodhew just shrugged. 'I can stop for an hour, and I'm guessing you can't.'

Instead of replying, she turned away and began filling yet another dustbin sack, this time from the fridge. He pulled a couple of black bags from the roll, stuffed one in his pocket and turned to the nearest kitchen cupboard. 'Any food that's opened?'

'Only if it's obviously inedible.'

They barely spoke until the entire kitchen was clear, vacuumed and smelling of bleach and detergent. So much for an hour. One room, two hours.

They'd retreated as they'd cleaned, and finally made it as far as the door leading to the hall. She passed him a can of Coke.

'Thanks.'

She tugged the ring-pull on her own can. 'I already know Shanie and Meg's cases are being closed. Dad told me.'

'I promised him I'd speak to you and Matt.'

Charlotte seemed surprised. 'You promised my dad?'

He replied, but she'd stopped listening; her thoughts were much further away. When she began to speak, her words were measured. 'When my mum was diagnosed, I didn't understand how it hadn't been found until it had spread so far. I really believed my mum would recover. I couldn't untie the idea that we were good kids and didn't deserve to lose her with the fact that cancer's indiscriminate. All my energy was being eaten up with injustice and anger, but I know I need to let it go.' Without warning, tears welled in her eyes. 'It feels . . .' She struggled for the right word, and her voice wavered. 'Selfish?'

'How?'

'As if I'm choosing myself above loving my mum. As if I've got to pick my future over my mum.' When the first tear fell, the others followed. 'D'you see?'

Goodhew nodded, and handed her a couple of sheets he'd ripped from the roll of kitchen paper.

'I knew we were going to lose her, and I couldn't face it. I wanted her to hang on. I wanted her to be there for me. Even when she was in so much pain, I wanted her to stay. I was with her when she died. The last time she was conscious, she just stared at me and, as her eyes closed, it was me she was still looking at, as if she wanted to remember me as she left.

'When Rosie and Nathan both died, Matt and Libby were convinced there was a bigger picture, and I wanted to believe them. I didn't want to accept that life, fate, whatever, was really that unkind. I wanted to find someone to blame. I've made it worse, I've discussed the possibilities with them, I even asked for Rosie and Nathan's cases to be re-examined. Basically I remained stubbornly open-minded.'

'That's not wrong in any way.'

She shook her head, indignant through the tears. 'I think I've made a mistake. Libby and Matt can't move forward and I've encouraged that. Then, with these new deaths, they've gone backwards. For me it's had the opposite effect: it's easier to accept them as suicides when those involved are almost strangers.' Charlotte's gaze flickered skywards. 'If my mum's up there somewhere, I have to trust that I'm moving on with her blessing.' She wiped the tears from her face. 'Sorry.'

'You're fine.'

'I don't know where all that came from.' She sighed. 'Of course I know, I just wasn't expecting it quite then.' She studied him for a couple of seconds, but it felt much longer. 'Actually, you're easy to talk to.'

'If you do want to ask anything about any of the suicides . . .'

She smiled – sad, reflective. 'No, thank you. Maybe if you'd offered a while back . . .' She stopped mid-sentence. 'I think I'll do some clearing out at home after this. It feels healthy.'

'I'll need to go now.'

'I appreciate the help.'

He reached the front door just as a knock sounded from the other side. Charlotte wiped her eyes once more and nodded for him to open it. He hadn't expected anyone to turn up, but when he recognized Marcus Phillips on the doorstep, he realized just how unlikely Phil's arrival seemed.

'Why the hell are you here, Phil?' Charlotte demanded, which summed it up quite succinctly.

There was a step from the street into the house, and just standing higher than Phil might have been enough to make him seem forlorn. One undone shoelace, uncombed hair and panda rings of tiredness around his eyes added to the effect.

'Who else is here?'

'No one,' Goodhew replied.

'Okay. Doesn't matter.' Phil glanced down King Street in the direction of the town centre, and for a moment Goodhew thought he planned to walk away. 'I wanted to see Oslo most, but I should see everyone else, too. Matt won't answer my calls so I thought I'd come in person.'

Charlotte replied, 'If he has your number, I'll let him know.'

Phil nodded then turned to Goodhew. 'Look, I wasn't planning this, but as you're here can I talk to you?'

'I was just leaving, so walk with me.'

Goodhew had intended to follow the same route back to the police station, but at the last moment decided to stay on King Street and find somewhere quiet to talk. 'It'll be easier to speak if we go in somewhere.' They were outside the Champion of the Thames and Goodhew reached out to push open the door. Phil chose that moment to retie his shoelace. Goodhew sensed some hesitancy. 'Something wrong?'

'No, only if you don't mind, I'd prefer the Radegund.'

'Why?' The St Radegund dated back to the 1880s. It was a crimson, flat-roofed building filling a tiny gap approaching Four Lamps corner, where King Street met Jesus Lane at an acute angle, creating a wedge-shaped plot. As the smallest pub in Cambridge it didn't take many punters to make it impossible to find a quiet corner. The fact that it was triangular left it short on corners even when empty.

'It's appropriate,' Phil replied.

Goodhew didn't ask him any more. When they arrived, they found themselves alone apart from one old guy who sat furthest from the door. All the tables were dark-stained oak, several marked with plaques bearing names of deceased customers. This solitary man had picked the smallest table and laid it out with a pint in one corner, tobacco pouch in the other and the crossword page from *The Times* in the centre; so perhaps they wouldn't be disturbed after all.

'Drink?' Goodhew asked Phil.

'Shelford Cryer, just a half,' Phil replied, before disappearing towards stairs that led down to the gents' toilet.

Goodhew ordered himself half a Pegasus, then chose the table furthest away from the pensioner and his crossword.

The ceiling was marked with names signed in candle smoke, similar to the way that wartime servicemen had signed the ceiling of the Eagle inn, in town. This place though, gave the impression that everyone knew each other. There were boat-club notices, press clippings and a post covered with pinned-on handwritten notes full of scrawls and doodles.

'So, why here?' he asked as soon as Phil returned.

Phil took the seat opposite. 'After Meg died I thought I'd go home for a bit, to clear my head. It's been tough.'

Goodhew made a non-committal grunt.

'I changed while I hung out with Meg.'

Okay. 'In what way?'

'We didn't mean any harm, but I think we were a bit full-on at times.'

'With other people?'

'Yeah, and when I went home and reflected on it, I think we probably hurt some feelings.'

'Like Shanie's?'

'Maybe.' He shrugged. 'It was like the riots, when some people thought afterwards about what they'd done and realized they'd behaved out of character.'

'And this relates to your boast of having sex with her?'

He nodded. 'I realize I look like a bit of a shit.' He stared at Goodhew as if he was waiting for words of understanding.

'Yes, you do,' Goodhew replied. 'So what's your point?'

Phil shifted uneasily. 'I actually liked both of them.'

Goodhew didn't bother to comment, just waited for Phil to continue speaking.

'Do you know about the King Street Run?'

'The drinking race? Of course,' Goodhew replied.

'We joked about the housemates all entering. Meg said she'd do it if she could drink Sambuca shots instead of real ale. Shanie, Jamie, Matt, Oslo and me – we reckoned we could drink some and still stagger the distance. We decided we'd feel that we were missing out if we didn't enter, especially when we'd end up watching it going on right outside our own front door, so we all registered and the race is Thursday night. I think we should still do it. For Meg and Shanie.'

Phil seemed too drained to consider participating in any race, even a drinking one, but Goodhew's slight sympathy for Phil's dishevelled condition was more than outweighed by the suspicion that any sleeplessness could be put down to Phil worrying about Phil. 'Why did you feel I should know this?' Goodhew asked.

'I didn't. You obviously wanted me to talk to you, and not to Charlotte.'

Fair point.

'I imagine Matt's a bit pissed off with me,' Phil continued. 'I don't know if he'll even turn up if I don't speak to him first.'

'I see.'

'It would be a good thing to do.'

'For the sake of your conscience?'

'That, too. What's your problem with me?'

Goodhew considered the question. Selfish, inconsiderate, arrogant Phil was another one who reminded him of a young Kincaide.

But it wasn't right to hold that too much against him. 'You're a liar,' he replied.

'No, I'm not.'

'Yes. You. Are.'

Phil glared at him, his eyes fixed with a *go-on-then-prove-it* expression.

Goodhew told him, 'Shanie Faulkner had made a conscious decision to remain a virgin. How come the word *virgin* makes you wince when you can happily sit there swearing? It was a commitment she had made to herself, yet you think nothing of boasting to others about sleeping with her.'

Phil shrugged. 'A bit unsubtle, if you put it like that, but she didn't say no.'

'It never happened – and the fact that she was proud to wait makes your claims highly offensive.'

Phil tried to bluff it out with a smirk, until he saw Goodhew wasn't joking.

'She really was a virgin, Phil.'

'Says who?'

'Little thing called forensics.'

'What, she'd never done it? Ever?' Phil was clearly finding the concept of virginity a tricky one to grasp. 'And I thought she just wasn't into me.'

'And Meg? Was Meg your girlfriend?'

'No, but at the same time we wound each other up when we went with other people.'

'But your relationship *was* sexual?'

'Yes.'

'Purely sexual?'

'No, we went out together too.'

'But she wasn't your girlfriend?'

'That's right.'

Goodhew centred his empty glass on the beer mat and frowned. Now it was his turn to find a concept tricky to grasp.

FORTY

Gully had showered, and dressed as far as jeans and a bra. She'd bought three new tops in the sales, then a fourth at full price and wanted to decide which one to wear before choosing how to style her hair.

She laid them out on the bed, then picked a stone-coloured blouse, the front embroidered with two panels of small red flowers, one on each side of the buttons. She left the top two buttons open and the mandarin collar stood up against the back of her neck.

She sat down at her dressing-table and combed her damp hair so that it settled softly on her shoulders. She had make-up ready too; there was no particular purpose to any of this except to occasionally remind herself that she could be feminine, and wasn't actually a police officer 24/7.

Her mobile rang just as she'd started on the mascara. She leaned forward to read the display: *Gary*. It would ring for about ten seconds before diverting to voicemail and she spent most of those trying to guess what he'd want. Only one way to find out.

'Hi, Gary.'

'Are you busy? Could you come over?'

She waited for an explanation, there wasn't one. 'Why?' she asked sharply. She sounded abrupt but in the mirror she didn't look anything but a silly blushing girl.

'I need some help with something.'

'Where are you?'

'My flat. Get over here and come straight in.'

It wasn't like Gary to ask for help or invite anyone round to his flat. So much so that even Kincaide would have been there like a shot, and she was pretty sure Michael didn't have any kind of crush on Goodhew.

'Twenty minutes, okay?'

She stared at the phone after she'd ended the call, thinking he'd call back at any moment and cancel. When he didn't, she changed into a T-shirt and baggy jumper, pinned her hair up into a pony-tail and headed back towards the centre of Cambridge.

Goodhew lived alone, occupying the top flat in an end-terraced property facing onto Parker's Piece. It had once been a single house, three storeys plus attic and basement. The correct description was no doubt townhouse, but it always felt like a mansion to her with its high ceilings and the huge empty rooms she'd glimpsed on the few occasions she'd been inside.

She'd never asked Goodhew whether he owned or rented, why he lived there and why no one else did. She knew it was none of her business.

But that hadn't stopped her delving into public land registry records either. The discovery that Gary's house was inherited answered very little. Why he confined himself to the smallest and least accessible corner of the building for one. Her best guess was that he probably couldn't afford to heat the rest of the place. And she could imagine that he liked his privacy too much to sell up and move into a three-bed semi like any normal person might.

She hadn't tried to find out more, with hindsight she'd felt sorry that she'd discovered anything.

Pushing open a front door and walking right in felt like intruding, even though that was exactly what she'd been invited to do.

She closed the front door behind her. 'Hello? Gary?'

There was no reply. Perhaps she'd said it a little too quietly.

She knew the ground and first floors were unoccupied, and when she peered up between the spiral of ascending banisters, the top floor looked unlit. She didn't call out again, just walked up the stairs quickly and quietly. She expected him to be in his flat behind its closed front door; instead she found an open door at the bottom of the final flight. Goodhew stood with his back to her, and was writing something across a large section of the end wall, the emulsion already defaced with lines of small block lettering.

'Hi, Gary. I'm here.'

'I know.'

'You could've answered.'

'I thought I did.'

Okay, move on. 'What's up?'

'Hang on,' he murmured, and carried on writing. It was only as she moved closer that she realized all the notes on the wall were related to Shanie Faulkner's suicide.

'What are you doing, Gary?'

He didn't reply, just continued to add names and dates, lines and arrows. Some were taken from the notebook in his left hand, but most seemed to be from memory.

The chairs had been turned to face the wall where Goodhew was working, and the coffee table and floor were strewn with photocopies of case-notes and duplicates of photographs.

She crossed the room and stood close to the wall itself so she knew he could at least see her in his peripheral vision. She slapped her hand on the paintwork and repeated: 'What are you doing?'

'Hang on,' he snapped, and scribbled two final names on the wall, then turned to face her. 'Remember your deal? I give you the gossip on Marks . . .'

'And I update you on the King Street deaths?'

'Well, I've had a change of plan.' His eyes shone darkly, the pupils dilated until the green of the iris was barely visible.

'You look angry.'

'It's wrong – that's why. Marks is wrong. There are too many reasons not to write this off as suicide yet. Do you remember Elizabeth Martin?'

'Of course.'

'She doesn't buy the idea that there's any connection between Shanie's suicide and the first two.'

'You went to see her?'

He waved his hand dismissively. 'Of course. She thought Shanie's suicide would need to be related to a traumatic incident.'

'Gary, she's not working on the case. Elizabeth Martin could be world class, but she doesn't have all the information.'

'She didn't pretend to know the case in detail, but her opinion is still valid. I've checked with Shanie's course tutor and fellow students. What they're doing is cutting edge, and Shanie was immersed in it all. Several of them, including Shanie, were already working online together and planned to continue to do so.'

'Doesn't mean she didn't do it.'

'Why does everyone come back to that? I want to talk to her parents, but I can't go in unofficially when I've never met them before and the case is as good as closed.'

'No, you can't. And if a conversation with Elizabeth Martin is all you've got, you shouldn't even be thinking about it. Don't forget there was a note.'

'Sue . . .' He looked and sounded disappointed. She blushed then, surprised it had taken until now for it to happen.

'I'll admit I've allowed myself to become involved in the details surrounding Nathan and Rosie Brett, but I'm still thinking clearly, you know,' Goodhew said. 'Phil claimed to have slept with Shanie. Libby overheard him rowing with Meg.'

'Hearsay, then?'

'At the moment.'

'Marks will lose it if you start questioning these people.'

'I don't want to. Phil also had a sexual relationship with Meg – that adds up to a good reason to interview him in relation to both. And on top of all that, Shanie was meeting someone who stood her up.'

'And what are you expecting me to do, Gary?'

'It's too soon to write Shanie's death off as suicide.'

'So go and see Marks. Tell him that. Then stop looking for

something that's just not there. What makes you think that all four of them didn't individually decide they'd had enough?'

'Too much of a coincidence.'

'Fuck it, Gary, didn't you do the maths degree? Throw enough coins, and heads will come up ten times in a row. That's not coincidence, it's just a statistical fact.'

'No.'

'No? Just like that? Rosie dies, Nathan killed himself – why not Shanie and Meg too? Come on, Meg was textbook.'

'Textbook?'

She'd regretted it as soon as she said it. 'I don't mean she ticked all the boxes therefore that's okay.'

He stopped mid-anger and looked surprised. 'I know you don't think like that, and I'm not angry at you, Sue. I discovered that there was a connection between Shanie and Rosie. Then I remembered finding Rosie dead, and it came back to me in such detail that I didn't understand how I could have ever put it out of my head. Whenever I talk to Matt and Libby, I can't escape the feeling that there's something lurking.'

'Lurking's an odd word. People lurk, not things.'

'Something adrift then. Like a fracture in a picture.'

Gully understood that: the cracked mirror, the multiple perfect reflections with none of them quite lining up to the rest. Fine when you looked at the individual sections, flawed and distorted as a whole.

Just because no one else could see the cracks, didn't mean they weren't there. She turned towards the wall, stepping back behind the nearest chair so that she could view it in its entirety.

Gary had drawn a box representing the student house in the bottom third of the wall and above showed the Brett, Faulkner, Stone family groupings.

He'd even noted his own head injury, with the date, and put in lines connecting it to Rob Stone and Charlotte.

'Thought you'd brushed over that?'

'I'm adding everything, and I'm not dismissing a thing until I can stand where you are and look at the picture as a whole. Besides, it hurt.'

'Okay, here's the plan.' She said it in a tone that was meant to instil confidence and make him pay attention to what she was about to say next. Problem was, until she heard the words come out of her mouth, she hadn't been too sure what they were going to be.

'I'm going to tell Marks about Phil, Meg and Shanie. I believe he'll be seeing Shanie's parents again, so give me any questions you'd like asked and I'll put them to Marks as my own thoughts. Then I'm going to do my best to gather up any details that I have: legitimate access to help you fill your wall. I'm not copying documents and I'm not going after anything that you couldn't have got yourself if Marks hadn't banned you from the case files.'

He began to thank her, but she held up her hand to stop him.

'I know being told you can't look has never stopped you before, but in return please, please, drop this as soon as you come back, and get yourself assigned to something else.'

'Thank you.'

'Seriously now, don't you think this is all a bit obsessive?'

They both stared at the wall and neither spoke.

Gary broke the silence. 'Compulsive, maybe, but I don't think it works to leave too much unanswered. I don't actually want someone on my conscience because I failed to be thorough in the first place.'

'Nice theory, Gary, but you know we can't be expected to carry burdens like that.'

'Unanswered questions don't go away.'

'You could decide they're not worth asking.'

'Or why not just ask? For example, why have you only put mascara on one eye?'

It was the one question from Gary that she couldn't answer at that very second.

FORTY-ONE

Goodhew locked the front door behind Gully, muted the phones and drew the curtains in his grandfather's library. He had more to add to the wall. He switched on the table lamps, the standard lamp, and turned the dimmer switch on the overhead lights until every shadow was washed away.

He'd already reached the point where everything he knew about all the people connected to Shanie Faulkner was displayed on the wall. What came next was deciding which information was missing.

He stood up close, pen in hand, then backed up until he'd put the greatest possible distance between himself and the wall. It was still no good; even when he was too far away to read some of the smaller words, his focus remained on them rather than the blank patches of emulsion in between.

He turned his back, and caught the eye of the *Girl on the Punt* as she stared out from her frame on the adjacent wall. She spent her days in a state of near chaos; caught in a precarious and unbalanced moment that threatened to dunk her in the Cam. Still she looked at him in amusement.

Coffee might be worth a try.

He went upstairs to the kitchen in his flat to boil the kettle, and that was when he realized what his grandfather's library had always been missing: music.

He sent Bryn a text, finished making two coffees and made it down the flights of stairs to the front door just as Bryn pulled up to the kerb outside in his Zodiac.

It took twenty minutes to move Gary's jukebox from his sitting room to the floor below. Bryn paused for a moment to look at the busy wall and commented, 'Graffiti works better with an aerosol.'

'Thanks, but it's my first time.'

'So you really didn't write *Miss Muir is sexy* above the urinals at primary school?'

'I don't think anyone did.'

Bryn pulled a face. 'I quite liked that stern schoolteacher thing she had going.' Then he winked. 'I also like that concerned visitor thing your friend Charlotte had going on. Shame you missed it.'

'I didn't miss anything.'

'You'd have missed it if you'd been conscious at the time. And that's one more example of how we're wired so differently. I'd have assumed I'd made an impression, the moment she cared enough to call an ambulance . . .'

'You're delusional.'

'Yep, happily delusional,' Bryn grinned.

Goodhew ushered him back to the mugs of tepid coffee. Goodhew drank his quickly, Bryn didn't hurry. 'I know you're rushing me. Don't tell me – things to do?'

'Something like that. Sorry.' Goodhew accompanied Bryn as far as the library door, leaving him to find his own way out.

Bryn glanced over his shoulder, flashing one of his best pseudo-hurt expressions. 'You blatantly use me then fob me off with a bad coffee and a quick goodbye.'

'It's not you, it's me,' Gary quipped.

'Damn it, I'm starting to feel like one of my own girlfriends.'

A few seconds later, Goodhew heard the front door close behind his friend, then the throaty and unmistakable sound of the Zodiac firing up. Goodhew shut himself in the library. The lights were still as bright, but now chrome from the Bel-Ami glinted in the corner. He selected random play and full volume, and before the end of the first track the outside world had vanished.

This was entirely the point; he needed to break free of the constraints of what he was allowed to look into – forget the job, forget the official verdict, just allow himself to detach and explore every angle signposted from the wall full of notes.

He worked through the night like that, diving on to his computer, trawling newspaper archives, sending emails and texts. Making notes. Adding comments to the wall. Scrubbing out questions, adding lines and arrows and more questions until the first light of morning began to show through the hundreds of watts burning in the library. His concentration broke then. He killed the jukebox, pulled back the curtains and stared out at the greyest of Cambridge mornings.

'The weather's crap.'

He spun round and found his grandmother standing in the now open doorway.

He wanted to ask how long she'd been there, whether she'd seen him in the throes of concentration.

She narrowed her eyes. 'Insomnia?'

'No, that's when you want to sleep, but can't.'

'Case fever, then?'

'Case fever? Did you just make that up?'

'No, I just saw you demonstrate it. It looked kind of intense.'

Questions answered.

'Breakfast, Gary?' She held up a bag.

'I was about to go over to Parkside.'

'Another day, another desk to ransack?'

'Who told you I was working through the night?'

'You mean there's more than one of your friends who has had their sleep disturbed by you?'

Her evasiveness made him smile. 'You're a tricky person to deal with sometimes.' Suddenly, the smell of Danish pastries and coffee hit him.

His grandmother changed topic. 'Will Marks be in yet?'

'I doubt it.'

'Twenty minutes then?' She said it with the certainty of a woman who wasn't used to being turned down. 'You can show me your art wall.' She swivelled the nearest chair next to the one Gully had

207

occupied the night before. They both sat and she passed Goodhew a cappuccino and a cinnamon swirl.

After several minutes of silently studying the entire display, she pointed to a dotted line that connected Shanie's mum, Sarah, with Amanda Stone. 'When will you get that answer?'

'I searched the local papers in Merrillville and Indiana, without luck, then texted Gully and emailed Sarah Faulkner directly.'

'Was that a good idea?'

'In the middle of the night it seemed fine.'

Behind them, a message arriving clicked into his inbox. 'Maybe we're in luck.'

He crossed the room. His grandmother stayed seated but watched closely for his reaction as he opened the email. 'It's not about that,' he said slowly. 'It's from Sheen.'

'At this time of the morning?'

'He's like that,' Goodhew replied, choosing not to glance up to catch the pointed look that was undoubtedly being thrown in his direction at that moment. Instead he brought the laptop over to her, and reread the message at the same time as she was viewing it.

Towards the centre of the wall were written the original four names: *Rosie*, *Nathan*, *Shanie* and *Meg*. He'd drawn a different coloured ring around each of them, then used those four colours to indicate connections between them and other events and people.

Sheen would have been proud of him.

But Goodhew wasn't looking at just those four names now; his eyes were following a wider arc. The widest. His grandmother's gaze was travelling a similar path.

'Oh,' she said finally.

Oh, indeed.

If he drew an embracing circle now, it would extend around the whole wall.

Sheen was already at his desk; he had papers spread across every inch. 'I've made a pile for each case,' he said.

Goodhew couldn't see any visible sign that the mass of A4 sheets, notes and photographs was any less random than it looked. He spotted a photograph of the stitches inserted in his own scalp and reached towards it.

'Don't touch,' Sheen snapped.

'Sorry.'

'So you should be. I know you've been in here out of hours, Gary.'

This time he didn't apologize; that would have been too much like promising not to do it again.

'You can try putting everything back exactly where you found it, but I'll still know. Why didn't you just ask me?'

'You weren't here.'

'Whatever.'

'Honestly, it was the middle of the night.'

Sheen paused to shove a totally dubious look at Goodhew. 'I'm not a fan of slang. *Phat*'s suddenly yesterday, and this week it's *peng*. It's all a pain in the *tush*, but whoever decided that *whatever* said it all was a genius. Next time, *ask*.'

Goodhew nodded. 'I will.'

'Stand there fidgeting as much as you like, Gary, it'll save you time in the long run if you're properly organized.' Sheen sorted a few more pages with an unrealistically patient expression plastered across his face. 'Fire, aim, then ready in your time, not mine.' Sheen slid a raft of pages on to his lap, and shuffled them into a neater pile before replacing them on his desktop, then followed suit with each successive cluster of paperwork. He placed each pile on top, and at a 90-degree angle to the previous one. When he had finished, he rested his hand flat on the top of them all, and Goodhew silently prayed he wouldn't need to resort to a snatch-and-grab to finally get them from Sheen.

'Each bundle is a death, sorted alphabetically by surname. Do your best to return them.'

Goodhew grabbed the pile. 'Thank you,' he grinned.

Sheen remained serious. 'And preferably in the same order, Gary.'

* * *

The door to Marks's office was closed as Kincaide stood waiting outside already.

'Is he with someone?' Goodhew asked, arriving.

'On the phone.'

Goodhew leaned back against the corridor wall and silently ran through the list of names of all the people mentioned in the files filling his arms. He wanted to be fluent with the facts when he saw Marks. Within seconds he gave up though, feeling sure the names would come to him automatically. This just couldn't wait.

'Have you tried knocking?' he asked Kincaide.

'What do you think? I opened the door, he looked pissed off and waved me back out.'

'How long ago?'

'Fucking hell, Gary, you're going to need to wait till I've seen him first.'

'This is urgent.'

'Urgent filing? Come on.' Kincaide's gaze skewed off to somewhere over Goodhew's right shoulder. 'Hey, Gully, hasn't Goodhew done wonders with the filing?'

Gully stopped in front of Goodhew, a single Post-it note in her hand. 'Wow, Gary, do you run errands too? Can I send you out for Jaffa Cakes?'

'Depends.'

She stuck the Post-it note on to the top of the top file, too close to his face for him to see it in focus. 'Half right, half wrong.'

'How?'

'Sarah Faulkner's American born and bred.'

'But?'

'Dad in the military, spent almost five years in the UK – same school class as Amanda Stone.'

Gully gave him the tiniest wink, and he guessed Kincaide hovered, quietly simmering in the edge of her peripheral vision, just as he was in Goodhew's own.

Kincaide waited until she'd gone. 'You're not supposed to be working on the Faulkner case.'

'I know.'

'What's that then?'

'Filing for Marks.'

'On that case?'

'Yes – and some interesting details about people connected to it.' Goodhew finally turned to face Kincaide fully.

'Like who?' Kincaide's tone was casual. Artificially so.

Goodhew heard Marks finishing his call. He shrugged. 'I really think it would be better if I saw him first.'

Kincaide hesitated, about to speak, when Goodhew pushed open the office door then kicked it shut in his wake. He expected Kincaide might hurry in after him, but nothing interrupted the sound of the paperwork thumping down on the desk.

'Sit, Gary.'

Goodhew dropped into the nearest chair.

Marks nodded towards the paperwork. 'What is this?'

'Every case connected to Shanie Faulkner. I'm sure she was murdered.'

Marks stared hard at Goodhew for several seconds before he spoke. 'I had some reservations about her death. Everything seemed on the level, and I might have put my doubts down to my other . . .' he paused to choose the next word '. . . preoccupations, except I couldn't quite overlook your instinct to look further into it. In situations like that, you're like some persistent yapping puppy.'

Goodhew's gaze drifted on to the files, not sure if Marks had paused to let him speak.

But Marks spoke immediately. 'Congratulations, Rin Tin Tin, because your yapping made me push for further tests on both Shanie Faulkner and Meg DeLacy. Meg DeLacy remains a suicide. Faulkner, on the other hand, was killed with an overdose of insulin – administered intravenously. The case is to be reopened with immediate effect.' Marks stared at Goodhew expectantly; whatever reaction he'd expected from him he clearly wasn't seeing. 'What is in that pile, Gary?'

Goodhew reached for the first one. 'More. Lots more,' he replied quietly. He laid his right hand on the top of the pile. 'See how these papers are bundled together? All but one relate to a death, and all of them are connected.'

Marks started counting.

'Ten deaths.' Goodhew pre-empted him. He lifted the first two piles. 'These concern Shanie Faulkner and Meg DeLacy, both suspected suicides and both sharing a house with Libby Brett, whose brother and sister had both killed themselves.'

Marks looked as though he was about to point out that they already knew this, but Goodhew pressed on.

'What I didn't know, until this morning, is that Shanie's mother, Sarah Faulkner, was a schoolfriend of both Matt's mother, Amanda Stone, and Libby's father, Tony Brett.'

He moved on to the next two piles.

'I was attacked outside the Carlton Arms – as was Joey McCarthy, who was also at the same school with Sarah, Amanda and Tony Brett.'

'And three of the four lived locally,' Marks interjected, 'within the catchment area of their old school, so the fact that they all attended is hardly a coincidence.'

Goodhew nodded. He understood the point but didn't agree. More importantly, he was prepared for this response. Amanda Stone's notes came next, and he extracted a printout from her pile.

Marks frowned. 'I hope you're not going to suggest there was anything untoward about Amanda Stone's death?'

'No, just that her close friendship with Sarah Faulkner was the reason Shanie happened to lodge with the other students.' Goodhew passed the paper over to Marks. 'This is the list of pupils from a particular year,' he continued. 'Those four didn't just go to the same school; they were all there at the same time. After that, I pulled all records on suicides, accidents and suspicious deaths from then until now, and there are a couple of other instances where two siblings died.'

'Why did you look for that particular pattern?'

For the first time Goodhew hesitated, as he knew exactly what was coming next. 'I made a list and realized that was the case, then with Rosie and Nathan Brett, I—'

'You decided to fit the data to the situation?'

'No.' It was actually a *yes* but he drew breath and ploughed on. 'The first two were former pupils called Aiden and Becki Stacy.' Goodhew pointed at the list in front of Marks. 'They were the children of Len Stacy, same school year. The other pair, John and Vincent Wren, were still at school and were the younger brothers of Rob Stone's current employer and old schoolfriend, Colin Wren.'

This time Marks stared down at the list without being prompted to do so.

'I know I've only looked at them because of Rosie and Nathan, but it started me thinking that perhaps Shanie and Meg fitted as yet another pair.'

'It's a big jump in thinking. You're suggesting eight murders, when we only have grounds to investigate one at the moment.' Marks stared at the remaining sets of papers. 'So what happened with the other four?'

'Accidents – two drownings and two drug related.'

Marks was usually seated very upright, both straight backed and sharp eyed. This time though, he buried his face in his hands and pressed his eyes shut with the tips of his fingers. 'Oh, shit,' he whispered.

Goodhew wasn't about to hazard any interpretation of this comment, so he stayed still and silent.

After a long pause that seemed to run on for several minutes, Marks drew a weary breath and leaned back until he appeared to be looking at the wall behind Goodhew. 'Once in a while it would be a pleasant change for the easy option to be the right one. Never turns out that way, does it?'

'Sir?'

'I respect your perseverance, Gary. I would have preferred a clear suicide verdict on both girls, and you might easily have reached the same conclusion. The fact that you haven't has been the result of more determination on your part than I myself have shown these last few weeks.' His attention immediately reverted to the papers. 'So are you familiar with *all* these documents?'

'Roughly speaking, I know what they deal with, but I haven't had time to read them all fully.'

'Okay, I will need to pull everyone off other assignments and get them back on to this case. I'll brief them later this morning, so we'll aim for eleven o'clock. In the meantime . . .' His attention wandered away briefly, then returned. 'In the meantime that gives us about three hours, so you go and visit Colin Wren, and I'll take Len Stacy.'

FORTY-TWO

Goodhew located Colin Wren with a single phone call.

He drove to Chesterton, pulled into the car park of Ferry House and left the police car next to Colin's van. He spotted Colin almost at once, standing precisely in the same spot as the last time they'd spoken, facing the far end of the garden as if he was still watching Rob Stone walk away.

When he'd said *I'm working at the same place* Goodhew hadn't guessed it had been meant quite that literally.

Colin turned to him slowly, his expression quizzical.

'No Rob today?' Goodhew asked.

'No, not today. I've spoken to him on the phone, and he seems okay. Says he'll be back on Monday.'

'D'you think he'll really show?'

'Probably.' Wren shrugged. 'We'll see. I'd like to think it'll be because his conscience will get the better of him, but he's more likely to turn up because I don't pay him if he's not here. Actually, that's not entirely fair – he's much better than he was.'

'Really?'

'Give him time.' Colin Wren's expression changed, as though he'd only then realized that the reason for Goodhew's visit might not involve Rob Stone.

Goodhew knew this was his cue. 'I'm here on another matter, Mr Wren. The death of your brothers.'

Colin looked stunned. 'Johnnie and Vince?' Their names were uttered in little more than a whisper. He took a couple of steps backwards, towards the nearest bench. 'Can we sit?'

'Of course.'

'Has something happened?'

Goodhew shook his head. 'Did you realize that Shanie's mother was at school with you?'

Colin frowned. 'I know she was acquainted with Amanda, but I don't know how. Who is she, exactly?'

'Sarah Sumner?'

It took him a moment to register that name. 'The American girl?'

'Yes, and it's the connection with your old school that's made us look back at other cases.'

Colin nodded slowly. 'I see, but it was twenty-eight years ago. How can there be a connection?'

'We don't know that there is, but I'd like you to tell me what you remember.'

'Don't you have the case-notes, still?'

'Some, the rest are archived. I expect they'll be waiting for me when I get back.'

'Checking my memory then?' It was a jokey comment and Colin tried to add a smile but it touched his lips too briefly to count. 'Obviously I have photos of Johnnie and Vince, but they're in an album. I saw one of those pictures recently and I realized they looked slightly different to the way I remembered them. In between one time I see the photos and the next, I think I do forget a little bit more.'

Colin leaned forward and plucked a broad blade of grass growing up alongside the leg of the bench. He had one elbow on each knee and split the grass from end to end with the nail of his thumb. He let the two pieces fall to the ground before continuing to speak. 'Nineteenth of April 1984. It was a Thursday, I remember that clearly. They were a year apart from each other in age, and I was five years older. That made me the serious older brother and them the two irritating kids. I mean, that's how it seemed then.' His voice

wavered as he finished the sentence. 'I had this Walkman –
they were expensive then and I'd saved for it. John nicked it from
my room a couple of weeks before and I'd caught them both with
it. I was angry, of course, and next time it happened I ended up
scrapping on the floor with Vince. Our house was like that – we were
timid at school but rough at home. My mum went nuts.'

'Because you hit him?'

'Not with me, just with them. She could see how angry I was, I
reckon. I never thought they'd do it again, after that barney.' He
sighed. 'What a fucking nightmare.'

'Then what happened?'

'Thursday the next week, they went down to Jesus Green, and I
know they had some cans of cider with them. Probably smoking,
too, maybe joints. I didn't actually know where they'd gone, but
when they didn't come back home that night, I guessed they might
have been down there.'

'So you raised the alarm?'

'No, Mum did. I found out they'd taken my Walkman again and
I was angry. Said I wouldn't look for them. Said they had better
bring it back, or else. "I'll kill the bastards" is what I actually said.'
He clasped his hands behind his neck, eyes shut, head down until he
felt it safe to speak again. 'They'd gone into the water, and the police
found the bodies the next day. Still had their clothes on, so they
reckoned one had tried to rescue the other. The Walkman was in a
carrier bag also in the water. Bag was knotted. Heavy enough to
sink I guess, but airtight. It still worked. Fucking thing.'

FORTY-THREE

Len Stacy worked as a brickie and was currently employed on a new housing development out on Cambridge's northern expansion. The building company was quick to let DI Marks know where to find him, but actually locating plots 108 to 120 on an unmarked and unsurfaced street somewhere in a warren of what felt like hundreds of similar streets took far longer.

In the end, Marks found Stacy at about the same time as Goodhew was wrapping up his interview with Wren.

Stacy was around five foot eight and stocky, the kind of tree-trunk physique that managed to simultaneously look both robust and unhealthy. He was working on the exterior wall of one of the houses. His back was to the road, but he'd turned to look at the approaching car before Marks had even slowed. By the time Marks had parked, Stacy had already reached him. Some people possessed a sixth sense that alerted them to any policeman within a five-mile radius; the fact that Stacy and Marks already recognized each other helped too.

'Who d'you want?'

'You, actually.'

Stacy planted his feet so he faced Marks more squarely. His first response was to look angry – some things never changed. 'Go on,' he instructed.

Marks didn't hurry. He wasn't intending to antagonize the man, but he knew that giving in to Stacy's bad attitude would provoke him as much as a slap across his cholesterol-filled face. During Marks's younger days, rounding up Stacy had been a regular event, especially during football season; luckily that only lasted for about eleven months out of twelve. Stacy had a dull and predictable repertoire: pre-match disturbance, swearing on the terraces, post-match scuffle, pub scuffle, domestic scuffle.

Stereotyping wasn't great but Stacy *was* that stereotype, right down to the never-to-be-removed England shirt, fuzzy Union Flag tattoo on his left forearm and a swallow tattooed on his neck. He was fairly adept at the bully stereotype too, flaring up quickly, facing off loudly and, when threatened, backing down at the last, scraping out of trouble time and again.

He had incurred a couple of minor convictions that dated back to his twenties, nothing since.

'I'm part of a team investigating two sudden deaths in the Cambridge area.'

Stacy's expression darkened, and he turned his head away. He then pulled a packet of Golden Virginia from his pocket and busied himself with the ritual of Rizla, tobacco, filter, and finally lighting up.

'And you want to talk to me about my kids, right?'

'Aiden and Becki, yes.'

'I thought that was done with.' His expression hadn't changed but now his glare was directed at his cigarette rather than at Marks. 'No point going over it. I don't think about it any more.'

'We're looking into the possibility of a connection between Aiden and Becki's deaths and another case.'

'There won't be one.' His voice was heavy with disinterest but then his gaze suddenly pitched sideways and landed on Marks. 'Or is this your way of saying you lot screwed up the investigation?' He realized how much that answer now made sense to him. 'Years since I've seen you, right?' He didn't need to wait for a reply. 'What are you now – DI or above, right?'

'Just DI.'

'You're too fucking senior to be down here, unless you've been sent to sell me some special bullshit. What really happened to my kids, Marks?'

The workers across the road were still now, tools in hand, staring over at the commotion.

'What do *you* think happened to them, Mr Stacy?'

'I don't think it was an accident.'

'Then what?'

'They weren't heavy users – someone gave them something bad.'

'But you knew they were using?'

'I guessed. All teenagers do it. They would've known what they were doing though. They just mucked around, nothing serious.'

Marks had heard the *It was just marijuana/steroids/Ecstasy*, delete-as-applicable, shock response from a bereaved *parent/friend/relative*, also delete-as-applicable, too many times in the past. It had ceased to surprise him years ago, but he felt increasingly angry every time it was trotted out.

'They weren't stupid,' Stacy continued firmly.

'I also wanted to inform you that we will be running further tests on the blood samples taken at the time.'

Stacy ground out the butt of his cigarette between his discoloured thumb and index finger and dropped the rest. 'Should have guessed you lot didn't look into it very hard. Couple of no-hope kids, what do you care?'

'Actually I do, and if anything has been missed in the earlier investigation I'll do my utmost to find it. That means I will stay in contact with you.'

Stacy shook his head in disgust and turned back towards the half-built house. After three or four paces he hacked up a mouthful of phlegm and spat it over his left shoulder. He cocked his head towards Marks and then shouted to a colleague, 'Old Bill reckon they've cocked up.'

Marks walked towards his car.

When Stacy reached the other men he turned again, and as Marks closed his car door, delivered his final volley.

'I lost everything, when I lost them. My kids were my fucking world.'

Marks retaliated silently, *No, they weren't. But they should have been.*

FORTY-FOUR

At primary school they called him Nobby, as in 'copper nob'. And by fifteen it had been shortened to Nob. Or variations. *Oi, Nob* or *You fucking nob* were the two most common.

He'd dyed his hair now and his teeth were no longer overcrowded, nor tipping back like king penguins the moment before they topple.

He'd still looked like that in the last school photo. It had been one of those whole-school roll-out efforts, the ones that seemed like a good idea, that parents bought then didn't know what to do with. Mostly they seemed destined to stay in some drawer, probably held tight by their original elastic band until either the rubber perished or the photograph was dug out in response to one of those 'Do you remember so-and-so . . . ?'

For Nobby it had been neither scenario. He'd never even thought about the school photo since the day it was taken. His mum hadn't bought a copy and he hadn't cared. What interest was there in a photograph full of the victims and the bullies and worse still, those who stood silently on the sideline. Those with their sympathetic expressions and too little courage to harness the power of majority.

It had been an airless July afternoon when he'd first clapped his eyes on the wretched thing. An hour earlier and it would have only been a school photo. By the time he saw it, it had become the answer, the map and the future.

He'd helped himself to that same copy without asking, and now it stood on its end on the shelf next to the TV.

He liked watching television, but sometimes found it impossible to concentrate on any programme until he'd opened out the photo and studied it one more time.

He didn't think it counted as either a trophy or the start of one of those obsessional collections of the newspaper clippings or hacked-up photographs that other killers seemed to collect.

In reality he didn't know much about any of it. He certainly didn't consider himself a criminal. That word belonged to the kind of opportunistic conscience-free scum who undermined society. He was on the other side of the fence – right over the other side.

One day he'd be arrested, charged and put on trial. There would be condemnation until they'd heard his side. The jurors would be the adult equivalents of one section of the kids in the photograph.

Two rows staring out at him, blank faced because of the unfamiliarity of it – but fully alert nonetheless.

Their expressions wouldn't change but finally their eyes would light up as they recognized the truth.

He doubted that he would be faced with jail, although he'd understand it if the judge handed down a custodial term. The law needed to maintain the illusion that this wasn't an acceptable way for good people to behave. He'd see the look of apology in the judge's eye and accept his fate like a man.

He was well versed at imagining every scenario he expected to face. The courtroom scene was a favourite. He'd even been to visit the court; he sat in the public gallery watching a wretched defendant named Bryant deny that he'd ever seen a succession of stolen vehicles – even the ones smothered with his fingerprints, DNA and trademark touched-up paintwork.

£120,000 worth of BMWs.

Bryant's defence relied on: 'Must be a mistake . . .'

Nobby's own defence would centre on the more challenging assertion: 'I knew exactly what I was doing and I never got it wrong.' He would take them back to the beginning . . .

He barely noticed himself reach for the photograph, but once it was in his hands, his fingers traced over the curve of the roll and the sheen of the glossy coated paper.

This photograph would definitely be Exhibit Number 1. The police would probably label it differently, by using a numeric reference that, for them at least, held a wider significance. But he would explain to them that it had to be Exhibit 1 and refuse to refer to it by any other name.

The moment had come to look at it again so he placed the end approximately three inches to the left of his left elbow and unrolled it from there. He knew this was the perfect position so that the group he wanted to view would appear directly in front of him.

And there they were.

He could almost hear Mr McCracken calling out their names with his Glaswegian growl swamping every syllable. The boys by their surnames, Brett, McCarthy, Stacy, Stone, Viney and Wren. And full names for the girls: Mandy French and Sarah Sumner.

McCracken never spat out all those names in the same breath – that was his own, minor embellishment. In fact, they weren't all in the same class or even the same school year.

But by luck they *were* all in the same quarter of this big roll-out picture, and Nobby loved the way they all stared out at him, unaware of the invisible rings that circled some, the lines that joined the circles, and the way they were close enough for him to cover their faces with the tips of his fingers and make them disappear.

Just staring at the picture brought back that summer: the sawdust and the disinfectant mix that was swept along the corridors to remove the smell of sweat and the trodden-in food scraps and dirt on the stair carpet. The stewed smell that hung in the air outside the cafeteria even when the school was silent at the weekends. And the holes the kids had cut in the six-foot fence to get them out, or in, at will.

The deserted playground and the sound of the football being kicked rhythmically against the science-block wall until Mr Groves, the caretaker, bustled over to tell everyone to get lost.

All of those memories had been nothing until the first and

subsequent unrolling of that photograph. Clichéd as it sounded, the day it was taken now seemed like only yesterday, and he wished he could fall into that scene, knowing what had really happened, knowing what he knew now.

He liked to think he would have killed them all.

He might have regretted that, for who would have suffered then? Their parents, their loved ones, but not them. Or he might have done nothing, and regretted that more.

His thoughts switched, heading off on a tangent, but always arcing back to the familiar . . . when he'd owned a dog once. And about the same time discovered Stourbridge Common.

On reflection it had been a stupid and inconvenient idea. He wasn't a 'dog person', and he had neither the time nor the interest in the animal to sustain more than a few weeks of long walks and bagging up its mess.

His brief stint of dog-ownership had been about a woman. Her name was Connie, a skinny blonde with drainpipe jeans that failed to reach as high as her bony hips. She 'fostered' animals, and had turned her home into a small sanctuary for three dogs and four cats.

They had sex the night they met – not the cat and the dog but him and Connie. And it had been far more satisfying than the get-it-over-with shag he'd been after. He hadn't even had the expectation of enjoying sex again – he wasn't even sure he wanted to, at first – but Connie did.

Connie had a practical approach, thought of sex like a bag of chips or a burger on the last bus home. It was something you grabbed when you felt the urge; it didn't need to be your whole diet and not worth beating yourself up over either.

He merely offered her a lift home but stayed for the whole weekend. Her bedroom looked out on to Stourbridge Common, and when he woke in the morning he decided it had to be the most sinister place in the whole city. The other commons like Midsummer and Newnham seemed tranquil; elsewhere in Cambridge the river-edges were moored with prettily painted narrowboats and the open areas criss-crossed by pathways that promised picnics and festivals. All these were views to stroll through or photograph. Welcome destinations. Postcards home.

Stourbridge Common, by contrast, was none of those things. Yes, there were narrowboats, but only the kind with the flaking paint and mossed-up windows hid down here. Even those that were halfway smart looked as though they'd fallen into bad company, tethered there between the abandoned and floating scrap-heaps.

He wondered why Connie bothered to foster her animals when every one of her charges seemed to have feral relatives scavenging from the narrowboats. Even the vegetation seemed stunted and twisted, the pastureland bursting with fat clumps of weed that sprouted from the cow-shit-heavy grass. Cows avoided eating it and no one had thought to introduce sheep.

Most of Cambridge didn't unnerve him, day or night. But even in the daytime on Stourbridge Common he found it hard not to look over his shoulder.

Connie didn't get it. She always walked the dogs last thing at night. Thought they would protect her.

They had lain in bed one afternoon and he tried to make some conversation regarding the subject.

'What d'you know about the Common, then?'

'What . . . like its history?' She turned her head just enough for him to glimpse the look of distaste on her face. 'Don't know. We're not here for the view, are we?' She made coquettish eyes at him. If she'd been twenty years younger, maybe they would've worked, but some women's faces were too world-weary to pull it off after the age of twenty-five, and she was undoubtedly one of them.

She read too many cheap magazines too, and her brain was filled with the idea that all any man wanted was a woman with an insatiable appetite for sex. She saw no reason to keep her past discreetly hidden from him and made love like she'd taken tips from a second-rate porn movie; she groaned, panted and said 'yes, yes, yes' at every orgasm.

Or every faked orgasm.

His fascination with Stourbridge Common and his interest in shagging Connie seemed inversely proportional. She had been there at the right moment to allow him to catch his emotional breath. She'd never been a keeper, more like the temporary muse whose sole purpose was to inspire his next steps.

His waning interest in her was also inversely proportional to her interest in him; she was the classic woman who argued the benefits of no-strings sex then wouldn't let go. So they lay on the bed, her head on his chest and her hand on his thigh.

'I started reading up on the Common,' he told her.

'Me too.'

'Really?' He felt pleased, but irritated too as though she'd stepped on to his territory somehow. 'What did you find out?'

'It was once where they held the largest fair in Europe.'

'Yeah, everyone knows that.'

His response disappointed her and she fell silent for a moment or two. 'Okay, smartarse, tell me more.'

He stretched it out, giving her the history from 1199 to the early twentieth century, when it finally ended. He deliberately missed out two things; the one she wanted to hear and the one he'd decided to keep to himself.

'Did you read about those London Hackney Carriages?'

'No, I didn't,' he lied.

She sat up, a manoeuvre which involved sliding her body up his and straddling him. She didn't have attractive breasts. They were small, which was okay but they sagged too, and the combined effect reminded him of the ears on the pigs' heads that she bought as a treat for her dogs. The largest dog, an Alsatian cross named Myrtle, always tore them off and snapped her teeth as she tossed them around the garden.

'The Hackney Carriages would be hired by ladies and driven around the streets.' She made the annoying quote gesture with her fingers at the word *ladies*. 'One shilling and sixpence, it cost.'

'For her to hire the carriage or for the men to have sex?'

'I don't know.' Connie scowled. 'They were making a profit or they wouldn't have done it.'

'I guess so. So why do *you* do it?'

'Oi! I'm not a slag.'

'Come on, you'd have loved wearing all that finery and a queue of men to pull the petticoats over your head.'

'Have you ever done it with two women in the same night?'

'No. Have you – with two blokes, I mean?'

'No.' She went quiet, probably thinking about the opportunities missed. She'd slept with more men than he met in the course of a year. If they were ten days apart or ten minutes, what was the fucking difference?

It wasn't exactly the moment he decided to kill her, just the moment when he realized he wouldn't mind.

He remembered reining in his thoughts. This was the first time the two halves of his brain had recognized the other's process of thinking.

There had only been one death so far, one which his conscious mind had written off as an act of passion. It hadn't been a mistake though, just unplanned, and on the one or two moments when he remembered what he'd done, Nobby knew it had been something very, very risky.

But his subconscious brain was a totally different kind of thinker, remaining quiet until that very second, the moment when the last part of the plan locked into place and it could be trusted with the answer.

The answer which had blown in from Stourbridge Common.

She was still astride him, didn't seem to care that he'd been staring blindly at the window for the last few minutes. He wondered if she had any purpose in life except getting screwed by a succession of men and nursemaiding a succession of animals.

He pushed her off him and on to the bed.

'Don't get like that,' she sulked.

There was a small tub-chair in front of the window.

'I want you to kneel in front of that.'

'Why?' Again the flirty, overgrown child voice.

'You want me to tell you something to turn you on?'

'Uh-huh.' She gazed at him seductively. Shit, now he'd used the quote fingers. This whole situation was weak and sleazy and pathetic and he wanted out.

'You're going to feel how it was to be one of those Stourbridge Common ladies. Now get on your knees.'

And just like that she did. He slid into her from behind, pushing her face down on to the chair seat and thrusting hard.

He stared out of the window, determined not to listen to her fake moans, her cries of 'yes' and the pretence that she was too tired to carry on. The Common was all he cared about; the sinister distortion of Cambridge didn't intimidate him now. It had given his subconscious every answer. Even the new children's playground down there, with its Pied Piper sparkle in the heart of this throwback corner had fed him.

He came quickly, pulling out at the last moment and letting it shoot on to the small of her back and dribble back along the channel between the flat-faced cheeks of her arse.

He kept the side of her face pressed to the seat of the chair, pushing her jawbone so it would be easier for her not to speak. If she started pushing him to tell her why he never ejaculated inside her and chipping at him with a new set of questions about upbringing, relationships, and on, and on, he thought he might lose it. Right now he needed to be alone in his head.

Her own head moved a little under his fingers, and her one visible eye was straining back to look at him. He released his grip slightly. She was nodding vigorously.

'What?' he demanded.

'I will, I will,' she sobbed.

'Will what?'

'Be quiet and give you headspace.'

He let go entirely then and she sagged on to the carpet, head down staring at the floor. Silent now as promised.

He stopped noticing anything in the room; he only needed to look out at the Common to feel calmness. Then clarity. Then he allowed himself his second thought.

The women took the men in carriages because the fair had rules against bad behaviour. The fair was for commerce, and every trader had their set of rules. Ale had to be sold in specific quantities. Meat had to be of good quality and bread a certain weight.

These rules would be announced at the start of every fair in a proclamation called the Cry.

Okay, the history was interesting – up to a point – and he never would have found it but for the discovery of this woman and the Common she lived beside. But, in the end, it all distilled down to four words: one line proclaimed in the Cry that repeated itself constantly in Nobby's ear. '*Under pain of forfeiture.*'

The photo, those words, the names, the playground and even Myrtle the dog locked into place.

Under pain of forfeiture.

The baker loses his stock, the butcher his meat and the potter his wares. Punishment not only to fit the crime, but punishment that cuts to the very heart of what the poor man needs in order to survive.

After a while he pulled Connie back on to the bed. She had been crying quietly but didn't say much for a while.

He didn't begin telling any lies, but he apologized in any case, and she thawed out quickly after that – which made him smile. She smiled back at him, the stupid cow.

'Can I adopt Myrtle?'

Connie's face clouded. 'She's my favourite. And the oldest.'

'I like her.'

'You know about the vet's bills, right? You've been listening?'

He shot her a glance of mock warning.

'One of the others would be easier.'

'Myrtle,' he said firmly. 'Perhaps I'll change her name.'

'No!'

He had laughed. 'I'm joking. And I know she's an expensive dog to keep alive. You don't need to worry.'

Nobby now re-rolled the photograph. His mind was filled with thoughts that flared and flickered and darted through his head. Sometimes he really struggled to keep them in check.

Both Myrtle and Connie had been dead since late in the autumn of 2007 – September, he guessed, so why think of them now?

He pulled himself up short.

Only two more deaths and he'd be done.

Libby, Declan – then he could rest. To kill Libby right away didn't trouble him, but Declan wasn't due for another three years, and that made him uncomfortable. Nobby had only to turn his face towards the city centre to feel that change was in the air. And that meant time was running short. It was adjustments and compromises that had kept him ahead throughout. Forget the old plan then; their time had come now.

FORTY-FIVE

Libby's Facebook page popped up to show that she had one new message. She'd never been a huge Facebook user, not one of those collectors of a thousand or more 'friends', none of whom they actually knew. She had seventeen – classmates in the main. Jamie-Lee had defriended her yesterday: that was okay, she understood. Meg's page had been turned into a wall of condolence and was packed with messages like *Miss you babes* from a bunch of other students. Mostly strangers. It prompted Libby to defriend Meg.

She was still friends with Matt and Charlotte, of course, and assumed the new message would either be from one of them or else an invitation to a gig from someone else.

She saw Zoe's photo appear first, and had to force herself to stop staring at the image and actually click open the message.

Talk to me Libby, was all it said.

She released the mouse but kept staring at the screen, imagining for one moment that more words were about to appear. 'Oh shit,' she mumbled.

Unless it was a joke. Like a practical joke. Obviously not a funny one.

No, that didn't make sense. Who would know that she'd been sending messages to Zoe? Who else even knew who Zoe was?

Libby's heart began to thump, because any one of her friends could see her other friends. Charlotte would have seen Zoe at school, and if she'd seen the photo she would have recognized the tragic meningitis victim from the year above. In being clever, Libby had overlooked the obvious. She scanned her list of friends again; only Matt and Charlotte had been to the Manor School. Zoe's profile was closed; no one except Zoe's friends could see her friends and Zoe's friends totalled exactly one. On top of that, no one would know about the messages. Unless they'd logged on as Zoe.

'Oh shit,' she muttered again.

Libby's mobile was next to her keyboard. She could ring Matt and ask him whether . . . whether what? *Hi, Matt, I've set up a Facebook account in the name of a dead girl my sister knew. I did it so I could talk to her, because I don't feel able to bother you or my mum and dad. Why not? Because you're all too screwed up and I need to stop myself going mad.*

She rested her fingers on her phone in any case, wondering who else might have been able to access her laptop and Facebook account. With her laptop it was easy: her usernames and passwords all auto-filled. Even without her laptop it wouldn't be so hard. Her password for everything except her online banking was RosieB1.

She opened her bedroom door and called downstairs. 'Mum? Have you been on my laptop?' She waited for a reply. 'Mum? *Mum!*'

She went and found a note on the kitchen table. *Gone to Dr's.*

Libby turned her mobile over in her fingers. She was tempted to ring her mum and ask why she didn't even communicate when they were living under the same roof. She guessed she'd first be diverted to voicemail.

Her mum had swung from the over-anxious parent to the frequently detached one. Overall, Libby preferred to stand clear in case there was going to be a major swing back again.

She pulled a can of Pepsi from the fridge, opened it, then left it on the kitchen table untouched. She was already dialling Matt's mobile and had made it halfway up the stairs by the time he answered.

'Are you okay?' It was always the first thing he said.

'Yeah, fine. I just wondered whether you used my laptop when I was staying over at yours?'

'Might have, I suppose. Could've checked emails or something.'

'Oh.'

'Isn't it working?'

'No, no, it's fine.'

'What, then?'

'It's like someone's been into my Facebook page. D'you think Charlotte . . . ?' She let the sentence fade away as soon as she realized how stupid it sounded. 'I mean, if she'd wanted to access Facebook, I'm not saying she'd snoop into my account or anything.'

'Why would she even go on your laptop when she's got her own? What's going on, Libby?'

Behind her was her open bedroom door, and from beyond that she could hear the familiar plinking of an incoming chat message. Then another, and another.

'Are you messaging me, Matt?'

'No.'

'Someone's just sent me three or four.'

'Who?'

'Don't know. I'm not in my room, I can just hear the messages coming in.'

She moved quietly to the top of the stairs and across the landing. Plink. Plink. Plink.

She stopped at the doorway so Matt wouldn't hear that she was close enough to see her laptop. But even from there she recognized Zoe's profile picture. 'Look, Matt, I need to go.'

She crossed her room and was in front of the screen as another message appeared. Each was one character in length and the message feed filled the right-hand side of her profile page. She scrolled to the top, and down again.

H
E
L
L
O
L

She replied, *Hi.*

'Libby?'

Yes, who is this?

'Zoe.'

Okay, no point in asking that again. *What do you want?*

'Just to chat. I read the messages you sent me.'

And?

'I feel really sorry for you. I know how much it hurts.'

I can't keep talking to you when I don't know who you are.

'You were happy talking to Zoe, so why not to me?'

The replies stopped, then the silence in the room was broken only by the sound of her own breathing. It was heavy – almost panting – and when she looked at her fingers still poised over the keyboard, the tips were visibly shaking.

Zoe's status changed to *no longer online.*

In one of the gardens nearby, a lawnmower was running, and further away still, the sound of the main road hummed constantly. Inside this house nothing moved. The air stagnated around her and even Libby's college life seemed too distant to belong to her.

The dead house would have been disturbed by the ticking of a clock if the batteries hadn't packed up and been left to leak for at least a couple of years. When changing two AA batteries turned into an insurmountable task for any one of the three occupants, it seemed clear to Libby that they were well and truly fucked. With a capital F.

A clear but quiet click reached her from downstairs. Could've been the noisy thermostat on the freezer – it sounded similar, but Libby wasn't convinced. She moved close to her bedroom door.

'Hello?' Her voice sounded small and wispy, it always seemed to sound that way when no one was listening.

She hesitated in the doorway for several seconds more. She was alone – and she didn't need to search downstairs to prove it. That's what she told herself, in any case. 'Mum? Is that you?'

She peered over the banisters as far as she could into the sitting room and the kitchen. Both doors were only half open.

She entered the kitchen first; its back door led out into the garden. She checked and it was locked. She exhaled and almost laughed out loud. Weird Facebook chat was one thing, but it didn't turn into a real-world situation. Even so, she still paused to listen some more. And that's when she heard the slight but distinct squeak of a shoe on the floor.

Oh fuck.

Libby rushed towards the front door, but as she passed the sitting room she saw a shadow move and darken the wall. She grabbed at the latch, but her fingers were suddenly too weak and stupid to open it. Someone was behind her and she had to get out. She held the interior handle and rattled it, just as it gave way and opened towards her.

Matt pulled her out into the fresh air. 'Libby, Libby, speak to me.'

Those words again. 'Did *you* send me those messages?'

'Libby, forget Facebook. I just heard you shouting.'

'Someone's in there. I heard them.'

'Who?'

'I don't know. I heard a noise, then saw movement in the front room.'

Matt pushed the front door open and crept into the hallway. Libby followed. 'We should stay outside,' she urged.

'No.'

Matt walked into the sitting room, then straight back out again. 'There's no one there, Libs. What exactly did you see?'

She pointed to the far corner, 'A shadow over there.'

'Like a silhouette?'

'No, just a dark blur. I'd heard something and ran for the front door – I just caught a glimpse.'

'Then I arrived?'

She nodded.

'Could it've been my shadow from outside?'

'No.' She shook her head, but wasn't so sure now. 'I definitely heard someone move.'

He slid his arm round her and she rested her head on his shoulder. He led her through the kitchen and turned on the kettle, all the time holding her tight with one arm.

'Coffee, then?' he asked.

'Thought it was supposed to be sweet tea you needed for shock?'

'I don't drink tea.'

'I'm the one who needs it.' It was meant as a light-hearted comment but instead her voice sounded shaky still.

She pressed her face close to his chest and put her arms around his waist. Now was the right time to come clean about Zoe, but she didn't want him to let go of her, so she stayed quiet. Which meant keeping the chat messages to herself too. She couldn't remember exactly what they said now, just the words *speak to me* – the words Matt had just used. And she knew better than to suspect him of anything. That was fear playing tricks on her.

Even as she drank her coffee and her gaze fell on the back door, she said nothing. Hadn't she checked? Hadn't it been locked? She was sure it was a yes to both, but she tried and it opened – and doubt spoke loudly in her mind. So she didn't comment, simply gave the key a turn to lock it once more, keeping her added fears to herself.

FORTY-SIX

Libby considered logging on as Zoe and then changing her password. In the end she didn't do it.

She wouldn't send Zoe any more messages now, but she kept the dead girl's Facebook page open and checked the inbox repeatedly, even though the volume on her laptop was turned up to maximum, so it seemed impossible for her to miss any kind of audible alert.

Her two-way communication with Zoe might have been fictitious, but it had felt *real*. There now had to be another way.

In the end she slipped into Nathan's room, trying to be as briefly there as possible, because dead teenagers' bedrooms were dangerous, too full of the kind of junky mementoes that could only belong to someone busy with the act of living. She pulled an unused notepad from one of the drawers in the base of Nathan's bed, then retreated into her own bedroom.

If the pad had meant anything at all to her brother, at least some of the pages would have been used, but that didn't stop her running her hand gently across the plain navy front cover before opening it. She sat down on the bed and contemplated writing on the unmarked first page.

It wouldn't be the same as messaging Zoe but yes, she could see this would work.

I'm back home again. How d'you think that makes me feel? But then what choice do I have?

Mum's here; her face is a mess of bruises and all she goes on about is reasons to excuse Dad for what he did. Illogically, it's him I feel sorry for. I'm not stupid – I know you can't go round hitting people every time it gets too much, but I understand how he feels. You get to the point when you run out of words and then you want to act it out – you want to find a way of demonstrating how much it hurts. Demonstrating how impotent it feels to be standing here and watching people around you dying.

Oh shit. I'm hoping it's over with them now. I want them to get divorced and stay away from each other, and not use me any longer as a go-between – or a weapon. But you know how likely that is – not one bit.

For my sanity I would have to choose one or the other, or split my life in two and refuse to let the time I spend with my mum influence the time that I spend with my dad, and vice versa. Eventually I'd have to turn away from them both. It wouldn't be about choosing between them but about choosing self-preservation over being ripped in two.

I wanted to go back to the house in King Street, but that too is over now. There's no way our parents are going to rent another home and no way we could go back to this one. One death is bad enough, but two will start to feel like 'Shit, who's next?'

No.

And I can't stay round Matt's. What would I do? Sleep on their sofa or share a room with Charlotte?

Or end up sharing a bed with Matt, and ruining things forever.

FORTY-SEVEN

The pedestrian bridge that crossed from Chesterton Road to Jesus Green clattered with a steady stream of footsteps and the click-click-click of unridden bicycles being walked over its span. It was like that most hours of the day, though first thing in the morning and last thing at night, the lack of road noise made every creak of the bridge more pronounced. Declan Viney knew it well.

Now it was late afternoon as he sat in its shadow, fishing in the weir. It was a secluded spot, just him and the swans and an uninterrupted view across to the city. The sides of the bridge were a shoulder-high lattice of welded steel, and they reminded Declan of the kind of walkway he'd seen between platforms at old London stations. Its geometry rippled in the reflection in the water. Sometimes he would see the smudge of a face reflected too, but he never felt that anyone up there noticed him and that was just one reason that he chose to sit in this spot when he should have been in school.

Year 11. And for Declan that meant the last days of classes were finally within sight. From there he was supposed to sign up for some form of higher education. He hadn't told his mum yet, but that battle was definitely on the near horizon.

She would throw the college prospectus at him yet again and demand to know why he now considered himself above any of the courses.

Truth was, he didn't.

And he didn't hate school either, because he'd selected the subjects that played to his strengths: art, literature, design and sport. And when that prospectus had first arrived, he'd immediately circled half a dozen possible courses. All of them interested him, but none grabbed him sufficiently to result in a completed application form.

Maybe if his mum hadn't suggested a second interview with the careers' advisor . . .

No, nothing had been put in his head that wasn't already there, though the words *Think about what you really feel most passionate about* had been the trigger.

Over and above the choice between graphic design, sports therapy or any qualifications in media studies, the thing he wanted most was to get to know his father.

There were questions that only his dad could answer. Questions of identity. He needed to know whether he'd inherited his dad's personality along with his wiry curls, skinny frame and aptitude for art. And, if so, was it inevitable that Declan would find himself similarly adrift in twenty years' time? What, then, would be the purpose of another two years of education?

It had been about ten months since he'd last seen his father and, even by his dad's erratic pattern, the man was overdue for a visit home. Last time, he'd stayed for a whole month, claiming he had a gap between contracts. *Contracts?* Declan had never worked out whether that was a euphemism for being between sofas or actually between jobs. When his dad was home they talked a lot but Declan never forgot that their conversation drifted seamlessly between fantasy, reality and wishful thinking.

And his dad was another reason for choosing this spot. It hadn't been the last place Declan had seen him, but it was here where they'd last spent time together. His dad had fallen silent as he often did, but this time Declan spotted *the* look in his father's eyes. *Resignation? Defeat? Loss?* He'd never found the exact words to describe it, but he knew it invariably meant that his dad would soon be moving on.

Whenever Declan sat here alone, he found it easy to imagine that his dad was sitting quietly next to him. Or would slip into view between the trees and join him here again one day. Declan had no idea what drew his father back to this spot time and again. The urge to be here was one more thing he himself had inherited.

He sensed someone approaching along the riverbank and glanced up. It was a man about his dad's age.

Declan dropped his gaze back to the water, but from the corner of his eye could see the legs of the man's jeans as he stopped walking, then took a couple of hesitant steps forward.

'Caught anything yet?' The accent was local, and the man used the low tone people adopted when they wanted to show you they had no intention of disturbing the fish.

'Couple of perch – small ones . . . Nothing else.'

'Is this a good spot?'

'I like it.' Declan screwed up his nose. 'I've caught rudd and roach in here. My dad got a big pike once.'

'Did he?' There was an edge now to his voice.

Declan turned, studying him a little more carefully. 'Yes, he did. There are plenty of pike in here.' The stranger didn't look convinced, or perhaps there was some other reason for his obvious tension. Declan turned back to his rod, suddenly hoping he would move on.

'Tell me,' the man persisted. 'Why is this such a good spot?'

Declan decided to take the path of polite responses with no embellishment, no eye-contact and therefore no encouragement for any conversation longer than the minimum. He shrugged. 'Dunno really, just is.'

There were voices on the bridge above; they sounded like a couple of teenage girls, and he suddenly felt compelled to excuse himself, pretend he knew them, wave and chase after them. Before he thought it through he stood abruptly and called the first two names that entered his head. 'Lucy! Jess . . .' He grabbed his rod. 'I need to go.'

The man ignored his ploy. 'I think I know your dad.'

Declan hesitated.

'Ross Viney?' the man went on.

Declan nodded.

'Sorry, you caught me off-guard with the mention of pike. Took me a minute to place you.'

Declan studied the stranger's face again. Perhaps he did look a little familiar.

'You're the image of your dad.'

Declan forgot about the girls. 'You've seen him?'

'Not for years. We were at school together.'

'Oh.' Declan didn't know what else to say, but he sensed there would be something more. Maybe something that might help him understand his dad a little better? He turned back to the water and concentrated on delivering his most expert cast, aiming downstream of the rushing weir.

He smiled to himself, no longer uncomfortable with the presence of this man who said he knew his father. The two of them said nothing for a while; voices from the bridge faded and he welcomed the coming lull of early evening. He would need to return home soon, but right now Declan was in no hurry to leave.

This was the closest he'd felt to his dad since he'd been gone. 'What was he like at school?' he asked.

The man didn't reply at first and Declan was considering repeating the question. But that thought was overtaken by the realization that the man's response was not about to come in words.

If the shops on King Street had shutters, some of them would have been locked down for the duration of the Run. The word *notorious* had often been applied to the event, but *chaos* was more apt. A crowd of students, a dash from end to end of a short, narrow street while consuming seven pints of beer each wasn't the formula for a sedate night out.

Shanie had liked the St Radegund pub, and as the last stop on the Run, it seemed fitting to Phil that they should meet there prior to the run. He suggested 5 p.m. even though the race wouldn't start for at least two hours. He wanted to be able to phone or text any no-shows and still have time to persuade them to change their minds.

After the first half-hour of waiting alone, Phil had been relieved to see Oslo walk through the door. Amazingly, the others had all soon followed – Jamie first, then Matt and Libby together.

Libby was the only one who seemed reluctant, but he hoped she'd at least show interest in what he planned to say. She meanwhile had one elbow on the table and her head bowed over her mobile, poking at it with the fingers of her other hand. Texting probably. She didn't look up when he started to speak, but thankfully the others did.

'When our idea of competing in the Run first arose, I don't think it was anything more than a joke.' He paused, suddenly feeling uncomfortable and hoping he wasn't misrepresenting Meg or Shanie in anyone's eyes. But now wasn't the moment to cave in. 'Okay, I'll be honest: I was fond of Meg, and I didn't know just how much until the last few days. I did some things I'm not proud of, and I wanted to do something to say goodbye to her.'

Libby glanced up, but her eyes were back on her phone by the time she actually spoke. 'And getting pissed is a good way to say goodbye? They both overdosed and your best idea is to get drunk?'

Matt reached over and put his hand on the arm of her chair. 'Libby's not running, but you know I'm up for it.'

Phil jumped back in at the first opportunity. 'Libby's right, my first thought *was* how inappropriate it might seem, but listen: can we ever think about living on King Street without remembering the girls?'

Jamie and Oslo both shook their heads. Jamie spoke: 'We were all there when we joked about entering. I didn't plan to come back, but I can remember both Meg and Shanie talking about it. It feels right to me.'

Libby didn't comment either way.

'I've thought hard about this,' Phil continued, 'and there were seven of us in that house, and there are seven pints to drink in the Run. One pint for each pub even though there are only five pubs left. So I'm thinking that it doesn't matter if we finish, as long as we drink the first two – one for Shanie, one for Meg.'

FORTY-EIGHT

The briefing had begun closer to 11.30 than 11 a.m., and it had filled a full hour. Goodhew's usual restlessness had deserted him and, like everyone else in the room, his gaze kept returning to the nine photos – Joey McCarthy and the four pairs of victims, pinned up to one side of DI Marks. Marks himself pointed to the corresponding photo each time he mentioned one of the names, and by the end of the briefing, Goodhew had the names and dates and faces fully memorized.

Marks's final announcement was the news that Tony Brett was about to be released from custody. 'We have no reason to continue holding him so he has been granted bail, but subject to the condition that he stays well away from his wife. He will be living with relatives in the area and has been made aware that we are reviewing the cases of Rosie and Nathan Brett. Goodhew, I would like you to accompany him and *tactfully* gather any questions that he'd like to ask. Kincaide, same for you with Sarah Faulkner. She and her husband will be heading back to the States as soon as they can arrange a flight. I'd like you to reassure them that we will maintain full communication and that they can contact me directly at any point.' Kincaide and Goodhew both nodded. Marks turned to address everyone else in the room. 'I think it is safe to assume that none of you will be seeing home anytime soon.'

* * *

The irony of Goodhew being the same officer who had arrested Tony Brett and was now driving him home was lost on neither of the two men. Brett looked like he was wearing the same clothes he'd been wearing on his arrest, but now he had the appearance of a man who'd spent twenty-six hours flying long-haul and needed a night in his own bed and a shower before he'd begin to seem coherent. He recognized Goodhew and grunted something like, 'You again?'

Goodhew had been told to drop him off at an address several streets over from Brett's own home. 'Are you staying with relations?'

'Yep.' Brett leaned his head back on the headrest. 'Wife's sister and her husband,' he added wearily. 'I can stay in their spare bedroom and use the downstairs loo. The rest of the house is out of bounds.'

Goodhew had a stab at sounding positive. 'At least they're taking you in.'

Brett grunted again and they both stared at the road ahead without speaking for most of the next mile. Goodhew was about to raise the subject of Rosie and Nathan but Brett beat him to it.

'You know they're looking at my kids' deaths again?'

Goodhew nodded.

'Is it simply a review to make sure nothing was missed, or is there really a serious reason to think someone killed them?'

Goodhew didn't reply immediately as he wasn't comfortable with either answer and was struggling at first to find the diplomatic way to reply. But then he couldn't ignore the question either. 'Did DI Marks explain that there are a number of deaths under review?'

'Yes. He said they were linked because of a connection to the Manor School. He didn't say more than that though.'

Goodhew could see that made sense. Marks hadn't divulged anything to Brett that wasn't already in the public domain; as long as the families were kept ahead of media briefing, all the information remained contained.

He glanced over at Brett for any sign that he felt aggravated because details were obviously being withheld. Brett's head was still tilted back and his eyes were almost shut, but Goodhew had no doubt that he was awake. 'If you have any questions, I can relay them to DI Marks.'

'No, I don't.'

'Or any thoughts that might help us?'

'Nope.'

'I'll leave you my number, and maybe after you've rested . . .'

They drove past the Carlton Arms, and Brett managed to open his eyes wide enough to stare across at it for a few seconds. 'Actually, I do have a question. What do Meg DeLacy and Shanie Faulkner have in common that connects them with the Manor?'

The pub slipped out of sight and Goodhew swung left into Perse Way. 'Meg DeLacy wasn't connected, as far as we know, but Shanie's mum went there. Sarah, Sarah Sumner?'

Perhaps Brett grunted again, perhaps not. Goodhew had the impression he'd made some kind of noise, but when he glanced over to see, Brett was back in his earlier half-asleep mode.

'You knew her?' Goodhew asked.

'Huh? No, not really. Hung out with Matt's mum Amanda at school.'

Somewhere in that last sentence the subdued lilt to his voice had slipped away. If he still wanted Goodhew to think he was disinterested, he needed to stop drumming his fingers against his thigh. Eventually he noticed what they were doing and stilled them, but whatever was now bubbling in his head needed an outlet so he started talking instead. 'Of course, they must have kept in touch. I saw Mandy right up to the end, you know, but she never mentioned Sarah.'

'You were good friends?'

'Matt and Nathan had been in the same class all the way through school. They were best mates. Mandy and I ran into each other because of the kids. But were we friends?'

Goodhew waited for him to answer his own question, but instead Brett just repeated it again with a little more uncertainty in his tone.

'Mr Brett, is something on your mind?'

'No.'

'You seem to have become agitated.'

'I'm tired, not agitated.'

'Is it something about Amanda Stone and Sarah Faulkner?'

'Like what?'

'That's what I'm asking *you*.'

Goodhew had pulled up outside Brett's sister-in-law's house, and his passenger's hand was already on the door handle. 'Sarah left Cambridge years back,' he said. 'And Mandy's dead.'

Goodhew pushed a card into Brett's free hand. 'Phone if you think of anything else we should know.'

'Appreciate the lift.' Brett slammed the door behind him and didn't look back.

Tony Brett's sister-in-law, Sandra, opened the front door and stood there with folded arms. She scowled. 'I only agreed to this for Libby's sake.'

From then on, her mood deteriorated and Brett resolved to ignore it. 'Is Libby here yet?'

'She's running behind, but she's on her way.'

'Did she phone you?'

'Texted.'

Sandra uncrossed her arms and pulled a mobile from her back pocket; she tapped the screen a couple of times, then pushed it towards Brett. He pulled it from her hand and held it away from his face so he could read it. *See you in 40.* 'That was almost an hour ago.'

'So call her.' She took her phone away from him. 'On your own mobile, not mine. Vicky dropped it off, it's in your room.'

Tony Brett retreated to the eight by seven box room that was now his palace and sat on the edge of the narrow single bed. From there he tried Libby's mobile four times. Her home number too; it went to answerphone – his own answerphone – and he left himself a message, asking for an urgent return call. In between calls his thoughts swung back to Amanda.

Each time he failed to locate his daughter, his sense of panic rose a little higher. Maybe he was being paranoid. He wasn't stupid – or perhaps he was. The drowning of Len Stacy's children had sent shockwaves through the estate. He imagined the death of his own had done pretty much the same, but he hadn't made a connection. Why would he?

He checked the street outside his window. No sign of her.

He'd thrown Goodhew's card on to the bed, alongside his clear-plastic bag of *personal items*. He didn't want to call the police; he owed it to himself to deal with this. Just so long as he knew Libby was safe.

He thought about Mandy again. She'd had cancer, had known she was dying. He understood what she'd done – it had come to him just now in the car, like a vision. Her sallow skin. Her fading days. Now he knew what she'd meant when she'd whispered that she wanted to leave everything in order. He'd replied, *I know, I know*. But he hadn't known at all.

He'd said it, anything to offer comfort.

He didn't even question what she meant. If he had, he would have assumed she was talking about her will, instructions for the children, maybe concerning the funeral. He'd had no idea what issues someone facing death felt compelled to address. Until today. Until the terrible truth had made the remnants of his world self-incinerate before his eyes.

If he couldn't get hold of Libby, maybe phoning the police was already too late.

He checked out the numbers on Goodhew's card, both a landline and a mobile. Or 999?

Libby, Libby, Libby . . .

His hands were shaking now. One last try. He dialled Matt's home number and after three rings, Charlotte answered.

'Is Libby there?'

'She left earlier.'

'When?'

'This morning. She's coming back after the race.'

'What race?'

'The King Street Run.'

'She's supposed to be here. She was supposed to be here over an hour ago.'

Charlotte had already adopted the tone of a telephone support worker, polite and only pretending to understand his sense of urgency. 'I just said, they're doing the King Street Run.'

'Libby's not. She's coming here to meet me.'

'She's with Matt.'

'She was. Now she's not. She's not here. She's supposed to be here. I need to find her. It's urgent. Get hold of Matt. I have to find her.' He finished the call abruptly, pressing the *end* button when their conversation had done one circle too many. Nothing had changed, except his decision. There would be no phone call to the police. Goodhew was well intentioned, Marks was diligent and knew about the Cambridgeshire force as a whole. But there was one thing for sure: not one of them would deal with the situation the way it deserved. He set his mobile to vibrate and dropped it into his pocket.

He wanted Libby safe, and he would kill to achieve it.

And if she wasn't safe, he'd kill for that too.

Charlotte replaced the handset in its cradle then continued to stare at it for several more seconds. She didn't know what to do. Either as a neighbour or as her brother's best friend's dad she'd known Tony Brett her entire life. Okay, so that didn't give her the same insight as a close relative or colleague could claim, but it gave her enough perspective to know that the man she had just spoken to on the phone was behaving like a totally different person.

Clearly, something had happened. An event that had affected him more than a period of custody. More even than the deaths of his two other children. His fear for Libby was palpable and all-consuming.

She texted *phone me NOW* to both Matt's and Libby's mobiles. Libby of all people knew what she put her parents through when she went out of contact. She'd been due to meet her dad and must have been planning to return here too – why else would she have gone off without her laptop?

It was on the kitchen worktop, next to the kettle. By the time Charlotte had dragged one of the kitchen stools across the room, she'd written off any moral debate about interfering with it. That laptop might hold nothing more than contacts, social chit-chat, emails, downloads and receipts of purchases – in fact, the typical life of the average seventeen year old – but Charlotte couldn't think of any better place to start. The police were hardly going to scramble the Force helicopter for a teenager running a couple of hours late and ignoring a couple of texts.

The odds of accessing Libby's computer were high. Charlotte knew that there was no password set on the screen name, and Libby had often explained the advantages of agreeing to let the operating system auto-save the login details for every website. Fine until, like now, when the intruder had charge of the laptop.

Charlotte started with the hard disk, scanning all the directories, from the newest files backwards, searching for anything that might prove interesting. Several Word documents had been recently accessed, but they were all college essays and most were incomplete.

Charlotte moved on to photographs, selected thumbnail view and browsed them all, scooting down the pages as swiftly as possible. The pictures that whizzed by were mainly of Matt and Libby. With friends. With their other housemates. Out and about in Cambridge. At their house or Libby's. Matt with Nathan. Nathan and Rosie.

Too many dead people for someone Libby's age.

Charlotte's heart began to thump and she turned off the stream of images, closed her eyes and drew a couple of deep breaths. She couldn't afford to cry right now. She was still fighting this surge of emotion as she began trawling through Libby's mailbox and web-browsing history.

The emails were bland, mostly updates from ASOS and Dorothy Perkins on their latest in *unmissable offers*, Facebook notifications and eBay updates. The Web-browsing history was illuminating but ultimately fruitless. Libby had spent more time on news sites and search engines than anything else. Her search parameters always included phrases like *Cambridge student deaths*, *patterns of teenage suicide* and *signs of suicidal tendency*. The next most frequently visited site was Facebook, and although the home page came up immediately, the username and password did not auto-fill. Charlotte used Libby's email address and made a couple of attempts at guessing the password; she applied her own habit of middle name plus year of birth. No luck. Charlotte stared at the log-in screen for a few seconds longer, willing the same inspirational luck that blessed characters in film and TV.

Nothing.

Except that seeing Libby's Facebook page now felt like a priority.

Charlotte reached for her mobile and tried both Matt and Libby again.

Nothing.

She tried calling Libby's home number then the number Libby's dad had used when he'd called her. No reply on either. That was weird. Surely he'd be desperately awaiting news. Or if Libby had turned up, surely he or Libby would have answered? It was too much for Charlotte to deal with. It wasn't for her to second-guess the seriousness of the situation, or to hope she'd suddenly see something that would give the answers.

She found DC Goodhew's number and called him, instead. And in the time between her pressing 'call' and the moment he replied, she reopened Libby's emails and went into the folder marked *deleted messages*. At the top of the third page, the title of an email caught her eye: NEW MESSAGE FROM LIBBY BRETT.

From? How did that make sense?

She opened it just as Goodhew answered. 'No one knows where Libby is,' she explained to him rapidly. 'I can't get hold of Matt, or her mum or dad. It's not making sense, and I've just looked on her laptop and found something odd.'

'Where are you now?'

'At home.'

'I'll be there in a couple of minutes. Bring the computer and come straight out.' He hung up.

She grabbed nothing but her phone and Libby's laptop, and waited on her doorstep. This time there was no convenient distraction that would stop her heart from thumping. The fear she'd just heard in DC Goodhew's voice had sounded far greater than her own.

FORTY-NINE

When Goodhew received the call from Charlotte Stone, he was still nearby.

Half an hour earlier, he'd dropped off Tony Brett. The more direct route back to Parkside would have been to turn right round and go back the same way. Instead, he drove straight on, thinking about Brett and wondering why the mention of Sarah Sumner had hit him so hard. This route out of the Arbury estate was lengthier, but at the next junction he realized that he was close to Arbury Road and therefore the Manor School.

It was a dated building, a low-rise development on the King's Hedges side of the road. A few years back it had had a poor reputation, but its recent fortunes had seen a complete turnaround and, apart from the location, Goodhew doubted there were many similarities between this school and the one Brett, Stone and the others had attended. Even so, he pulled into the empty school car park in order to call Kincaide.

'Are you still with the Faulkners?'

'Just leaving.'

'Tony Brett seemed strangely shocked that Mrs Faulkner was the same person as the Sarah Sumner that he'd known at school. Something rattled him, possibly connected with Amanda Stone.'

'Did you actually ask him?'

'Yes, I actually did and he wasn't up for discussing it. Can you bring up Tony Brett and Amanda Stone with her and let me know whether Brett's reaction means anything to her? Ring me back as soon as you can.'

Kincaide didn't sound pleased but agreed.

Goodhew finished the call and stared across the car park to the dimly lit buildings. One of the side doors opened and a short man in a boilersuit raised his hand as he walked in Goodhew's direction. Goodhew stepped from the car and waited.

The grey-haired man looked about sixty. He wore Buddy Holly glasses and Doc Martens that looked as though they were polished regularly. 'No evening classes tonight, sir, they've been cancelled.'

Goodhew introduced himself. 'Do you work here?'

'Caretaker. Harry Groves.'

'I'm wondering whether there are any teachers here who would have been here in 1984.'

Harry Groves thought. 'Mr Durant, maths, and Mrs Lawrie, geography. And me, but obviously I don't teach.'

'Would you remember pupil names that far back?'

'Names like Johnnie and Vincent Wren?'

Hearing their names caught Goodhew off guard, Groves gave a small smile and continued without Goodhew saying anything. 'That's all that year became. The kids were traumatized, even the ones that didn't know those boys. It was the worst year we've ever had for children changing schools, also for kids fighting with each other.'

'I'm curious about some of the other pupils who were here at the same time.' Goodhew reeled off the names.

Groves nodded at each. 'Yes, can't get all the faces clear, but Stone and Wren were mates. The two girls hung out together too, sometimes on their own but often with the boys. You named three, there was a fourth. You know they were a particularly tricky bunch.'

'Tricky?'

'Let's just say I'm charitable. I know Joey McCarthy died but I'm not even sure I can put the right description with the right name. Have you got a minute or two?'

Not really. 'Fine.'

Harry Groves led him into the foyer and flicked on a panel of overhead lights. The walls displayed framed school photos going back about thirty years. Goodhew wondered how the younger students felt if they had to face a dodgy adolescent snapshot of one or both of their parents each time they sat outside the Head's office.

Groves found the 1984 photo and almost pressed his nose against the glass as he studied the tiny faces. 'There.' He had picked out Len Stacy. 'A thug. Not without his good moments, but liked to talk with his fists. I didn't have much of a problem with him; I knew where I stood and he was never smart enough to get away with much. That one . . .'

'Joey McCarthy.'

'Thought it might be. Nasty boy – and I rarely think that. Most have redeeming features, and maybe McCarthy changed, but I doubt it. Spiteful child. Selfish but charming too. It was the charm I hated. When he wanted something, he had no conscience. The other two were younger.' He moved his fingers, one in between Len and Joey and the other to a scrawny kid in the row in front. The in-between kid was Tony Brett, the one in front Goodhew was sure he'd never seen before. Groves tilted his head to one side, frowning until the missing answer found its way into the correct part of his brain. 'Tont Brett and Ross Viney!' He sounded triumphant. 'Younger than the other boys. Stone was hot tempered, but not that tough. I could understand why he hung around with the other two, I suppose. No doubt looked up to them in some way, but that kid . . .' Groves tapped the boy's face. It was hard to see detail, but it was obvious that Ross Viney had been small for his age and his complexion was the shade of pale pink that went along with freckles. 'Always so quiet, tagging along with the others like some sort of shadow. I don't think many people even noticed him.'

'Any idea what happened to him afterwards?'

'No. Once they've left it's only the spectacularly successful or the spectacularly criminal that we hear about. And sometimes when they die.' He shrugged. 'There's about four hundred and thirty kids in this school and I've been here for twenty-eight years now – you work it out. I'm shocked I remember as many as I do.'

Fair point. Goodhew thanked him and headed back to his car. Groves followed and Goodhew had opened his door before the caretaker spoke again.

'Course, Ross Viney's lad Declan is a pupil at the moment.'

Goodhew turned slowly. 'His son? How old is he?'

'Final year, so fifteen or sixteen.'

Goodhew nodded, shut himself inside the car, out of earshot of Groves, and contacted the control room. 'I need the address for a Declan Viney. Age fifteen or sixteen. Pupil at the Manor School, King's Hedges.'

'Hold on.'

'It's urgent.'

A pause. Background noise. Hesitation.

'I'm patching you through to DI Marks.'

'No! Just give me the address.'

But his call was already being redirected. Goodhew started the engine and spun the car round until its nose was poking out on to the Arbury Road. *Come on, come on.*

The line opened. 'Goodhew?'

'I need—'

Marks cut him short. 'Control just explained. Where did you hear the name Declan Viney?'

'We need to find him. He could be in danger.'

'He's dead.'

Two simple words but Goodhew couldn't digest them. 'He can't be.'

'Pulled out of the Cam an hour ago. Possible ID only in the last few minutes – and then *you* phone. I need you back here fast.' Goodhew flicked on the vehicle's lights and sirens, and accelerated towards the city centre.

'We need to find Libby Brett at once!' Goodhew shouted.

'We're looking for her already, Gary.'

'Okay, okay.' Goodhew didn't make it as far as the next junction before his mobile rang, and the fear in Charlotte Stone's voice was present from the very first word.

FIFTY

The record for completing the King Street Run stands at fourteen minutes and five seconds. Many, students in particular, suspect it's not so tough. But most of those don't make it beyond the third pub in that time and soon realize that the last pub, the St Radegund, may as well be in the next county.

The last of the daylight had gone as Matt leaned his back against the wall of their old student house and slid into a squatting position. It wasn't the quantity of beer but the combination of adrenaline and an empty stomach that left him feeling happier now that he was closer to street-level.

He wrapped his arms around his knees and waited for Oslo, Phil and Jamie. And, despite knowing she'd gone to meet her dad, he kept watching for Libby too.

For him, the last half an hour had changed everything.

Initially Matt hadn't really cared whether he made it beyond the second pub, and he didn't think the others did either. For once they'd united, and saying goodbye to Meg and Shanie was all that mattered. Libby had stood on the pavement – okay, so she wasn't racing, but she was there and it meant a lot to him.

He had walked across and given her a hug. 'Thank you.'

She'd shrugged. 'I'm glad I came. I understand now why this is a good thing.'

He'd hugged her again, tighter this time, relieved that she couldn't see the inane grin which had just appeared on his face.

'I texted Aunty Sandra so she knows I'm running late. But I'm only going to hang on until you have run the first two pubs.'

He'd nodded. 'I'll text you when I finish.'

'Finish or give up?'

'We'll see, but I'll carry on as far as I can. I think four pints is the max for me.'

Libby had tapped him on the arm then to remind him that Phil, Oslo and Jamie were standing next to them. She'd been a little self-conscious as she spoke to them all. 'I'll be gone by the time you finish, so I'd better say it now. I think Shanie and Meg would be pleased you've all done this.' With Oslo and Phil, the goodbye had been brief and still a little stiff, but as she'd held Jamie tightly, the affection between them was clear. Then she took a couple of steps back and watched as the starting whistle blew and the whole pack ran to pint number one.

When Matt emerged from the first pub, D'Arry's, Libby was on the same spot. She'd waved and he was able to pick her voice from the rest as she shouted encouragement. The second pub, the Bun Shop, was across the road and the crowd had moved with the bulk of the runners so she'd now been closer. Again she waved.

That was all the pubs and pints he'd needed to do, one for Shanie and one for Meg. Matt's knew how to drink too much, but usually lager, shots or a combination of the two. Pints of ale were a different game and just the second pint had left him feeling full. But the idea of the third pint being for his mum and the fourth for Nathan had casually entered his head and hadn't felt like leaving since.

At two of the pubs the runners had to drink two pints to make up the seven, since a couple had closed down. He'd decided that if he could do that at the Champion of the Thames, maybe he could accompany Libby to visit her dad, and then they could both go home.

He'd managed to rush pint three, and swallowed number four as quickly as possible. Suddenly the only person he could think about was Libby. He'd felt himself sway as he made for the door. It wasn't a stagger yet but it was headed that way. He wasn't in the right state to see Libby's dad at all.

He must have been slow getting through the pub doorway; some runners barged in, some barged out but he didn't think to move and instead drifted back and forth in the opening like a loose strand of door curtain.

He'd studied the spectators with care; he'd known he was drunk and that meant she could be right under his nose and he might not see her.

But no, she'd gone. He'd stepped from the doorway at last; for him the race was over. And the only thing left was realizing how much he hadn't wanted her to go. He scanned the crowd standing further down King Street, but she wasn't there either.

It felt like she'd just vanished.

He'd shivered apprehensively, but the feeling continued and it remained with him as he finally sank to the ground.

FIFTY-ONE

A silver Vauxhall Astra had almost reached the centre of Cambridge at the same time as the King Street Run began. Nobby was careful to stay one or two miles an hour beneath the speed limit. He watched the road but his mind was full. There were too many questions raising their little mole-like heads, popping up from the darkness too quickly to be dispatched by well-directed answers.

He knew Declan Viney's body had already been found, but had it been identified?

Connected with the other deaths?

Were the police looking for him yet?

Did he have the time to take Libby?

The questions began to pile up in his head. He couldn't afford the distraction, but then he realized that only the last question mattered. There had been times when reaching the end had seemed an impossible task, but then he reminded himself of how clearly he knew it to be right when he set out. Now he mustn't rush, since failure to get them all was failure. So he pressed on and, one by one, they'd all died.

But now that he was close to completion, his mood had changed. He buzzed with anticipation; the final weight would be lifting from his shoulders.

One more death.

Then arrest. But he wouldn't confess to murder and that would mean the full courtroom circus. The chance to tell his story. To be vindicated.

And to ensure that, he had tried to kill with compassion. There was no need for them to suffer much. People wouldn't understand if he did that.

Nobby coughed to clear his throat. He felt as though he hadn't spoken to another human being in an age. 'One, two, three.' He sounded a little croaky. 'One, two, three.' Better.

He reached the end of King Street, only to find that it was temporarily blocked off. Obvious really: the road was narrow on a normal day, so filling it with drunks would mean emptying it of cars. He hadn't considered that.

He parked the car as near as he could then typed a text before getting out. He didn't press 'send' until Libby was within sight. He watched her fish her mobile from her pocket and see that her mum had sent her a text. *I NEED TO GO TO HOSPITAL. I'M HERE BUT CAN'T FIND YOU. MEET ME AT THE CAR. I'VE PULLED UP ON DOUBLE YELLOWS AT THE START OF SHORT STREET. MUM X*

He'd examined her previous texts, and Libby's mum texted all in caps, with full sentences. She always signed off with an 'X'.

Looking at Libby hurrying off to find her family's car confirmed to him that she suspected absolutely nothing. Bless her.

FIFTY-TWO

Tony Brett ran for home – his home, not his sister-in-law's eight-by-seven charity box but the real thing. He needed to grab the car, work out where Libby was, and get her safe.

He reached his front door and banged on it, for the one thing that hadn't been returned to him on his release was the door key. When there was no reply, he bent down and shouted through the letter-box.

He looked up the street; he had no doubt that there were noses twitching behind some of those curtains. Neighbours he'd known for years. He didn't think he could turn to them now.

His own car was outside their house; Vicky's wasn't. It hadn't even occurred to him that she would be out. And his car keys would be hanging up in the kitchen.

He went to the side of the house, picked up a brick and smashed through the nearest window.

Fuck the restraining order.

It was the least of his problems.

He scrambled through, into the kitchen, and grabbed the bunch of keys from their hook. He was heading for the front door when he noticed the answerphone flashing. On the off-chance that Libby had left a message, he went over and pressed 'play'. A message from yesterday, from Matt: *Hi, Libby, it's me, de-da-de-da* . . .

Tony pressed '*stop*' and listened. He heard nothing, but pushed the door open to the sitting room. Then: 'Oh fuck, Vicky.'

She lay face down, a pool of blood around her head and a thick, immobile trail of it visible through her matted hair. 'Vicky, *Vicky*.'

He reached out and found she was still warm. He put his ear close to her mouth and heard the faint sound of her breathing. 'I'll get help. Stay with me, Vicky.'

He eased her into the recovery position, grabbed the house phone and hit 999, saying, 'Ambulance.' He gave the details of her injuries but stopped short of telling them who had done it. Whatever he said now, he'd probably still get the blame. Only Vicky could decide whether he deserved it.

This time there'd be no running from the responsibility. He knew it was his.

Her lips moved a fraction. 'Don't talk,' he told her. 'I know who did this. I need to find Libby.'

She opened her nearer eye a couple of millimetres, and mouthed what looked like a soundless '*Matt.*'

He tried again, but her eye reclosed and stayed that way.

He hurried from the house, leaving the front door wide open. 'Vicky needs help!' He shouted it twice, as loudly as he could, and prayed the neighbours really were as vigilant as he believed.

Tony Brett uttered a second prayer as he swung out into the main road and saw the ambulance headed towards him. Time was everything, for all of them, right now.

Had Vicky thought that Libby was still with Matt – was that all she meant? Or was there more? He could have misread the word on her silent lips.

He drove towards the city in any case, instincts pushing him towards Matt and King Street.

Several times, he glanced at his phone which sat beside him on the seat. Could the police really find Libby more easily? They might not even believe him, especially once they discovered he'd just driven away from the home of a seriously beaten woman.

He pulled over into a layby on Victoria Avenue, next to the dome-roofed public toilets. He was within sight of Four Lamps Corner and the end of King Street, but he could see the crowds there. It made more sense to ring Matt, one final shot at working out what Vicky had meant; after that he'd call the police despite his misgivings.

He opened his contacts list, sure that he still had Matt's number in there. He wasn't like Vicky with her lilac iPhone and consistent formatting of every name and number. He'd rung Matt and was waiting for it to connect. It was all he could do to sit still. Vicky's phone even had a photograph against each contact. He thought of her picture of Matt, a sunny day and the rarity of his smile.

It switched to voicemail. That didn't matter. Tony now knew where Matt's photo had been taken and knew why Vicky had tried so hard to whisper his name.

Tony swung the car round in a wide arc. He knew exactly where he was headed and the idea of calling the police was instantly gone.

FIFTY-THREE

Goodhew had spotted Charlotte the moment her house came within sight; she was standing next to her front door, bare armed, with a laptop clutched across her chest. She'd hurried to the kerbside as soon as she saw the blue light. Her first words were, 'Libby's missing.'

'We're already searching for her,' he'd told her, but doubted that did anything to ease her fears.

Now she sat in the seat next to him, laptop open, as they wove through the streets. 'I can't open her emails until I get on the Internet.'

'It'll be easy at the station. Just tell me what you've found.'

'Messages between Libby and a girl named Zoe. Doesn't matter about Zoe right now – she was a fake profile Libby set up on Facebook just so she had someone to talk to. There are pages of it, and that's all Libby was doing, talking – like you would to a therapist, I suppose.'

He asked again, 'What did you find?'

'That's just it – I don't know. Her dad phoned me, panicking because she hadn't turned up. I couldn't get hold of her or Matt. I didn't know what to do so I went on to her computer and found this. I started reading, but there's so much and I knew there wasn't time. It's too much for me, too impossible. I rang you because I didn't know what else to do.'

'Where's Matt?'

'In town. Phil wanted them all to join in the Run.'

'Phil told me that too, but said no one would speak to him.'

'Right.' She pulled a rueful face. 'Phil phoned our house and I answered. I actually thought it was a good idea. I talked them round.' She paused. 'Saying goodbye's important.'

Goodhew glanced away and concentrated on the road again, but he could clearly hear the distress rising in her voice.

'So Libby went too?'

'Yes, but only to meet them beforehand. She must have decided she'd show her support. But if she found out her dad was being released and she'd promised to be there, she wouldn't let him down.'

'How would she travel from King Street to home?'

'Bike – but, no, not today. She and Matt came into town together, and his bike's still at home.'

'Bus, then?'

She nodded.

'D'you think she'd accept a lift from anyone she didn't know?'

'Absolutely not. She's very careful that way.'

He considered that for a moment: being careful was such a dangerous game.

Safer to be a lone pedestrian at night, or take a lift with a friend who might be driving drunk? Safer to meet a stranger in public or secretly meet someone you think you know? Safer to keep it secret than feel embarrassed, in case the friendship is misconstrued? Sometimes it took luck as much as judgement. Especially with people you barely know.

More so when, like Shanie, you're thousands of miles from home.

The police station was in sight now, meaning little time for a major switch of topic. 'Shanie said she met someone for a drink but they never turned up. Any idea who it was?'

'No,' Charlotte shook her head, 'but Libby and Matt talked about it. Shanie said she'd wasted her money . . .'

'. . . because she'd bought a drink for the person already?'

267

'Yes, so they reckon it would have been someone she knew quite well . . .'

'. . . otherwise she wouldn't have known what type of drink to buy.'

'Exactly. Don't keep finishing my sentences.'

Goodhew didn't reply. He pulled up to the front of the station instead of driving into the car park. The image of Shanie buying an extra drink was floating in his head, and somewhere in the back of his mind was the other half of that picture, the anchor that would hold it all still long enough to tell him where to go.

Charlotte started to speak but he turned his head away. He stared at the lamp-post in the centre of Parker's Piece.

Reality Checkpoint was the name given to this lamp-post that stood on the spot where the paths crossed; its four curled arms pointed to every boundary to the city. The ancient buildings, the research, every possible subject, the edge of science. Past, present and future. A small city that touched the whole world. All the answers were here and he just wanted one, one snippet of Cambridge Trivia.

The Rain Check Tree.

He grabbed Charlotte's wrist. 'Take that in, ask for PC Sue Gully. Only her. Tell her I need her to read it all now.' He leaned across her and opened her door. 'I have to go.'

Goodhew floored the accelerator and cut through the lights on red; he then drove up East Road, riding the white line and trusting the siren to clear the way through the next three sets of lights too.

The next left took him on to Maids Causeway, and from there he'd have a straight run to the end of King Street and the St Radegund. The traffic was busy but moving freely, and he had no trouble weaving through the cars all the way to Four Lamps, the closest spot to the pub. He jumped out and dashed into the throng of competitors and spectators who were filling the pavements outside the pub doors.

Why hadn't he remembered the Rain Check Tree? Why hadn't he noticed it there when he'd gone in with Phil? 'Police, let me through.'

A few stepped aside, he repeated himself and pushed forward, through the doorway. And for a moment wondered whether he hadn't noticed it because it had gone.

'Move aside!' he shouted.

But he knew it would be there. Notes promising drinks had been pinned there for years. A round to say congratulations. A pint bought for a baby at birth, redeemable on their eighteenth birthday.

A sorry-I-missed-you drink.

Goodhew was only a couple of feet away from the bar when he saw the first of the white memo-block squares pinned to the upright beam. 'Police!' he yelled. 'I need to reach the bar.'

Someone chipped in with, 'Queue like everyone else.'

A couple of his mates laughed.

No one moved much, there just wasn't the space. Goodhew pushed through the final gap between the two nearest drinkers and started snatching at the squares of paper.

The landlord stopped serving. 'What do you need?'

'Anything recent.'

The landlord came over and grabbed a handful; Goodhew did the same. 'How recent?' the man asked.

'Last four weeks,' Goodhew told him.

'They don't always get pinned on top, so check them all.'

Goodhew nodded and pulled down the next clutch of notes. The man standing next to him did the same. Goodhew reached for the sheets. 'Here, let me.'

The man held them out of Goodhew's reach. Began shuffling them haphazardly. Protruding from under the man's thumb were the letters 'S-H-A'. 'Hand it over now!' Goodhew barked, snatching the message from the man's grasp.

She'd written across it diagonally in large block letters, *YOUR ROUND NEXT TIME!!* And at the top of the sheet, in much smaller writing, the man's name.

Goodhew held it tightly and turned for the door. Despite the crush of people, their noise and their pub-crawl-addled wits, he broke through in moments, bursting out to Four Lamps and his car.

Now he understood Tony Brett and what the conversation had meant. And he knew why Tony Brett had had no plans to share the identity of the killer of his own children.

Why would he, when Tony Brett thought he could reach the killer first?

FIFTY-FOUR

Matt was still sitting slumped on the pavement when he saw the pulse of police lights against the walls of the whitewashed houses at the Midsummer Common end of the street. He wasn't particularly curious. He couldn't imagine the King Street Run taking place without at least a minor emergency. Even so, he gave in to the basic urge not to miss out on anything, and clambered to his feet.

Then he spotted the man pushing through the drinkers and heading into the St Radegund: DC Goodhew.

Now it was Matt's turn to push forward.

There were two doors to the pub, and he chose the closer. He'd caught his first glimpse of inside just as Goodhew broke away from some activity at the bar and pelted towards the other exit.

Matt backed out of the door and chased after Goodhew, but the detective was both quicker and probably completely sober. By the time Matt arrived at the police car, Goodhew was already inside with the engine running. Matt threw himself in front of the bonnet, shouting, 'Stop, stop!' – until he realized that Goodhew was shouting into his radio and simultaneously reaching across to open the passenger door.

'Get in.' Then, to the radio, 'I've got Matt Stone.'

From the radio: 'We're running his van through ANPR, see if we can track it.'

They signed off and Goodhew turned to look at Matt properly

for the first time. His expression sobered Matt in a heartbeat. He had no idea exactly what he was about to hear, but knew it was going to alter the course of his life.

Not Libby . . . no, not Libby.

Goodhew already had the car in gear, handbrake off, foot over the accelerator. The moments before Goodhew spoke seemed to stretch for an eternity. Matt understood: he had to listen carefully, respond accurately. Goodhew was looking at him to make a difference.

'Matt, we need to find Colin Wren immediately. You've known him a long time. Where would he go?'

'His house – our house if he's with Dad.'

'Does he have a key?'

'Knows where to find it.'

Goodhew radioed that through. 'Where else?'

'I don't know.' Goodhew hadn't driven off yet, so Matt knew he wasn't giving the right answer. 'Oh, shit, yes, the allotment. Arbury Road.'

That was enough: they shot forward, accelerating towards Arbury.

Goodhew spoke to the radio: it spoke back. Some of it passed Matt by but he understood enough: helicopter scrambled, cars going to multiple locations, ambulance and police in attendance at 57 Brimley Close.

A jolt of shock went through him. 'What's happened to Libby?'

Goodhew's eyes were pinned on the road. 'We don't know.'

'But she's hurt?'

'We're trying to find her.'

No, no, Matt wasn't buying that. He needed to know. 'Don't hide it from me. They've just said there's a fucking ambulance at her house.'

'Her mother's been attacked. Her dad's missing. His car has gone from outside their house.'

'And you think Colin's behind it?'

'Yes.' Flat, matter-of-fact.

They were rounding Mitcham's Corner now. Matt had been round here a hundred times in Colin's van, helping him with planting. Helping his dad to help Colin. And helping his dad keep his job with Colin – that lifeline they'd all been thrown by his dad's best friend from school. He didn't want to believe it. The man had been like family, and all the time . . . 'He killed Nathan?' His voice hovered between doubt and disbelief. 'And Rosie? And Meg and Shanie?'

'Meg really was a suicide. Shanie was killed with insulin, there was none present for Meg.'

'Okay.' Matt didn't know why he said that. It was just his mouth running solo for a minute, while his brain tried to lock on to something else. He just didn't know what.

'Matt?' He swung the car into Milton Road. Goodhew's voice sounded urgent. 'Matt?' he repeated.

'What?'

'I said, "Does Libby's mum have her own car?"'

Matt scowled back. 'Yes. I thought you people had records of these things.'

'What's she got?'

'Astra. Silver. It's old.'

'Registration?'

'No idea.'

'How long's she had it?'

'Couple of months.'

'Shame she didn't put it in her name,' Goodhew muttered as he passed the sparse details into the control room. In the distant sky Matt saw the flying dot of the police helicopter. 'Insulin is a registered drug?' Matt didn't know whether Goodhew was asking Matt himself, or the radio. Just as he turned to look at Goodhew, the car swung across the road, through 180 degrees and accelerated back towards Mitcham's Corner.

'What?' Matt gasped, then shouted, 'Turn round, you're going the wrong way!'

'Which is Colin Wren's biggest contract?'

'Ferry House.' By far the biggest, hence the innumerable van journeys between home, allotment and Chesterton, passing through Mitcham's Corner.

'Is that the only place with their own greenhouses?'

'Yes, two greenhouses and a small workshop. It's part of the deal. Colin uses them like they're his own.'

'And you know your way around?'

Matt nodded. 'I've worked for him on Saturdays and school holidays before.'

'So it was Colin who encouraged you to study horticulture?'

'Yes. And because I love it.'

'Do the staff and residents trust him?'

'Absolutely.' Matt's tutor had banged home the importance of backing an answer with evidence. He scooted round his brain for the right anecdote and it hit him like a smack between the eyes. The very thought he'd been unable to grab just a few minutes earlier.

Reading labels, unscrewing jars, reaching on top of cupboards.

Some of the residents lived without the intrusion of nurses and carers, independent apart from the security of an on-site warden. Most of them trusted him enough to let him in their flats, to offer him a coffee and ask him to give them a hand with an occasional five-minute job here and there. Five-minute jobs like helping them count out their pills and check on how many days were left until they needed to renew their prescriptions. He could almost hear the barely disguised puzzlement in their voices: *Really? I thought I had more left than that.*

And Colin hadn't been keeping Matt's dad away from the residents for their own benefit; he'd done it for his own. How many misplaced insulin doses had been dealt with quietly rather than risk an accusation that the resident was showing signs of becoming unfit to cope alone?

He nodded. 'And Libby would probably trust him too.' Goodhew was back on the radio, telling them where he was now heading. Matt waited until he'd finished. 'How d'you know that's where he's going?'

They came off Chesterton Road, on to the roundabout at the junction of Elizabeth Way and off again at the turn for Chesterton High Street. They were getting close now. 'How do you know?' Matt repeated.

'I don't. All we can do is cover as many places as we can, as fast as we can. You shouldn't even be in the front of the car like this, but now you're here . . .'

'What does he want?'

Goodhew shot him a glance. It was enough to convince him that Matt could handle the truth. 'To kill Libby,' he replied.

Matt felt a double bolt of pain, heart and stomach twisting in unison. 'He'll never get away with it.'

'He doesn't need to. She's the last one.'

FIFTY-FIVE

Sue Gully was alone in the room with Charlotte Stone, and on the table between them was Libby's laptop. Charlotte could see nothing but the open lid and a partially obscured view of the young policewoman's face.

From Gully's side of the table the view was more interesting. Libby's dialogue with the fictitious Zoe ran on for several pages, but it wasn't exactly a novel and Gully's first question sprang up before she'd even started the first page. 'Have you read any of this?'

'Just the first page. When I realized what it was, I called DC Goodhew.'

'Why were you worried if you hadn't read it?'

'The girl, Zoe Kipfer, used to be at our school. She got ill and died several years ago, so I knew the messages were fake. My first thought was that someone was posing as her to trick Libby. That's why I panicked and rang him.'

'And you read enough to work out that Libby was essentially messaging herself?'

'That's right.'

'Why not read on?'

Charlotte's attention dropped on to the back of the PC; maybe she was trying to stare right through and catch up for lost time. After a few seconds her gaze jumped back to Gully. 'I'm not sure. I knew Libby was missing and I just stared at the words and none of them seemed to sink in.'

That made sense. Gully reckoned everyone had that threshold.

She went back to the laptop and started reading. Nothing sprang out at her the way she hoped; there was no 'don't-tell-Matt-but-I-always-meet-his-dad's-best-friend-in-the-gazebo' style confession.

Instead Gully was hearing Libby's anguish, her longing for the truth. The girl was baring her soul in these messages, and she turned out to be bolder and braver than Gully ever would have guessed. Libby had known the picture of Rosie's and Nathan's deaths had been wrong. Gully imagined her fear as she held on to that truth when no one official would take her seriously. It was uncomfortable reading. She wished Libby had reached out to her, asked her for help the same way as she was telling Zoe.

Could it have been different?

Gully scrolled down and her frown deepened. She glanced across at Charlotte then back to the screen.

She reread the paragraph, and inside her head her thoughts screeched to a standstill, making the kind of internal sound similar to when her grandmother used to drag the stylus off an old 45 before it had finished playing.

'Kincaide?' she blurted.

Charlotte looked startled. But guilty.

'Michael *fucking* Kincaide?' Gully didn't swear out loud. There was a time and a place, after all, but she was almost overwhelmed with the desire to blurt out every rarely used profanity that she'd ever heard. 'You and Kincaide?' she asked again, even though there was zero chance that she and Charlotte weren't on the same wavelength at that moment.

'I asked him for advice about Rosie and Nathan.'

'And he said what? "Let's discuss it after sex"? I don't think so.'

'Look, it wasn't like that. He seemed okay, approachable – that's why I thought he might be prepared to help. I explained I just wanted him to have one last dig, see if anything seemed wrong.'

'Cut the innuendo.'

'Actually I didn't mean it in that way. The whole thing was a

277

mistake and I don't know why you're so angry about it. At least I didn't know he was married – there's no way you don't know that.'

'Of course I know, why do you say that . . . ? God, you don't think *I've* ever had anything going on with *Kincaide*? Is that what he said?' At that moment his name became more repellent than an entire book of expletives. 'I'm not interested in *him*, and I'm not angry at *you*. But I'm livid that he abused his position. You were vulnerable, and he took advantage of that.'

'Right, but I really don't want it raked over any more. You drop him in it and that won't help anyone. It won't help his wife and it certainly won't help me.'

Gully shook her head in frustration. *Focus, Sue, just focus.* She didn't reply instantly, turning back to the screen.

She read a couple more paragraphs. 'And how long did it go on for?'

'A few weeks.'

'Then what?'

'I worked out what he was really like.'

Gully screwed up her nose. It must've been fun while it lasted. It wasn't even black humour material. *Gross.*

She started reading again, then stopped.

Charlotte looked at her expectantly, 'What?'

Right now it seemed the perfect time and place to unleash some profanities after all, and it took all of Sue's self-control to condense it down to, 'and Gary *flaming* Goodhew.'

Charlotte looked instantly shaken. 'No.'

'Libby didn't think so when she wrote this. I've seen the way they look at each other when they think no one else is paying attention. I doubt they were just talking when they were alone in King Street.'

'That's mad. Nothing happened. Shit, sorry. There was no way I was going to get him in trouble.' Charlotte blushed. 'I mean, I do like him.' Gully reddened more.

'Sometimes perspective is lost,' Gully began coldly, but then apologized. Now was the wrong time for any of this.

The door opened just then and DC Charles leaned in and

addressed Charlotte Stone. 'Your brother is with DC Goodhew, and DI Marks would like to speak to you.'

At that mention of Matt, or Gary, or maybe both names, Gully saw hope appear in Charlotte's eyes and disappear again when she finally realized it was DI Marks who wanted to see her. It wasn't Gully's place to judge her; people would do a great deal to protect their loved ones. She gave Charlotte a smile of encouragement. 'Don't worry, I'll come too.'

Gully closed the laptop and brought it with her. Charlotte could deny whatever she liked but Libby's messages were evidence, and Kincaide and Goodhew wouldn't be getting away nearly so lightly.

Bastards.

FIFTY-SIX

Tony Brett drove towards Chesterton with his mind clear. He kept moving rapidly, dodging through the traffic with just enough pushiness to provoke shouts and hoots from other drivers.

Behind him, Vicky's life hung in the balance and somewhere ahead was Libby, facing the ultimate punishment for something that wasn't her fault. And for reasons she wouldn't begin to understand.

The blame lay at his own door and he wasn't avoiding any part of it now. He understood that mistakes had to be paid for, the debt remained until then. But the lesson was twenty-eight years too late and now he'd been made to pay with interest on top.

He'd been down by the river, all those years ago, with Len, Joey, Ross, Mandy and Sarah. It had been pissing down with rain but Joey didn't mind, therefore none of them did.

They were huddled in a group on the Jesus Lock footbridge; the sides were a metal trellis, and they had spent most of the afternoon either blocking it or making snide comments at anyone who crossed. Rob didn't understand what teenagers thought it achieved. Superiority? Strength? Respect?

He didn't understand it even now, but he hadn't understood it then either.

Depending how you looked at it, Joey was in charge, but Len was the muscle – and it often seemed to Tony that it suited Len that way. None of that mattered now, apart from that day on the bridge.

Tony had spotted them first; he remembered liking the idea that he was about to get listened to for once. 'Look at that.' He pointed at the two figures walking up the avenue of trees on Jesus Green. 'Nobby Wren's kid brothers.'

They all hated Nobby Wren. He was one of those gangly kids with an Adam's apple that protruded so far that it looked like his neck had an extra bend in it. He grew plants, for God's sake. He was nervous, studious, and scored below halfway in the looks department too. An ideal candidate for bullying.

And, if they bullied Nobby Wren, there was no way that Johnnie and Vince were crossing that bridge without hassle. Things escalated; he didn't think Sarah and Amanda had even been listening when it all kicked off. Tony remembered them looking up when Len grabbed the carrier bag that Johnnie had been clutching with a bit too much enthusiasm. 'What's in here, Johnnie?'

'It's my brother's.'

'Your brother's what? Dildo? Blow-up doll?'

The two boys looked miserable. Tony had never been sure that they even understood the words but they recognized the mocking tone well enough. Johnnie hung his head. 'It's Colin's Walkman,' he mumbled.

Vince chipped in, 'We're taking it home before he finds out we had it.'

An expression that was both nasty and playful grew on Joey's face. He pretended to let them pass but then stopped them when they were just a few feet on to the bridge. He caught Len's eye and Len kicked off with a bit of rough-housing.

Mandy and Sarah had fallen silent, smiles drying on their rain-damp faces.

Ross Viney made one feeble attempt at protest. 'They're only small.' He got glares back and said nothing else. Tony knew Ross had still done more than he had himself.

And what Len was doing wouldn't have been so bad if Vince and Johnnie weren't so small; they were at least four years younger and this was a world apart from being pelted by chewing gum in a boring geography class.

Len grabbed the bag and held it through the trellis. It dangled about ten feet above the water and Johnnie started to snivel right there and then.

'Give it back,' Vince demanded.

'Or what?' Len replied.

Joey started to walk away. 'This is getting boring.' The girls and Tony had followed; Ross seemed more hesitant. 'Chuck it in,' Joey ordered.

'*No.*' The boys were in unison but Tony heard the bag hit the water from where he stood. Then little Johnnie's sobbing grew louder.

And the whole time it felt like Cambridge had abandoned them. No doubt it wouldn't have happened if it hadn't been for the rain emptying the streets all around, and that bloody Walkman that had meant so much to those boys that they'd gone in after it.

Their gang had fallen apart after that, but there'd been an unspoken understanding that they had to say nothing. And, to his knowledge, that silence had never been broken.

Of course he'd heard what had happened to Joey. They'd been more than acquaintances, but less than friends. Joey was cocky and pushy, and there were plenty of punters at the Carlton who'd have been happy to give him a good hiding. He'd heard about Len's kids, too but never thought it might be connected.

And since Rosie and Nathan had died he wasn't too sure that he'd thought anything through very much at all. At least not until today, when Goodhew revealed that the Sarah Sumner who'd sobbed in the rain years ago was the Sarah Faulkner whose daughter had just been murdered.

And, yes – he thought clearly now – Ferry House was around the next corner. Vicky had been almost unconscious with just the name 'Matt' on her lips, but he'd known what she'd meant. The only place they both knew which connected Matt to Colin.

Had Colin taunted Vicky, told her what he had planned for their last surviving child? Had Vicky stayed alive just long enough to be able to pass him that message?

He parked in a nearby street and slipped in through the side entrance of Ferry House. A few of the windows were still lit. He scouted the grounds, keeping to the grass to stay silent, and followed the line of a gravel track until he caught sight of the night sky reflected in the panes of the greenhouse. The ridge of the roof continued in darkness and he realized that only half its length was glasshouse; the rest extended into a workshop-style building.

The perfect place to wait.

He risked a couple of cautious steps across the noisy gravel towards the double door facing the house, and looked back over the grounds. No one switched on lights or cupped their hands to their windows to see better. He reached for the catch and was relieved when it simply unhooked. The door gave a low moan as he opened it but as soon as it was wide enough for him to sneak through, he slid inside and pulled it shut behind him.

The place looked smaller from the outside; he made out the shape of a ride-on mower to his right and another vehicle to his left. He stepped sideways and his foot clipped a long-handled tool of some kind that toppled to one side then clattered to the ground.

He needed to chance some light, just long enough to find a place to hide. He pulled his mobile from his pocket; it didn't have a built-in light but the screen lit up a little whenever he unlocked it. He pointed it towards the middle of the workshop. It hit the lawnmower. He swung it on to the other vehicle and froze. It was Vicky's Astra.

He lifted the phone higher and moved its weak beam slowly along the back wall. If Colin and Libby were already here there had to be a door to another room, or maybe through to the greenhouse. There were tools on the opposite wall too, less cumbersome than the long-handled forks and spades on this side. He needed to be armed and moved closer, shining the light in front of him, looking for a blade or cosh of some sort. That was the moment Colin chose to speak. 'You won't need a weapon.'

Tony spun to his left and could just make out Colin's silhouette framed in a doorway. Tony darted forward, knowing he'd always been fast. He really believed that his anger and strength would be enough to bring Colin to the floor. He burst through the open doorway, straight into the side edge of a spade swinging into his shins. He buckled, and it was immediately followed up with a kick in the ribcage, and the flat side of the same spade descending on his head.

He was on all fours as Colin flicked the light on. Tony raised his head and found himself staring straight at Libby. She was huddled to the wall, her skin glistening with sweat and her body racked with shivers. She stared back, but her eyes were unfocused and her expression said she'd already gone off somewhere else.

FIFTY-SEVEN

Libby had found her mum's car but there was no one in it. She'd looked around and noticed Colin Wren standing about ten feet away, as if he'd appeared from absolutely nowhere.

Looking back, it was obvious she should have run.

Then maybe she wouldn't be here right now. Wherever *here* was. Actually, in terms of geography she knew exactly where this was: the shed adjoining the greenhouse at Ferry House, Chesterton. She meant wherever in time, or more specifically where in her lifetime; she couldn't decide if she was still at the start of her adulthood, or within minutes of the end. And she was having trouble keeping herself propped up as she sat against this wall. It was cold for one thing, and the ground felt slightly on the tilt.

She tried to study Colin's face, to see if she could read what he was planning.

She'd been here a couple of times in the past, when Matt had helped out with the potting on a Saturday morning. She'd always thought Colin liked her, and even now she was finding it hard to accept that he actually wanted her dead.

She knew it was vital to stay awake, so that was when she began replaying everything that had happened since her arrival at her mum's car.

She'd been confused for a second. She had worked out that his presence was more than a coincidence, but couldn't actually understand why he stood there with her mum's lilac mobile in one hand and her car keys in the other.

'Is Mum okay?'

'Not really,' he'd said, and handed her Mum's phone. He'd unlocked the front passenger door and opened it while she unlocked the phone. The screen had filled with a photograph. She'd looked away even though she couldn't distinguish much in the picture. The phone had almost slipped from her hand so he'd taken it from her.

'Hop in' he'd said with the kind of easy assertiveness that she'd automatically obeyed. Why, she still didn't know.

She'd watched him walk to the driver's side then get in next to her. *Surely this wasn't the behaviour of a man who . . . ?*

She hadn't even finished that thought in the car, but she finished it now, *a man who had murdered her brother and sister.* She finished it now because she knew it was true.

Her heart started thumping even before he handed her the phone again. He leaned over to flick the screen slowly through the next three photos. She broke the contents of the photos into four: carpet, skin, hair and blood. She repeated the four words in her head, refusing to let the more obvious four take their place: *my mum is dying.* No, no, Libby, just say what you see, like that old TV show catchphrase – say what you see.

'Your poor mum,' he said. 'I think she's been through a lot.'

She held the phone, hoping there'd be a way to use it to call for help.

'I took the SIM out,' he said, as if he'd read her mind. He reached into the side of his door and waved her mobile in the air. 'And yours isn't switched on either.'

She didn't even know when in the last five minutes he'd taken that from her.

She'd reached for the door handle then.

'Don't do that. You have too much at stake. Whether she lives or not is down to me now. I did it to her to make sure you would behave.'

He drove quickly, and it wasn't until they'd arrived at the

roundabout joining Elizabeth Way and he'd gone straight across to Chesterton that she'd finally understood that she wasn't being taken to her mother.

The anxiety was hitting her so badly that she felt as if she was about to vomit. She found her voice. 'Did you message me on Facebook?'

He glanced at her without answering at first but she could tell by his expression that he was pleased to be getting the credit for it.

'How?' she demanded.

'From your own laptop, Libby. You know me, in and out of Rob's house just like one of the family. Charlotte and Matt don't think twice when I pop round to see their dad. Why would they?'

'So you just picked up my laptop and started using it.'

'Exactly.'

'Why are you doing this?'

'Because.'

'Because?'

He sighed. 'Let me show you something.' He slowed, then pulled over to the side of the road. 'In the glovebox is a small envelope. Pass it to me, please.'

She'd leaned forward to look. At first she couldn't see it but then she realized there was an envelope at the very back of the compartment. She reached further in, then recoiled in shock as she felt a syringe stab into her right buttock. 'What was that?'

'Insulin. An overdose.'

Twice she could have run, twice she didn't. He'd driven right through the gates of Ferry House and straight into the workshop; the doors were open in readiness. Maybe she could have tried it then too, before the insulin kicked in.

What was wrong with her?

But then she understood. Discovering the truth about Rosie and Nathan had been all-consuming; it was too much to drop it, even now. She was committed – she just needed to go with this, and hope to survive.

'How did you kill Rosie and Nathan?'

'Same way.'

'No. Rosie went to meet someone, but that wouldn't have been you.'

'Rosie liked the cinema, she liked the duty manager. Once you know someone's likes and dislikes, their habits and regular activities, how hard is a chance meeting? I'll tell you, it's easy. And when you've talked your way into someone's car, it's easier still. And Nathan? A couple of drinks inside him and all I needed to say was *I have something to tell you about Rosie.*'

Libby heard him repeat the line two or three times. She didn't try to run, instead she sat next to him and waited until he'd switched off the engine, helped her from the car and led her through the darkness to a small storage room beyond.

'Don't worry,' he said. 'I won't leave you on your own.'

She just stared at him. Did he really think he was doing her a favour? She knew she needed to walk around, keep moving, but instead she just sank to the floor – and right then she decided she was pathetic.

It was a few minutes after that when she heard the outer door opening. She tried to call out, but no sound came. Moments later, she heard Colin's voice. Then the sound of a couple of swift blows and the sight of her dad sprawled on the floor, struggling back on to his knees.

She should have run when she had the chance. She wished *he* had.

She made one last attempt to speak, but the words were slurring even before they left her mouth.

Oh God, she felt so cold.

She stared at her dad, and his lips moved too. He was telling her something. But she couldn't work it out. Then there was Colin again. He was bending over her father and listening.

It didn't matter now. She tipped on to her side and her eyes shut.

FIFTY-EIGHT

Wren's allotment and his house had both been checked, and the other police vehicles were headed in his direction. Goodhew had additionally requested a second ambulance then spent the last few minutes of the journey silently trying to tot up the amount of head-start Wren had on him.

'Did Libby drink any alcohol?' he asked Matt.

Matt had remained silent too. The adrenaline had now subsided, leaving him white faced and scared looking. He shook his head. 'Why?'

'Insulin acts faster along with alcohol. You'll find a bag on the floor.'

Matt grabbed it up and looked inside. 'Jaffa Cakes?'

'No, the Lucozade. We'll need to get sugar into her as quickly as possible. There's some rubbish down there too, so see if you can find any sugar sachets. Then tip them into it.'

Goodhew barely slowed through the gates of Ferry House, sweeping along the arc of gravel that led to the greenhouse.

'Stay in the car,' he ordered Matt, as he scrambled out. And when Matt ignored him: 'At least stay behind me, then.'

Goodhew had parked across the front of the double doors. As the two of them approached the workshop. Goodhew knew he should wait for back-up, knew he should send Matt back to the car, and in fact knew Matt shouldn't have been in the car in the first place. Goodhew also knew he was about to ignore all those things.

He banged on the greenhouse door with the heel of his hand. 'This is the police! Open this door.'

No response.

He banged again. 'This is the police! Stand back, I'm coming in.' He rattled at the door, and it gave way a little; he shone his torch through the opening and the light fell on Vicky Brett's silver Astra. He looked down to see the chain and padlock that prevented the greenhouse door swinging open any wider.

'I'll go through a window,' Matt volunteered.

Goodhew was already back at the boot of his car, and returned with bolt-cutters. The chain fell away easily and they stepped inside.

'Find a light switch,' Goodhew instructed. Meanwhile he flashed the beam around the room, stopping when he spotted the door. He reached the threshold as Matt found the lights. 'Through here!'

The door opened halfway down the long wall of a narrow storeroom. Tony Brett lay on the same side as the door, his daughter against the opposite wall, within touching distance if they'd been capable of it.

Goodhew tilted Libby's head to look into her half-closed eyes. 'Libby? Can you hear me?' Her pupils gently contracted. 'Libby, listen. Matt's going to give you something to drink. Try to swallow.'

He patted Matt on the arm as they swapped places, Matt nodding understanding at what he needed to do.

Goodhew knelt beside Tony Brett. He could hear sirens in the distance now and spoke into his radio, aiming to give them as much pre-arrival information as possible. 'No sign of Colin Wren. Two further casualties, one female age seventeen, probable insulin shock. Barely conscious.' He checked Brett's breathing; it was shallow. He felt for obstructions in his mouth. 'Second casualty, male, early-forties. Head injury. Shallow breathing.' Goodhew pulled off his T-shirt and applied pressure to a large gash in Brett's scalp. He glanced at the floor, trying to pick the bloodstains from the dirt. 'Heavy blood-loss, appears to be from the head injury. He is not conscious.' Then to Matt, 'How's she doing?'

Matt sounded scared but in control. 'She managed to swallow some.'

'Keep going.'

'She mouthed *Colin*, I told her you already knew.'

'Hang on.' Goodhew had his T-shirt pressed firmly to Brett's head, but he could still feel the blood beginning to seep through. 'He's stopped breathing now,' he shouted into his radio. He carefully rolled Brett on to his back and began mouth-to-mouth resuscitation. Less than a minute later the paramedics came swarming in – four of them, followed by Marks, Kincaide and PC Kelly Wilkes. It had been a long minute of waiting. He watched as the paramedics worked quickly to stabilize Brett, and Goodhew guessed it would be touch and go for some time yet.

He turned back to Libby. The other two paramedics were with her; they had already inserted a cannula and a drip was being connected. Matt held her other hand. 'I asked her about Colin,' he said. 'She told me he'd promised to stay until she died.'

Goodhew knelt next to Matt and managed to get his face into Libby's field of vision. He thought he saw a flicker of recognition from her. 'Why did Colin leave?' he asked.

She formed the words carefully, making sure he'd worked out one before she moved on to the next. 'Dad. Told. Him. Something.'

'What?'

'One. More. To. Kill.'

'Can you tell me anything else?'

'No.'

Marks was standing outside. 'Wilkes is going along with Matt and Libby to Addenbrookes,' he said, then he scowled. 'Get your shirt on, Gary.'

'It's probably in an evidence bag by now.'

'Michael, find him something to wear.'

Kincaide pulled a *why-me?* face then yanked off his jumper and threw it towards Goodhew.

'One of the residents spotted Colin Wren running off on foot.'

'In which direction?'

'Out of the main gate.'

'He can't get to Matt, Charlotte or Libby. He can't go home or to the Stone house without being arrested. Any other thoughts?'

Goodhew turned his back on the home's main entrance and took a few steps down towards the river. The air wasn't actually cold, but a slip of cooler air pressed against his back as he drew closer to the Cam. Colin's brothers had drowned on 19 April 1984 – and that was the answer to everything happening here. There had been six in their gang: Joey, Len, Tony, Ross, Mandy and Sarah. Only Mandy's children had escaped. *One more to kill.* Colin Wren had planned to stay and watch Libby die. He knew he'd been found out and only left when Tony Brett had convinced him he had to kill one more time.

The big question was, *who.*

Had Brett endangered someone random, and also innocent, in an attempt to save Libby? Right now that was an impossible question to answer.

But Brett had had just one shot to sell the idea to Wren. With only one chance, who would he choose?

Goodhew turned to Marks. 'I think he's going to kill Len Stacy.'

FIFTY-NINE

Marks redirected every car in the area towards Len Stacy's home address, then told Goodhew to take them both there. Goodhew listened to the radio chatter for a minute or so then asked, 'Has Ross Viney been told about Declan yet?'

'We found him. Lives in a sheltered accommodation in Slough. Unfortunately he has some long-standing psychiatric problems. He will need support before he's told about his son.'

'He needs to know.' Goodhew nodded to himself. 'He really needs to know.'

'What's on your mind, Gary?'

Goodhew was thankful when the radio cut in and prevented Marks pushing it further.

The helicopter's thermal-imaging camera had picked up a man approaching the gardens at the rear of Stacy's house.

The arrest had been made by the time they pulled up. Goodhew saw the footage later, showing how Wren had scrambled over the final fence straight into the grasp of three officers. It seemed simple at the end.

As he was cuffed and put in the back of one of the marked cars, Goodhew stood nearby, and just before the door shut, Wren looked up at him. 'I should have done him first.'

Goodhew watched the car pull away, lights flashing. The blue flashing left streaks on his retina and gave the impression that colour had been left behind, streaking the night sky. He didn't notice that Marks was now standing next to him.

'You were about to say something in the car.'

'I hate secrets.'

'Are you talking about Christmas and birthdays, or something else?'

Goodhew turned slowly; a choked feeling had gripped his throat. He didn't understand where the emotion had come from, and he didn't know if he could trust himself to speak either. 'People usually deal with the truth. How can they hold on to terrible lies without it eating away at them?'

Marks stared back. 'That's rhetorical, isn't it?'

'Probably.'

Marks nodded. 'I think you should sit in with me while I try to take a statement from Wren.'

'I reckon he'll talk easily. Any news from the hospital?'

'Nothing yet.'

Perhaps he was being over-imaginative, but Goodhew thought he recognized a particular expression that some killers wore straight after their first arrest. They often leaned forward, eyes alert, keen to gauge every expression from anyone looking at them. They knew what they'd done, but the difference now was that other people knew too. Observing this change in other people's demeanour was part of the transition to their new status in the world.

Colin Wren showed no hint of this. Nor was he deliberately staring away in a show of non-cooperation. Colin Wren was just Colin Wren.

Marks sat directly facing Wren, while Goodhew sat back a little and to Marks's left. 'Seven counts of murder.' Marks let the words sit for a second or two. 'I'd like to start with the deaths of your brothers.'

Wren gestured at Goodhew. 'He visited me, we talked about it then.'

Marks looked across at Goodhew. 'Detective?'

'You and your brothers lived alone with your mum.'

Wren nodded.

'How did she take their deaths?'

'How you'd think?'

'Devastated?'

'Of course.'

'Were you able to talk it through with her?'

The corners of Wren's mouth gave an involuntary downwards twitch. 'We tried.'

Goodhew studied Wren for a moment then pulled his chair closer. 'I don't think it's ever been your plan to hide what you've done, has it?'

Wren just looked at him in silence.

'You would be telling me everything if you felt you'd finished, wouldn't you? But in your eyes there's one more to go.'

Wren nodded slowly.

'Please, start with your mum.'

Wren thought for a moment, and when he began speaking, his words were measured. 'It was hard for her. She couldn't understand how it had happened. Why they'd even go in the water. But when the police found that bag containing the Walkman, I knew what had happened. I couldn't tell her though.'

Goodhew shook his head. The handles of the plastic bag had been twisted around Johnnie's fingers so he'd found it before he drowned. Goodhew wondered if Wren knew.

'I was sixteen. That lot bullied me at school. Those aren't excuses but sometimes I was harder on Vince and Johnnie than I should have been. I thought then that they'd been so scared of me, they'd risked their lives . . . *lost* their lives . . . just for a Walkman.'

'Is your mum still alive?' Goodhew asked even though he knew the answer.

Now Wren shook his head. 'Stayed at home all day with the curtains closed, eating, watching TV, and not much else until her heart packed up.' He pressed his lips together for a moment before adding, 'Yep, killed her too, I think. I kept my head down, working on people's gardens. I never considered a family of my own – didn't think I had the right.'

'Until Amanda Stone was diagnosed with terminal cancer?'

Wren glanced across at Marks. 'Doesn't miss much, does he?' Then back at Goodhew. 'Go on then, tell me how it was.'

'I can't put words in your mouth.'

'No one's going to do that.'

'Amanda is married to Rob, and Rob was your best friend from school. You've been part of her whole marriage, and the guilt has weighed on her throughout, so when she realizes she's going to die, she decides to tell you the truth. Just to clear her conscience.'

'Yes, putting her house in order they say, don't they? Her house always was, because she was a really loving, decent woman. She loved Rob and their kids. Going round theirs was like sending a hungry man to sit alone at the best table of the best restaurant, then only letting him watch the other diners eat.' He tapped his fingertips on the table-top, the first sign of agitation they'd witnessed. 'I wasn't in love with her, nothing like that, but I too could've had all of that if . . . if . . . if . . . if . . .' He sucked in a long hard breath. 'I'd like a drink of water, please.'

Afterwards, he put the empty plastic cup back on the desk. 'They'd all of them been there, hanging out in the rain on Jesus Lock Bridge, when Johnnie and Vince had come walking back from town. Joey picked on them just because he picked on me. He threw the bag in the water because it was mine. Amanda told me he shoved Johnnie in after it.' Wren paused, then made a fist and pressed it against his sealed lips. 'I could see there was more she wasn't telling me, but I think she looked at me and decided I couldn't take any more either. I killed Joey that same evening. I don't even think I planned it – something just snapped. And when I woke up the next morning, I realized that I was still suffering – but Joey wasn't.'

'And what better way to make someone suffer than leave them thinking their child has killed themselves? You gave them just what they'd put you through, all those doubts and feelings of responsibility.'

296

Wren tapped his finger on the desk. 'They weren't children when I killed them. Except Declan, but I was running out of time.'

'Fair game once they're eighteen?'

Wren looked off to one side, frowning at the same time as his eyes widened. For the first time he wasn't looking so comfortable with what he'd done. His gaze pivoted back to Goodhew and his head slowly followed. He stared, unblinking.

'What did Tony Brett tell you?' Goodhew asked.

Wren shook his head. 'You ask *him*.'

'I can't if he dies.'

'He's not dead – because you said seven. Joey and the kids – they make seven. You would have said eight, or nine with Connie.' Goodhew noticed Wren's speech pattern was changing.

'Connie?' Marks frowned, writing the name on his notepad.

'No last name. A woman I saw a few times; I met her on a dating website. Collected strays – like me I expect.' He didn't smile. 'She had insulin for her diabetic dog. I injected her and watched what happened. I needed to make sure I knew what I was doing.'

'Tell me what Tony Brett said.'

'No.' Colin Wren leaned forward. 'Sarah, Tony and Ross were all there. Hearsay from me will mean nothing in court. My brothers deserve this to be done properly.'

SIXTY

Tony Brett's bed was the only one in the hospital room. He lay with the head of it raised by several inches and with two bags attached to his drip. Goodhew and Marks moved two visitor chairs over to the same side of the bed.

Marks spoke first. 'We've just checked on Libby. She's stable, that's all we know.'

Tony Brett mouthed, 'Okay.'

Goodhew pulled his chair in closer. 'Mr Brett, you said something to Colin Wren that made him leave suddenly.'

'How do you know?'

'Libby told us. You wanted him away from Libby, because there would be no risk of him intervening to hurry things along, then. Right?'

Brett gave the smallest of nods.

'Sarah Sumner is mid-flight, Ross Viney is ill. Right now, I think you are the only one who can tell us what really happened to Johnnie and Vince.'

'We were only kids, old enough to know right from wrong. But still kids.' He told them the same story they'd already heard from Colin Wren; there were parts that tallied with the police report and plenty that didn't. 'Joey dropped the bag through the metal trellis on the side of the bridge. Johnnie and Vince ran to the bank. They were on the side where the hotels are facing the river, but there are bushes and trees between the road and the river, so no one could see them unless they were coming from the Jesus Green side. And no one was over there because of the rain. Joey and Len followed them down. Joey was wired by then, just full of it, and he pushed Johnnie into the river.

'We laughed at that.

'All of us.

'Johnnie could swim – no one thought he was too far from the bank to reach it – but he didn't just want to get back out: he wanted that bag. That bridge goes over the lock and the weir – it's a dangerous spot. Len and Joey wouldn't help; I was too scared – Ross was too. It was little Vinnie that couldn't stand it any more. He flung himself from the bank and splashed over towards Johnnie.

'The rain had got heavier, and even though Ross and I were just over the other side of the bridge, we couldn't hear everything. Mandy and Sarah were further back still, huddled by the trees. I remember them hanging on to each other.

'Seemed like Vinnie had been in the water for ages when he finally made it back to the bank. Johnnie still hadn't come back up. He looked at Joey and Len. They were standing beside each other, just staring at him. I couldn't hear what he said. They never reached out to help him and I could see Joey start to panic. Then suddenly Len knelt down and I thought he was about to help.'

Tony's speech had accelerated, but now he stopped and just stared across the room. He took a breath, then another. He closed his eyes then finally gave a sob. 'Len drowned him. He held him under and none of us moved. None of us talked about it again, ever. We just pretended we weren't there.' Tears ran from his eyes. 'Len drowned him, and we all kept quiet.'

SIXTY-ONE

Goodhew's grandmother reckoned a good night's sleep put things in perspective. For the first time in days, Goodhew felt rested – but no more. The case had saddened him in a way he'd never experienced.

He arrived at Parkside Pool before its official opening time and completed his regular one hundred lengths by 7.30 a.m. He then went to the station, straight up to the second floor, and plonked himself into the chair opposite Sheen, who was sitting at his desk.

'I hear that was a tough one?'

'It wasn't good.'

'Nice line in understatement, Gary,' Sheen said. 'Len Stacy's been charged, I hear.'

'Tony Brett's making a statement, so is Shanie's mother, Sarah Faulkner. Ross Viney can't, but you know what? He's spent most of his adult life receiving psychiatric care, and each time he's been released he comes back to Cambridge. He's drawn back to Jesus Lock Bridge, then bang! The whole cycle starts all over.'

Sheen nodded then held out his hand. 'And more importantly, I assume you've brought my files back.'

'No, actually they've gone into evidence.'

'The whole lot?'

'Yep, they were that good.' The comment was supposed to sound jokey but he just sounded worn. 'Mostly closing a case feels positive, there's a sense of progress, but this time . . . I don't know how I feel.'

'Empty?'

'Yes. It is that kind of feeling, almost like I've lost something. Is that normal?'

Sheen sat back in his chair and thought for a moment. 'There are two ideas I've never bought into,' he began. 'First off, there's that saying my mum always used: *Least said, soonest mended.* It's crap. Keeping things bottled up doesn't work. Whether they're big things or small, it's the unspoken ones that cause the damage. Second, this warning that you mustn't get emotionally involved. Nice idea, but sometimes you can't block out empathy for other people's pain, and you wouldn't be human if you did. So you feel crap about this case? Well, good for you.'

Despite himself, Goodhew smiled. 'I wasn't expecting anything quite so new age from you.'

'New age? It's common sense, son.'

Sheen's desk phone rang. He picked it up, then passed it to Goodhew. It was Marks. 'I want you and Kincaide in my office at eleven,' he snapped, then hung up.

Detective Constables Charles and Young had been sitting at desks in the incident room while Kincaide was spouting on about his plans for the weekend. Sounded like they even included his wife.

Goodhew was trying his best to concentrate, assuming that Marks wanted paperwork, and the best way to do it was just to do it. Obvious really, and actually less stressful than his previous habit of avoiding it for as long as possible.

Kincaide had been trying out yet another unimaginative and inevitable joke about Goodhew's topless ten minutes. Sometimes Goodhew just wished the guy would get himself a life.

Then Gully had come in with a stack of papers and dumped them on the nearest desk. She looked uncomfortable and tipped her head in the direction of the doorway.

He caught up with her on the landing. 'Sue?'

'Glad you got the hint. I need to talk to you.'

'Go on.'

'Not here.' She'd led him into the nearest empty office, and had started speaking as soon as she closed the door. 'Charlotte Stone.'

She let the name hang in the air, watching to see his reaction.

He thought he managed to remain expressionless. 'What about her?'

'You like her, I see it on your face.'

He nodded slowly then. 'Yes, actually I do. It's awkward with the trial coming up, but—'

Sue wasn't listening. 'When I went through the messages on Libby's laptop, I discovered that both you, and Kincaide, were involved with Charlotte Stone.'

Goodhew's stomach lurched. '*Kincaide?*'

'You didn't know?'

He shook his head. He opened his mouth to speak, then just shook his head again.

'Well, I feel doubly awkward now. I'm sorry, Gary, but I think it's fair to let you know I've reported you and him to DI Marks. I just handed over the files and he's going to take it from there.'

'I see. Didn't you feel you could talk to me first?'

She looked at her hands. 'I just felt really let down, because I had this crush on you.' She blushed a little, not her usual full-on redness but a hint of pink. 'It's over now, but I thought you wouldn't do that.'

'I wouldn't.'

'But you did.'

'No. Whatever Libby wrote, she misunderstood. I liked Charlotte, I still do – and too much really, considering. And it had crossed my mind that once the case was over . . .' He let the sentence drift away. The irony of him finding Charlotte attractive when she'd secretly been seeing Kincaide wasn't lost on him.

It wasn't lost on Gully either. 'You and Kincaide?'

'Don't.' He'd tried to make light of it, but it was too soon for that.

Neither of them spoke for several minutes, then Gully turned to go. 'I'm sorry, Gary, I've really messed up.'

'Handing that over to Marks is fair enough. I'm just sorry you thought I'd do anything like that.'

And now he sat here alone with Marks. Kincaide had gone in first, and the word *disciplinary* had made it out to the corridor more than once. Now Gary himself was in the hot seat.

Marks looked surprisingly placid, however. 'Nothing went on between you and Charlotte Stone, I assume?'

'No, sir.'

'She came in to see me, assured me it hadn't. She's asked me not to put Kincaide through any kind of disciplinary, either. If they both deny any wrongdoing, I'm scuppered. More to the point, she's had enough. She wants to be left to get on with her life, and I can respect that.'

Lucky Kincaide.

'I actually wanted you here so I could explain something to you.'

'Oh.' Goodhew wasn't sure why Marks would want to confide in him.

'I know you feel uneasy about having become overly involved in a case.'

'Sheen spoke to you?'

'I appreciate your concern about how distracted I've been lately. Several years ago, I too became over-involved in a case. I took it home with me, literally. I started behaving . . . well, like you, really. And I hadn't done that for years.

'I then made a mistake. A serious one. And, as a result, a man who should have received a life sentence was jailed for only ten years. He's now served just over half, and I've recently found out that he's soon going to be released.

'It preys on my mind. I am convinced he'll re-offend, and someone out there will become a victim because of it. Because of me.'

Now Marks's burden finally made sense.

'But there's another side to it,' Marks continued. 'My mistake probably saved someone's life. I can't separate them out and have one outcome without the other. When you run around breaking the rules, you risk getting more involved than you should. In those situations, when you make a mistake, you have to learn to live with it. Don't expect to stay unscathed, Gary. It's not going to happen.'

EPILOGUE

The funeral was today.

And the last time I'll write is also today. That makes sense to me.

I woke up this morning and expected rain, or at least a heavy sky, but the day was beautiful. And, after the constant rain of the last few weeks it felt as though the sunshine had come out just for us.

Mum hung on until the week before Christmas – 20 December, to be precise.

She never regained consciousness.

You could wonder at the point of her having those extra weeks when, despite treatment, prayers and goodwill, we still had to let her go.

But Dad and I did a great deal, so they weren't weeks of nothing. We visited her every day. I talked to her and read to her. Dad and I talked properly, too, openly and for hours.

When he first visited, he held her hand. Initially I think it was out of guilt and duty, but at the end I could tell it was because he wanted to, as though he finally thought enough of himself again that he could allow himself to find comfort in her touch.

'We went through a lot together, didn't we?' I was standing in the doorway to her room when he said that. I slipped back out into the corridor and left them for a while. When I returned he'd fallen asleep in the chair, tilted forward with his head on her bed.

I'm not a stupid romantic who thinks they could have patched things up. They were never a great couple – I reckon they were mismatched from the start. But when it came down to it, either of them would have died to save me – and that's a real bond.

We'd been home just about an hour on the nineteenth when they called us back. We played music quietly and talked off and on for those final five hours, and by 1 a.m. she'd gone. We'll never know whether she heard anything either of us said, but I choose to think she did.

Dad and I spent Christmas morning alone with the curtains drawn and the phone muted, but we knew we couldn't carry on like that. Dad looks back at all the other years, and his verdict is that healing doesn't just happen; you must let it happen, and even help it along sometimes.

Dad had already decided on a cremation. He said Mum hadn't cared either way. She'd always said she had no plans to go before she'd lost her marbles, so it didn't really matter anyway. So much for plans. On the grounds that she'd never expressed a preference, Dad made the choice.

The crematorium is north of Cambridge, on the A14, close enough to the road so you can see the traffic shooting past. I think Dad chose it simply because we'd pass both the spot where Nathan died and under the bridge from which Rosie fell. It's right we face these places now. And today we're saying a proper goodbye to them too. That's why there were three wreaths on Mum's coffin.

The crematorium is six miles outside Cambridge, so it meant we avoided the interlopers who think they can learn something about life by spying on someone else's misery. They wouldn't have destroyed it for me, in any case, as the defining moment of today occurred as we turned in at the gate.

The crematorium reminds me of an old schoolhouse; it is symmetrical, with a circular flowerbed in front and a little tower that could house the school bell just behind. It's plain and not imposing in any way. The approach is straight up a driveway cut through the apron of grass at the front. Bare trees lined the route, and the sky beyond was an untouched winter blue.

The hearse went in front, carrying Mum and our three wreaths, and we followed. I sat in the middle of the rear seat with Dad on one side and Matt on the other. At that moment I appreciated the balance, and I felt hope. I knew I was ready to say goodbye.

The service was short. I gave a reading. I wore that nail polish and my fingers trembled, so I put the notes down and did it from memory. I wasn't word perfect but I don't think it mattered either. Plenty of people were there for Mum, and I could see how much that moved Dad.

The police were there too. We appreciated that more than they could have known. DI Marks, PC Gully and DC Goodhew – the one who tried to save my sister. Their presence showed respect, and as Rosie said, it's the only thing of value you can give the dead.

I carried Mum's wreath to the memorial garden, Dad carried the other two. At the last moment Dad called Goodhew and asked him to take Rosie's wreath.

Right now we're back home. Everyone's gone except Matt.

When I came out of the coma Matt was there. When I came out of hospital he was there. We discussed how we felt about each other, and agreed that we shouldn't risk wrecking our friendship by dating. Then we kissed because the truth was, we'd gone beyond being only friends a while ago.

He and Dad are downstairs, and I've slipped upstairs to write this, to remind myself of the good things I feel today, in case I have days when I forget.

Requiescat in pace.

Enough tears now.

Goodhew had picked the St Radegund, and they'd been lucky enough to get a table before the main onslaught of customers. It seemed to Goodhew that whenever his grandmother and Bryn were in the same room, Goodhew himself was the wallflower. The other two talked cars, or played pool, but this evening they'd gone over to the bar and ended up shouting answers in an impromptu trivia quiz set by one of the regulars.

He didn't mind at all.

He was grateful for the company, but glad of the space. And maybe they'd worked that out.

Today was the first time he'd seen Charlotte Stone since the day after Wren's arrest. They'd both known they had feelings for each other, but maybe because they'd never been expressed, it made it easier for them to say goodbye.

It's because of Kincaide, isn't it? she had asked.

It wasn't just that, but that alone made it impossible. Goodhew had nodded apologetically. Maybe it wouldn't have bothered some people, but there was no point in pretending he was someone he wasn't.

He was glad he had attended the funeral. Marks had decided it would be appropriate, and had invited him and Gully along. They still had the court case to face, and they'd be seeing most of the key mourners again in court. There would be two trials: one for Len Stacy and the other for Colin Wren, if he proved fit to stand.

Goodhew had noticed Colin Wren's agitation bubbling through, but mostly he'd been calm and forthcoming in making his confession – until it came time to give details of the death of Declan Viney. The psychiatrist said it could have been the trauma of killing him in the same spot where his brothers died. Goodhew himself was convinced that it was because Colin Wren had broken one of his own rules by killing a child.

Of all the victims it was Rosie he thought about most often. In his dreams he saw Colin guiding her to the parapet and Rosie too drugged to resist. Time and again he watched helplessly as she toppled into the traffic. Still crawled under the lorry to reach her, but when he spoke to her she spoke to him. And when he woke later, he still felt bereft. He missed his grandfather now more than at any time since his death all those years ago.

'Vera Lynn?'

He looked up and realized his grandmother was there with a glass.

'It's a Vera Lynn ... Lynn for gin,' she explained. 'Bit of a speciality in here, apparently.'

Bryn stood just behind her, pint in hand and a *go-on-indulge-her* expression on his face.

Goodhew obliged. 'Happy now?'

'Anything to cheer you up a bit,' she replied.

'I don't even like gin, so how's that going to cheer me up?'

Bryn held up his glass. 'We're shaking you out of your comfort zone. And we've invited Sue to join us.'

'Gully?'

'Why not.'

He shrugged – there was no reason now why not. Once they'd started speaking again he had sensed that, through the awkwardness, their friendship had been cemented. She still blushed regularly, but less often around him.

By the end of the evening they'd found a pool table, and Bryn started trying to help Sue improve her game.

Goodhew smiled to himself at the sight.

His grandmother sat opposite him. He'd asked her twice more about her sister's death. *It was a long time ago, Gary. I should never have mentioned it.*

'I think I hate secrets,' he'd said.

'So do I, but some exist for good reason.'

'You do realize I know nothing about my family tree beyond you and Grandad?'

'But *you* know who you are, and that's all that matters.'

He left it there. She was wrong but also right at the same time; and for someone who found closeness to other people so challenging, he'd done well.

He glanced across to the pool table in time to see Gully slam the black into an end pocket. 'Your round, Bryn.'

Bryn demanded a rematch. Goodhew's grandmother demanded a game of doubles.

And so it went on for the rest of the evening. It was a good night.

Then he walked home alone, with the blur of streetlamps illuminating his way through the icy Cambridge fog. He knew every step of the way, so visibility could have been zero and Cambridge would still be there, clear and bright in his mind. It was other things, things he couldn't quite see, that fed his insomnia, or visited his dreams once he managed to sleep.

Tonight, he knew, he'd stay awake.

ACKNOWLEDGEMENTS

My first thank-you is to Jacen, Natalie, Lana and Dean for all your encouragement, good company and music in the workplace.

There are many friends I'd also like to thank for small favours and great kindness at various times: Claire and Chris Tombs, Sue Gully and Gary Goodhew, Richard Reynolds, Christine Bartram, Jon and Gabrielle Breakfield, Kelly Kelday, George Wicker, Jane Martin, Rob and Elaine Watson, Elaine McBride, Liz Meads, Genevieve Pease, Charlotte Prince, Martin and Sam Jerram, Tim and Diane Slater, Alison Hilborne and Kimberly Jackson.

During the writing of *The Silence* I was lucky enough to be able to have some great support from the Royal Literary Fund and specialist knowledge from several generous and helpful people including Dr T. V. Liew, Dr William Holstein and Tony Ixer.

Thank you to the team at Constable, in particular Krystyna Green, Rob Nichols, Jamie-Lee Nardone and Jo Stansall. And my thanks also go to Joan Deitch, whose comments were greatly appreciated.

I've had great fun at events this year, with talks at libraries, reading groups and literary events, and the opportunity to meet so many readers in person has made it a very memorable one. Also, to the readers and other authors I've met during my first year on Twitter, @Alison_Bruce; it's been a joy getting to know you all. One person deserves singling out for a special mention: @milorambles; Miles, thank you for all your support.

And finally a huge thank-you to my lovely agent Broo Doherty, whose kindness, common sense and words of wisdom I truly value.

THE SOUNDTRACK FOR
THE SILENCE

When I write a book I find there are songs that can inspire me as I write a particular scene or chapter. By the time I finish I have a playlist that belongs to that book alone and some of those tracks will have been played several hundred times. These are the twelve songs I listened to most as I wrote this book, my soundtrack to *The Silence*.

'Change Your Mind' – The Killers

'Find My Love' – Fairground Attraction

'Have Love Will Travel' – Hot Boogie Chillun

'Hot Love' – Brian Setzer

'Indigo Blue' – Jacen Bruce

'Long Black Shiny Car' – Restless

'In Dreams' – Roy Orbison

'Nobody's Guy' – The Blue Devils

'Perfidia' – The Ventures

'Someone Like You' – Adele

'Tail of a Rattlesnake' – The Blue Devils

'You Don't Love Me' – Bo Diddley

For more information please visit www.alisonbruce.com.